SALVINGTON'S

SOLDIERS:

DESCENSION

For Rosemary,

Thank you for
the support!

Printed in the United States of America.
Second Edition.

Cover design & Illustrations by Hanna Weiss.

ISBN: 9781792985232

To Mom, for being the first to believe in this project from the very beginning.

To Dad, for reading draft after draft I sent him without complaining.

To all of my glorious beta readers, who took the time to read this and suffer through its errors.

To my friends and family, who asked over and over when this would finally be in their hands.

To Grandma and Grandpa, who gave the best feedback and suggestions I could ask for.

To Kojo and Amanda, as well as all of the Questers, for giving me the inspiration to write this story.

To Miss Erin, who started this entire thing.

To Hanna, for keeping up with my ridiculous requests.

To Justin, who hung out with me as I finished this book for the eighth time.

To Parker, for letting me include him in this adventure.

To Kabir and Rana, who inspired an amazing protagonist.

I hope you're all proud of what I've created.

PROLOGUE

"You've got to be kidding me."

"I can assure you, I am not."

"You actually want me to do this? After everything I've done? I thought you hated me."

"Hate is a false word. I am asking you to do this because you mean the most. If anyone else were to do it, the message wouldn't be clear. You, however, have the farthest to go."

"So you're letting me walk free? Roam the universe as I did before?"

"I'm placing a great amount of trust in you. This is your final chance. Don't waste it."

"Fine. What about the others?"

"I can only choose one of you, unfortunately. In time, you may have to face them."

"And when I do, what happens then?"

"You will show them the Light."

1

"With grace, keep your mind awake." Kiran Andon watched closely as the man, dressed in full black, mask and all, twirled his blade. The silver katana the man held spun hypnotizingly, a silver circle

repeating itself over, and over. At any moment he could strike, and it would surely be deadly.

"But do not be deceived by your opponent's tactics. He is deceptive, and that is his goal." Kiran readied his own blade, a silver broadsword, the signature of the Academy Warriors. He kept his head high, and his knees bent as the moment of attack neared. He had to shake himself free of the man's hypnosis, each time falling closer to unconsciousness.

"As your opponent nears, block his attacks even before he sends them." The silver katana burst into action, a flurry of silver swipes snapping the air, each one ending in a satisfying *clash!* Kiran held his own, blocking the ones that endangered him and leaving the rest to fly elsewhere. After the last strike, Kiran went for a charge of his own.

"With a counter, be firm." Kiran's sword broke through the man's initial defense, tearing through his outer clothes. For a moment, Kiran hoped he had exposed what was underneath but was dismayed to see even more black clothing. The man lept backward and gingerly touched his cut area. Kiran could not see the eyes beneath that mask, but he could feel a sharp glare.

The man did not attack again but kept his blade pointed forward. He spoke, voice changed by his mask.

"No matter how long you protect her, her Reign of Terror is no more." His words were deepened beyond human nature, a thin line of static in between each one. He rose and fell in jagged form with his syllables.

Kiran observed the man, thinking. He paused for a few moments, then responded:

"Reign of Terror? Is that what you're calling it? Seems hypocritical for a group like you!"

The man growled, sounding much like a lion. "You do not know us. We have seen worse than what we will bring."

"Leave," Kiran said. "Before I tear you up even more!" He felt the frightened eyes of the crowd on him and knew all of their lives may very well depend on his own. A few feet behind him stood the President, accompanied by her trusted guards. Even they, however, could yet not withstand the might of an Anarchist.

"Beware your leader...we are all her pawns."

"I do not want to hurt you," Kiran warned. "But if I must-"

The man disappeared in a black poof. Dust fluttered to the stage floor, and it was soon swept away by the wind. This was the third Anarchist appearance in the past week, all resulting in widespread panic. Kiran turned slowly to the President, and their eyes met.

Topia City was in unrest.

2

Two weeks later.

A cloaked figure, without emotions and practically invisible to others, stood within the angry crowd. No one around him seemed to acknowledge his presence, acting as if he wasn't really there. Even though he appeared unrecognized, the crowd kept a weird circle around him. Not a single person stood within four feet of him, the bare ground empty aside from usual garbage.

It was if the space around him was his and his only.

A brown cloak shrouded the figure entirely, reaching the ground beneath his feet. His hands were put together, covered by sleeves. No skin was showing. His hands were tightened into fists under his long sleeves, hoping to keep them there.

No punches thrown is a good day. Gabriel's going to lose that bet.

He waited for a particular moment, the same one as everyone else in the crowd: a speech about an ongoing crisis. One person, speaking to hundreds, perhaps thousands-on screen-of other people.

Sure enough, at the stage in front of the crowd, leveled ten feet high, there stood a woman of importance.

The cloaked figure knew all people of importance have something to say, whether it be wise or not.

That's why I'm here, he thought. *This one woman is who will speak of the crisis. She, one human being, will offer a solution to the problem that affects nearly a million others.*

So, in one sudden wave of a hand and tap of a microphone, the crazy activity halted.

The woman stood dominantly, hand still outstretched, and scanned the crowd slowly. As the last word in the mass was spoken, she smiled slightly.

The smile felt warm to all those who saw it, the woman's teeth glimmering white. The figure, however, could see blatant worry beneath. Each twinkle in the woman's eyes sparked hope for the crowd but brought uncertainty for the figure.

The figure was not pessimistic, however.

I'm just not naive, like the others here might be, he thought. *She's worried, but it's sensible.*

The woman adjusted herself, icy blue eyes bright, and spoke:

"As much as I enjoy these gatherings, having so many loyal citizens in one place, we assemble today upon a much more...dismal setting.

"It is my concern, and my associates' concern, that the Anarchist Rebellion is nearing a toxic and perhaps nuclear state."

A few angry yells rang out from the crowd.

"Sorry," the woman responded, "Poor choice of words considering my address two weeks ago. We are all still a little sore from that, but the Anarchists have taken their disagreements too far. We at the capital have received threats against civilian housing and public centers, which is entirely unacceptable from a group who considered themselves a political party up until a short time ago.

"My associates and I now call upon the Anarchist Movement to stand down and surrender, as soon we will have no choice but to declare war on those who threaten us. You are being considered as a Class Two threat, meaning our security around the city is on high alert for your presence. Surrender yourselves now and give up your hatred."

The woman then became silent, seemingly awaiting a response. The hooded figure observed her carefully, noting the woman held an unusually calm posture considering she had just taunted the Anarchists. Curiosity filled him, for he had never seen such a bold move.

It could be bravery or ignorance. What it is will be decided in a matter of moments. On the one hand, I hope it is bravery. On the other, if it is ignorance, I will make my first move.

He waited, envisioning both scenarios in his head. Both intrigued him, and either would be beneficial. Of course, if it were to be bravery, then there would be no point in the figure's presence. For as he envisioned the second one, there was no need.

For, in two split moments, a roaring fire of a gun sounded, a single bullet was shot. The figure watched it in slow motion, despite his hood still up and his eyes closed. It cut through the air with shrieking precision, aimed directly at the woman's head.

But the bullet never reached the woman atop the podium.

For the hooded figure, in a flash of blinding light, appeared just before the woman, hand raised, the bullet snugly caught between his index and middle finger.

No one dared move a muscle.

The redheaded boy could not believe his eyes. He blinked several times, the previous moments playing out over and over in his mind. Something he had never expected to see in his life had just happened, and he didn't know where the situation would go from there. Nothing had prepared him for this in the slightest.

It's...unheard of.

The railgun fell limply from his hands, switching off as it hit hard concrete. Its blue glow faded, but the boy didn't look away from the stage.

From his view, nearly forty feet above the crowd, he could see everything clearly. A bird's eye view gave him direct sight, precisely what he had needed for sniping. He could now see the President Leila Lanondek atop her podium, still alive and well, even after his fatal shot had been fired. Her face held shock greater than his own,

10

as she knew her life had been decided in less than a second. Her once sky blue eyes turned a chilling, icy turquoise.

He could see the guards in utter confusion, contemplating rushing to help or stand in silence. Even Gabriel Lanondek, the man who was thought to know everything, stood speechless.

For a figure cloaked in brown had caught a bullet, fired from the red-haired boy's gun. It smoked slightly between the still figure's fingers.

The Anarchists are gonna be pissed, he knew. *It's not really my fault, though. I dunno who this guy is.*

The boy couldn't see anything beneath the figure's hood, but the fingers holding the bullet were white, but not as a skin tone. He could see them be a regular person's skin, but the longer he looked, the more he found an unnatural golden coloration.

It's like he doesn't have a race at all. He's raceless. Is he even from around here? He must be...there's nowhere else.

Finally, the lengthy silence broke. Even so, no one knew what to do but yell and scream. Many whirled around searching for the shooter, while others rushed the stage. All were thrown into complete confusion. Raging crowd members yelled out in horror that the Anarchists were going to bomb the entire plaza, while others shouted for the sniper to be found. Guards motioned for crowd control, but there was no hope. A few of the higher-ups on stage backed off, disappearing down the back stairs.

The boy, knowing his time was short, took off the bag strapped to his back. He unzipped it hastily, keeping an eye on the crowds below. Several officers guarding the stage had rushed down from it, and into the masses. They knew where the shot had come from.

Pulling a small black device from the bag, the boy smiled. Resounding confidence rushed through him quickly, but it was soon replaced by haste again. He clipped the device to the railgun and pulled another object from the bag. This next object was a box with a red button.

Again, the boy felt a rush of security. He glanced up once more, and seeing the guards now gone from his view, knew there were only moments before he would be found. No mercy would be shown toward him, and his entire cover would be blown.

He left the bag on the floor and stood up. He flipped his black hood up quickly and turned. The red buttoned-device in hand, he ran down the building's unfinished staircase. His footsteps pounded against the concrete, but there was no one around to hear.

Adrenaline and the run of mad joy sparked the moment he went out the side door. He sprinted behind the building and didn't look back. Trees obscured his being as he ran behind the market square establishments, making the job of any officer difficult.

With the press of that big red button, the construction site lit up with flames.

And the boy was never caught.

3

"He what?!" Kiran exclaimed through his communicator, hardly believing the words he had just heard. "That's not possible, my dude. You must be losing it. You know, there's an insti-"

The person on the other end of the line reassured him. "I saw it with my own eyes! It was in slow motion basically. Insane. Reflexes faster than any human in the city. This guy could be some sort of god."

Kiran could almost feel a shudder on the other end of the line. He noticed the upcoming intersection and began to quicken his pace. He crossed a few smaller streets with ease, dispersed crowds nearby. People passed him in ones and twos, hardly ever in a group larger than four.

"Ethan, bro," he said.

"Yeah?"

"This is ridiculous. I'm not believing you until I get some proof. Even so, the Anarchists are surely going to kill off this guy next. He's too big of a threat to them if he can stop a bullet with his bare hands."

"Okay, I can get you evidence," Ethan sighed in annoyance. "But...I have a suspicion. What if he's...the new prophet? What if there's no way to stop him?" He grew quieter. "This could be something absolutely impossible, but there's something bigger to consider."

Kiran fell silent, dumbfounded. He rolled his eyes, despite Ethan not being able to see it. *Sure...*

"We have to bring him in, right?" asked Ethan. "There's no way we can leave him loose, right?"

Kiran thought about it for a moment. "Yeah, Gabriel will want to talk with him ASAP. Let's hope he pops up again soon. If not, we can't find him." A pause followed.

"Where did he go after the speech?" he continued.

"President Leila said he disappeared into the crowd not even a minute after he caught the bullet. No one saw his face, so he could be walking among us at any time! He could be an Academy student, even."

"That's a stretch."

"It isn't'! Think about it, how well do you really know your former classmates?"

Kiran frowned, memories clouding him that he didn't wish to visit. Whatever the case, Ethan had a point. Not every classmate of his was who he thought they were.

"I guess you're right...but I need some evidence before any assumptions are made. Is the footage at HQ?"

"I think so. I won't be there for a little while so you'll have to find it without me."

"Should be easy."

The call ended with a quick beep, leaving Kiran in silence. He adjusted the golden badge pinned to his official red suit, letting the sunlight glint off gloriously. He stepped into the crosswalk with ease, a bounce in his step. Few cars were out, all awaiting his passage.

The day was busied with news of President Leila's second speech. It had only happened three hours ago, at about ten o'clock.

Now, all news of the mysterious figure had spread through Topia City. Everyone was forming their own opinions at this very moment.

So many people are being influenced by this. A Wizard hasn't been seen in years, and even this is beyond wizardry. Ethan could be right, this is all too powerful for a time like this. As if the rebellion needed more tinder.

An angry driver honked, and Kiran quickly jumped across. As he turned the corner onto Cobalt Street, pedestrians began to flood the sidewalk. Tens of people dressed for work moved about, signaling Kiran's entrance into the Capital of Topia City, also known as Lanon. The area opened up wide as a large circle, top of the line businesses occupying every space except for one.

The place where Kiran's life had been changed in an instant, and now his very workplace, The Academy.

The massive building stretched seven stories high, each for a level of rank in the guild. The building sat center in the circle of Lanon, entirely because it signaled dominance to of all of Topia. The Academy Warriors, the famed students themselves, acted as police to an extent, as they followed the command of Gabriel Lanondek, right hand to President Leila.

Even despite the Warriors being capable of handling small-scale disturbances, the president had called upon a drafted army to deal with the Anarchists. They were inadequately trained before being sent out, all under the command of General Timothy MacArthur. It had caused unrest, as men with families and jobs were uprooted and called to the capitol, a couple blocks north.

They're untrained, and most are stubborn, Kiran thought. *They don't deserve swords. But then again, neither do the Anarchists. All we can hope for is some sort of resolution.*

He strolled along the bustling sidewalk, head held high. He grinned as passersby cautiously glanced at his badge, meeting them with serious glances. Many people nodded to him, but they all held hesitancy.

There's a level of fear that didn't exist until the brink of the rebellion. Now, anyone sees themselves as a suspect. They're lucky, though. Not just anyone can be arrested.

Then he realized, the time was approaching.

He had known a particular moment would come, but the precise time wasn't clear to him. He knew the event would begin loud and distinct, as it always did. For the past six days, it had. Today would be the last warning, if it did come. It would be the final declaration of war.

And so it happened.

A loud and sudden scream came from the group of people passing just in front of Kiran. A rustle of complicated movement could be seen, and Kiran slowly made his way over. A solemn frown spread across his face. He rushed through a few passersby and was greeted by the slow crowd that came before him. Gasps ensued, muffled by frightened hands.

Just like routine, he thought grimly.

His hand quickly reached up behind his head, where a cold metal hilt lay waiting. He grabbed it and pulled it swiftly, the blade attached sliding smoothly from the sheath strapped to his back. The sword gleamed silver in the day's light, and Kiran brought it confidently forward.

The crowd in front of him parted instantly, all fearful of his newly revealed weapon. Their clearance let the screamer be visible, and Kiran rushed to aid. It was a young girl, around twelve years of age, grabbing at her neck. A black-clothed arm was wrapped around her neck, keeping her fixed in place. She clawed at it frantically, twisting her throat as she did.

Kiran, ten feet away from the two individuals, looked up to the face of the perpetrator. The entirety of the person's body was covered in black clothing, even his face. The mask covering the person's face shone of carved silver, two darkness-filled eyes staring blankly. His other arm held a glistening knife of massive size, moving toward the girl's face threateningly.

Kiran moved slowly toward the two, preparing for a quick but dangerous encounter. He raised his blade accordingly and watched the individual's knife as well. The girl looked to him with eyes of fear, but Kiran kept his focus on the perpetrator.

As Kiran stepped within six feet of the two, the individual's blade darted quickly to the girl's face. It stopped just before touching her skin, but it still hovered less than an inch away. She looked to the blade, and her lower lip started to tremble.

Kiran stopped, wary.

"You come here every day," he said. "Why?"

He waited, not sure what to expect as an answer. Any sign from the individual's masked face would serve to be a response, but no movement occurred at all.

So Kiran continued.

"Everyday you run this same routine. Every day you scare some poor child half to death. You put a knife to the child's throat every single time, but you never kill. Are you afraid?"

The crowd hesitantly awaited, watching as Kiran taunted this possible murderer. They expected any second for a flash of blood; a sickening sight of death on the streets.

The individual looked at Kiran curiously, as if waiting to see what the young Warrior would do next. After a few tense moments, time nearly standing still, the being spoke.

"I do not come here. We come here," he said suddenly, his voice dark and clouded. Scratchy, almost. "I do not kill. They do." He paused.

"In seven days the capital will fall," he continued. "In seven days the Academy will be destroyed. In seven days, all of Topia will be taken into the right hands."

Then, in one swift motion, he began to slit the girl's throat. The girl screaming with blood-curdling fright, Kiran threw his blade at the individual's head. It spun, metal gleaming, and stopped inches short of his forehead.

The blade stopped short for one simple reason, and it was a reason no one in the crowd could possibly explain, understand, or question. Everyone watched, half-frozen in fear, and now, time seemed as if it had indeed halted. Kiran didn't even lower his arm.

A single finger held the tip of the blade in midair.

Kiran's eyes followed the finger down to the owner's arm, shoulder, and eventually, face.

Gleaming blue eyes stared back at him, golden blond hair accompanying. A brown cloak ran down the boy's body, hood down but very much present. His other hand was as well outstretched, but to the left, where a single finger as well held the tip of the black-clothed individual's knife less than an inch away from the girl's neck.

Two lives saved at once.

Kiran forced himself to blink multiple times before finally believing his vision. His mind struggled to conceive of such forces allowing the blades to stay suspended. Gravity had ceased to work, and he half expected himself to start floating. But, alas, he did not.

Has gravity somehow switched off in those two places? No...it's some sort of magic...but no magic is that powerful. His fingers should've been stabbed clear through. And where did he come from at all?

Instantaneous, invulnerable, and young?

Upon Kiran's third blink, the blades clattered to the floor.

The black-clothed individual let his grip around the girl weaken immediately, causing her to finally overpower him and escape. He darted away with surprising speed, disappearing into an alleyway nearby. The boy did nothing to stop the being from leaving. He merely looked to the girl.

"Are you all right?" he asked softly, a caring in his eyes not of a teenage boy, but of an experienced father. A remarkable maturity maintained his posture as he consoled the girl. The girl had a little trouble catching her breath, but otherwise, she was fine.

Kiran slowly approached the boy, glancing to the crowd around them. He noted fearful but impressed reactions in each person, as in himself. A great confusion, however, was within him. He came within a normal speaking distance from the boy, but focused first on the girl.

"I can call someone if you need," Kiran told the girl, who merely shook her head. Her eyes were red with tears, but a smile said she was grateful. The boy kept one hand on her shoulder.

The girl looked to both boys separately, thanking them quietly, and started to walk off. Kiran motioned to follow, but she disappeared into the crowd quickly. He nodded, hoping she would return to her parents safe and sound. Under any other circumstances he would've followed without hesitancy, but this time, he had a separate matter.

He then looked to the boy and met eyes with him for the first time. A silent but absolute conversation ran through their heads, taking Kiran off guard. In one instant he saw a playback in the boy's bright blue eyes, a rewind of what had just happened. Those impossibly suspended blades flashed through his mind time and time again.

After seeing the unbelievable instance a few more times, Kiran suddenly felt the tens of eyes gathered around him.

"Look, you better come with me," he said quietly.

The boy nodded.

4

Kiran and the boy entered The Academy minutes later. They stepped inside the very loud and crowded first floor, many men and women moving about hastily. Almost every person was dressed as Kiran was: an entirely red suit with black boots and gloves. None of them paid attention to Kiran nor the boy.

"This floor is usually the busiest," Kiran said. "Everyone has access to it. Even outsiders."

"What do you mean, access?" the boy asked, scanning the room thoughtfully. He noted everyone held sheathed blades much like

Kiran's. Kiran had since retrieved his from the sidewalk and had it sheathed once again.

"Well, every Academy Warrior has a type of rank. Our rank is equal to how many of the seven floors we are able to visit and operate on. I'm rank four, so I can visit floors one through four without anyone questioning it." Deep within him, there was an odd curiosity of what lay on the upper three floors.

"Hm," the boy said, placing a finger to his chin. "Reminds me of a place."

"Yeah? Where?"

The boy looked to him carefully, as if deciding whether or not to answer. He instead slightly ignored the question, looking off to the side.

"So where are you taking me?"

Kiran hesitated, noting the dodging of his previous question. He decided quickly to not press further.

"Just for a tour upstairs."

The boy again turned to him as they walked toward the stairs, expression blank.

"You could've just told me I'm being taken in for questioning," he said, sighing slightly. "Not the first time." He scanned the room with penetrating eyes.

They reached the staircase, which was oddly empty of people. The stairs spiraled upward to the next floor and went on for five more after that. They split the center of a grand atrium, a glass skylight in the ceiling. The day's sunlight shone down, illuminating the stairs. A few colored panels filtered the light into yellows, greens, reds, and blues.

Kiran appeared surprised. "Well, most guys don't respond well to the knowledge they're being questioned. It's usually followed with escape attempts, requests for lawyers, and even resorts to violence. The latter end the most poorly. Even so, your questioning isn't guaranteed to happen, but I have to take you up there anyway."

"Wise."

They moved up the steps in an orderly fashion, Kiran making sure the boy went first as protocol. Their footsteps thundered against the white marble steps until they reached the second floor.

"This is where we stop," Kiran said. The boy nodded and began to walk down the first hall. Kiran followed close behind.

The second floor was bronze in color. Everything appeared hammered and sand-like, mostly for aesthetics. Photos and paintings hung on the walls, all of Academy Warrior moments in history. The boy noted one to his left, featuring a dark-skinned man with golden eyes, holding a shining silver sword. The man stood on a frozen lake, with glaciers surrounding him.

The boy stopped. Surprised, Kiran stopped abruptly as well. The boy looked over to the picture.

"Who is that?"

Kiran glanced over to the picture, keeping a straight face.

"That's Master Bosun, one of the original Academy Warriors. They say he could teleport."

"Teleportation? Is that normal for Warriors?"

"Not really. I can't do it, that's for sure. It sounds incredibly nauseating." He touched his stomach gingerly. "No one else I know except for Gabriel Lanondek can do it. And the Wizards....I suppose."

The boy nodded and turned back to the hall. He and Kiran walked forth a little more before turning left into the nearest hallway. Kiran found it a little unusual the boy knew exactly which way to go. Even so, he didn't feel the need to intrude. Enough weird things were already happening.

They entered a hallway with black padding on the walls, leading to a door at the end. The boy assumed this was the interrogation room, speculating the walls were soundproof.

Two doors stood on either side of the hallway as well. The boy again took instinctive initiative and went to the right door, impressing Kiran once again.

"How do you-" he started.

"Lucky guess."

Right, Kiran thought, wondering more and more who precisely this boy was. He realized he hadn't even asked for his name yet, but decided not to as he would ask in the interrogation.

It intrigued him, however. Would this boy have a name of legends? There were few, but still plenty that might fit.

He could be another Bosun, after all. Or, perhaps his name is Buerbune, one of the Wizards. An Archer...perhaps Merrick or Arjun.

He smiled a little at all the possibilities.

They entered the room. Inside awaited seemingly nothing but two chairs, a table, and a dim light in the center of the ceiling. The area smelled of dust and stale air. A small vent was embedded in the upper corner of the room, feebly creaking every now and then.

The boy sat down in one of the chairs, and Kiran sat in the one across.

Kiran tapped a button on the underside of the table, and it beeped loudly.

"What was that?" the boy asked.

"Just calling in Gabriel," Kiran responded. The boy nodded, beginning to scan the room. He noted the sheer bareness of everything, an absence of movement, sound, and even life. Two dark, foldable chairs leaned against the corner nearest the door, dust settling upon them. Gray walls surrounded them, dark and without decoration. A window was the only thing on any of the walls, but nothing could be seen through it.

It's one-sided, the boy presumed. He imagined the people who might be behind it, watching his every breath. But as soon as the possibility became apparent, the door swung open.

A short, slightly plump individual stepped through, but he carried his weight with ease. He was bald, and his eyes shone bronze. They met the boy's immediately and narrowed. They flickered with recognition.

After a split second, the man grabbed one of the chairs by the door and brought it over to the table. Dust fell off the chair quickly as the man unfolded it, placing it next to Kiran's. After breaking the boy's gaze, he turned to Kiran.

"Ethan isn't here?" the man asked, disappointed.

Kiran shook his head. "He said he'd be late. Had some other priorities I take it."

"Fair enough. As long as he arrives."

The man and Kiran both turned to the boy. A momentary silence fell over the three of them, replaced by tension.

The man reached under the table, pressing another button.

"This is Gabriel Lanondek, Head of Department of Secrecy and Law Enforcement. Class Four Academy Warrior Kiran and Class

Three Academy Warrior Ethan are both permitted. Commencing interrogation."

Kiran nodded and turned to the boy. "State your name, and age."

The boy hesitated, thinking. *I knew it would happen eventually. I always could, I guess, easily break out of here. This Kiran though...he could be the first.*

"Michael Nebadon, 14 years."

Kiran repeated the name in his head, glad he finally had a name to match these blue eyes and blond hair. It was not a name of legend, but it was one nonetheless. Knowing this boy was a year younger than him but possessed powers and emotions so advanced caused him to shudder visibly.

"You alright, Kiran?" Michael asked softly. Gabriel looked to him oddly, as if wondering whether to interject or not. Kiran nodded his head in response.

"Just cold, that's all," he said. "Moving on. What were you doing in Lanon today at around noon?"

Michael frowned. "Lanon...that's where we are now, right?"

Gabriel and Kiran looked to one another, then slowly turned back to Michael. Gabriel stared determinedly at Michael, biting to ask a specific question. He could not ask it with Kiran in the room, however.

"Have you not visited Lanon before? Have you not heard of it?" Gabriel asked, the question he wanted to ask being pushed farther back into his mind. He hoped for the answer he did not expect, but it was too much to ask.

"Never. This place is entirely foreign to me," Michael answered, fulfilling Gabriel's fear. He glanced at them casually, but then noticed the ominous expressions upon both of their faces. Gabriel's face turned disapproving, but Kiran remained shocked. "Is something wrong?"

Kiran took a hesitant breath. "Where do you live in Topia, exactly?"

Michael raised an eyebrow. "Topia? Oh, I don't live here."

Again, Kiran didn't know how to answer. He struggled to form an explanation, a reason how this 14-year-old boy wouldn't know of the city he's lived in. Gabriel, meanwhile, started fuming. He glared at Michael but kept his mouth shut. *I cannot risk it with Kiran here,* he thought.

Finally, Kiran managed an answer.

"Michael...Topia is the last city on this planet. Everything else...is gone.

Ethan Catanzaro burst into the room, cheeks red and sweat glistening off his forehead. He quickly grabbed a chair from the corner of the room and began carrying it over. He collapsed in the chair, sighing of relief.

"Sorry...sorry," he said, breaths quick. "Had some...other work to finish. So..."

His expression faltered as soon as he saw the strange silence occurring between Kiran, Gabriel, and who he presumed to be the suspect. He slowly set the chair down beside Kiran and sat with equal caution.

"Kiran, you good? What's wrong with you?" he asked, leaning slightly into the boy's view. Kiran had no response, just a blank stare over at the suspect. Gabriel instead stared down, expression contemplative. Both were utterly still as if they were frozen in time. He waved a hand in front of both of their faces, but nothing happened.

Fearfully, he placed a hand over Kiran's chest. For a moment, he heard no heartbeat, but then the thumps began. They were slow, but there indeed. He did the same with Gabriel and gained the same result.

He followed Kiran's gaze over to the suspect, and figured the suspect might be in the same "stupor." He flinched, finding striking blue eyes staring back at him. As he stared longer, he became more and more entranced.

It's like there's a whole universe in his eyes...

The suspect blinked, and Ethan snapped from his thoughts. *He isn't frozen like Kiran and Gabriel! What...if he's the one who's keeping them from moving?!*

"So," he said slowly. "What have we covered so far?"

The suspect ignored Ethan, looking back to Kiran and Gabriel. He watched them blankly, and Ethan did not appreciate it.

"You're mute? Is this a joke or something? Because it isn't amusing."

There was no response from anyone. Ethan then sighed, running his hands up through his red hair.

"Alright then, guess I'll join in."

He stared mockingly at the suspect, hoping his time doing this would be short. Concentration immediately failed him, and he found himself looking all around the suspect instead of just the eyes. His gaze swept the blank walls, instantly bored. Finally, it landed back on the suspect.

A sudden familiarity reached him in the small way the suspect's skin was colored.

It's...tinted gold? I've seen that before.

His mind, however, failed to recall the exact memory. A lot had happened this morning, and those events had shaken up his mind quite a bit. Sounds of explosions still rattled in his brain.

He lost focus on staring and grew exasperated once again.

Sighing loudly, he glanced up to the ceiling. Gray nothingness looked down to him.

When he looked back to the suspect, he found the boy's eyes were focused on him now.

"Do I finally have your attention?"

The boy nodded exceptionally slowly.

"Name and age?"

The boy's eyes grew condescending, and he answered:

"Michael Nebadon, 14 years."

Ethan grinned slightly, his movements ever so slowly as if a sudden move might revert everything back. He took a slow breath and cautiously resumed questioning.

"What's wrong with them?" he asked, jerking his head in the direction of Kiran and Gabriel. They remained still.

"Just paralyzed by information, I believe."

Ethan narrowed his eyes, suspicious.

"What did you tell them?"

Michael tapped his fingers in unison on the table. He tilted his head slightly.

"I didn't tell them anything. I *showed* them."

His eyes sparkled, and a sudden headache slammed into Ethan.

5

Gabriel was the first to break from the stupor. He wasn't particularly fazed by it, but he still held some surprise. He looked to Michael and glared once again.

"What were you thinking?! Making yourself an established threat on day one?! You could've died immediately, and all would've been lost!"

Michael, taken aback by Gabriel's forthrightness. He had spoken in such an open manner.

"I would've thought you to be proud, Gabriel," the boy said. "After all, perhaps my decision to be timid last time was a mistake."

"Your death was no mistake, and you know it," Gabriel hissed.

"My death was necessary, of course it was! That was not the mistake! I didn't leave a good enough impression on this world...that is my only regret. My followers died off after putting my words to paper, and even despite the traditions passing on through quite some time, they were translated. The words were turned, muffled."

"So now you hope to establish yourself as what, a lower god? You're copying the rebels."

"Heavens no, Gabriel!" Michael assured him multiple times, bringing his hands up. "And if you are criticizing me for being too direct, then the cameras recording us right now are not hypocrisy?"

"They are off, of course. I would not be that foolish."

Michael frowned, glancing away. He let himself cool a little, breathing slowly. *Rage is the source of all mistakes,* he reminded himself. "You would never think me to join the rebel ways, would you?"

"No," Gabriel admitted. "That would never be a possibility."

Michael smiled slightly, confirming. "Then, have confidence. I've been thinking this plan out for years upon years. What I did this morning was only the first of many calculated moves."

Gabriel grinned broadly.

"What shall I do, then, in all this chaos?"

Michael smiled, and his tone turned poetic.

"Oh Bright and Morning Star, your post is unguarded at this moment. However might you suffice?"

Gabriel laughed deeply. "I will return one day, but what of my presence at the moment?"

"I'm sure they will not think it surreptitious."

Gabriel smiled again, this time slyly. "No, they shall not."

A thoughtful pause struck the two, halting their conversation. Gabriel narrowed his eyes and looked to Michael, who in turn, copied.

"Is something off?" Michael asked.

Gabriel did not answer at first but kept his expression. He felt his serious attitude beginning to fade away, and could no longer hide his joy.

He laughed again, and Michael smiled.

"What is so funny now?" Michael asked, amused.

"It's good to see you back here, that's all."

"It was a promise I was sure to fulfill."

Gabriel nodded slowly. He stood up from his chair, gears turning within his mind. It was a moment he had waited for nearly fourteen years. A moment when he was finally given the order to return home.

"Are the seraphic transports ready?" he asked, preparing himself. The cold remembrance of teleportation rattled him, seeming so foreign even despite the countless times he had done it before.

"Indeed they are. Only one will be required for you," Michael answered, envisioning the magnificent swirling portal hundreds of miles above them.

"I'll see you soon," Gabriel said and motioned for the door. A swift turn of a knob made him disappear in a flash, leaving golden sparkles flickering in the air.

"Seraphic physical deception is always enjoyable," Michael commented and smiled.

He turned to Ethan and Kiran. Noting they remained frozen, and knowing they hadn't witnessed or heard anything of his previous conversation, he made the decision.

With a quick snap of his fingers, Ethan and Kiran sparked to life.

6

Ethan grabbed at the table ferociously immediately after being set free, a wild craziness bursting through him. Breaths turned short and rapid, his heart rate spiked. He clutched onto the table for security. Willing it not to fall from reality, he blinked multiple times, the vision still burned into his eyes.

Kiran, on the other hand, slumped back against his chair, as if a great weight had been lifted from his shoulders. He commanded himself to breathe slowly, and Michael began to see a significant difference between the two boys.

Michael waited for the both of them to calm themselves, as they were overwhelmed intensely. He noted, however, the disparity in reaction.

Such a difference. They will do nicely.

Ethan looked to him first, eyes now filled with anger and disbelief. He wasn't angry because of what he had seen; he was angry at the boy who put him through it.

"What..." he started, pausing to breathe. "The hell...was that?"

Michael turned to him oddly, not understanding.

"Hell does not exist."

Ethan shook his head as if attempting to fix his hearing.

"What?"

Michael ignored his question and looked to Kiran, who remained staring blankly at the table. His chest rose and fell with deep breaths, mind struggling to contemplate what he had seen.

Ethan began to open his mouth, but Michael interrupted him first.

"Your questions have no need to be answered. You have seen it all, if only for a fraction of a second. Be-"

"That was less than a second?!" Ethan interrupted back.

Michael nodded and answered thoroughly.

"Indeed. Even so, you were immobile for some time."

Ethan's eyes widened, and he looked to Michael as if he were crazy. He remembered entering the room what seemed like days ago, and seeing Gabriel and Kiran immobile. He flexed his fingers, looking down at them.

"You froze us?!"

"A crude way of putting it, but yes."

Ethan sat further in his chair and looked to Kiran. He grabbed the warrior's shoulders and looked him dead in the eyes.

"Kiran, we have to leave now."

Kiran did not respond, only looking back at Ethan without emotion.

"Give him time," Michael stated calmly.

Ethan shook Kiran to break him from his stupor, but it failed. Kiran was indeed conscious, but he was still processing what he had seen.

"No! We have to go!"

Michael snapped his fingers, and Kiran flared to life completely.

He instinctively shoved Ethan off him, startling the redheaded boy. Ethan fell back over his chair, ambivalent. On the one hand, he felt glad Kiran was moving. On the other, he felt pissed that Kiran had pushed him.

Kiran slowly turned to Michael.

"Why?" he asked, not out of fear, but curiosity. A sense of drive and purpose ran through him, and he could now comprehend his vision. Ethan called out to him, but all focus was on Michael Nebadon.

"Kiran," Michael started, grateful but expectant of the boy's serenity. "In time you will come to understand the meaning of what you have seen. Even as you understand it in a physical sense, there are three other planes of existence for you to truly comprehend."

Kiran didn't respond, hesitant on accepting this answer as fulfillment. His understanding still felt a little...unfinished. *The Light is pure, and it is true,* he recalled. Even so, there was finality in Michael's statement. He knew the boy would be void of help beyond what he had already gained.

His narrowed drive widened suddenly as a great banging sounded behind him. He whirled around in his chair to see Ethan desperately pulling on the doorknob, every few seconds taking a moment to bang on the door itself. Ethan's face turned fearful, causing Kiran to slowly approach him.

Kiran stood, and made his way over to his raging friend. Just as he was about to confront Ethan, Michael spoke.

"Be wary, for he may react poorly to consolation," he said, remaining still. Kiran glanced back to him halfway, but the statement added nothing to his caution. Situations like these were destined to happen with Ethan, but Gabriel was often present to pacify.

He then stopped dead in his tracks.

Where's Gabriel in the first place?

He glanced about the room slowly, taking in the information out of oddity. His gaze then settled on Michael, who raised an eyebrow. His mouth opened to ask, but words never came.

Instead, he turned to Ethan again.

"Ethan," he whispered. "Where's Gabriel?"

Ethan suddenly looked to him, realization kicking in. He looked about the room frantically, confirming the fact that Gabriel was indeed gone.

34

He became locked in Michael's blue vision, and rage engulfed him.

"What did you do with him?!" he exclaimed, stepping away from the door. He marched to the interrogation table, leaving Kiran behind. The chair blocking his path was quickly knocked by a solid kick, leaving what would later become a bruise on Ethan's shin. Adrenaline empowering him, he put both hands on the table.

"Where is he?!"

Michael looked to Ethan with curiosity tinted with disappointment. *He's doing his best...but he's spending energy on the wrong plane.*

"Before I answer, I will ask you to divert your energy from one plane to another."

Ethan, taken aback, looked to him with his brow furrowed.

"What the *f* does that even mean?! You better lose the fancy talk soon, or I'll be sure to pummel your wise self into the wall!"

Michael frowned, growing serious. His voice deepened slightly.

"Understand what this means-"

Ethan's hand darted back, grabbing the dark hilt over his shoulder. A quick flash of silver marked the drawing of his sword, and less than a second passed before he sliced at Michael with it.

Kiran's eyes widened, and he reached out. It was futile but would've made no difference had he been quick enough. Ethan gleamed with malicious intent, and Michael saw a tip-off sign within that could not be ignored.

Michael, seeing the blade come for the side of his head, spent the last moments before it struck contemplating whether or not he needed to block it.

I need not feel something like that again, he thought, and made his decision.

Five times quicker than Ethan's strike, Michael's hand stopped the blade in its tracks without effort. His arm shot up, flexing just as the sword came in contact with it. A flash of light jumped out from the clash, but it died quickly. Ethan's blade bounced away, and the Warrior clenched his grip tight. He gritted his teeth.

Michael and Ethan's eyes met, and both held a great revelation, and neither could ignore it.

Both knew they had met one another before, and both knew the exact circumstances.

"No..." Ethan said quietly, letting his grip falter. The sword clattered to the ground next to Michael.

Michael did not feel bleeding whatsoever from the block and was once again grateful. He glanced at Ethan with dark eyes, instilling unintentional fear. Ethan backed away, ignoring Kiran's attempts at communication. His hands tingled with past memory, and he rushed back to the door.

This time, the door opened quickly, and Ethan ran out like a startled cat.

7

The door of The Academy burst open suddenly, just as the sun began to arc downwards across the sky. Passersby and employees alike glanced worriedly to the individual sprinting outside, but no one made any effort to stop him. The redheaded boy wore a badge that signaled to all:

Whatever he's doing, it's none of my business.

Ethan ran down the sidewalk, making no attempt to stay out of anyone's way. Even so, again the crowds parted for him, and despite his disheveled appearance, no one thought him unofficial. His hair had been thrown distraught on his way out, and his eyes flickered with panic.

His mind became set on the destination he needed to reach, narrowed from his encounter just a few minutes ago. Michael's little ability to stop his blade...with his hand nonetheless, was something he needed to inform others of immediately.

By others, Ethan meant his unknown superiors, not the general public. They had already seen this "Michael" in action at Leila's Speech, but they did not know of his other abilities. It would be better if it stayed that way.

However, this would be excellent for Ethan's people to understand. It had entirely confirmed what everyone had feared: something even more powerful than the magic of the Wizards.

He sprinted forth, turning two corners before ducking into a dark alleyway. His heart pounded from continuous adrenaline, thoughts still jumbled. He glanced down the grimy depths of the alley, hoping the area would be without rats and bums. Dumpster bins held gross smells and shadowed shapes.

Ethan stepped closer to the center of the row, cautiously glancing about. A sense of urgency remained within him, but he still felt wary of what could be hiding in the darkness.

"What are you doing, Ethan?" a voice asked from behind him. He jumped slightly, tensing up. He kept his back to the individual, hoping they could be referring to a different Ethan.

Of course, that was of minuscule chance, which he quickly realized. Slow steps sounded behind him, eerily coming closer and closer every second. Ethan began to turn, mind racing for escape options.

He tilted his head up slightly, now facing the individual. He smiled, began to open his mouth to speak, but never got the chance.

Even before he could identify the person, a great dark force pummeled the figure out of the alleyway. The mass slowly settled itself down, turning to Ethan in a great stroke. It was a dark, shadowy hand, disembodied except for an arm that stretched from nowhere. Ethan jumped as it turned to him, palm open and fingers wide. It expanded, soon covering the entire alley opening.

Ethan backed up slowly, suspecting it was the work of his master. Frightened but grateful, he dropped to one knee and bowed his head. Waiting for acknowledgment, he closed his eyes.

The hand expanded, palm and fingers fusing until they touched the walls of either building, blocking all light from entering. Soon, the top of the hand skyrocketed upward, turning into a ceiling. All light from above was then covered, and in a split second, the alley opening behind Ethan was covered.

An entirely new room was created, devoid of light, but not devoid of consciousness. An abstract reality hidden from the outside world, a power nearly no one could possess or counter.

A figure stepped from the first alley opening, the darkness following and clinging to him. He approached Ethan swiftly.

"STAND," he commanded, voice booming. It rattled the fake reality around them, little sound ripples in the walls. Ethan did as he was told, and immediately plead his case.

"Master, he's greater than we thought. He holds power-"

"POWER? ALL POWER IS IN MY HANDS. ANY POWER HE HOLDS IS NONEXISTENT, A RUSE. ANYTHING HE HAS DEMONSTRATED PALES IN COMPARISON TO MY POWER." The being paused, and added: "SOON, HE WILL FEAR EVEN YOUR POWER."

Ethan looked curiously to the figure's face but found it could not be seen. This was not surprising to him, but he still found it intriguing. A hood covered the figure's eyes, appearing non-material. Even so, he knew anything around him could be fake, editing so he would not see the truth.

A source of gravity seemed to emanate from the figure, drawing everything closer. Ethan felt pulled to his presence, commanded. A small part of him wished to step away, but he knew it would not be possible.

"If I may ask," Ethan started, voice weak. The figure did not respond, signaling he may continue. "What power will I gain? What will I be able to do? Will others bow to me as I to you?"

The figure lifted his head slightly, but still, none of him could be seen. An odd pause settled between the two, and Ethan awaited the ultimate answer. He was always aware of the energy that raged around him, creating this pocket dimension.

The figure then spoke, voice obsessive.

"ETHAN, YOU MAY NOT UNDERSTAND NOW, BUT YOU SOON WILL. THIS ENTIRE PLANET WILL FALL UNDER YOUR CONTROL, AND YOU WILL BECOME IMMORTAL. THE

LOWLIFE CREATURES HERE WILL SEE YOU AS THEIR GOD, THEIR RIGHTFUL RULER. SOMEDAY YOU WILL POSSESS THE ABILITY TO CEASE OPPOSITION WITH A FLICK OF YOUR WRIST, AND THE LIGHT WILL NEVER CONTAMINATE YOU EVER AGAIN."

Ethan grinned, but a sense of hesitation lived inside him. The sounds of becoming godlike and having ultimate control were easily tempting. He craved the day where people like Kiran and Gabriel would fall under his command. He envisioned thousands of Academy Warriors kneeling before him in a great assembly, their every will, his own. No longer could he be cast aside, another worthless face in the crowd.

The light will never contaminate you ever again, he recited in his head. It seemed superficial, and he took it as such.

"What do I need to do, master? How can I acquire this...control?"

The figure turned slowly, his cloak dragging across the dark ground. It dissipated on contact, like a steady smoke following his wake. He moved closer and closer to the wall of blackness, before stopping just in front.

"THE BOY, MICHAEL," he hissed disapprovingly. "HE IS WEAK, BUT HE POSES A THREAT TO YOUR OWN LIFE. IN A MATTER OF HOURS, HE WILL ASK OF TWO WARRIORS TO ACCOMPANY HIM ON HIS QUEST. YOU WILL VOLUNTEER."

Ethan swallowed visibly. "Yes, master. Anything else?"

"WHEN OUR END IS NEAR, AND MICHAEL THREATENS TO OVERTAKE ALL WE HAVE CREATED, YOU WILL BRING HIS END, AND ALL WHO STAND BY HIS SIDE."

Ethan's eyes widened, and he had to be sure. "You mean..."

"YOU WILL KILL EVERY SINGLE ONE OF HIS FOLLOWERS, AND THEN, HIM."

Kiran Andon adjusted himself in the waiting room. He looked into the mirror, dark eyes accompanied by brown skin staring back at him. His red Academy Warrior uniform fit perfectly on him, his badge polished and gleaming gold. Bronze cuffs attached to black gloves covered his hands; bronze cuffs with black boots covered his feet. His sword was sheathed, shining silver hilt protruding over his shoulder.

He smiled broadly, photo ready. At every assembly there was at least one photographer, and there was nothing that could be done about it. Only private meetings deemed by Gabriel were void of picture-taking.

The intercom above him crackled.

"One minute until gathering," it said, hardly understandable. Kiran, however, had heard the words enough to correct them in his mind. He did not know who continued to send the messages, as it was far from his department, but found it oddly consistent throughout all his years.

The gathering of Warriors could only ever be brought to fruition in times of great need. They had been called together four times in the past two weeks. This, being the fifth, marked some disturbance within Kiran.

Of course, he was the person who had incited such a meeting, as Gabriel's disappearance and Michael's "entrance" were both of intrigue. Word had spread quickly that a person of interest had been brought in, and it was the bullet-catcher.

The gathering had been announced within minutes, and all Warriors throughout Topia were notified. Everyone's city-issued motorcycles sent out urgent messages, and no one ignored them. Each Warrior was aware that in times of rebellion, each presence was crucial. Those who took days off were released from duty.

Of course, Kiran was never late. By being the right-hand man to Gabriel Lanondek, all eyes were always on him. He loved the attention but knew any screw-ups would be publicized immediately. Two years ago, when he was thirteen, he made a mistake that would cost the life of a girl his own age.

Why think of her now? He wondered. *At such an odd time, this is when I am reminded of her?*

He shook the thoughts of that event from his head and continued preparing himself. Even so, her name lingered in the back of his mind, ever so present. A much bigger and more obvious thought took his attention: the intercom.

"All Academy Warriors due in the gathering center at once! Any who are late risk being uninformed of current events!"

At the same time, a dark-skinned man popped his head into the doorway. Kiran noticed the man's hazel eyes through the mirror and turned his head slightly.

"What is it, Walter?" he asked.

"I've come to present you on stage. The council is settling, but we must be quick."

Kiran glanced toward him, no longer looking into the mirror. "Present me?"

Walter nodded. "The three of us must be representatives for the entire council today. We will be doing the majority of the speaking on stage."

There was a blind sound to his voice, Kiran noticed. He then realized Walter did not know of Michael or any of the events that had happened recently. He doubted the man was even aware of the meeting's purpose.

Ethan stormed outside, Michael appeared out of nowhere, and Gabriel is just...gone. Ah, that's right...

Walter had as well said, "The three of us," about himself, Kiran, and Gabriel. Kiran frowned upon realizing this, as the news of Gabriel's sudden disappearance was indeed important, and the meeting was going to start any moment. He hesitated to share the news, but figured it would be bad if Walter were told in front of the entire council.

"Walter," he said, turning around fully. "Gabriel isn't with us-"

Walter's face grew panicked. "He's dead?!"

Kiran rushed to correct him, noticing his choice of words was not the best.

"No! No, no, no. I just meant...he's, well..."

He struggled for words, as there wasn't a great way to phrase what had happened earlier. He figured the meeting would serve well for explaining who Michael was, as he was the reason Gabriel had disappeared. When Kiran had asked Michael of Gabriel's location, the boy had given him a very cryptic answer:

"Back home."

Kiran started to continue speaking, watching as Walter's face grew more and more puzzled.

"We...don't know where he went."

Walter chewed his lip, turned around slowly, and stopped in the doorway.

"Better find out soon," he muttered, and left the room.

8

The meeting room was flooded with Academy Warriors all alike. The majority were dressed for duty, swords sheathed and uniforms on. They stood in a sparse crowd, small groups of similar Academy Warriors forming. They talked as they waited for the meeting to start, stories being shared. During this time of rebellion, none of the Warriors kept consistent family lives. They were always on call for raids and defenses, breaks rarely being taken.

Male members were more common than female, which was expected in the community. They outnumbered the female warriors five to one, but none found this surprising. Even though there were fewer, the female warriors were still to be reckoned with.

A large amount of the Academy Warriors had been chosen from an early age. They were often recruited straight from the Junior Academy on the second floor (an exception to the ranks). Kiran had been as well. All from the Junior Academy were hand-picked by Gabriel Lanondek. They consistently showed signs of determination, bravery, and most of all, loyalty.

The man had an unusual interest in loyalty. Kiran would make a note of every time Gabriel mentioned someone's "trustworthiness or loyalty" as if there were always seeds of betrayal spreading. He now saw that with the Anarchist Rebellion, it made sense to find loyal soldiers, but Gabriel had been recruiting for it from the very start.

Kiran had heard many stories of Junior Academy students being put through test after test of obedience, their allegiances being revealed over and over. Some students were impeccable, with every test bringing positive remarks. Walter, Kiran remembered, had been one of those students Gabriel had found impossible to fail a loyalty test.

He walked from the preparation room swiftly, following Walter to the stage. The senior Academy Warrior trotted into the meeting room as if he were a celebrity getting ready for an awards ceremony. A wry smile made its way onto Kiran's face as he watched Walter move, hoping not to shatter the man with more of the weird news he brought.

The fact that Gabriel was gone now did not seem to faze Walter. In fact, he had left the panic and worry behind...

Or so it seems, Kiran thought. *He could be putting on a show for the crowd. They deserve to know the truth though. If we leave anyone out of the loop, chaos could spread across our communications like wildfire.*

As they entered the room, everyone was seemingly already captivated by the stage. Everyone looked as if they were incredibly pleased and entertained. They nodded at whoever was speaking from the stage. Walter stopped dead in his tracks and listened to the figure speaking.

Kiran nearly bumped into him, moved out of the way, and took a look for himself. He shouldn't have been surprised, but he did stand still for a moment, thinking. He nearly started laughing, but the sounds would not overtake him.

A blond haired Academy Warrior from the middle of the crowd glanced up and saw Walter. He smiled brightly, motioned to the others around him, and called out.

"Hey! Come hear this plan!" he yelled, interrupting whoever was speaking. The speaker did not resume afterward, as if waiting for Walter to respond as well. The Academy Warrior who had called out grinned expectantly.

Walter glanced at the speaker and sized him up. The speaker was a young boy, shorter than him, with strikingly blue eyes. The boy exerted overconfidence so strong Walter nearly thought he could see it in the air, but it was immature overconfidence. He thought he could see childishness.

He stepped from the hallway and onto the stage, aware of the eyes placed upon him. He ignored those in the crowd and approached the boy first.

"Mind telling me why you're here?" he asked, like an annoyed adult finding a suspicious child loitering in his front yard.

The boy glanced around him and at Kiran. He raised an eyebrow when he noticed Kiran was covering his eyes and mouth with one hand, with a disappointed-parent look as well. He then switched his attention back to Walter, and acknowledged him.

"I'm Michael Nebadon. It's a pleasure to meet you," the boy said, with a slight accent Walter had never heard before. It nearly threw him off, not expecting this sort of language from such a young boy, but regained composure quickly.

Instead of introducing himself back, he repeated his question:

"Mind telling me why you're here?"

Michael appeared confused and glanced once again at Kiran. Kiran was now only covering his mouth, eyes revealed. Their eyes locked, but Kiran did not make any effort for communication. Michael kept looking at him with Walter in his peripheral vision. He was aware of the danger this man possessed, but understood the crowd would not take kindly to violence.

I am safe here, he knew. *This man would not hurt me.* He spotted the sheathed sword strapped to Walter's back, and hoped the Warrior would not be so quick to draw it.

So once again he placed his focus on Kiran. He still failed to understand why Kiran wasn't speaking, as if he were frozen in time. He connected it almost back to when he had shown Kiran "the vision," except now it didn't have a reason.

Kiran's mind was starting to figure something out.

There had once been a time where Kiran Andon felt true sorrow. He had been born and raised in the middle-class sections of Topia City, labeled Desertia Towns, until his ultimate acceptance into The Academy.

Almost all of the students accepted into the Academy came from extraordinarily ordinary and traditional backgrounds. They were raised well, and schooled within their own homes as per usual. Families often had both parents, one working outside of home and one taking care of schooling. This set a high and stable standard for recruits, which attracted both positive and negative comments from the press.

Some praised the selection process, stating it was "exclusive, sensible, and wise," while others said it was a "flawed and selfish" process.

The only kids who were recruited had to meet these requirements.

Except for those like Kiran.

Kiran lived with both his parents for the majority of his childhood. Of course, childhood meaning the younger years of his life, as he was still fifteen years old. He was ahead two years in regular education, considered a top of the line student.

Then, all hell broke loose. My father died, and my mother fell mentally ill. Everything crumbled through my fingers.

He glanced up at Michael once more, seeing the caution in the boy. Walter stood beside him, still at a standoff. Kiran knew Walter had nearly no idea what to do, as Michael wasn't listening to anything he was saying.

Time paused; frozen still as Kiran plunged into his memories. Michael's shining blue eyes called him back to previous times, as he saw such an immense resemblance to a man he had known up until thirty minutes ago.

The connection is so weird, so bizarre. It's as if Gabriel and Michael were the same person, but forty years apart. They must be related...

No. The way they spoke to one another was as if they hadn't seen each other for a hundred years.

It's more like they're the same person in two different bodies.

Gabriel Lanondek, Michael Nebadon...

He played back Michael's words in his head, noting the way the two spoke was eerily similar. Their mannerisms, movements, even the way they breathed was nearly identical. He glanced back to the ground.

Why have I focused so much on this? he wondered. But then a voice within himself reminded him:

He saved your life.

Five years ago, Kiran's father had been killed by a force he could not explain in the slightest. He didn't have the chance to see it himself, coming home to the madness after a long day out with friends. He found him seemingly unharmed, but with the echoes of pain and death consuming him. A dark essence could be felt in that room, one that surely drove Kiran's mother insane.

She had cried for days, having seen the moment herself. She could not explain it; no one could explain what had happened.

The Academy Warriors themselves had no clue about the cause of death or even the signs of the person who had done it. It was as if the life was drained away after extreme agony was dealt.

It was an odd feeling, having his father's life taken in one moment, but it was as if he could still not conceive of it; one day his father might walk through the front door of the house as he always did, home from working at the most significant banking firm in Desertia Towns. The fact that no one really talked about what had occurred made the death almost feel less real, fake, nearly.

He didn't want to believe it, because there was even the chance it wasn't true. Even so, every time he let his mind run away with those thoughts, Kiran thought of the body he had seen, and it was genuinely lifeless. He always knew, deep down, that it had happened, and it was over.

A week after the event, Kiran's mother was clearly not well. She had been taken in for therapy, but since the therapist could not explain it better than anyone else, there was almost nothing that could be done. Kiran was left waiting for news, for his mother to become sane and sensible again, but that never happened.

He remembered spending days, just thinking. His schooling had been put on halt for lack of a teacher, and despite being able to support his own needs around the house, he had no connections to the outside world. The therapist assigned to his mother would bring her home after a long morning of care, but that was all.

This went on for three weeks. Hope was running thin, as Kiran, even with the slight help he received from the therapy firm, was low on resources. He had scavenged the whole house for food multiple times, but because his mother remained ill, nothing came to his rescue.

They had no outside sources. Any extended family was nonexistent, and Kiran's father's bank had nothing to provide. Horrific thoughts came pressing in:

What if I die from starvation? Will I have to become homeless before then? Why won't anyone help me?

His questions, however, were only just about to be answered.

For three weeks and two days after the event, a man named Gabriel Lanondek stepped through Kiran's front door. He was supported by a team of two men dressed in uniform and armed, but he himself was not. Unbeknownst to Kiran, Gabriel had taken an interest into the case only three days after it had happened, investigating it promptly. He had known of Kiran's existence, but did not know of the terrible conditions the boy was being held in during the aftermath.

Kiran's mother had been home, but it hadn't mattered. She was quickly whisked away, and that was it. Kiran hardly cared; he had been slowly forgetting about her and focusing on himself as the days passed. She no longer took care of him, and she was unresponsive to his words, so he began to ignore her. His sympathy for her became

50

nothing more, and his only mourning had been for his father. Even that, however, had been brisk.

Plus, when Gabriel had stepped through the door, his eyes had immediately landed on Kiran Andon. A young boy whose father had been killed, his mother driven insane, and left on his own after the previous events.

Gabriel had approached him right away, squatting so he could meet eye to eye with the boy. They exchanged a long staring contest, of which Kiran was the winner. Kiran smiled but did not show excitement for his victory. Instead, he asked a question:

"Are you my new father?"

Gabriel did not answer right away, but glanced around the dimly lit and musty house. He then replied,

"I must be."

Then, Kiran looked into Gabriel's shining blue eyes and forever remembered the shine. The very same shine that he saw in Michael's eyes now, the shine of stars. The shine of the night sky as cosmic bodies danced their stellar ways, and it all led him to a conclusion:

That's no coincidence at all.

9

Michael saw Kiran's shift in realization moments before the action took place. He noticed the swift change of pace in his thinking, Kiran's eyes flaring to life as he turned to Walter.

Kiran placed his hand in front of Walter to prevent him from advancing toward Michael. He thought of questioning Michael right then and there, asking him of the stirring resemblance. But he shook his head visibly.

Later.

"Walter," he said, looking at the Academy Warrior. "Why don't we at least hear the plan he has to share?"

Walter did not look away from Michael. "He could be wasting our time."

Kiran glanced at the crowd, then back to Walter. "The crowd seemed to love it."

Walter grunted, and pushed Kiran's arm away. He stepped to the edge of the stage, facing the entire audience.

"Who here believes this boy's plan is possible?!"

A significant amount of the Academy Warriors raised their hands. A few did not, some because they did not want to oppose Walter in the slightest. Those raising their hands were mostly genuine as well, but some band-wagoners did exist in the crowd.

Walter sighed, and placed his hands on his hips. He glanced at his feet, half disappointed and half annoyed.

Kiran, however, was even slightly surprised himself. Confidence had been present when he spoke to Walter, but it was somewhat exaggerated. The ratio was much larger than he expected at all. Out of nearly the one hundred Warriors in the room, almost ninety supported Michael.

He glanced at Michael and saw a bright grin on the boy's face. A single thought passed through him:

What did you say to convince so many people?

But the thought did not last long, as Michael opened his mouth to speak, and the crowd shushed immediately.

As they did with Gabriel, Kiran noted.

Walter stepped away, still annoyed. He shot a glance at Kiran, who ignored him.

Michael started, and Kiran was in no way prepared with what he would propose.

"Since most of you here have already heard this, I promise to not repeat myself in a way that will sound monotonous."

He paused, thinking. The words passed through him once again, and he made sure not to say the exact same speech.

He nodded and continued.

"I have only been in this city for less than a day now, and before you interject, it is not a situation I can explain at the moment. Do not question it! Perhaps, once we are finished, I will tell. Even so, do not think it odd! Similar events have happened in this world, as I know from firsthand experience.

"Your strategy for handling the Anarchists is inconsistent and passive. The Academy Warriors possess great abilities and potential, but you are being restrained. It is your own fault. The Anarchists began as a purely political party, but now they are appropriately a rebellion. Their political standings weren't excellent to start with, and I am surprised at how shocked you all were. Their betrayal could've been predicted easily!

"Now, the rebellion has only existed entirely for two weeks. Even so, they've been a rising threat for perhaps even a month. A preemptive confrontation would have handled the situation, but instead, you've let it worsen over time. You left an infection to take over without batting an eye.

"Soon, in a matter of days to weeks, I can predict a war breaking out.

"This war will start only because the Anarchists will gain equal power to Topia City. They will assume a new nation upon themselves that can no longer be seen as docile or dormant. Their soldiers will flood Topia's streets, and civilians will be either harmed or converted to the Anarchist cause. And do not be deceived by the 'nation' I speak of. That is not their way. They will instead form a loose agreement, for as soon as the government is broken down, chaos will ensue."

He spoke on for about another minute, but Kiran's mind started to wander. He noted that Michael, as soon as the attention was on him, had left any remains of childishness behind. The boy was younger than him, but he could hardly tell by listening to his words. The audience remained captivated even though they had heard the plan once before. They seemed not to treat him as if he were a young teenager, but a young man on equal footing as them, or even above.

He looked to Walter and saw a sharp glare on his face. It worsened the more Michael criticized the methods of the Academy Warriors, and while Kiran expected Walter to eventually interrupt, the man never did.

A little while after mentioning that the Anarchists were supposedly giving Topia seven days to prepare, Michael continued:

"The Anarchist leaders are unknown, which is incredibly worrying. How can we defend ourselves against masked faces? How can we arrest criminals who have no identity? How can we even begin to plan, if we have no clue who we are fighting? We cannot, so, therefore, uncovering the identities of any Anarchist leader would be a priority before any major combat breaks out. In fact, their leaders could be...."

He turned his head slightly, eyes glancing back at Kiran.

"Within our own organizations?"

This seemed to unsettle Kiran more than it did anyone else, as Michael had looked to him as the words were said. No one else apparently noticed the glance, as Michael turned to the crowd once again soon after.

Does he think I'm with the Anarchists? Kiran thought. He bid the idea ridiculous. Michael would have exposed him as a leader if he had been. The tone of Michael's voice sounded accusatory indeed, but for some odd reason, Kiran didn't honestly feel as if it was aimed at him.

Or is he suggesting someone else, and warning me instead?

He scanned the crowd, noting faces as he went. Some people he recognized, hearing their names in his mind as he passed over them. Walter, of course, stood beside him.

Jeremy Gonzalez...Sergio Rontoza....oh, Ethan's back as well.

He saw Ethan deep in the back of the crowd, near the doors. Dark circles loomed under his eyes, and his red hair remained disheveled. He seemed to struggle to stay awake, as if he might pass out any moment.

Still not doing too well, I see.

He went back to matching names to faces, but no one really stood out to him. One girl next to the right wall, Dynai Riddenwood, held a concealed knife in her left hand, which seemed suspicious to Kiran. Her face, however, showed focus as deep as the others around her, listening to every word Michael said.

She was always fascinated with her weapons, he remembered. She had been in the Academy with him, but in the two cohorts that had divided the students, she and Kiran had been separated. They had only encountered one another on all Academy missions, where Kiran remembered Dynai always being the first one to have her sword out.

She seems so loyal about it, though. I'd be surprised if she were an Anarchist. In fact, not many of the people here seem dangerous enough to pose that much of a threat. Most of them have been training as Academy Warriors for years and years. Some are in their twenties, thirties, and have decades of service.

Maybe Michael's just proposing a possibility after all.

He turned back to Michael and listened to the end of the speech.

"If Topia falls, and the Anarchists take over, this city will descend into a Dystopia, without light, and without order. Your people will fall to chaos and crime. It is already rather unfortunate that now, even as I speak, areas of your cities are unprotected and poor. People already roam the streets as homeless and on the brink of insanity, so imagine what the entire city may become if that spreads."

He's referring to the lower class areas...the Smith and Hookhorse Districts. They're already Anarchist-flooded, thought Kiran.

"Your businesses will turn corrupt, your civilians starved and in destitution. Wildlife poisoned and killed, air too noxious to breathe.

Thousands of years of evolution will slowly be wiped away, and everything will turn to darkness."

Kiran started to see Michael's true worry unearth itself. His voice began to grow direr, ranting on and on. The crowd grew more interested with every passing second, and they were not left hanging.

"A greater evil may rise from beneath, one I myself faced a many, many years ago. He will call upon his allies, and take advantage of your lacking in organization. This planet will turn to fire and ash, and all will be left behind."

He stopped, letting the words sink in. Kiran glanced at Walter once more and saw that his expression had not changed. Now, however, Kiran was surprised. Walter would still hold his grudge over information that now confirmed the Anarchists' potential!

"But..." Michael started. "There is one final option, one that I will elaborate more on as the higher-ups are now listening. This option may or may not be possible, depending on how brave some of you are.

"I will first warn that this mission will be dangerous. That will not be kept a secret. We will be going places unknown to this city. Anarchists may be watching us at every turn, and their leaders will know us by name and face.

"So then, I offer the opportunity for two Academy Warriors to accompany me on my ultimate goal of stopping this rising darkness. And keep in mind, we must do this in seven days, before the Anarchists are certain to attack."

Michael looked out to the crowd with curiosity.

"Anyone who wishes to volunteer, raise your hand."

After a few moments, he counted the hands.

Zero.

10

Ethan Catanzaro held a cold hand to his face, eyes wet with anger. He wanted to hate himself for this decision. He wished to run out of the building as he had done before, but this time with nowhere to go. He wanted to run straight back to the Shadow Lords, no, *straight back to his home*. His burnt, crispy home that sat in rubble and ash in Mysti District.

He thought back to that day, that bitter, horrid day. He held the tears in with difficulty as he was thrown back five years.

Once again, he opened his sleepy eyes to a darkened living room. The TV was switched on, muted but full of color. Characters moved across the screen in dramatic action, as they battled to compete in Topia's newest hit: *Alliance*. He realized with horror that he had fallen asleep in the recliner, which was frowned upon in the Catanzaro household.

A small creaking sounded from behind him, behind the cold leather of his father's recliner. Mr. Catanzaro loved his Sunday afternoons away from work, spending hours in the recliner watching TV and drinking. Sunday nights were always bittersweet, knowing he could relax now, but had to work the next day.

Ethan froze still in the recliner, pretending to be asleep. He prayed his hair wouldn't be visible above the top of the chair, for if his mother were to see him still down here...

He knew the odds were slim, but if his mother had come downstairs for some unrelated reason, he might not be seen. She might've forgotten to do something for work, or maybe she just needed water from the kitchen.

Whatever it is, Ethan hoped, *Just let it be quick.*

It was a Tuesday night, which meant an early morning the next day. Ethan would be punished for staying up this late. Being grounded meant no TV, no dessert after dinner, and no allowance. All things he needed to survive, supposedly.

As he stayed still for what seemed like ten minutes, but was really only thirty seconds, he had yet to hear another creak. It seemed odd for what his mother would usually do if she had come down here with a purpose.

One didn't merely stand still in the middle of a hallway, in the darkness.

Ethan slowly peeked over the edge of the recliner, moving as slowly as possible. His eyes scanned the darkness with worry, wondering what he might see. He continued to pray whoever it was would not notice him.

A dark shape stood in the hallway to the front door, but the door was wide open. Ethan's eyes widened themselves, now convinced the person was an intruder. He frantically began to glance around, but kept his slight focus on the figure.

The figure was unmoving. It stood there, only a silhouette from the light of the TV and the stars outside. Ethan's ten-year-old heart raced, pounding in his ears as the blood rushed. Adrenaline spiked, and fear with it. His vision became blurred, and he struggled for solutions.

His eyes flashed to a small object on one of the numerous coffee tables about the room. A little red light blinked on top of it, and Ethan assumed it must be one of the house communicators. He recited the emergency number for The Academy in his head, realizing that he could easily rush over and grab it. He also knew his parents were asleep upstairs, and waking them somehow would help, of course.

He waited a little while longer, not sure what the figure might do if he made such a deliberate move. He felt the minutes tick by and came to a horrible realization.

The figure could be watching HIM.

He became frozen with the thought, unable to move at all. His eyes locked on the figure as if watching him would keep him still. He thought about waiting until daylight came, and the light flooded through the door, followed by his parents coming downstairs. He hesitated on the possibility but knew that it would be impossible. Time felt nonexistent.

Daytime will never come unless I make a move.

So his mind fell to other options. He thought, for a split second, that it all might be a dream, a horrendous nightmare. Maybe, in a few minutes, he would suddenly snap awake in his bed upstairs, no longer in danger. He would open his eyes to the sunlight streaming in from his windows, illuminating the red blinds that hung there.

He would rise up from the bed, and hear his parents making breakfast downstairs. He would see his father straightening a tie to go to work at Catanzaro Financials down the street. His mother would sit down at the dining room table, welcoming Ethan with a bright smile. Vibrant orange locks of hair would fall on her shoulders, glowing in the morning's light.

Ethan would sit down, and he would smile back.

But then, in one swift moment, it would all shatter. A torrent wind of reality would tear him from that pleasant scenario, ripping the seams that held it all together. The figure still stood in the hallway, a dark essence surrounding him that made Ethan queasy.

In the figure's blank face Ethan thought he could see jagged green eyes glowing, staring back at him. He could see them with his cursed imagination, as they looked into his soul and his mind. Green claws of the same shape, jagged and torn, grew from the figure's arms, lengthening until they touched the floor.

The green claws detached from the figure, a dark trail of smoke following, and began to crawl like spiders. They made their way down the hallway with ease, straight at Ethan. The boy shrunk back into his chair, not knowing at all what to do. His mind raced once again for an option, but there were none.

Luckily, he did not need one.

The claws suddenly lept right, straight onto the staircase that led upstairs. They scurried up the steps, growing larger and larger.

Ethan panicked. He knew where they were going: straight to his parents' bedroom. He could only imagine what they might do.

He jumped up from the chair spastically. He fell to the ground, banging his knee hard. Adrenaline allowed him to ignore the pain, and out of desperation, he ran at the figure. Sudden bravery combined with fear-if that made any sense-rushed within him. His footsteps pounded as hard as his heart did, and as he drew nearer, the claws ran farther upward.

He did not follow the claws, however. He ran directly at the very figure who seemed to summon them. Black tendrils still clung to the figure's arms. They ran up the staircase as well, following the claws until ultimately connecting to them.

Ethan wanted to run barehanded at first, but the last, tiniest bit of reason made him decide otherwise. As he searched slightly for a weapon, he noticed the only thing in the path between him and the figure.

An umbrella basket.

His fingers closed around one of the umbrellas at random. There was no time to choose the best one. He grabbed it and reared it back like a bat. Intending to only make contact, whether it be blasting the figure's head off or smashing the tendrils apart, he swung.

Contact was made, but in the worst of places.

Ethan's eyes opened, as they had been closed when he swung, and looked upon the scene before him. The umbrella was jammed in the gleaming sword of the figure, seeming to float in midair. He struggled against it, trying to pull away or unlock the umbrella, but nothing worked.

Out of more desperation, he kicked at the figure. Throwing his entire weight into the kick, he figured it would be his last chance. He closed his eyes once again and prayed some damage would be done.

His leg fell right through the figure, as the shadows departed around it. They congealed and formed elsewhere, but one black tendril remained attached to Ethan's leg.

It threw him with enormous force, and the umbrella was torn from his hands. Following it almost immediately, he felt a sickening slash of a sword across his face. A deep cut opened. He had no time to react and ended up on the doorstep outside. Cold air rushed into him, and as he reached out to crawl back inside, the door slammed shut.

A scream came from inside the house, followed by a deeper one. Yells and loud noises followed, hurting Ethan every time as he laid helpless.

Then, the top of the house glowed orange, and a fire blossomed.

Nothing remained after it burned. Ethan laid there, tears flowing from his eyes and blood from his cut, already determined to kill the murderer inside.

And now, as he stood with his face covered by a wet hand, he felt the scar rough against his palm. He slowly brought his hand down, fingers running over it.

That's why I'm an Academy Warrior. I will hunt down that figure and personally be his doom. He took what was mine, so I will return the favor.

Then, in horrid realization, as he snapped back to reality, he saw his other hand was raised.

Kiran was the first to notice Ethan's hand. It was alone among the sea of others, pale and shaking. Ethan was not looking up, but still down at his other trembling hand. Kiran could only imagine what Ethan might be thinking. He raised an eyebrow, the events of earlier flashing from his memory. Something must've changed for him earlier. Something big.

No one else had even budged. Not one single man or woman, besides Ethan, of course, had raised their hand. Even after, no one joined with him. In fact, they parted around him with a wide berth.

Kiran ran through the people he had seen earlier in the crowd. Both Jeremy and Sergio were watching Michael, waiting to see the boy's response. Dynai held her dagger much more firmly, watching Ethan. She took what Kiran recognized as one of the Academy Warrior conflict stances, but her fingers were positioned in a way he had never seen. Even so, he had no time to truly focus on it.

Walter stood silently beside, not surprised. He knew that despite the "ground-breaking" speech Michael had given, no one would follow through. Michael was merely a boy with bright intentions, and he had no real standing. Walter himself would decide the plans overall. He would dismiss this plan shortly.

Only one person even has remote faith in this...boy. And that person seems to be on the edge of insanity.

Look at him, crying. He doesn't have to do this, I hope he realizes. Ah, well. I guess it's his fault if he wants to make foolish decisions.

Poor kid's been through a lot. A fire killed his parents, made an orphan at the age of ten. Probably the worst time to become one. You remember just enough, but you haven't gone through enough to survive it.

And look at the toll it's taken on him now. It's made him insane!

Michael looked down upon Ethan with the greatest curiosity he'd experienced so far. Wonder surged through him, and he was even a little confused. He recalled what Ethan had done earlier, storming out and all, but was now beginning to understand.

Ethan remained trembling, and Michael wished to observe him a little more. Everyone else seemed to be watching either him or Ethan, often switching back and forth. Michael, of course, kept his gaze on the redheaded boy, but was well aware of the eyes on him. He noted many of the ones he had expected to raise their hands kept their sights on him, and he suspected it was out of example.

*I have one member...*Michael thought. He looked about the other potential candidates but knew the other Academy Warrior he needed was right behind him.

The chaotic one makes the first move, he noted. *How will the peaceful one respond?*

Walter stepped forward.

"Well! As far as I see it, only one little boy stands with you, Michael. That's unfortunate on your end, but now your spotlight is over." He walked over to Michael and began motioning for him to move.

Kiran, however, had other plans.

Just as Walter was beginning to take charge, he walked to the front of the stage.

"Actually," he said and paused. A momentary flicker of doubt showed in him, but he pushed it away before his mind could change.

If Ethan can do it while he's broken and in tears, I can do it right now.

"Actually," he said again. "He has two little boys."

Michael grinned broadly. He looked to the crowd expectantly, letting them take in the two volunteers. He himself, however, showed no surprise.

It's exactly as I've expected! They will do well, I'm sure.

Walter looked to Kiran as if he'd been offended.

"You've got to be kidding me," he muttered. Kiran heard it and ignored without a doubt.

"Walter," Michael said, catching the man's attention. "Would you fetch Ethan for us?"

Walter hesitated, wanting to say no very badly. He gritted his teeth, glanced at the redheaded boy in the crowd, and sighed angrily. He nodded reluctantly and walked to the edge of the stage.

The crowd parted for him to jump down, and in a swift moment, they all created a path to Ethan. Walter attempted to make eye contact with any of the other Academy Warriors, knowing some might be on his side about this plan still being insane. He thought the idea of only two men, *boys*, accompanying Michael would be suicide. They needed an army to confront the Anarchists.

A good one, too. Hopefully, then, Michael will be leading these two on a suicide mission, and I won't have to worry about them interfering.

No one wanted to look at Walter, it seemed. They kept their focus now on Ethan, who struggled to gather himself. He wiped tears from his eyes, but his face was still stained with them. Blotches of red on his skin showed, and only Kiran knew it was from worry. His hands still shook violently, and he finally lowered the one in the air.

Walter got to Ethan quickly. He grabbed the boy by one arm and began pulling him toward the stage. Ethan struggled against it slightly, but he didn't have the energy to resist. A pulsing pain echoed from his wrist where Walter held him, but he didn't cry out. His memories were louder than that.

Michael and Kiran awaited them. Kiran walked over and stood by Michael's right side. He expected Ethan to do the same on the left.

Ethan looked dead in the eyes as he was half dragged-half led across the stage. They met with Kiran's, but no connection was made. He still felt as if he were staring off into space, his mind a blurry mess and his eyes failing to work.

Walter let the redheaded boy go as soon as they reached Michael's left side. Ethan fell to his knees, utterly collapsing.

Michael turned to him, tilted his head, and knelt down. Ethan refused to look at him.

"I know I cannot replicate what you are feeling," Michael whispered. "But you don't have to go through this now."

Ethan grunted, and his shoulders fell limp.

"You've proven the validity of your decision. There is no need for more reluctant strength."

Ethan grunted again in response. He finally began to refocus his eyes and started to glance up at Michael. Michael, however, only appeared as a blur of brown cloak and blond hair. His blue eyes seemed to expand and contract in Ethan's vision. They started to swirl and began to form as galaxies. Ethan saw stars upon stars within them, and he fell into another stupor.

"Ethan," Michael whispered again. "I'm going to need you to do something, okay?"

Ethan did not respond, locked in Michael's eyes.

"Ethan..." Michael said.

Still no response at all. Ethan remained looking into Michael's now universal gaze, starting to see further and further.

Michael remained perplexed, and frowned. He raised an eyebrow. The crowd continued to watch, but no one said anything. They were all focused in stupors themselves.

Michael started to realize his eyes had not moved for the longest time. They were as locked in Ethan's as Ethan's were in his. He was tempted to jerk away and break the staring contest, but he didn't want to disturb Ethan more than he already was. Instead, he began to take an advantage into the situation. Again, he plunged himself into Ethan's mind and relived that night for him.

He saw himself not through Ethan's younger eyes, but as a floating being nearby. The flashback passed quickly, with the claws scurrying up the stairs at a blink of an eye and the house burning in an instant. But even after Ethan was thrown outside, slashed across the face, the flashback did not end. Everything froze for a split moment, and then all actions reversed.

The claws came down the stairs, the figure backed away to the door, and Ethan walked back to the leather recliner.

It started all over again.

It's madness, Michael thought. *A cycle.*

He snapped into focus and began moving. As he did, the moments slowed, and Ethan did not dart from the recliner as he had before. Michael headed steadily toward the back of the recliner and glided around it.

Ethan could now see Michael, but he was still hazy. Michael now appeared as a golden shine in the air, standing before him. He still remained in his trembling state, but Michael created an aura of warmth in the cold night.

Then the creak sounded behind him, and he once again became tempted to look over the edge of the recliner. Michael urged him not to, whispering:

"Don't. We are the only ones here. There is no one else."

Ethan resisted the temptation and looked away.

"Look at me," Michael commanded. Ethan complied, but with puffy eyes. "Good. Now, focus."

As Ethan kept his gaze on Michael, the darkness of the night faded away into new Light. The gold from Michael flooded outwards, enveloping all. The TV turned to shimmering dust, and the walls followed. The staircase fell as shining sand, with the ceiling dissipating into thin air.

After that, only the recliner remained.

"Ethan," Michael said. "Be the Light."

The seat beneath Ethan crumbled, and he fell.

His eyes in the real world snapped open, and as he regained his consciousness, Ethan felt a hand grab his own. He was pulled upward onto his feet, and for the first time that day, felt remotely stable.

Michael looked to the crowd and smiled. Having Kiran on his right and Ethan on his left let him know the plan was working. He spread his arms toward the masses.

"I present my two volunteers. Kiran, Ethan, I welcome you to a new age! You are sacrificing much to join me, and I will be forever grateful."

Kiran turned to him.

"But how are us three supposed to take down the whole rebellion?"

Michael remained looking at the crowd but responded anyway. He grinned broadly, blue eyes sparkling.

"I was just getting to that."

11

Kiran couldn't interrupt Michael quick enough.

"Hold on hold on!" he yelled, waving his hands. "We can't do that!"

Michael stopped speaking, and looked to Kiran, confused. He paused for a moment, wondering what exactly Kiran was referring to, and awaited a further explanation.

"What do you mean?" he asked.

Kiran started to speak faster, and he knew the crowd was growing antsy, but he restrained himself.

"What I mean is..." he glanced away, and for a moment, he saw Walter watching him intensely. The man had both hands clenched, and he appeared red in the face. Now, true anger filled the Warrior, much more than before. He was only a few seconds away from attacking Michael.

"We can't leave the city!"

"At all?"

"Not at all. It's been a rule for the longest time."

Michael raised an eyebrow and turned to Ethan. He and Ethan exchanged glances, and Michael found what Kiran was saying was the truth. He turned back and frowned.

"So no one can leave the city?"

Kiran started to say no but paused midway.

"Well, people can, I guess. If they wanted to."

"But there's nothing out there," added Ethan quietly. "It'd be suicide."

Michael looked to the crowd.

"Is this true? Is the land beyond desolate?"

A quick murmur ran through the crowd, and many heads nodded solemnly. All eyes fell to the floor.

Michael shook his head. "But how can you know? Have you searched?"

"There's no need," Kiran said. "After what Leila Lanondek revealed a few weeks ago, the whole mess that started the rebellion, we know for sure everything is gone."

"So what I'm hearing is that you've never looked? No one has even tried?"

Kiran sighed. "People have tried, and they've never returned."

Michael put his hands together and closed his eyes. Kiran and Ethan watched curiously as he touched his fingers to his forehead, nearly saintlike. He whispered soft words that flowed through the air like a swift breeze.

"In my words of serene zephyr, I speak to you. Offer me something, what more can I ask to convince those who stand before me?"

Everyone, unsure of who he was speaking to, remained silent. They watched on as Michael's eyes squeezed themselves shut, as if a splitting headache was running through him. His breathing became much heavier and drawn out.

Then, in a sudden moment, his eyes snapped open, and his hands lowered. His eyes shone brighter than they had before, with everyone looking on.

He then spoke to every person in the room, his voice vibrating and echoing about, his words repeating in hundreds of different voices.

"The world beyond Topia is not empty, of that I can assure you. The people who have left are out there, where else would they have gone? Your history is dark indeed, and I have watched it unfold, but it cannot stop the future. We will leave Topia City tomorrow at sunrise, just the three of us.

"Now, who can tell me about the people who have left?"

Michael then stopped, his eyes dimming and his focus waning. He began to feel lightheaded, with his vision blurring more every second. He shook his head over and over, attempting to rattle himself back to reality, but nothing worked.

Too much energy! I mustn't be so reckless.

"I will awake," he whispered, raising his hand high into the air, and toppled backward. Kiran's eyes widened, and he lunged to catch the falling boy. It was no use, and Michael slammed against the stage.

Kiran glanced up to Ethan. "I'll take him home. You gather the missing person's reports. Find everything you can on those who have left the city. We need as much info as we can."

Ethan glanced at Michael's unconscious face. The golden Light he had seen from him still remained in his eyes.

He looked back to Kiran and nodded grimly.

"Whatever you say, pal."

Two hours later, Michael opened his eyes to reveal a room he had never entered. His mind hazily started to recall everything from before, and soon, he became fully conscious.

Of course, he had woken up the moment Kiran had carried him out the door of The Academy and remembered every second past that. He had decided to remain "asleep" out of curiosity, merely wondering where Kiran might take him. Experiments like these were to live for.

He even felt the eyes of everyone watching as he passed, despite his own eyes always being closed. He felt the swift breeze of dawning evening rush over him once outside, and could picture an orange sun making its way down the sky. Kiran lowered him into the backseat of some sort of vehicle, in which they drove off.

The ground rumbled beneath the vehicle's wheels, and soon, Michael thoughts started to drift away.

His consciousness drove in two, one part of him still hearing and breathing the world outside, the other delving into moments that had occurred years before.

Voices entered his head, the first being one of a young woman:

"What are you thinking, Michael?"

He looked to her, but there was no one there. There was only the darkness of his closed eyelids.

"I think it's time," he answered, but his mouth did not move. His voice rang out from behind his head, more profound and louder than he remembered it.

The voice asked another question:

"Time for what, my dear?"

He paused, mind biting for an answer, but he did not know. Any chances of an answer sat on the tip of his tongue. He could tell the asker was awaiting his response, and even though she did not seem impatient, he struggled with haste. He came to realize he wanted to answer more for himself than for her.

"I-I don't know," he wanted to say, but as he did, he could not hear the words come from his mouth. As he lay, confused, his other mind listened to the running of cars and felt the bumps of the road. They turned onto different streets several times before eventually stopping.

Kiran walked back to him and carried him once again. They entered another building, one much different than The Academy. No people were bustling about, just a rhythmic, quiet sound from far off. It was almost like a rumble.

They turned quickly and went inside yet another room. This one, however, did not stay still. Kiran said a few words that Michael couldn't understand, and the room lurched upward. Michael's other mind started to fuse back with this one, but after a moment, they separated again. The place then moved upward slowly for about five seconds.

A *ding!* sounded, and Kiran stepped out from the room.

Michael's other mind retook control.

"It's time to return," he told the young woman. There was then silence, which he assumed would be the woman thinking. He didn't quite understand what he meant himself, but found it better to let the flow continue.

"It's been so long since those fateful days," he continued. *"I want to check on them."*

An unsure but trusting *"hm"* came from the woman, and Michael dearly wished to see her face. He always knew facial expressions could convey more than words could, and now he had only a slight idea of what the woman was thinking.

But even so, he had a sort of feeling that this conversation had already happened. It was as if it was over many many years ago, and everything they were saying had once been told. He could feel a lifelessness in the conversation.

It was dead, and it was in the past. Even so, he sincerely wished for it to go on, for he was weirdly curious as to what he would say next.

"There's another reason," the woman said. *"I know you have an ulterior motive."*

Now it was his turn to pause and think, finding this incredibly confusing. How was he expected to answer when he did not know what he had been saying before? There were too many missing pieces in this puzzle. He could not answer, but his past self could.

"Dear, I care for that planet," he said.

"I know you do. I do too, and so do many others. 'What of Amadon?', they asked so long ago. And, a long time after that, they asked of you."

"So they did, and I am grateful."

"They asked of YOU, for it was YOU who chose that planet."

"So many terrible things had happened there."

He grew ever more confused, but so, so intrigued. Some of the words were familiar to him, and some he could even remember saying. It was like some weird version of Deja Vu. The moments were right there, being played back to him, but there was a blur. He could not see it without his glasses, and right now, both lenses had been shattered.

"Even so, I do not blame you," the woman continued.

"Thank you, dear."

"It isn't your fault they rebelled."

"Now, don't get started with that."

"It isn't your fault they laid waste to Satania and caused that war. It was never on yourself to bring them to the Light. What you did was of your own purest volition. But...you seem worried?"

"L-"

"Do not mention his name! He doesn't deserve it..."

"But he's exactly who I'm worried about."

He could nearly see the disappointment on the woman's face. Her tone was growing sourer as he was growing tired.

"You can't be serious," she said, exasperated. *"After what strength you've gained, you still fear him?"*

"Fear is a crude way of stating it."

"It's how THEY would state it, on that planet, THERE! That is their language, and if you go down there...it's how they'll see you."

"Dear, come with me."

"Are you crazy!? I-"

She paused midway, and Michael could feel her starting to leave the room they were in. He could envision her throwing her hands in the air, and storming out.

Most of all, though, he knew who she was. He could feel it now, and remember her voice. Her face appeared so simple in his mind, but even so, it was changing. He could not remember her one way or another, only that she was there, with him.

Or that she was still out there, letting him see what he's done now. As he thought, his separated minds began to fuse back into one. He could feel himself now laying down once again, but this time the material against his back was not leather. Instead, he could feel it as a smooth fabric, much like a chair or a couch.

In the distance, he could hear someone, presumably Kiran, moving around. There were a few clangs of metal, but not like the ones of swords. A few beeps sounded, and a warm smell began to reach him. Comforting spices.

Heavy footsteps thumped the floor nearby, drawing closer. An object was set down lightly to his left with a glassy clink. The smell was much stronger now, and Michael presumed it was from the glass itself.

76

A drink. The first I may have this time around.

His eyes fluttered open, and he was greeted by a beige ceiling. It was spotless, and as he slowly sat up, he realized that would be the norm here.

Everything in the room was clean. The place appeared to be a type of apartment, with the kitchen off to the side and dimming natural light flooding in from all directions. Michael's view came from the corner of the room, and glancing down at his body, he noticed the soft turquoise couch beneath him. His skin appeared pale, and as he checked himself for warning signs, he found none.

Kiran sat on a matching blue chair across from him, observing. Michael was reminded of the interrogation earlier and felt a similar tension now. Even so, it was only similar. Something in the air was different.

Michael looked to Kiran. Gesturing to the room, he asked, "Your home, I presume?"

Kiran nodded, stroking the white cup in his hands. His knuckles had been white from gripping the cup tight, but now they were beginning to fade.

"You live alone, then?" Michael asked. Kiran glanced away, hoping to hide his reaction to the question. It was too late, though, and Michael easily saw the flash of pain in Kiran's eyes.

The pain of the past. He will move on.

Kiran did not cry, for he bid himself to never. The tears couldn't flow, and he never wanted them to. He never cared enough to even entertain the possibility. Only bitterness and resentment followed. It was such a simple question with such a simple answer, and as far as Michael was concerned, it had already been answered.

"It's a story for another time," he muttered. Michael nodded.

"I understand," he responded. The conversation with the unseen woman flashed in his mind, and he heard much of it over again, only fast-paced. There was still a biting mystery of it, and he wanted it to continue. "I have stories as well, some I am still telling myself."

Kiran smirked, and he made eye-contact once again. He stared at Michael for a long time, some deep understanding beginning to form. With every word the boy spoke, Kiran felt he saw more and more.

He glanced at the untouched cup next to where Michael was sitting. It remained steaming, but not nearly as much as before.

"Drink it," he said, a little too vaguely. Michael raised an eyebrow. "On the table," he added.

Michael looked to the cup for the first time, and he once again recognized the smell of strong spice. It already warmed his chest just looking at the steam. He reached out, and let his fingers curl slowly around the handle.

"What is it?" he asked, looking deep into the light yellow liquid. A little bag attached to a string sat inside it, filled with a compressed substance. The string connected to a flap that lay outside the cup, dangling.

Kiran took a sip of the same drink in his own hand, but his own had cooled much quicker. He hadn't been sure when Michael was going to awake, so he had waited a little longer to take Michael's drink out of the microwave.

"I like to call it 'tea,'" he said. Michael continued to eye it weirdly, as if he'd never seen such a thing. Kiran noted the boy was especially interested in the tea bag, and began to draw it out of the cup.

"Be careful with that," Kiran cautioned. Michael dropped it suddenly, eyeing it even more suspiciously now. "Sorry, that's not what I meant." He laughed. "The bag has small herbs and spices in it. That's what gives it the flavor. "I gathered the materials myself, and found the recipe among my father's hidden scrolls. It's supposedly a very old tradition."

"Impressive," the blond boy responded.

Michael picked up the tea and began to bring it closer to his face. He sipped it slowly, and his brow furrowed. He never remembered tasting anything like it in the past. A spicy but somehow sweet sensation rushed through him, followed by warmth.

He put it back on the table and nodded. Kiran watched him expectantly. Michael noticed, and said finally:

"It's good."

Kiran smiled and finished his own cup. Michael leaned back against the couch, and sighed. He thought back to the speech he had given at the Academy, and where it had ended. It was finished in an unsatisfactory way, with a question that still didn't have a sensible answer.

However, Michael thought. *Kiran might hold information that is crucial. And Ethan is gathering data as well, if I remember correctly. Now's a good time as any, I suppose.*

"Kiran, tell me a story."

Kiran frowned, then a slight grin crept its way onto his face. "What?"

Michael leaned in suddenly, and his tone turned serious.

"Tell me the story of why no one leaves."

Kiran placed his cup down and began to think. The very story popped into his head instantly, and found it was perfect to tell. He had been involved in it himself, after all. He contemplated it for a little, not wanting to reopen old wounds.

But after a few moments, he decided he needed to hear this story once more himself.

"Alright, Michael. I'll tell you the story of Rachel Donovan."

12

"Rachel Donovan was magnificent, one of the greatest students in the Academy. She never faltered; she held Gabriel's attention day after day until she no longer needed it. Her sword skills surpassed every boy and girl, myself included. I even heard that she could stand against Gabriel himself for a minute in sparring without taking a hit-"

"Is that good?" Michael asked. He had never tested his sword skills in such a way.

"Crazy good. I myself could barely last fifteen seconds." He cleared his throat.

"Anyway, everyone was extremely impressed with her skills. You see, she came from one of the weirdest families in all of Topia, the Donovans."

Michael raised an eyebrow and made a mental note of the name.

"The Donovans were, and still are, the most famous family in the city," Kiran continued. "They were upper class to begin with, but that wasn't the reason for their fame. The parents themselves were odd."

His voice turned low, and much quieter. "Rumour has it both of them led double lives. Double as in normal mom and dad one second, secret conspirators the next. No one knows exactly what they did, but the eldest son Frederick claims he could hear the parents leaving at night and not coming back for hours."

"Did he ever question them?" Michael asked.

Kiran nodded. "Yeah, and they managed to dodge the question time after time. It was weird though, for this went on for years. Apparently, it grew more and more sporadic over time. They were never caught breaking the law though, and no one could ever find them at night. No records at nightclubs in the south, or testimonies from witnesses. Absolutely no sign of their existence."

He leaned in close, and Michael did the same.

"Then, one night, they just disappeared forever."

Michael moved away from Kiran and glanced into the distance. "What do you mean, disappeared?"

"One night they went out, but they didn't come back as usual. After that, no one ever saw them again."

Michael sat back on the couch, deep in thought. He touched a hand to his chin and held it there.

"So what did the children do?"

Kiran's fingers touched together and began to fidget. He kept his eyes away from Michael's.

"Even though I called Frederick the eldest, he was barely."

"What do you mean?"

"He, Rachel, and their other brother Leo were all triplets. Frederick and Leo were identical. All three of them were recruited by Gabriel at the age of eleven. Rachel, as I said, was an immediate hit, but to say it ran in the family would be a stretch. Leo quit first after two months, going to work at the business his father had, serving in an extremely young internship. Apparently, one of the high associates there took him in, and that was it. Later on, he received a partnership with the capitol, but I don't have those details.

"Frederick stayed around for a year and a half, before being offered a job with Timothy MacArthur in the government. Again, with him only being twelve, MacArthur had to serve as a parental figure, and it helped Frederick immensely. Unfortunately, his departure left Rachel alone at the Academy.

"I remember her vividly," he said, a sad smile crossing his face. "We actually arrived around the same time, but I only truly met Rachel two years after that. It was late one night, after training had passed, when we first talked. I remember her sitting outside by herself in the night, staring off into space. Her brown curly hair was beautiful. I walked up to her, and..."

He stopped. Michael's brow furrowed, and he tried to gain Kiran's attention multiple times, but Kiran did not respond. After a few moments, he snapped back into focus.

"S-She told me she was planning on leaving the city. I, of course, said she was insane, and that was suicide. But she persisted, and there was nothing I could say to deter her away from the idea. Eventually, she said she wouldn't. I believed her and slept soundly that night.

"....but the next day, she was gone."

A minute passed, and neither of them said anything. Michael sighed quietly and opened his mouth to finally speak. No words came out.

If I say that, and I lie to him the same way, what will it do to him? Evidently, he didn't follow Rachel out there.

Would he follow me?

"Kiran, where did Rachel go when she left?"

Kiran took a moment to respond, finally looking up again.

"Well, she went west of the city, toward the only forest in sight. She was presumed dead days after."

"How can anyone be sure?"

"They called her insane for doing it, and doubted she would survive. She even left her sword behind, and that sold it for many. She didn't leave to find something new. She left to die."

And that's the simple difference, Michael noticed. *I have a reason, she didn't.*

"Fine," Michael said. "We'll rethink the plan tomorrow morning." He looked out the window nearby, watching as the orange sun drifted closer and closer to the horizon. The sky began to turn colors of deep red and even purple to an extent, something Michael felt he saw for the first time. He recalled many sunsets and sunrises before, but none that turned this beautiful.

"It's turning late, anyway," he added.

Kiran nodded, standing up with a sigh. He took both his and Michael's cups from the table and walked to the kitchen. Michael spun around on the couch so that he was laying on it the long way, already ready to sleep. It was a tradition for him to rest as the sun went down and darkness fell over the earth, believing most work done at night is evil.

Of course, there are many exceptions, he thought.

Kiran placed the cups in the sink and immediately began washing them. The countertops were spotless otherwise, with all dishes in the drying rack or packed away in an overhead cupboard. He finished cleaning them and walked back to the living room.

"Hey, Michael," he said, but as he glanced at the blond haired boy, he found Michael already asleep on the couch.

But Michael had a side reason to going to sleep early.

Nine hours later, at 4:30AM, he awoke.

Kiran barely heard the front door close.

Michael felt no regret as he snuck out of Kiran's apartment that night. The moon shone bright overhead, and the sky was littered with stars as the blond haired boy moved about. He snuck under the darkness of an overhang that covered every apartment doorway, and found himself three stories above the ground.

He started to spread his hands apart and began to breathe in. His knees bent down, and the air began to swirl around him. He prepared to jump, and-

Out of the corner of his eye, he noticed a small black circle on the wall. It appeared round, with a slight glare from the moonlight. It looked eerily like an eye.

I'm being watched, Michael realized, and immediately ceased his coordinated movements. *Gabriel said to never reveal abilities to those who cannot understand them.*

So instead, he decided to use manual transport until he could be sure there was no one watching. A slight detour of the plan, but it would not stop him.

He peered over the edge of a metal railing that spanned the walkway, looking down. A courtyard laid beneath, little patches of green grass hidden in the darkness. A large, twisting tree stood in the center, rising up nearly to the third floor.

Michael glanced to the side and saw two mysterious metal doors at the end of the hallway. He started to go to them, hoping it would be an exit, but then noticed a staircase down the opposite corridor. He hurried over to it, turning right and then going straight. He moved with haste, quickly reaching the bottom of the spiral staircase.

Standing now on the sidewalk next to a busy street, he noted the sheer absence of privacy. He began to consider a worse possibility.

I might have to wait until I'm outside of the city. Only then might I be...oh!

He looked down the street before him. It traveled straight for the most part, but at one point, it broke off into a tiny street. And while there were lights all up and down the main road, there were none in this smaller one.

Few people walked about, and the ones who did passed by Michael without question. He figured it would be too dark for anyone to notice his face, and those who did would only know him from the speech yesterday morning.

And my hood was up that time.

He then noticed the people were ignoring the tiny street as well. Walking right by it without a clue.

Perfect.

He started to cross the street, not having the collective knowledge to look both ways. Luck was with him though, and no cars were on the road that night. Or at least, not at the time. He crossed swiftly, turning left as soon as he reached the sidewalk. More apartment complexes seemed to be nearby, but Michael paid them no attention.

He will follow.

But will he?

He will.

How do you know?

I don't.

He reached the tiny street and ducked inside. A rotting smell filled his nostrils, forcing him to gag slightly. He pinched his nose and continued on. Damp puddles covered much of the ground, which Michael stepped carefully around.

He ducked behind a large metal container which harbored the smell even more, but it was enough. He released his nose and gagged once more. The area reeked of sewage and mold now.

Again, he started to breathe in slowly. A cold shiver ran through him. It was more torturous with the smell so powerful, but he forced himself to manage.

"What're you doing 'dere boy?"

Michael lost focus and jumped back, banging against the metal container. A sharp pain shot through his side. He glanced around frantically for the voice and found it almost immediately. A man was walking toward him, dragging one leg awkwardly. Michael couldn't see his face in the darkness, but by the sound of the voice, he was old.

"Who are you?" Michael asked. The man limped toward him more, breathing heavily with effort.

As the man moved closer, Michael forced himself to use an ability. He held his palm out in front of him, and after a few seconds, it shone goldenly. Light glowed from it as if his hand was a flashlight.

He raised the light up first to the man's face, just to at least see it. The man raised his hands instinctively, hissing from the bright light. Through his rough fingers, Michael could see a scraggly gray beard and wrinkled skin, confirming his guesses.

"Turn dat light off!" the man exclaimed, trying to see anyway. He stopped moving to regain himself.

Michael brought the light away from the man's face, and let it fall on the man's injured leg instead. His eyes widened as the light illuminated a bloodstained slash on the man's thigh. The area of his gray jeans around it was soaked red.

"Sir, are you alright?" Michael asked, keeping the light stable. After the man did not answer (he assumed it would be a solid no, if the man had), he turned to a different question. "Who did this to you?"

The man limped forward more, his heavy breathing becoming louder and louder. It had a thin gasping sound to it, as if the man was straining for every breath. Michael moved out of the dumpster corner and into the open alleyway.

"Sir, do you need my help?" he asked. Goosebumps began to pop up everywhere on him, and a chill ran down his spine. Something wasn't right, and this man had more to him than met the eye. Michael's thoughts immediately ran to the man being involved in a small-scale robbery, but he had a feeling that it wasn't the case.

"No..." the man gasped. He suddenly stopped moving, and Michael realized the man's voice had changed as well. "Not at all..." He then moved his injured leg back to a standing position, and, to

Michael's surprise, put half of his weight on it. In fact, it seemed completely fine now.

Michael's other hand lit up, and he shone both lights at the man. There was no hissing this time, only a dark snarl of insanity. No longer caring about the man's wishes, Michael put the light on the man's face. The man screeched from the light.

The man's features were nearly dissolving, peeling away bit by bit. Underneath Michael could see the man's specific features; he could see darkness underneath. The man's eyes turned black, as if his pupils encompassed everything else.

Clumps of the man's beard fell to the ground, and the chin beneath turned darker than the man's pupils.

Michael's light had no effect on the man now. He brought his hands down, and suddenly felt eyes upon eyes staring at him. By instinct, he glanced up.

Five dark figures crouched on either roof. They held gleaming silver blades, all poised and focused on Michael. *So these are Anarchists,* Michael realized. *Perfect.*

"I just needed your attention," the man growled. "Get 'im, boys!"

All of the Anarchists jumped down, but as they did, Michael jumped up. He felt three whooshes run by him, each one frighteningly close. All of the Anarchists hit the ground smoothly, awaiting Michael to join them. However, he did not.

As they twirled their weapons, glancing around for the blond-haired boy, confusion settled in.

"Fools!" the man yelled. "He's above you!"

The Anarchists looked up, taking fighting stances. Michael stood above them in reverse fashion, standing over their heads now.

Oddly enough, while the night had cloaked the Anarchists, the starlight illuminated Michael. They faced a stalemate at first, but after a few seconds, hell broke loose.

Michael jumped backward as silver daggers implanted themselves in the edge of the roof. They stuck in only because of brute force, but the lack of aim showed promise to Michael. He turned away from the alley and sprinted across the flat roof, his footsteps thundering over the apartments below.

Moments later, more footsteps followed. Michael noted them. *Four, five...six...*, he counted, still sprinting forward. Bounding over a small metal box, he realized the roof was growing short. He was running out of space, and the Anarchists were close behind. A quick glance to the next roof put any roof-jumping thoughts to rest. He was not fond of flying into the street just to avoid the Anarchists.

He figured the damage would be equal anyway.

As soon as the edge of the roof was mere feet away, he stopped. He heard pounding footsteps behind him and came up with a quick idea. He ducked down.

A loud bang crashed behind him, and one of the Anarchists went flying over his head. The man whirled his arms in a futile attempt to stay on the roof but ended up dangling over the edge of the building. Michael knew he could've kicked the man's trembling fingertips off the edge if he had wanted to, but decided against it.

I won't stoop that low.

Instead, he jumped up from his cramped position. As soon as he looked up, he ducked immediately. A silver sword slashed the air above him, wielded by a cloaked Anarchist. Michael quickly snapped to attention and followed the sword with his eyes.

"*Enhance Archer Perception,*" Michael whispered. A blue wave consumed the roof.

As if the sword was moving in slow motion, he reached up and grabbed the wielder's hand. Prying the sword away, Michael had the instinct to punch. His free hand closed into a tight fist and shot forward at the Anarchist. Michael let a great breath time it correctly, but as his fist came within an inch of the Anarchist's cloaked abdomen, he stopped.

"*I'll bet you can't get through the mission without throwing a single punch,*" *Gabriel had told me,* he remembered. As his fist hovered a moment away from contact, he fought to make a decision. He felt the Anarchist started to pull away but kept his grip firm.

I'm not losing that quickly.

A glint of silver alerted him of a throwing dagger even before it had left a one of the other Anarchist's hand. He brought the sword down hard to block, Anarchist still holding on. He followed the fashion he had been taught with a sword, trusting himself and the Anarchist to keep steady.

Rowing the boat, flowing down the river, and OVER THE FALLS!

"*Academy Three!*" the Anarchist's blade glowed for a split second before fading.

He whipped the sword forward to intercept, but the Anarchist tugged back. This was unfortunate only to the Anarchist, however, and the dagger shot right into the man's exposed wrist. He yelled in agony and dropped the blade, leaving Michael to the others.

Michael felt the Anarchist fall limply to the ground, weaker than he had expected. He turned to the other four, who stood in a half-circle around him. He did not know which one had thrown the dagger, but it didn't matter.

90

"Leave, Anarchists," he ordered. They only solidified their stances and gave their weapons an extra twirl. *Stubborn. It is not to their advantage.*

He glanced over at the fallen Anarchist, moonlight spilling over and illuminating his blond hair. The Anarchist lay clutching his wrist, breathing sharply in pain. Michael looked to the slashed area of the black glove, where it was bright red. He clenched his own fists and heard a voice.

"Every drop of blood you spill is power to the Shadows," the voice had said. It had been female, dark, and hissing. Michael wondered why it sounded of the Shadows itself, even though it appeared to be warning him. Whatever the case, it was correct.

The Anarchists remained at a stalemate with him, broken between their knowledge of legends, impression, and physical truth. One glanced at his damaged comrade, palms growing sweaty.

Michael looked up to the night sky, his hands rising to his center. The Anarchists readied themselves once again, confident he would attack.

"Enough has been done here. I have let myself become occupied with them," Michael whispered. He breathed in through his nose, and out through his mouth. Hands rising up, the Anarchists watched in interest.

Michael brought his hands apart, inhaled, and began to bend his knees.

"Appear!"

He launched himself into the air with a sharp exhale and spun. As he did, a blinding light erupted from him for only a moment, and after it did, he was gone.

The Anarchists looked on, none of them confused. The one with throwing daggers attached to her belt punched the one next to her in the arm.

"You let him charge his ability for too long! Idiot!"

The punched Anarchist yelled angrily and backed away. Rubbing his arm, he said:

"Me? You didn't do anything either!"

"At least I tried! He's some sort of Wizard, Warrior, *and* Archer!"

Meanwhile, in Kiran's house, a communicator rang.

13

"H-Hello?" Kiran asked groggily, rubbing his eyes. He sat up on his bed, holding the communicator to his ear. He hoped whoever was called would have a good reason. Several times had he been taken by someone selling something, to which he had only hung up immediately. He wished to ignore them, but a higher rank Academy Warrior was required to answer every call might it be someone in need. And now, with Gabriel gone, he was the highest of ranks. He even made a mental note to visit all seven floors when he had the chance.

"Get to the station! Now!" a familiar voice exclaimed. *Ethan.* He said it nearly like a hiss, as if he didn't want others to hear him.

Kiran was jerked a little more awake by the sound, but still remained sitting. "What? Why?" He yawned.

"If I were next to you I'd dump this glass of water on your head, Kiran. It's Michael again. You wouldn't happen to know where he is?"

Kiran slowly began to stand up. That had caught his attention. "Uh...he's supposed to be in my living room."

"Better check again."

Kiran walked out of his bedroom and into the hallway, where all of the lights were off. He flipped the switch nearby and waited for the entire hall to light up before continuing. He kept the communicator close to him. It gave him a sense of comfort.

The living room was dark as well, but the blind-lacking windows were beginning to let the rising sunlight in. Even so, it was still very faint, as faint as it could be at 6 AM. He glanced about the room, his eyes finally landing on the couch.

Empty. There was no blond-haired boy in sight.

"Crap..." Kiran muttered. Ethan heard him and nodded to himself on the other side of the line.

Kiran noticed the absence of Michael's robe, which had been flung over a dumpy coat rack by the front door.

Speaking of the front door...

Kiran's eyes laid themselves on the doorknob, which was unlocked. That confirmed Michael's sneaking out, as he always locked the door at night.

My mother always made sure of it. Of course, in the end, it didn't protect her or my father, but it's something small to hold onto.

He brought the communicator back to his ear.

"I'll be there shortly.

As the sun dawned over the horizon, and pale light enveloped Topia City, a cold breeze rushed through the air. It washed away the remnants of last summer, calling fall to its new reign.

Just as Kiran was about to walk into the front doors of The Academy, the door opened the other way. Ethan Catanzaro walked out, giving Kiran a side glance. Kiran stopped and followed Ethan. He took a quick glance through the glass doors and saw no one inside. One of the hallways leading to the conference rooms was lit, but otherwise, the place was desolate.

"He said Michael just disappeared," Ethan reported. Kiran then glanced around him, making sure no one outside was eavesdropping. Much like inside The Academy, no one was actually in sight, as the only people about at 6:20 were heading to their jobs.

"Who?" Kiran asked.

"The Academy Warrior who was a witness to what he called the 'weirdest rooftop brawl he'd ever seen.'"

"Rooftop brawl?"

Ethan nodded. "He reported seeing seven figures, six in black and one in a yellow shirt. There was a chase across the apartment building roof, leading with one of the figures in black nearly falling off the edge. No casualties were reported, and after a few flashes of light, the figure in the yellow shirt disappeared."

"Michael..." Kiran whispered. Ethan nodded.

"And...it was the apartment building across the street from yours."

Kiran didn't think much of that. It was expected, after all. He started to pace back and forth, piecing everything together.

"So Michael leaves in the middle of the night, without telling me, and goes to the building across the street? Then, by some serious bad luck, he gets involved in an Anarchist scuffle?"

"I mean, who knows," Ethan said. "Maybe with all that he did yesterday, the Anarchists found out about his plan. I know if I were a leader of the Anarchist rebellion, I would aim to take down any posing threats."

Kiran was too busy in thought to really process the last sentence. "He's just a boy. Our age," he said, still pacing. "Why would the Anarchists go after him? Even with the power he has, he isn't any greater than President Leila."

"Maybe they know more than we do about him."

"Perhaps..."

Kiran paused. He let out a deep sigh and placed his hands on his hips.

"Whatever," Ethan said. "We need to find him, right?"

Kiran didn't respond, still lost in whatever he was thinking about.

"I can send out a search party. He couldn't have gone far," Ethan continued. "He has-"

"No need," Kiran responded. He looked to Ethan, hand to his chin. "You know, I bet he's doing this on purpose to spite me."

Ethan narrowed his eyes. "You know where he is?"

Kiran nodded grimly. *That trickster. Right after I told him about Rachel.*

"I can't believe I'm going through this again."

14

The road beyond Topia was shattered and broken. It had not been used in nearly a hundred years, the cobblestones cracking from time. Moss grew in the broken spaces, struggling to survive but thriving all the same. Legend had it that it was once used to trade with outer villages, but those villages had all died off long ago.

The rising sun now over the eastern horizon sent orange glow over the road, giving the moss a warmer color. Streams of light poured through the city and out, with the buildings creating looming shadows that covered some of the roads. The sky grew lighter, and day had come.

The blond haired boy stared back at it all, now shrouded in yet another brown cloak, a much newer one. He watched the sun move above the great city of Topia, turning the silver buildings into blinding orange. There were no skyscrapers in the city, but Michael could quickly pick out where the capitol sat. The capitol building held an odd spire atop it, with an enormous silver sphere that shone brightly.

A few blocks south, The Academy stood taller than any other building, despite being only seven stories. He could imagine Kiran and Ethan now realizing where he had gone, and hoped they would follow. They were probably there now.

Behind Michael stood a supermassive forest, visible to all of Topia. Trees towered higher than any building in the city. Over half shot hundreds of feet into the air, with the tallest being near four hundred feet tall. Their leaves formed together to create a canopy over the rest of the forest, turning into one large, bush-like area.

Michael turned, looked up to the highest of the trees, and stepped forward. After a few more steps he passed through a transparent barrier, phasing through without notice.

He walked about the forest, having a clear directional goal but no time manner to get there. He frequently stopped to take in the air, breathing it in as if it was sacred. It smelled of fresh pine and other herbs he could not describe. Birds sang quiet songs to the swaying movement of the canopy, which Michael stopped to listen a few times.

Eventually, he crossed into a grass clearing. Rolling hills of green shades went on for quite a while until finally meeting with the forest again on the other side. To his left, the clearing dropped off suddenly. He glanced up, and-

There it is again, he thought. *The Crescent Island.*

Where the clearing dropped, there was empty space. Soon followed by that, however, was a towering waterfall, as tall as the tallest trees. Glistening blue water gushed down into the lake below. The waterfall's edges curved around into a crescent moon, and the lake surrounded all of it.

"It's beautiful, isn't it?" asked a soft voice nearby. Michael continued looking at the island, watching the water rush down wave after wave.

"They say when it stops flowing, the Sisterhood dies," the voice said. Michael found that superstition to be logical, because after all, where did the water come from?

The sky, perhaps.

"You're ready then, I presume?" he asked, still without turning away. After no response for several seconds, Michael felt forced to turn to the voice. He closed his eyes slightly, in knowledge of what he would see.

It took ten whole seconds for Michael's eyes to adjust. A blinding white light surrounded the figure who had been speaking, covering all of his/her features. Steadily, the light dimmed, and the figure was revealed.

Michael still felt overwhelmed by the sheer beauty of the figure, which he attributed to the eyes he now possessed. He recognized her in millions of others he had seen before, but this was the first in this age.

She'll blind any mortal she doesn't warn, Michael realized, his vision still a little damaged. *I'll have to warn Kiran and Ethan when they show, if necessary.*

The light dimmed to its max, with only a faint glow around her body and a brighter light emanating from her pearl wings.

Platinum blonde hair ran down the woman's shoulders, falling to her back. She wore standard seraphic attire, a light blue on white, a pearl dress that matched her wings flowing beneath. Her hands sat interlocked below her waist, waiting.

She nodded to Michael and began to lead him away from the edge of the forest. Her wings flapped slowly, letting her glide across the ground. Her feet hovered, shiny blue shoes covering them.

Only now, as Michael followed, did he realize how tall this "woman" was. She neared six feet herself, with the extra half foot of her floating. It was a little unsettling, as every other Seraphim he'd ever seen were minuscule to him.

He followed the woman across the clearing. They approached a hut made of wood. Three others sat behind it, but the one in front was definitely the largest. The woman grabbed the door handle and opened it, letting Michael walk inside. She soon followed.

The hut was only lit by openings in the roof; there was no electricity at all. A small table was the focus of the room, being one of the only few objects. Two chairs sat on either side, perfect for a conversation. Michael took the chair to the left and expected the woman to sit across.

She did not, however, and a look of realization passed Michael's face.

"Right," he said and stood. He nodded apologetically. The woman nodded halfheartedly in response.

"When Celestia arrives, then you will sit with her," the woman said.

Michael glanced back toward the door, which remained open. Sunlight streamed in, and the twinkling glimmer of the waterfall could be seen.

"Does she know?" Michael asked.

"Oh no, not yet," the woman responded, slight worry in her voice. "She only understands what I am, and never that we are the same."

"I will be the one to tell her, then..."

"Yes, but you must be careful. She cannot find it surprising, and therefore must be prepared for such news. She must lose everything, before that knowledge. She must feel the lowest of her existence, and then become what she truly is. To know that you are something greater is an interesting thing indeed."

"Of course. You are well, then?"

The woman nodded. "I am still myself, still Elara. And I've been here for years. It's you who should be asked about. Your return was quite the shock-"

"Shhh," Michael hissed, placing a finger to his lips. "No one else knows, and Celestia is approaching."

The woman named Elara turned her head to the doorway. Michael waited, feeling the outsider's steps grow closer and closer. There was the sound of rustling metal with each movement, the sure sign of armor. Michael smiled.

It's her, the next one.

The doorway darkened, and from the outside stepped another blonde woman, extremely armor-clad and wielding a large silver sword. A brown cloak similar to Michael's own hung off her shoulders. Her and Michael's eyes met, and Michael grinned slyly.

Celestia Triton, my newest apprentice.

"Ethan, get back in here!" Walter yelled, his head leaning out of the open front doors of The Academy. Ethan and Kiran still stood in thought, Kiran pacing and Ethan racking his mind for solutions. "We've-oh, it's you," Walter growled, noticing Kiran. "Ethan, come on inside. The council's gathering."

"Perfect!" Kiran exclaimed. "Ethan, actually, wait here," he commanded, but in a sarcastic-sweet voice. He turned to Walter. "I need to speak with the council."

Walter, taken aback, glared at Kiran. "You don't *need* anything. You're staying outside. The little stunt you pulled with that kid yesterday messed up everything. Now we're being forced to find-"

Kiran ignored Walter's protest and tugged at the door. Walter pulled back but was overpowered. He stumbled a little as Kiran walked inside.

Kiran immediately began walking to the council room, the same one Michael had been speaking in the day before. He found the door, and, aware Walter was following him, made sure the door would close before the man could reach it. Of course, Walter opened it after anyway.

"Attention everyone!" Kiran shouted to the crowd before him. It was much smaller than the previous day's group. Only the higher council members were in here now, the ones considered as Gabriel's trustees. They all looked to Kiran now.

"Thank you all for being here," he continued. Walter stood beside him, still glaring, and began clearing his throat loudly. Kiran pretended to not notice and addressed the crowd only. "It's been a weird past few days, hasn't it? Anarchist rebellion, Gabriel's disappearance, and now some young boy with a crazy idea shows up. We're experiencing an odd time, so it calls for odd measures."

Everyone stared at him, many eyebrows raised and brows furrowed. Each one awaited what he might be suggesting now.

"Michael Nebadon disappeared early this morning, as you are all aware. He did not leave as silently as believed, and we can conclude with near certainty that he was involved in a 'rooftop brawl' across my apartment in Desertia Towns. After that, we have reason to believe he fled the city as he said he would do."

Many could now see where this was going.

"Ethan and I have no choice but to follow him."

A few angry mutters came from the council, but no one openly objected. Walter, however, began grinning.

"Well," Walter said, turning to Kiran. "I wish you-"

"One more thing," Kiran interjected, keeping his focus on the crowd. "Jeremy, Sergio, you're in charge. Main task: send a smoke signal if the Anarchists betray their word. We'll return as soon as we see it. Everyone else, follow protocol."

Walter's grin faded. "You-you can't do that!" he exclaimed. "I'm supposed to be in charge, not you! And, especially, not them!"

Kiran laughed slightly, winking at Jeremy and Sergio. Their faces lit up, and they both winked back. They fist bumped one another and kept grinning. Kiran turned away, leaving the room. Behind him, he heard Sergio loudly tell Walter he could go as well.

Kiran smiled on his way out of the building, where he met a confused Ethan.

"What happened?" the redheaded boy asked.

"Doesn't matter," Kiran responded. "Let's go."

"So you think I'd help those fools?" the woman named Celestia said. "They don't deserve it."

She sat across from Michael at the small table, shaking her head at Michael's words. Her armor rustled as she placed a weak fist on the wooden surface. Elara was no longer there, and the door was now closed.

Michael sighed. "You're right. They don't." Celestia stared at him, mind searching for sarcasm. She found none and remained confused at Michael's agreement. Moments ago he had been convincing her to join with him to save Topia, but now...nothing.

"Okay then," she said. "What else do you want from me?"

"Just the ability to stay the day and night. I find the land out here much more peaceful than in the city."

Celestia pondered for a moment, then nodded. "Of course. I'll have it arranged." She hovered on the last word, something still nagging at her. She pushed it aside.

"Rosemary!" she shouted. After a few seconds, the door swung open to reveal a small girl with curly hair. She grinned broadly at Michael, who found it a little unsettling.

"Yes, Celestia?" she asked, her voice ridden with high-pitched mischief.

"It won't be needed until tonight, but prepare the spare room for our guest, please," Celestia responded.

The girl skipped off like the small child she was, letting the door close slowly again. Celestia turned to Michael and felt the nagging question still. Michael could feel her withholding the matter, and raised an eyebrow.

"Ask away," he said casually, leaning back in his chair.

Celestia felt this almost confirmed what she had been wondering, and now thought it only necessary to ask.

"Why did Siona let you in?" she asked, hazel eyes sparkling with intense curiosity now.

"Siona?"

"Yes, Siona. She grants a cosmic barrier around this forest so no one can enter."

"But I did."

"Somehow, and there are only two exceptions. One, you're female, which obviously isn't true, or two, you're a master."

"Well, that explains it," Michael responded. "I'm considered a master, of course."

Celestia nearly began laughing. "Of what?"

"Same as you, Celestia."

Celestia immediately stopped smiling. She sized up this fourteen-year-old boy in front of her, somehow a master, and shook her head. Now he claimed to be what Celestia was herself.

We'll see about that, she thought. Her right hand rose into the air, fingers nearly trembling. After a few long seconds, her fingers snapped.

A wave of blinding light shot out from her hand, intended to temporarily falter the vision of anyone around her. Only someone of equal power in the Light would be able to withstand it.

Sure enough, Michael remained unfazed, his blue eyes still very focused. He raised his own right hand and gave Celestia no time to sit in awe. His own fingers snapped, and the exact same wave of blinding light shot from it. Everything else in the cabin lit up.

"But you're just a young boy," Celestia muttered.

"Age can be deceiving," Michael answered, bringing his hand down slowly. "For instance, you might appear to be the age of a mere eighteen-year-old, but that isn't true, is it? I can see it in your eyes, Celestia. You've watched over a hundred years at least of Topia's growth, all here in the forest."

Celestia stood up suddenly. Her hands shook, so she clenched them into fists. She stared into Michael's eyes again and found herself losing control.

No...I'm always in control. This b-boy won't break me from it.

She tore her gaze away, turning to the door. She grabbed the handle and opened it, each movement difficult. Michael's eyes were still on her, still emanating that cosmic gaze.

"One more thing," Michael added. "Topia City isn't going to survive without your help, and if you don't the Sisterhood will die."

Celestia paused. "What?"

"I know all about where your comrades are now. Searching for life beyond here, that is where the entire Sisterhood is. They've left you behind to hold down the fort! But that means they have entrusted you to embody all of their wishes. Be grateful!"

"Do not lecture me," Celestia growled.

"Oh, but this is only to awaken your reasoning! Imagine, if Topia dies off, then the new Anarchist society will have even less care about your ideals. With no rules in that city, a Dystopia, they won't listen to anything you have to say. But now, if you help me and the others within the Light create the new age, then your words can be spoken."

Celestia wordlessly stepped outside, shutting the door. Thankful Michael could no longer see her, she relaxed a little. Upon realizing her heart rate had spiked during those moments, she started to breathe a lot slower.

Look at the water...relax...

Soon, though, she could see Michael's eyes in the rushing water. They were the same color. She glanced away again, this time finding the strength to step away from the cabin.

That boy is not typical. What he speaks of is true, but he wants more than I can give him. Helping Topia would be my last course of action...

She walked off, still not entirely convinced.

"Yo Z, they're just on the edge of the city."

The man named Z crouched low on the rooftop of a building in the outskirts of Topia City. His body was cloaked in black, but not like the crude suits the Anarchists wore. Instead of their plain pirate-style tunics and coats, Z's outfit was fashionable. Silver streaks ran down the sides of his rippled clothing, optimized in movement as much as appearance.

Despite being in broad daylight, there was no need to worry about being spotted. If anyone were to confront him, escape would be easy. After all, neither the Warriors nor the Anarchists cared. Besides, his targets were now walking blindly out of the city itself.

"Fools," he muttered into the communicator on his neck. "Continue keeping tabs," he commanded.

"Yeah we'll need a trace dart for that," the communicator responded.

Z grunted in response and adjusted the black bow over his shoulder. It blended in with his black clothes, nearly invisible except for the part extending upward. He steadily slid it from his back, keeping one eye on the two figures walking below. Archer vision allowed him to make out their appearances.

Kiran Andon and Ethan Catanzaro, just as it said on the bounty. Anonymous placement as usual, but no matter.

I'll get my coin.

He positioned the bow and prepared himself. His opposite hand reached slowly toward his arrow quiver but ended up bypassing all of the arrows. Instead, he reached into a tinier pocket on the side of the quiver and pulled from it a small dart.

As he brought his hand back with it, he glanced at his wrist. Another small black device was attached to it.

Too long range for a wrist launcher. I'll have to shoot it from my bow.

He readied his bow and placed the dart on the string. It clicked into place, and he started to aim. A shift of movement here, there, every angle being captured with his sight. Then, he fired.

The dart streaked through the air, Z losing track of it immediately. Soon after, though, he was confident it had buried itself in Kiran's calf. Kiran continued walking as if nothing had happened.

Z smiled slyly, satisfied.

"That good enough?" he asked the communicator.

"Perfect, Z. Well done as usual. We'll follow out later tonight."

"Sounds good."

Z stood and swung his bow back over his shoulder. As he turned away, the wind ruffled the collar of his jacket, revealing a tattoo underneath.

There, in dark blue, was a tattoo of a circled B with an arrow plunging right through it.

The Bulls-Eye Brotherhood begins its hunt again. The Academy's best faction, the Archers, return once more.

Celestia Triton stood proudly atop her hill, sword in hand. She stared off into the distance, mind wandering. She adjusted

her grip, feeling every groove of the leather surface. Her sword point just lightly touched the green grass, as it had years ago.

She then fell into the motions, her eyes closing and past mind taking control. Her movements reenacted the same scene in this same place-

Ten years, forty-seven days.

-long ago, feeling each clash and strike as if it was happening all over again. Her sword bounced off the blades of invisible attackers, but she barely felt those. More importantly, when her sword was not stopped by a force she could not see, she felt it all. Feeling that successful strike plunge and tear at some foolish enemy-

They shouldn't have come.

-that was only doing what they were told. Mindless servants attacking blindly for some higher being, never for themselves. Zombies, slaves, whatever might fit their purpose. There were hundreds-

Thousands, it felt like.

-of them, a wave of terrible men rushing to terrible fates. Horde after horde threw themselves on her, only to die by her blade. When they thought she had been caught off guard, she found herself unable to be hit. Even bullets could not reach her. They shot-

Foolish again, how I prayed for them even as I slew them.

-, only to be redirected by Celestia's great sword, the Tritonyx, and therefore it became known as that very weapon. A sword that could redirect objects traveling at unbelievably high speeds. No one could explain-

A simple technique, really.

-her ability.

But now, as Michael watched Celestia reenact her past moments, he knew precisely what technique she had used. In fact, he recognized it as she was doing it now.

And in her head, she said the same words Michael had been thinking.

Rowing the boat, flowing down the river, and over the falls. Academy 3.

And in her vision, despite her eyelids closed, she could see it all in her mind. Her sword spun in a silver blur, tiny metal objects flying into the mess and turning into sparks. They flattened on impact, flinging off in the direction they had come from. Some, if lucky, caught Celestia's redirection phase, firing back at the shooter with nearly double speed.

Michael smiled again and knew she would be perfect.

It took Kiran and Ethan two hours to reach the forest. Of course, not all of it had been walking. Kiran routinely glanced back at the Academy for signs of smoke, and was blissfully relieved to see none each time. Perhaps the Anarchists would stay true to their deal.

As they were within a mile of the forest, Ethan bent over suddenly.

"Cramp," he said, clutching his side. Kiran frowned, reaching into the bag strapped around his shoulder. He took one of the numerous water bottles he had brought with him and handed it to Ethan.

"This is all we have," Kiran said apologetically. "C'mon, we're nearly there."

Ethan took the water bottle and unscrewed it. "Why did we have to walk again? It's blazing out here." It was true. Even despite the oncoming fall, summer's last heat waves were making a stand. They wouldn't last too long, thankfully.

Ethan promptly then poured a large amount of the water over his head. He sighed, finally feeling the heat leave. It was only temporary bliss, however, and the sun soon penetrated once again.

"Dude, we only have so much water," Kiran told him. "And anyway, I have a weird feeling that riding here on motorcycles would've displeased Michael."

Ethan glanced up. "That's a load of BS. Plus, 'displeased?' Jeez, you're starting to talk like him too."

"It's his aura or something. It's getting to me I think."

"Sure."

Ethan stood up straight, screwing the cap to the water bottle back on and storing it in his pocket. He motioned he was ready to continue.

Kiran walked alongside him, the grand forest growing closer and closer. It had been a wonder no one had ever looked into the area, but Kiran figured that wasn't truly the case. In fact, he was almost sure the Anarchists had knowledge of the place.

Them, and whoever was considered insane.

There was, as well, a little bit of unsettling hope in the back of his mind. He turned to Ethan, hesitant.

"Do you remember Rachel Donovan?" he asked.

Ethan raised an eyebrow. "Uh, sure. Why?"

"This is the same direction she went," Kiran reminisced. "I'm starting to think that's why Michael chose this way."

Ethan frowned. "How would he even know who she is? She's a bit of a legend, but not big enough to hear about on your first day. If he's even telling the truth about that…"

"I told him," Kiran countered. "Last night, when he finally awoke, he asked me to tell a story. So I did, and Rachel Donovan seemed appropriate. He wanted to know why no one leaves the city."

"What did he think about that?"

"Leaving the city?"

"Yeah. I mean, it looks obvious now, but what did he say last night? Did it seem like he'd follow in her footsteps?"

"I suppose," Kiran said. He struggled to remember their exact conversation, but he did remember a few key points. "It actually seemed as if he was more interested in the Donovans as a whole, rather than just Rachel."

"So you told him about the Academy?"

Kiran nodded. "I explained Rachel's impressive skills, and what happened to Leo and Frederick. Oh, and I told him about the parents as well."

"What if…" Ethan paused, thinking. "What if he's searching for all three of them?! Frederick and Rachel are out here, if not dead, but Leo's alive, right?"

"Well, Leo's still in the city, so Michael couldn't be looking for him. I heard he lives in Mysti now, in some old house down south. Or, at least, that's what Jeremy's told me. I've never visited."

"You never liked him, did you?"

Kiran sighed, crossing his arms as they walked. "He just…didn't click with my mentality. He was always about material gain, making money in the end. It's fitting that he ended up as a businessman. He would've made a terrible Academy Warrior."

"And there's that time when he broke your hand on accident."

"There's that as well, but I don't hold a grudge. It was useless for a long time, but my hand's completely healed." He flexed his fingers for effect.

Ethan nodded. He fell silent for a few moments, but then asked a final question:

"Do you think Michael could find her? Rachel, I mean."

Kiran knew that option would be the most positive reason, but Rachel had been gone for a little over two years now. Two years out beyond the city...he couldn't say for sure she was even alive. She hadn't left with food nor water, and no survival skills to assist.

But if anyone were to survive out here, it would be Rachel Donovan. She always was creative.

"That's something to ask him ourselves."

They walked along, the sun now directly overhead. The forest drew closer, and with that it grew larger. The sheer size of the tallest trees was astonishing.

"How do trees this big even live out here?" Kiran wondered. He didn't expect Ethan to respond, as neither of them were particularly educated in plant life. The parks in Topia were all they had ever seen of trees, and those were ant-like compared to the ones before them.

To Kiran's surprise, however, Ethan said something:

"Must be that Garden of Eden crap Gabriel's talked about," he said, looking up. Noticing Kiran's confused expression, he looked over. "Y'know, the place that can 'harbor all life.'"

Kiran had never heard of such a thing, and therefore questioned how much he had really listened to Gabriel's teachings. Some of those teachings had been wild enough for Kiran to lose interest, thinking they were always metaphors and analogies.

Evidently not literal, at least.

"I don't remember him mentioning that," he said, noticing Ethan was watching expectantly. It confused him, a little, that Ethan would be so excellent at recalling one of Gabriel's teachings.

"It was one of his lectures he'd go on any time we visited a park," Ethan explained. "Remember? He'd stand up tall and preach to us about the glory of plant life. He'd speak of bizarre purple and pink plants from places we'd never heard of. I'm surprised that, you, of all people, don't remember that."

Kiran shrugged. "Whenever we went to parks, I was the first to start training. While he was speaking, I would usually cartwheel in place. My hearing wasn't always the best at those times."

Ethan laughed slightly in response, and they fell into silence.

They continued on, finally reaching the forest. It now towered just over them, spanning their entire visions. As they passed the first treeline, Ethan yelled out.

"What the heck?!" he exclaimed, clutching his forehead. He clenched it in pain, and Kiran started to walk back, confused. He glanced around the forest of trees, finding it unusual, but not hostile.

"What hit you?" he asked.

Ethan regained himself, still wincing slightly. "I was just walking, when-" he reached out, but found his hand could not pass a certain point in the air. He gingerly pressed his palm flat in the air, smushed against something. He then tried to force his way through, using every option he had available. He attempted his legs first,

114

entire body, and even just a single finger, but nothing could pass through this barrier.

Weirdly enough, Kiran had no restriction to passing through. Even as he stepped onto Ethan's side, he found himself able to move back and forth without issue.

Then, as Kiran began to follow the "forcefield" with his eyes, he could see it outlined the forest itself.

"It's a shield," Kiran concluded.

"No kidding! Why'd it let you through?" Ethan asked, slightly accusatory. Kiran could only shrug. He looked back into the forest, taking this sign as something was off here. He smiled, but it wasn't of complete happiness.

"Why are you smiling?" Ethan asked. "I need a way through this thing!"

"Wait here. I'm going to find Michael."

"Wha-"

Kiran walked off, leaving Ethan at the forcefield. His boots crunched through the dirt beneath, and he was confident that at least someone was in this forest.

Maybe even Rachel herself.

15

Ethan Catanzaro stood outside the forest alone, staring angrily at Topia. Eyes glazing over, Topia City a mass of silver rectangles, he sighed. He leaned back against the forcefield, taking advantage of his inability to pass through, and crossed his arms.

Why'd he leave me out here? This is ridiculous.

He understood Kiran's curiosity, but he wished they had spent a little more time thinking of a way to get through. After all, Kiran had passed without issue completely.

So why can't I?

He sighed again, standing up straight. He turned around, facing the field. Through it, he could clearly see the entire forest, silent even in midday. A few birds flew through the area, but not often. Ethan reached out to the field once again, feeling it push back.

To him, it literally felt as if there was a brick wall before him. The forest behind opened up so plainly it was infuriating. It was literally there, just beyond his reach. He smacked the shield hard, turning away before slamming his fist into it.

The pain only irritated him further, forcing him to use his other hand. He slammed that one into the field as well, bringing it back with equal pain. His knuckles stung, appearing red and rushed.

Curse this barrier. I'll find a way through even if it kills me.

He brought his right hand to his back, searching for his sword hilt. He found it quickly and drew his blade. After a quick shift of weight, he slashed at the field. One cut followed by another, he delivered blow after blow. He rammed off Academy Warrior techniques from all over his knowledge, certain one had to work.

His face began to turn redder as he put more energy into every strike, exerting stronger breaths. Adrenaline kept his power up for the time, but through all of his efforts, none were working.

Eventually, a voice interrupted his work.

"You know, no matter how long you do that, it won't work," the voice from behind said. "Only an idiot tries the same thing over and over again, and expects a different result."

Rude, Ethan thought, finally ceasing his onslaught. He let his sword drop down, and noticed it had a red glow now. He began to turn around.

"Save the comments-"

He paused, noticing no one was there to match the voice. He found himself only staring back at Topia City, along with the tattered road he had followed but soon lost. He brought his sword back up, and used his opposite hand to wipe the sweat from his forehead.

"Listen, bud, I know you're there," he said, keeping his gaze fluid. Out of the corners of his eyes he hoped to see through this invisible magic but found no immediate answer.

After 30 seconds, he dropped his guard. The voice hadn't spoken again, and it seemed whoever owned it would not be showing themselves anytime soon.

He began turning away, ready to start attacking the field again. Even if it was just to spite the ghostly figure, he prepared another onslaught. He raised his sword, shaking his head at the odd voice. He went to strike-

As he tried to slash, his arm resisted. He found bringing it passed a certain point to be incredibly difficult. He forced his movement harder, but something held him back. Then, he noticed the tight feeling of rope around his arm. A quick glance at his arm confirmed what he'd feared.

A tight, brown rope was wrapped around his forearm. He attempted to turn once again away from the field for a look at the source of the line, but another cable caught his other arm. He was completely restrained.

"Crap," he whispered. "Well, then-"

He grinned. A quick flash of movement followed by slashes of his silver sword severed both of Ethan's restraints. He flexed his wrist soon after, already feeling the adrenaline wearing off. He now faced the previously invisible attacker, who revealed himself.

The figure materialized in the air, distorting the area around him. He was dressed in dark black clothing, but not Anarchist style. His robes connected together, restricting their tendency to blow in the wind.

The ropes snapped back at the man's command, drawing back to what appeared to be a black bow. They disappeared momentarily, but reappeared instantly again, ready to be fired.

The man looked at Ethan with a hardened stare, his dark eyes swirling ominously. Femininely long brown hair fell straight down, but the exact length was hidden by the man's clothing.

Ethan kept his sword at the ready.

Kiran better get back soon.

"Hey, buddy," Ethan said, hoping to somewhat console this hostile man. "Is there something you need from me?"

The man raised his bow, sliding a thick arrow in as he aimed. He drew back, and Ethan readied himself.

However, a small detail caught his eye. A blinking red light was coming from the end of the arrow, and Ethan's confidence dissipated.

Crap...exploding arrow! He's an Academy Archer!

He dove to the side, time slowing as the arrow was shot. The point plunged deep into the invisible field, the light blinking twice before stopping.

A rippling explosion hit the forcefield, sending a shockwave throughout the entire forest.

Ethan blacked out.

Kiran stumbled into the clearing, feeling the ground rumble beneath him. Pausing, his knees bent, numerous thoughts ran through his mind. With certainty, he concluded it wasn't an earthquake, no. It was an explosive.

He glanced back at the forest in worry, but no explosions followed. The trees swayed in the slightest, but there was nothing more. He hesitated, knowing Ethan may very well be injured, but fought the urge to go back.

If I find Michael first, he might be able to help Ethan more than I can.

He turned to the clearing he had just entered, gaze landing on a small assortment of huts. Each one seemingly offered a different purpose, with Krian assuming the largest one would be his best option.

Even so, he hesitated again. This was confirmation that some sort of life lived out beyond Topia, human or otherwise. It was clearly intelligent, and Michael had apparently been interested in it. Kiran kept his sword hand ready to draw and began approaching.

The forest had been relatively silent when Kiran had passed through. Of course, he hadn't stopped to look at anything; he had been intensely focused on his goal. Now, with the explosion that had just occurred less than a minute ago, the forest seemed to wake.

He drew nearer to the huts, vision broadening to all of the clearing. He felt a very odd weight nearby as if he could sense someone's...presence.

He reached the large hut, sword hand hovering back and other hand reaching for the door handle. His fingers closed around the metal ring and pulled.

His sword hand grabbed hilt, and he stepped into the hut. Immediately, he felt four eyes staring back at him. Whoever they belonged to sat across from one another in chairs, seemingly in conversation.

To his right sat the familiar face of Michael Nebadon. Kiran was starting to grow used to seeing this boy in the most unusual of places, but was relieved now. Michael did not seem surprised in the slightest, as if he was telling himself it was fate, with a content smile.

To his left, however, sat a young woman of formidable appearance. She had blonde hair nearly shinier than Michael's, but she lacked the same blue eyes for hazel ones instead. A brown cloak covered her extensive silver armor, and Kiran could see a glimmering sword underneath it as well.

"Another master," the woman said. She looked to Michael. "You didn't say there'd be more following you."

Michael smiled. "I was unsure, but sure enough. This is Academy Warrior Kiran of Topia City." He turned to Kiran. "Pleasure to see you've followed."

Kiran nodded to Michael. He looked to the woman. She glared at him oddly, not exactly hateful, but scrutinizing. He felt her watching his every mannerism, and knew the expectations were high. He would need to act like Michael.

"I am indeed Kiran. Who might you be?" he asked, using a formality he felt was expected now.

The woman's dominant hazel eyes turned swiftly from Kiran to Michael, then back to Kiran. She did not hesitate.

"I am Celestia Triton, leader of the Sisterhood."

Kiran nodded. *The Sisterhood? There are legends...but never truth of one existing!* He began to pose a question but didn't get the chance.

"Where is Ethan?" Michael asked suddenly. "Did he falter in faith?"

Kiran frowned. "He's...outside of the forest."

Celestia looked to Michael curiously. "There's another?"

Michael nodded. "And he hasn't been deemed a master by Siona, it appears. Quite peculiar indeed. I wonder if that rumbling was him as well."

Kiran's eyes widened. "Oh, right. I was going to ask if we can-"

Celestia broke through. "He does not need our help. If he can survive out there for long enough, perhaps he will be deemed worthy to enter the forest."

"Still," Kiran pressed. "What if he's dying?"

Michael raised his eyebrows. "You doubt him that much? He's come far enough already."

"It's not that," Kiran said. "But if Ethan or someone else is causing explosions out there, shouldn't we try to figure out what's going on? We should check..."

Celestia sighed. "I'm sure that if anything incredibly dangerous is happening, Rosemary will take care of it."

"Rosemary?"

"She's the scout I keep around in the forest. She watches everything with the purest of precisions, and I trust her words. If anything is happening to your friend, I will eventually find out."

"I didn't see anyone in the forest."

Celestia nodded. "Good. That means she's doing her job well. I'm sure though, after the explosion your friend has caused, Rosemary will be aware soon if not already."

Kiran finally felt slightly assured. He glanced away from the two sitting before him, still thinking of this odd place. Here it really was: a civilization beyond Topia. Humans living outside the city entirely.

Rachel could very well be alive. Perhaps she even came here! There are so many questions I want to ask.

Celestia adjusted herself in the chair and gestured to Kiran once again.

"So, I am curious to hear about the Academy. I've heard all the legends of Gabriel Lanondek, and the Wizards, Warriors, and Archers. You say you're a Warrior, but your appearance is abysmal to what I've imagined. Perhaps you're more than meets the eye, I hope."

Kiran waved aside the odd stabs at his physique. "The Academy is well known across all of Topia, and it serves as a beacon of peace. The unification between the Wizards, Warriors, and Archers is long gone, sadly. The Wizards and Archers defected in a simultaneous event, both leaving to begin their own organizations. The Archers now have-"

"The Bulls-Eye Brotherhood," Celestia finished. Her face turned frustrated.

"You've heard of them?"

"Of course. Those fools once dared to stand on my doorstep, asking for something ridiculous. Something about assassinating a public official. How they ever found their way out here is beyond me."

Kiran raised an eyebrow. *The Bulls-Eye Brotherhood has left the city?! And they know of the life here?*

"Something troubling you, Kiran?" Michael asked, breaking his silence.

Kiran hesitated, but he knew he had to spill it.

"The Brotherhood has always been secretive, but leaving the city is a daring feat. I wouldn't be out here if it weren't for the Anarchists threatening to send Topia into ruins. It just seems odd that the Brotherhood would willingly leave, and then come back. This job that they wanted to be done...it must've been so important they couldn't do it alone."

"They weren't happy when I rejected their offer," Celestia said. "The shield worked well, but they hung around for days. I had to knock one unconscious before they finally yielded."

"Did they say who they wanted to be killed?"

Celestia shook her head. "Only that they'd be back to take revenge. I highly doubt that, however. It's been almost four years, and they haven't returned. Those archers are-"

Another explosion rattled the ground, and Kiran stumbled back. Celestia bounded to her feet, letting the chair behind her fall to the ground. Her sword was drawn faster than Kiran's, but Kiran was at a disadvantage anyway. He grasped at the door for support, barely keeping himself standing.

"That can't be only Ethan," Kiran said, breathing heavily. "No way."

"Whatever it is, Rosemary will report back here soon enough," Celestia assured.

Kiran wasn't too convinced, and soon, smaller shockwaves crossed the land.

Four, five, six, seven, eight, nine-I'm out.

Z ceased his fire, waiting as the smoke started to clear. He had shot every last one of his exploding arrows, hoping something would leave a dent in the god-forsaken forcefield.

He looked on at the forest protected by it, certain the one they called Michael Nebadon was hiding inside.

A coward.

Z shouldered his bow, walking calmly to the chaos his arrows had made. The field was unmarked, but Z could clearly see where the smoke was flowing from. Small black shards of his once arrows lay scattered around the area, evidence of his failed efforts.

He now stood less than a foot away from the field, staring into it. He glared at the forest beyond, but nobody was there to receive it. He reached up to slam both hands onto the field, but much to his surprise, nothing held him up.

He fell right through the field.

As Z slowly stood up, he glanced at his hands. *They-they passed right through! So..all of that was for nothing?! But...*

He glanced back at the redheaded boy, who was still unconscious. He was trapped in Z's own net, but he didn't appear to be moving anytime soon. The boy's blade sat shattered on the ground, a broken mess of silver.

124

Z turned away, stepping into the forest. He slid the sleeve over his wrist up, revealing his communicator, and double tapped it. He crouched low, crunching dead leaves beneath him.

"Team, you there?" he asked, keeping his voice down.

"Ye, Z. Wassup?"

"Begin securing the area outside. I was able to bypass the forcefield somehow, and now I'm making my way toward the target. I'll capture him tonight and bring him out. Be ready."

"Sounds good. Well done, Z."

"Oh, and also, there's that ginger kid outside. You might want to watch him closely, but for now, he's out cold.

"Z, signing out."

The line went silent, and Z stood. He turned the communicator off, concealing it once again with his sleeve.

He flicked his wrist smoothly, and three tiny spheres of silver launched out. They fell to the ground, morphing into little robots no more significant than Z's thumb. They skittered off into the distance.

Spy bugs. Black-market items, and incredibly useful.

Z listened carefully for the signal. After five seconds, a low ringing sound vibrated through the entire forest, but the birds in the trees weren't disturbed enough for it to cause a difference.

Then, after a momentary silence, one single, high-pitched beep made its way through the forest. This one made Z strain to hear it, but that was the point. Hopefully, no one else would be able to notice it as well.

And that confirms there is at least SOMEONE else in here.

He took a few slow steps farther into the forest, his concentration settling in stronger. His steady movements allowed his appearance to slowly phase into clear, turning seemingly invisible. It was magic Z had first doubted long ago, but now it was second nature. The Archers held magic not even some Wizards could replicate.

He then darted through the forest, careful not to touch any trees. Coming in contact with one would destroy his invisibility, and speaking would as well. He ran until the first signs of humans came into his view, noticing a clearing with several village-like huts in the middle. A magnificent waterfall ran behind them, but it did not distract Z.

So it's true...there IS civilization out here. I suppose this is why they want Michael captured or killed. He's going to crush the rebellion with people the Anarchists didn't even know existed. Of course, I'll have a job no matter which side wins.

He slipped his hand into his pocket, pulling out a small black device. It snapped into a pair of hi-tech glasses, which he promptly slid onto his face. Looking through, everything turned into the product of a thermal scanner, allow Z to easily see inside the huts. Two of the shelters were empty, but the third shone unnaturally bright. Two of the signatures were much more vivid than any human Z had ever seen, nearly blinding in fact.

What? That's not possible, both of those people should be dead with the heat built up inside them. I suppose I'll have to investigate even further than planned. One of them has to be Michael, however. This kid isn't human!

The third signature, however, resembled a normal human being.

Must be that other Academy Warrior. He must've found a way through the force field as well. I wonder how it decides it's judgment.

Obviously, it isn't moral, or I would be in here. It could be a measure of skill or even desire.

Then, to make sure the signatures were correct, Z took a quick glance to his bag. He rummaged through it, hand sliding past cases of variations of darts and knock-out powder. Soon enough, he grabbed ahold of the trace dart detector, and with a quick look, the identity of that third signature was confirmed.

Just as I suspected. Now, it's only a matter of time before nightfall.

Kiran was thrown back off the hill, shoulder digging into the dirt. He winced, feeling as it scraped against the ground, but knew giving up would be a failure. This first impression wasn't going well, and he was now determined to show this girl who's boss.

His wrist already felt sore, and he flexed it a little. Remote pain flashed up his arm, but he could deal with it. He bent down to pick up his sword and prepared for another clash.

"Academy Warrior!" Celestia shouted from atop the hill, sword drawn. "Prove your title!" She readied herself, bending her knees and holding her weapon with both hands. She bounded off the hill, leaping into the air gloriously. The sun illuminated her in the sky, shining light pouring from her every angle. Blonde hair became golden, and her sword shone pristinely.

Kiran didn't have enough time to dodge and instead attempted to parry Celestia's fall. It did not work to his advantage, as her blow launched him several feet away. Celestia landed hard on the ground, a small shockwave emanating from her feet.

"I have heard legends of the Academy Warriors' power, but you fail to meet those legends!" She said. "Prove yourself!"

What legends? Kiran wondered. He lifted his sword, feeling exhaustion dawning. His breath grew heavier and drawn out.

Celestia slammed into him at lightning speed, their swords interlocked as they flew backward. Momentum launched Kiran into the ground again, Celestia diving over. She crouched low to the ground, back to Kiran. Standing slowly, she looked back to him.

Kiran now lay stunned, energy-sapping every second. His sword lay inches from his fingers, but he was making no effort to grab. Hope began to fade.

Celestia watched this mockery of an Academy Warrior lay defeated, shaking her head. "The legends aren't true, I see," she muttered quietly.

Then, with finality, she leaped once again, this time higher than ever before. Her sword raised itself to the sky, sunlight glinting off. Her entire being sparkled with Light, and she began to descend sharply.

Michael stood nearby, arms crossed. He watched on, seeing one of his greater fears come to fruition. However, he now saw Celestia's power and that it rivaled his own. He closed his eyes slowly.

It only rivals in a minuscule way.

As Celestia came within feet of destroying Kiran outright, Michael made his move. A quick flash of Light accompanied by a zipping sound signaled his action.

Celestia's sword was thrown from her hands, spinning back until finally stabbing into the cold dirt nearby. Celestia herself flew back from Michael's force, but she did not fall easily. She skidded on the ground, sliding nearly to her sword.

128

A steaming red mark had appeared on her chest plate, right under the solar plexus.

She glanced up to Michael, eyes furious.

"That was quite enough," Michael told her calmly. "I still need him alive."

Celestia stood, wiping the sweat from her forehead. "That boy behind you is no Academy Warrior."

"Perhaps not," Michael agreed. "He is, however, still a master."

Celestia glanced away, sighing. "What does Siona see?"

Michael smiled. "Siona has some of the greatest judgment I've seen in a Finaliter."

Celestia sighed again, walking over to her sword. She tore it from the ground, seeing the large incision it had left. She frowned, knowing Rosemary would not be pleased. She hesitated on calling her over, seeing as this might not be the best time.

She walked over to Michael, who was now crouched over Kiran caringly. He inspected the wounds on his body and found there were none to actually be worried about.

"You are quite impressive," Michael told Celestia, even though he was looking away. "You've been practicing a lot, I presume."

Celestia ignored the compliments. "This mockery of an Academy Warrior has turned me away from joining whatever you're doing, by the way."

Michael did not respond. He remained crouched, but his attention was turning away from Kiran. A disappointed look crossed his face, but it only masked his understanding.

"I never asked you to follow him. I asked you to follow me," he said. Celestia, a little surprised, did her best to not falter in response.

"In that, you have a point. If I do agree, which is unlikely, I will only follow you, for you are more worthy."

Michael nodded. He focused once again on Kiran, who still lay stunned. The boy's eyes were frozen, and everything he could hear was clouded and muffled. Shock. Michael himself had been a little impressed, but it wasn't entirely surprising. The Sisterhood and The Academy had been created equal, but their environments had definitely changed their prowess.

Michael stood, interlocking his fingers. He took a final glance to Kiran with neutral eyes, proceeding to walk away. Celestia followed soon after.

"You're just going to leave him?" Celestia asked, sheathing her sword.

Michael laughed, noting this immediate care for Kiran Celestia had spontaneously adopted. He spoke without turning, keeping his eyes toward the cabins.

"He's in shock, not dead, Celestia," he said. "Does it matter to you now?"

Celestia sighed angrily, not choosing to respond. They walked in silence back to the hut.

16

Z couldn't believe his eyes. He looked on from his cover in the forest, standing in shock from the aftermath of what he'd seen. The powers of this armored woman and Michael himself were astonishing, and the Academy Warrior Kiran had lost easily.

If that woman gets to the city, I don't know what the Anarchists would do. He smiled oddly. *It would be fun, that's for sure. I can see it now.*

He kept his shrouded cover, still awaiting night to fall. His gaze was mostly on Kiran, who lay on the ground for nearly 15 minutes. He almost considered going over and capturing Kiran right then and there, but decided against it. His mission was not to catch Kiran, but Michael. Risking that in broad daylight would be a rookie move.

When Kiran finally stood, he fell to his knees soon after.

Z could only imagine what was going through Kiran's mind at the time, but he thought it was along the lines of utter shock and confusion. Z himself knew the Academy Warriors were prized fighters in the city, feared by many in the Brotherhood. Ever since the great divide of Academy classes, the Warriors had definitely become the most intimidating.

And this woman nearly killed one of the best in the association with ease?

Z could nearly see the confidence draining out of Kiran's mind. And as it did, the sun fell closer to the horizon. It streaked across the sky in slow motion, drawing nearer to the end of the day. The moon followed, ultimately placing itself in the sun's spot in the sky. Tonight it was full, a great glowing sphere high above.

He smiled upon seeing the tons of stars in the sky but soon hated himself for doing so. Forcing himself to look away, he thought: *Keep those simple thoughts away! Stars are just eternal explosions. They're nothing magical or cosmic, just science.*

Time passed, Kiran eventually leaving the open field and everyone residing in their respective huts/cabins.

Z crouched low, waiting. The sun had set, nightfall taking over the land. The air turned cold, and the forest grew eerily quiet.

While it sat in the back of his mind, Z did not allow the unsettling feeling of the dark woods behind him become a distraction. He remained poised for action, an assassin stalking his target. He watched as his thermal ray glasses showed Michael's blinding heat signature, indicating the boy had entered his smaller hut and sat down.

From what Z could tell, the boy was in an odd cross-legged position, but that was just another quirk he showed. Z planned out his actions in his head, making sure everything would go according to plan.

A light drizzle began to fall from the sky. It marked the transition into a fall season, the heat making a last stand and the trees soon turning. Z hated it all, for change was upon him. Something big was happening with Topia City, either with the Anarchists taking over or the Government finding enough power to hold them down. Either way, the Brotherhood would have jobs, but there were always more jobs in the chaos.

Just as this one, Z thought. *I wouldn't be in this forest if it weren't for the war. I can see the propaganda posters down in Smith right now. Full of blasted nonsense. But it makes people mad, and those are the people I can always work for.*

He glanced at his bag, seeing the neatly placed objects he would need for this task.

Knock-out powder, a net, anomaly disruptor, hooded cloak. Everything needed.

He started by taking the Anomaly Disruptor, a crystalline pink heart necklace, and wrapped it around his neck. Scowling at the feminine nature of the jewelry, he then followed with the hooded cloak, allowing himself to be completely shrouded in black. It would protect his identity as soon as he made contact with Michael, but it wouldn't do as good of a job as his stealth did. Invisibility was a gift, but not a gift that could evade everything. He grabbed the knockout powder and net.

Attaching the bag back to his hip, Z stood. Then, in the silence of the forest, he began sneaking toward Michael's hut. His glasses alerted him that the boy remained in his meditative posture.

That was good for Z, and he assumed this was just the way Michael slept at night. A quick glance to the other cabins showed two more heat signatures, assumably the Academy Warrior Kiran and the powerful blonde woman. Z nodded, noticing both were still as well.

This should be easy.

He crept up to Michael's cabin, silent in the shadows of the night. Not even the grass moved beneath his feet, and therefore no sign he was even there.

He moved around to the front of the cabin, continuously sweeping the area for movement. He pulled the door open swiftly, moving it just enough before slipping through. His stealth dissipated, and now he only had his hooded cloak for cover.

The cabin was dark, but Z had to whip off his glasses. Michael's signature had been blinding enough earlier, but up close it was genuinely vision-erasing. It took a few seconds for Z to regain his focus and full sight, but still, a faint red had been burnt into his vision.

This better not be permanent, or Michael's really going to deserve what the Anarchists do to him.

He looked to the boy, who sat peacefully atop a white bed. Michael's legs were crossed, his eyes closed. A faint glow surrounded his silhouette, giving his features a warm color. Moonlight struck it as well, pouring in from the window. They combined, making Z nearly want to leave him be.

That won't get me paid, he countered.

He clenched the package of knock-out powder in his hand, face growing serious. His dark eyebrows bent inwards, and his eyes flared. He crushed the bag with one hand, launching it at Michael's face. It exploded on impact, white/yellow dust settling all over. Z clamped his non-contaminated hand over his own nose and mouth.

After a few moments, Michael toppled backward, the glow fading entirely and his legs losing their posture. Z smiled from beneath his makeshift filter and nearly laughed.

That easy?! I expected more resistance.

Z looked unsurely to the net now in his hand, collapsible in an instant. He glanced at Michael again and quickly pocketed the net. Surprisingly, no need for it. He instead promptly walked over to the unconscious boy and picked him up. He placed him over his shoulder.

Z carried Michael out of the cabin, again opening and closing the door with practiced stealth. He rushed over to the forest, struggling now with this added weight. As soon as he passed the treeline, his pace slowed by a significant amount. He slowly made his way back to the area he'd come from.

After a minute, he found himself lost. Every direction he looked in appeared the same. Dark trees clouded every area, and sight became minimal. Z reached for his glasses but found they were in the same pocket as the net. He pulled the net out, dropping it to the ground. His glasses went with, and he cursed.

He would be forced to place Michael down, the only way of picking up his glasses. As he set the blond haired boy down, his vision was blocked momentarily. When he turned to grab the glasses, they were gone.

Z stumbled back, surprised as he glanced up. Standing over Michael was a small girl, brown curls touching her shoulders. She smiled sweetly, but a dark hint of deception twinkled in her eyes as she did. Z drew his bow in an instant, arrow notched and everything. He aimed straight for her forehead and knew he could kill her with ease.

The girl did not at all seem frightened by Z's weapon. She even dared to step closer to him, turning her head slightly in interest. Her dark green dress dragged itself across the ground as she continuously walked.

Z's aim began to falter as the girl approached, arrow tip trembling. He backed away slightly, hesitant.

She's moving me away from Michael...

The girl grinned a little more broadly and lifted up Z's thermal glasses. She spun them on her hand, a child playing with a toy she did not understand.

"What are these?" she asked playfully, holding them up to her face. "Some of that tec-techno-ligee? From your mysterious cit-ee?" She laughed and spun them faster.

Z began to pick up odd vibes from this girl, causing him to back away further. He kept his arrow pointed as well as he could, but the girl showed no reaction whatsoever.

The girl suddenly dropped the glasses to the floor, glancing down at them in mock clumsiness. She put her hands together, looking up to Z.

"I just realized I never introduced myself," she said quietly. "I'm Rosemary, by the way." She smiled again, this time even more unnervingly. "And who are you?"

Z stared worryingly at this even weirder child, not sure to treat her as hostile. She had never been seen on his thermal glasses sweeps, and he had never spotted her in the clearing otherwise.

The most terrifying part about this child is not knowing if she's going to attack me or not.

"Z," he said, voice low. "My name is Z."

Rosemary frowned, her eyes turning saddened. "No it isn't," she responded. "Why did you lie to me?"

Z's eyes widened, wondering what sort of lucky guess this was supposed to be. He pulled his arrow back further, this time ready to fire.

"Z is my real name," he pressed. "You have no proof otherwise."

Rosemary walked closer, Z's arrow point nearly touching her forehead. She looked up at him with possessed eyes, and as Z looked on into the darkness, he could only see black in them.

"Still," Rosemary said softly. "Z's an unusual name for a girl."

Z fired, and the arrow pierced Rosemary instantaneously. Instead of it stopping in her head, however, it launched directly through. Rosemary collapsed into grey smoke, dissolving into the air.

Z notched another arrow, and a chilling girl's laugh ran about the woods.

Doppelganger magic, Z deducted. He now sprinted through the forest with Michael over his shoulder, thermal glasses to light his way. He ignored any signs of stopping, fatigue or otherwise.

Not many can perform that inside the city...what that small girl just did is a power beyond what I've seen in all my years of business. She must be a high-level Wizard. No one else could even come close to that power. Is this indeed what the Wizards have now? Perhaps they're more frightening than the Warriors after all.

He dodged roots and fallen trees on his way out of the forest, feeling the watching eyes of Rosemary on his back. Any second he expected the small girl to materialize before him, with curls and wide eyes. Even if she were to, Z promised himself he would run her over like a bulldozer.

Soon enough, he cleared the treeline, launched himself and Michael out of the forest and through the forcefield.

Ethan awaited the two of them, a burnt mark on the left side of his freckled forehead. He held the remains of his shattered sword attached to his hilt in his hand, as if that would do any good. He started to take a step forward to Michael, but Z bounded to his feet quickly.

"How'd you break free?!" He exclaimed, swinging his bow into fighting position. He glanced at the slashed net nearby and cursed.

"Wasn't that hard," Ethan taunted. "What else ya got?!" He bounced back and forth on the balls of his feet like a boxer getting ready to step into the ring. Z shook his head disappointingly and laughed.

"Three more brothers," he answered in a low voice.

Just as Z had said, three more figures materialized in the thin air behind Ethan. They all wore an assortment of assassin type clothing, suitable for stealth and capture. Two held bows much like Z's, but one appeared defenseless.

The one seemingly without weapons grabbed Ethan from behind, restraining him with a practiced chokehold. Ethan dropped his broken sword and clutched the arm holding him, but the Brotherhood member was much stronger. He lost most of his strength instantly, falling a little limp.

The Brotherhood member smiled.

"Well done, Z."

The other two Brothers crowded around Michael, who remained unconscious. Z, hands on hips, watched their amazement form.

"It's really him," the one said. "Dang, bro, that worked out nicely."

"We're gonna get paid a ton," the other responded.

Z nodded. "Yeah, well-"

A loud clanking noise came from behind, and Z whirled around. He gritted his teeth upon seeing the source.

The great blonde woman stood at the edge of the forest, sword drawn. She glowed in the darkness of the night, giving light to the soon to be battlefield. Next to her, sword drawn as well, stood Academy Warrior Kiran. They prepared themselves, knees bent and swords held high.

Z cursed loudly. "Prepare yourselves, men!" The Brothers complied, drawing arrows. The one holding Ethan walked back a little for some space.

Then, in between the two sword wielders, from the shadows of the forest, walked a much shorter and happier figure.

And such Z made his second meeting with the girl who called herself Rosemary.

"You know," the little girl said, stepping carefully onto the center of the battlefield. She placed one foot in front of the other, heel-toe, heel-toe. It was nearly hypnotizing.

She stopped. "It's not such a bad thing...being who you are..."

Z fired an arrow on instant. It streaked through the air, and just before it struck Rosemary, sparks flew and the now curved arrow was flung away. Celestia moved from her protective position over the young girl, sword poised, and charged Z.

More sparks exploded as Celestia deflected all of Z's shots, with her shortening Z's range every second.

Celestia sliced at Z's bow. It snapped clean in half, but Z disappeared in an instant after. As the pieces fell to the ground, Celestia noticed a smoky powder in the air where Z had just been. She growled.

Meanwhile, Kiran struggled to move forward at all. Arrows flew from the two Brothers guarding Michael, keeping his every move on deflecting. He prayed that eventually the archers would run out of arrows, but didn't know how long he could actually handle this.

Celestia watched the area for Z, knowing stealth could only last so long. She kept Rosemary behind her.

Walking back in the darkness, an appearance of Z out of nowhere would be deadly. Celestia's vision was good, but even in the night, she had trouble spotting objects that weren't moving.

Kiran felt an arrow cut into his left hand, forcing his sword to become one-handed only. He winced, itching to clutch at the wound, but had no time. More arrows rained down on him.

He stepped back in panic, nearly falling. The arrows all bounced off a transparent barrier and fell to the ground weakly. He closed his eyes momentarily, thankful. This proved the Brothers weren't classified as masters to Siona.

But the one that captured Michael...he's a master? Kiran questioned. He got up to his feet with his good arm, glancing to the other. He closed his eyes, and quickly pulled out the arrow. A wince followed, but it was necessary. He dropped the bloodied arrow to the floor and flexed his hand.

It'll be fine, he assured himself. He glanced up to the battlefield, staring into the darkness, and prepared himself to return.

Celestia smashed into the Brother who had shot Kiran, leaving Rosemary to her own devices. She glanced at Kiran, who stood watching, and glared.

"Get back in here!"

She whacked the second archer with the flat of her blade, sending him to the ground instantly. She stood alone over Michael, looking for the other attackers.

"STOP! STOP, or I'll kill him!" a voice shouted. Celestia whipped around to the source and reinforced her grip. The man seemingly without weapons still held Ethan in a chokehold, one arm tightly wrapped around Ethan's neck. Ethan was on the verge of unconsciousness, eyelids heavy.

Celestia did not drop her sword. There was no blade in sight at first, but the man soon produced one. It was a shining knife, definitely capable of killing. At the sight of that, Celestia kept her sword down.

Kiran took a few slow steps forward, just behind Celestia. "YOU!" the man yelled. "STOP!" Kiran complied, holding his hands up. He could feel a slight trail of blood running down his left arm now. He let his sword fall to the ground.

Of course, Kiran thought. *Of course Ethan gets himself captured like this. If I had just gone back for him earlier, this battle would be over now.*

The man's eyes were wide, trembling with the stability of a terrified animal. Men like these were unpredictable, perhaps having nothing to lose.

The Bulls-Eye Brotherhood are known for recruiting men with no family, no job, and no ties to anyone at all. They feed off of these animals of men, Kiran thought.

The man smiled oddly, putting both Kiran and Celestia on edge.

"Step away from the boy," he ordered. Kiran and Celestia looked to one another, and Kiran prayed this would work. He winked, and they both stepped to the side, away from Michael.
Instead, however, Rosemary walked from in between them, Kiran observing her. He awaited the reaction of the man to her, praying this wouldn't trigger Ethan's possible death.

Rosemary smiled sweetly again, looking to the Brother. She only walked a few feet from where Celestia and Kiran were, standing still with that mischievous twinkle in her eyes. Even Kiran hesitated to trust her at this point.

The man stepped away, lifting his chin up and tightening his grip. Kiran tensed on the sight of this, but nothing followed. Ethan's eyes opened fully for a moment, but they closed immediately after.

"Do you want to be told something?" Rosemary asked the man. "Something that could change your view of your leader?"

Speaking of Z, he was still nowhere in sight. Celestia continued to watch for him, knowing Rosemary had quite the trigger information. The small girl had told her of Z's unknown gender only less than fifteen minutes ago, waking up to the news suddenly. She nearly found such a topic humorous.

A woman pretending to be a man? Why would she need to do that at all? I'll have some choice words for her if I don't kill her immediately.

"Stay back, little girl," the Brother holding Ethan said. "You're too young to be involved in this!"

Rosemary laughed, a sly grin overtaking her face. "You see, how can you be called a Brotherhood when your leader isn't a Brother at all?"

The man stopped, face blanking. "What did you say?" He started to try and make sense of the situation but came up empty.

An arrow plunged itself into the side of Rosemary's head, but again it fell to the floor in a cloud of smoke. Doppelganger.

"What she said was true," Celestia said, the brother turned to her. "Your leader, Z, is no man. She infiltrated our shield, which only allows women and masters through. There are no exceptions, and-"

Another arrow came from out of nowhere straight at Celestia, who caught it with her free hand. She snapped it clean in half, letting the pieces fall.

"And she is no master."

The man slammed the hilt of his knife into the side of Ethan's head, and the boy fell entirely limp. He let go, and Ethan slumped to the ground, unconscious. The man looked past both Kiran and Celestia.

"Z!" he shouted. "Show yourself!" No response. "Prove them wrong!"

A figure materialized in the shadows behind the two sword wielders, tackling Kiran. Celestia, no longer with the dangling threat of Ethan's death, kicked the figure off the Warrior. He went flying, slamming into the ground and rolling over several times.

The figure stood, clutching his side. It was Z, of course, gasping.

Kiran got to his feet quickly, hardly feeling his pain. He dashed over to the unconscious Brotherhood archers and grabbed an object off one of their wrists. He snapped it over his own.

After a quick second of Z stumbling forward, Kiran fired a net from the wrist launcher he had commandeered. It wrapped around Z in an instant, binding him tightly.

Celestia walked over and kept Z from falling. Kiran and the Brother walked over as well, all looking to Z.

"What's the truth, Z?" the man asked.

"And the point is?" Z growled, and Kiran noticed something a little odd. Of course, since he now knew the truth, it became apparent, but now he could indeed tell. Z was struggling to keep his voice low, as to sound manly. Kiran laughed.

"You're giving them time over this useless matter!" Z exclaimed. "Shoot them now!"

The man's eyes turned grim. "You know better than anyone else what our rules are. If you live in suspicion this long, no one will trust you back at the 'hood."

"I'll explain everything after we complete the job!" Z surrendered. "Just get me out of this situation!"

"And let you get the pay?" the man asked sarcastically. "I think not. I've been fed up with you for a long time, Z. Everyone knew you didn't deserve your high rank. You've given me too good of an opportunity to pass up."

He slid his sleeve up his arm and revealed a dart launcher. He dug into his pocket for ammo and pulled a small dart out. He slid it into the launcher and fired.

"You know what truth darts do, Z. This isn't worth dying over," he said. The dart sank into Z's arm, and the effects started to take instantly. Z felt weakness fall over him, muscles relaxing.

The first part of this blasted drug, he cursed. *Next...oh, no.*
He began coughing, but only with slight consistency. He knew if he started lying, the coughing would overtake him and made his lungs collapse. It would kill him in no time at all.

The Brother motioned to speak, but Kiran interrupted him.

"Interrogation is one of my specialties," he explained. The man glared at him a little, but yielded. He knew he would easily lose any conflict at this point. Celestia towered over him in height, and even though she was busy holding Z up, he had no intention of fighting her.

"Let's start with the basics," Kiran said. "Name and age."

Z held back, but he could feel his breathing falter. He let out a forceful cough.

"I am seventeen years old, and my name is...Z."

He coughed harder.

"I didn't say nickname," Kiran pressed.

Z didn't respond, and the next cough made him bend over. He began a fit, gasping for air. Celestia frowned, beginning to question how far Z would go to hide the truth. She fought to hold him up, but he continued to slump forward. The violence of his coughing increased, and his face grew incredibly red and pained.

Is this how I'm going to die? he asked himself. *From a blasted truth dart? And for what, dying just to hide this secret I've spent my life guarding?*

Not MY life...I guess. I've been protecting the life of someone I've created in my head.

"My-" he gasped, feeling the truth coming up his throat like vomit. Here he was, about to throw up the poisonous truth he'd been holding in his gut for two years.

"My name is Zoey!" he strained, feeling the chest tightness leave him. "Zoey...Mitchell." His voice transformed itself, leaving the low gruff it used to be and growing more comfortable.

The Brother exploded with rage. "So it is true! You...you traitor! Just wait until Captain Parker finds out! He'll have a bounty on your head when the sun rises! You'll never be welcome anywhere in Topia ever again. Goodbye, *Zoey.*"

He stomped off. Celestia let Zoey fall to the ground, and she motioned to follow the Brother. Kiran stopped her, however, by placing an arm in front. Celestia glanced questioningly to him, and he shook his head.

"If we kill him and the others, the Brotherhood will only send more."

The Brother walked over to his unconscious companions and slung both of them over his shoulders. He looked to Michael for a moment, but decided against it. There was no use at this point.

He walked away from the group and turned one last time.

"We'll be waiting for you in the city. Or die out here, it won't matter to me."

He faded into the air, his companions with.

Michael's eyes snapped open the moment he left. He smiled, saying: "I love pretending to be unconscious."

17

"*You're sure?*"

"*Of course. There is no doubt in my mind.*"

"*But is it really the time? You've waited for a long time in between other cycles. Millennia, in fact. The previous cycle was not that long past, are you certain?!*"

"*Yes! Keep faith in me. I must at least observe...if not act.*"

"*I understand it is entirely your wish, but to begin it like this? The fifth cycle? The stage that is an enormous step for your universe?*"

"*I will begin this struggle there. With those mortals, who have gone through so much, I will spread the Light to the far ends of the universe. My mortal life started and ended there, and now it will begin once again.*"

"*But why there? So many other planets have mortals that are brilliant.*"

"*...*"

"*Michael?*"

"*...'What of Amadon?', they asked! That planet was chosen by me many years ago. The history there is incomplete, and I must finalize it.*"

"*...*"

"The matter is settled. I am going, and the Light will blossom there. The Light will spread to the far corners of the universe, and the fifth cycle will be complete. Darkness will never overtake those loyal, Light and Life will be all. I ended my last cycle with that planet, and now I will begin my next with it."

"As you wish."

Michael's eyes opened to the starry night sky, staring up into infinite space. Familiar stars twinkled to him as if saying hello. Michael so dearly wanted to say hello back but found he could not.

Not until I do what must be done.

He sat up, tossing the dark blanket off of him. He could only make out his group of now five individuals, all visibly sleeping. Rhythmic snoring came from Kiran as he rose and fell. Ethan lay next to him, a welt on his left temple. Aside from that, however, he appeared to be sleeping soundly.

Michael smiled, but it wasn't genuine. He questioned the fact Ethan and Kiran were still loyal to him now, and he wondered what they may be like during the morning. The night had already been hectic, and now with the sunrise in the next hour, it had been quick as well.

Once everything had settled down, Ethan had only woken up for a few minutes before falling asleep again. He was breathing normally and didn't show any signs of long-term damage, but even Michael didn't know what would follow.

Rosemary had disappeared for a while, but now she was curled up near Celestia, covered in a blanket as well. On the other side of Celestia was Zoey, "Z," herself.

Celestia had appeared ready to lecture Zoey on her fractured beliefs, but there was no time before Zoey had passed out. Since she

147

had barely slept before the chaos, Celestia found herself very tired as well.

Michael sat back, looking to the stars once again. He imagined Gabriel watching down on him, and wondered if he'd be pleased.

I, myself, am not entirely. So far, everyone who I've desired to join has, but could they be true soldiers? Is my judgment genuinely correct?

He brushed the blond hair from his eyes, feeling the oiliness of it now. He realized it would need to be washed, another material obligation he had to attend to now.

I liked it more when my hair glowed like starlight. When it shone like diamonds, its own star in the night sky. But even so, do I deserve that now? She...she would tell me I don't...not until I please every being in the universe.

Well, I will. And once I do, she'll trust in me once again. She'll look to me as she did before, and we'll work side by side as I always wish we had. So here is where it'll begin, the new age that will start with one planet, but encompass all.

I better get more sleep.

The next morning became the next time of travel. The group rose from their makeshift beds, nearly all still tired. Michael was what would be called a "sleepless elite," so he was wholly rested even after his six hours. Ethan, on the other hand, refused to awaken.

Kiran shook him vigorously. "Get up!"

Ethan groaned, rolling away. He clutched his silk blanket tighter, as to make himself a chrysalis. Then, like a forceful butterfly, Celestia came over and tore the blanket right from under Ethan.

"Let's go," Celestia growled. She turned to Michael. "Where are we heading, anyway?"

Apparently, she had subconsciously decided that she would accompany Michael and his group of followers. *I have to remember what he told me, however,* she thought. *I am a follower of no one. Not even him. This will be a new age of the Sisterhood that dawns on the world.*

Kiran noticed this to be odd. "Celestia, you're coming with us?" An unsure smile crossed his face.

"Of course," the Sisterhood leader answered. "I see honor in Michael. And in you, I suppose, despite your lack of legendary skills that I've heard of. Plus, I will keep an eye on Zoey here."

Kiran nodded and fell silent.

Michael glanced at Topia City, a silver mass in the distance. Morning haze covered the tops of the tallest buildings, and he could see the supposed capital Lanon easily. Deeper in, he could imagine President Leila watching the Anarchist forces moving in steadily. With every day that passed would the rebellion grow stronger. If the Anarchists kept their promise, they would attack in four days.

Then, he turned his attention left, seeing a high mountain range quite a far distance away from the city. It was veiled in haze, hardly visible, but definitely there.

"What's over there?" Michael asked Celestia. She looked to it, brow furrowed.

"I've never checked. I'd assume its a desert beyond that."

Michael glanced back to everyone else. "Anyone know what might be over there?"

All of them shook their heads, but Kiran gained a spark of hope once again.

Rachel could be over there, he knew. There was this biting disappointment she had not been in the Sisterhood, but after all he had seen, the possibility she was alive grew higher. Now, in some obscure mountain ranges, he could imagine her there. She would probably find a way to hunt with her sword skills, dominating whatever odd life-cycle existed over there. Even though she had left her sword behind, it could've been a ruse. Just to throw everyone off, only to make a new weapon once outside the city.

Even though no one had any knowledge about these mountains, it was exactly what Michael was looking for. He turned away, announcing,

"And so there we are headed!"

18

There was plenty of initial questioning about Michael's decision, but the reasons were all laid out simply. Zoey had no intention about heading back to Topia, Celestia was eager to go elsewhere, Kiran still kept his hopes peaked for Rachel, and Ethan had something else on his mind.

The group traveled along as Kiran and Ethan had before, but now as the six of them. Michael led the way, Kiran close behind. Ethan followed after that, but his pace slowed incredibly compared to those in front. Rosemary skipped happily behind Ethan, no one knowing if it was her real self or not.

Zoey glared at the young girl from behind, Celestia restraining her with one arm. Every now and then Zoey would purposefully misstep, as to annoy Celestia. After the fifth time, Celestia questioned letting her fall flat on her face.

"You're really pushing it, aren't you?" she barked. "I never thought disrespect reigned so highly in Topia."

Zoey spat on the ground next to Celestia's boots. The next moment, she was on the floor, gravel bits on her face from the road. She propped herself up with her elbows and smiled bitterly. She stood, brushing herself off. Celestia grabbed her arm again, and they continued on.

"You're ridiculous, you know that?" Celestia hissed. "Doing what you did for so long, it's disgraceful."

Zoey didn't respond, keeping her dark hair to the sides of her face, nearly like a shield.

"But there's one thing I don't understand," Celestia continued. "Why? What was the true point?"

No response.

"I have three more truth darts, Zoey."

Zoey sighed angrily, gritting her teeth as she glanced away. Her chest still hurt from the coughing yesterday, not something she wished to go through again.

"Women are weak compared to men," she stated. "I wanted to be strong."

Celestia brought her hand around fast after that statement, smacking the side of Zoey's face with power. Zoey winced, but nothing more.

"That's the dumbest thing I've ever heard. Do you even know who I am and what I do?"

"Would I care if I did?"

"My mother, Siona, founded the greatest women-power organization in the galaxy. The Sisterhood, she called it. She wanted a new age where women were equal on every level to men, the only true form of balance." She spoke proudly, heart and soul put into these words. They escaped from her as if she'd been storing them for years. "I was the first to be made a leader of the Sisterhood, and I served well for many years. I made my mother proud, and spread our vision far and wide.

"Well, you both did a crappy job in Topia," Zoey remarked.

"You like getting slapped across the face, don't you?"

Zoey sighed. "What I meant was: there is no such thing as equality in Topia. It's a blasted lie, and that's all. People advocate for causes that'll never catch the government's attention. The Anarchist takeover might change all that."

"And what, leave everything worse off?" Celestia's voice lowered to a whisper. "You see, Michael doesn't know this yet, but I'm not here to protect the Government. I'm here to...prevent an Anarchist rebellion."

Zoey looked oddly to Celestia as if picking up on the subtle hints.

"Are you saying..." she started.

Celestia nodded. "Who's saying we can't bring upon our own revolution, Zoey? One where there is no superior sex. One where men and women sit equal on the council. Rights, jobs, respect, everything. And I don't mean weaklings like Leila Lanondek. She may be President, but she's a figurehead at best. The men make all the real decisions.

"But soon, women will be warriors just as much as men are, and perhaps even more."

For the first time in a while, Zoey questioned her decision of joining the Brotherhood. With them, she killed and captured and nothing else. "Rode the wave," as Captain Parker had said.

Now, though, she might finally bring on change, man or woman. It sounded terrific, but she still doubted the reality of it.

"How are you so sure?' she asked. "You are one person, an in the eyes of men, you are one *weakened* person."

"Well, long before now, I was not alone in my endeavors. Nearly two hundred sisters lived on Crescent Island, all as strong as I. My role to them was only as a guide, to help point them in the direction of the Light. However, six months ago, they all left." She sighed. "It was for a good reason, and they chose me to be the one left behind. I had begun the Sisterhood reign, and I would end it. Rosemary stayed with me because she was young, by far the youngest out of any sister. We became responsible for taking care of Crescent Island, and...here we are now."

"Why did they leave? Seems like a jerk move."

Celestia narrowed her eyes, not understanding one of Zoey's words, but she got the message. "A few of the older sisters had begun to hope for life beyond Topia. They wanted to either find a living city, or find ruins to begin a new one. I haven't heard anything from them since. It has, however, always been the Sisterhood dream to start anew from Topia, but it is an unlikely one."

"That's quite the goal."

Celestia nodded and smiled. "Ever since they left, however, I've always wanted to start another Sisterhood. But for a long time, I hadn't met anyone worthy.

"You might be the first," she concluded.

And they walked on.

19

The group then walked on for an hour before taking a break. The mountains grew larger as they grew closer, but they remained eerily far away. The sky slowly filled itself with sunlight. With fall dawning, however, the skies became overcast quickly, and there seemed a possibility of rainfall.

When the first drizzle hit, Ethan's stomach started growling. He ignored it for a solid five minutes, but after that, he could not resist to at least ask.

"Kiran..." he started. Throughout the trip so far, he'd been dealing with the aftereffects of his blow to the head, signs of perhaps a minor concussion. Dizziness forced him to stumble a few times, but he could always keep himself on his feet. And, of course, losing his sword didn't help his spirits.

"Kiran, where's the food?" He grabbed at Kiran's bag, unzipping the pocket. Kiran shrugged him off.

"Jeez, let me at least take the bag off!" He exclaimed, sliding it off his shoulders and handing it over. Ethan stuffed his face quickly, helping himself first to the bag of potato chips Kiran had packed.

Kiran himself took an apple, and upon seeing Rosemary catch up to them, tossed her one as well.

Celestia and Zoey made their way over, but neither were hungry. Celestia let go of Zoey, who promptly sat down. Rosemary sat down next to her, smiling. Zoey moved away a little.

Kiran turned away from the group, looking for Michael. "Hey, Michael! Do you…" he trailed off, noticing Michael was nowhere in sight. He placed his hands on his hips, not sure whether this was funny for Michael to leave again.

"Where is he?" Ethan asked, and his grin started to fade.

Kiran clenched his fists. He turned, and Ethan could make out disappointment in his eyes. "Gone."

Zoey laughed, quite entertained. Celestia looked to her bitterly and looked in the direction of the mountains. "Does he usually do this?"

Kiran and Ethan both responded in unison.

"Unfortunately."

Zoey laughed again but ended up going too far. Her weak lungs forced her into another coughing fit. Kiran glared at her, but she did not notice.

The rain began to grow heavier, coming from drizzle to light rain. Clouds above gathered, becoming steadily darker. Kiran frowned. He looked to the mountains, still a considerable distance away. He suspected they would arrive close to midday tomorrow if they continued at a steady pace.

He sighed. "I think it means we need to follow him again."

Ethan looked at him incredulously. "You'd think he'd give us a little heads up?"

"It's the second time he's done this. The first worked out fine."

Ethan sat down again. "Whatever. I think it's time we rest for a while. Who's with me on waiting? We've still got like...four days?"

"Considering if the Anarchists keep their promise," Celestia growled. "I wouldn't trust murderers."

Kiran surprisingly agreed with Ethan. "So far they've been reliable. If anything had gone wrong, we would've heard from the Academy. They've been notified to release a smoke signal if anything happens."

Celestia glanced over to the city, sweeping her gaze over its skyline. Sure enough, blue skies with dotted clouds were unaccompanied by any smoke. "So, we're just going to rest in the middle of our travels?"

Ethan grinned. "Of course! Sit down, sit down. We deserve a break."

Celestia sat beside Zoey, and Kiran beside Ethan. They all looked to one another awkwardly before Celestia addressed Kiran.

"You never told me about the Wizards," she said. Kiran raised an eyebrow. "Back in the Sisterhood, when you were explaining the present times of the Academy, explained the Warriors and Archers. Not the Wizards, however. And, since Ethan here is so adamant about us taking a break, it's a good time to get a word in."

Kiran nodded, understanding finally. He reached into the depths of his mind and brought forth what he could remember.

"The Wizards, as you know, were harnessers of the Power Cosmic. My understanding of the Power Cosmic is slim, due to Gabriel's short teachings of it, and because of that I can't explain very much of it. Based off what I've heard, the Wizards don't truly understand it themselves, but they use it anyway."

"Review," Celestia grumbled. "What's new about them? Why did they defect?"

Kiran scratched at his chin, feeling a thin line of stubble begin to blossom. His razor was back at his apartment, but thankfully, he didn't grow facial hair too quickly. "The Archers left first, so I understand it was partially using the momentum of that. The few Wizard students we had, ones that Gabriel has vaguely spoken of, disappeared within a matter of days. They were nowhere to be found in all of Topia. We sent search parties from day until night for a straight week, but came up empty."

"They left the city," Ethan interrupted.

Kiran shook his head slightly. "I don't think so. That's been a rumor among the students for a while, but it doesn't line up. They were powerful beyond the strongest Warrior and Archer, so fleeing would've been a waste of talent. If anything, their disappearances were supposed to be deceptions."

Celestia narrowed her eyes.

"The Wizards were famous for magic," Kiran began again. "Much of that magic was cloaking, the art of stealth-"

"-Which they stole from the Archers," Zoey said. "We invented it." Kiran looked to her oddly, then resumed:

"Their mastery of stealth helped them blend in when needed. Even so, it only lasted for a short amount of time, or it had some easy way to penetrate it. For example, a hooded cloak, even with magic, can't prevent someone from looking up the hood's face. Or, with stealth, touching anything would reveal you immediately."

"Where are you getting at all of this?" Celestia asked. "This side tangent better be worth it."

"What if..." he looked to Ethan, then back to Celestia. "What if the Wizards used all of that as deception? What if they showed us every trick so that we would look out for it? So, that when the time came for them to truly disguise, we wouldn't be able to do anything at all."

Ethan grunted a laugh. "You can't be serious."

"I am! What if it's an exact parallel of the Anarchist leaders? We don't know who they are, but Michael himself speculated that they are hiding in plain sight. If the Wizards did the same thing, we'd never know. There could be Wizard masters living as citizens all throughout Topia. The question is...what'll bring them out of hiding?"

"It sounds to me as if you're suggesting that the Wizards are the Anarchist leaders themselves," Celestia added. "That's a big accusation on circumstantial evidence."

"Makes sense though," Ethan said, agreeing for the sake of his ulterior motive. If he supported Kiran's crazy theory, it could detract from any suspicion toward him. If there even was any.

"It could be possible," Kiran urged. "The Anarchists hold power we've never seen before. The magic of the Wizards, it seems like."

"It is only the power of the Shadows."

"The Wizards thrive off Shadows."

"They are not naturally cruel like the Anarchist leaders are."

"You've never met an Academy Wizard."

"I know the legends."

"You yourself said that they lie."

"I merely-"

Celestia's statement was broken off abruptly by a cackling laugh. It was soon followed by a coughing fit, so violent Zoey had to bend forward. Once she was done, however, a broad smile crossed her face. Her chest thumped a few more times but then stalled.

Ethan frowned. "What?"

"Through all of this, you never bother to ask the Academy Archer? Do you not remember what the Bulls-Eye Brotherhood does? We have tabs on every person in the city. That includes every Wizard we can find. And oh, there's many. Not to say they're hiding or anything, but they definitely exist."

Celestia looked to her. "What are you saying?"

Zoey smiled unsettlingly at Kiran, who gritted his teeth in return. "Kiran, your idea is half-right. I won't tell you which half, however."

"Why?" Celestia asked harshly.

"Because..." Zoey paused, drawing the word out. "It's confidential."

Kiran glared at her and sighed angrily. "We have to find out which side the Wizards are on soon. They could decide the fate of the war." He looked to Ethan and stood. Brushing the dirt from his pants, he readied himself for more traveling.

"Hold on," Ethan protested. "She could be messing with us!"

Celestia gestured to the backpack. "There are more truth darts," she offered. Zoey hissed in response.

"No," Kiran said, voice low. "Let's not waste them."

There's that look in her eyes.

It's just like when she stole from me.

20

Michael stepped swiftly into the dark cave, the high sun overhead now. He left that sun's light and walked into the darkness, nothing visible inside the cave at all. He heard a few squeaks of a frightened animal, probably some sort of bat. Michael had never truly encountered such creatures before, but based off what he had always heard, they were harmless.

He rubbed his hands together as he walked blindly in the shadows, feeling them grow warm. Slowly, they glowed a faint golden light. He held them up to guide his way, and he moved forward into the cave. He walked slowly and carefully, each footstep thundering about.

Water leaked from the ceiling, coincidence to it still raining outside. It dripped in a consistent pattern all throughout the hall Michael now walked through. He stepped in light puddles as he moved forward, and left them behind at an equal pace.

In the distance, he sensed movement.

A slight pang of regret had touched him when he had left the group, but he knew now more than ever they would follow. Kiran would lead them, and Celestia would hold the line. It was only a test that was needed.

He still wondered a little about Celestia's motives for joining. Of course, at one moment she had been entirely against such an idea, but when it was time to leave she made no effort to stay behind. Had it been truly been Zoey? Rosemary?

But both Zoey and Rosemary weren't openly committed as the boys were. Zoey was obviously being forced along, and she herself barely knew her own identity. If not for Celestia, she would've run off at the very beginning.

Michael continued to struggle with understanding Rosemary. She seemed so innocent, the young girl she was, but the way she acted nearly seemed inhuman. And maybe she wasn't human at all.

Celestia may be the only answer to that, Michael speculated.

Then, just out of Michael's light, the roaring fire of a gun sounded, and a hailstorm of bullets unleashed upon the blond boy.

Michael found himself dodging, twisting, and turning with every attack. Bullets flew faster than he could catch them, sparking off walls and bouncing. A few grazed his hands, leaving hot skid marks.

He lashed out with flashes of light, hoping to blind the attacker, but it seemed of no use. Whoever it was appeared to fight very well visually impaired, if not blind. Even after each bright blast of energy, the attacks kept coming.

Michael clasped his hands together, pulling them apart at a quick speed. Glowing gold energy blasted out from all directions, but mainly in front of him. It spanned wall to wall of the hallway as a glimmering shield, catching all the bullets that flew.

Each metal shard exploded on impact with the shield, red balls of flame afterward. Michael's brow furrowed at the sight of this. No bullet he had ever seen was so infused with fire, so much it seemed influenced or unnatural. To add, he knew of no gun that could shoot that fast. The ones the Anarchists supposedly held only shot one bullet at a time before needing to be reset.

He backed away from the hallway entrance, moving into a larger, more circular, cave room. He knew that this figure fighting from the darkness was indeed who he was looking for, but the fight being put up was much more than he bargained for.

I'm even impressed. The Wizards have truly trained a worthy apprentice.

At last, the firing stopped. Michael slowly made his way back to the shield he had put up, awaiting that comforting sound.

Click! Click!

A small object was thrown to the floor in frustration, and Michael could hear it skidding toward him. He dropped the shield steadily and moved through. Still using his hands to slowly light the way, he listened for any movement. The steady drip of water continued, the only sound in the entire cave system.

He moved into another cave room, this one the biggest so far. He could see pointed cones of crystal forming into stalactites and stalagmites across the room, water running down them from the ceiling. The water congregated into pools on the ground, sporadically placed about. Then, in the very center of the room, Michael found precisely who he was looking for.

"I've heard many great things, Frederick Donovan."

Frederick Donovan crouched in the center of the cave room, a glowing ball of flame in one hand. Still poised for attack, he stared deep into the dark hall, lightly illuminated by some shining being. Around him hung more stalactites and stalagmites made of crystal, dripping water as usual. More puddles surrounded him, and torches hung on the walls.

He had lit the torches himself long ago, with the very flame that sat in his right hand. It could not disappear or die out; it was eternally burning. What Frederick could do, however, was make it much, much, smaller.

If it was a curse or not, Frederick had no idea. Ever since he had left, four years past, it had always stuck with him. Perhaps it represented his life, or his siblings' lives, who knew.

He waited now, knowing the shining being who had somehow survived his onslaught of bullets was still there.

And so, after only a few more moments of waiting, a little boy entered the room. Little, of course, was a stretch, but he seemed two or three years younger than himself. Not to mention three inches shorter. Or..two...one?

This is the first person to enter this cave in two months. *Measurement...isn't my strong suit right now.*

"I've heard many great things, Frederick Donovan," the boy said. His words flowed calmly, sending them out as a swift breeze. Even though his choice of words seemed ominous, the way he said them was not.

"How do you know my name?" Frederick asked. "Who told you?"

"Many of those things have proved in the past few minutes, but never did I expect you to be hiding in a cave," the boy continued. "You're an impressive Wizard, after all. Your gun was impressive as well, and I'm surprised you kept power for that long. Normally, as I've seen, a gun can only fire once every so often, but yours could fire multiple times nearly every second."

Frederick backed up a little, the ball of fire bouncing steadily on his hand. It sparked orange and red, mixing together. He glanced at his gun, astray and empty.

"What happened to your family was terrible, or so I've heard," the boy said. He stepped closer.

"What do you know about my family?" Frederick snapped. "They're dead, all of them. In the past, forgotten."

"Oh, they aren't forgotten, Frederick. Very far from it in Topia. In fact, I heard of them on my very first day in the city."

Frederick did not respond. *First day? What does that mean? First day alive?*

"I'm going to need you to start from the very beginning. Tell me what you've heard in a clear manner, and maybe I won't burn you too badly," Frederick demanded. He flexed the flame in his hand for effect.

The boy smiled, pristinely white teeth shining. Blond hair fell down his forehead, little spikes just above his eyes.

His blue eyes sparkled, and so he began.

"First off, let me introduce myself.

"My name is Michael Nebadon, and I am fourteen years old.

He explained it all.

21

The group reached the outlying peak (Kiran's supposed name for the mountain) an hour or so later, just as the sun began falling from the sky. A thick glaze spread across the land, turning everything into filtered orange. The colors of fall dominated, and the green fields beyond the mountain glowed. Topia City itself shone with seemingly innocent light, but deep within, Kiran knew the darkness was slowly rising.

Of course, they had yet to see any signs of smoke, signal or not. Perhaps this was indeed the Anarchists keeping a deal alive, but Kiran did suspect that the southern half of Topia was still falling deeper into their trap. It was odd, however, that they would not take advantage in the northern half of the city.

The group unanimously decided to rest at the base of the mountain for the night. Kiran and Ethan were both tired from the previous night's shenanigans, and Zoey would take any chance to delay reaching Topia City. Celestia had some uncertainty about staying, but it didn't take much to convince her.

Celestia lit a small fire using her light abilities, and the group circled around it. After a few hours of mismatched talking and slight movement, only Celestia and Kiran were awake.

Kiran looked across the blaze alit in the night, the glow casting undertones across his dark face. His eyes reflected the flames themselves.

"How big was the Sisterhood again?" he asked softly. "Before they all left, I mean."

Celestia glanced up at him, a little surprised that he had broken the silence. She was bent over with fatigue, but she could not sleep. Too much was crossing her mind, and perhaps this was the distraction she needed.

"There were nearly two hundred loyal members. Each one was a woman of harmonious ability."

"Do you remember every one of their names?"

Celestia nodded slightly. She looked into the fire. "I'll never forget."

Kiran breathed deeply, hoping he would gain an answer he was searching for. He almost hesitated at asking, as an unsatisfactory answer might only worry him more. "Did you...ever have a sister named Rachel?"

"Rachel is a common name."

"Rachel...Donovan. She's probably seventeen or eighteen now."

Celestia thought for a moment but shook her head. "She was not a sister of mine. Was she close to you?"

Kiran silently cursed. "She was, even if our friendship was short-lasted." he quickly explained Rachel's story of leaving Topia, only sparing some of his feelings toward her.

Celestia stayed silent for a little while, as if spacing out into the flames. When she finally moved to speak, her eyes remained trained on the burning tinder.

"I understand why she left. In fact, it's almost the same reason why I did."

Kiran looked at her incredulously. Celestia's eyes flicked up to his, meeting them boldly.

"Don't be so surprised. I had to grow up somewhere, right? Of course, the old Topia was very different. I hardly ever think about it anymore. I don't even know if I can."

"You do know why the Anarchists are rebelling, right? It's because of the past Topia, and what they claim is terrible about it. President Leila made a speech a few weeks back, explaining a little bit of how Topia was created. All of Topia's history drew from a main fact: war. Deadly war, too."

Celestia nodded, her eyes now again fixated on the fire. "There was war, and the Anarchists have a right to be angry about it." She sighed. "But, of course, they are hypocrites. They will destroy the world in hope for a better one. It is pitiful."

Kiran had never honestly seen it that way. "What was the war about? How were you involved in it?"

Celestia frowned, her face distorted in unease. "I have never told anyone about those days, not in detail. If I were to remember anything about how I lived back then, and what I did, I would die." Her voice turned grim. "I can never forgive what I've witnessed, so I pledge to not reveal it.

"Someday, maybe I will explain and die from it. If so, let it be that fate I reach. But as of now, I can never, never, explain. And please, do not speak of this again. If it must be done, I will choose to do it on my own accord."

Kiran nodded and promised to never bring it up in the future. He turned over and willed himself to sleep.

Celestia was the last to be awake. As she sat, hunched over the tiny flames, time passed uncontrollably.

She could feel Elara watching from above.

The next morning came surprisingly quickly. Once everyone was awake, Kiran announced they better get climbing soon. He explained that the fastest way over the ranges would be scaling the sides, and walking around would take forever.

"To hell with that!" Ethan exclaimed, staring up at the large mountain in front of him. "Might as well walk back to Topia at this point!" He turned away, hands thrown in the air.

"Hell doesn't exist," Rosemary chimed in. She began skipping up the side of the mountain with ease, leaving the rest of them behind.

Ethan rolled his eyes. "Now she's saying that as well? Well, to hell with that too!"

But Kiran was already climbing up after her, apparently intent on not coming back down until they found Michael. This first part was only a steeper incline, much more a hill than a mountain. He trudged up it, backpack and all. Zoey watched him closely and began to follow even without being told.

Ethan looked to Celestia, who was looking up the mountainside. She chewed at her lip with discomfort.

"Where does that little girl learn stuff like that?" Ethan asked her. "What kind of childhood did she have?"

Celestia swallowed visibly. "Sometimes I'm never sure. I found her on the outskirts of the city four years ago, and as far as I can tell, she's quite the special kid."

"Special is an understatement," Ethan muttered. He looked up the mountainside, watching as Kiran, Zoey, and Rosemary began climbing higher and higher. As they did, the climb became much steeper.

"Again, to hell with that. I'm going around," he declared and promptly turned. "See you all on the other side!"

Kiran glanced back, frowning. *What?* "Seriously?!" he shouted. Ethan shrugged and didn't answer. Kiran shook his head, continuing to climb.

Celestia watched as Ethan started walking down the much longer path of around the mountain, following a dirt "road" through a valley. Weeds of all shapes and sizes grew wildly around the area, probably full of snakes and lizards. She looked back to the mountain once more.

The top seemed incredibly far away, staggering in the lowest levels of clouds. It reminded her of the trees back in the forest, ones she had never dared to climb. Those had always been for the other Sisters to prance around on. Rosemary would spend days up in the canopies sometimes when time slowed. Celestia, on the other hand, would rather stay grounded.

So she followed after Ethan, but kept her distance. She let the redheaded boy lead the way, knowing now was the best time for her to be alone.

The sun moved directly overhead, tiny rays streaming through the overcast. The rain had stopped, but a drizzle passed periodically. Celestia walked through the widening valley, Ethan far ahead.

And, after a split moment, Elara was by her side. The pristine, angelic being had shown up in a flash, her movements at the speed of light.

"What's wrong, my dear?" The Seraphim asked, gliding next to her. Her sky blue eyes were full of caring. They seemed knowing something about Celestia was very much off. Celestia's brooding disposition was no longer present, now she held a chaotic personality.

Celestia stared forward solemnly, watching as spots of water appeared on the dirt path. They were infrequent, never within a pattern or standard. Some fell bigger than others, and a few even merged together.

But, even so, no rain fell from the sky, and only Elara knew that the drops on the ground were Celestia's thoughts. Broken, without matches, and weirdly shaped. And as Elara looked into the ones Celestia was stepping over, she could see them very clearly.

In one she saw herself, but apparently in a past time. Her hair was braided, unlike it now. In another, she saw a younger Celestia, but no younger in a physical sense. It was a memory as well, but she had not physically aged. In fact, that was one very unusual thing Celestia and Elara had in common:

They never seemed to age.

"I'm wondering if this is really what the Sisterhood was meant for," Celestia answered finally. "Is conquering the right idea?"

"The Sisterhood does not conquer," Elara answered. "It spreads."

Celestia smiled. *Siona's quote, engraved on the side of my cabin. There is truth in it even now.*

But even so, there is never a full truth. I will only ever see fragments of it, for my perspective may always be flawed. The mortal mind is funny, and therefore mine is.

"Elara," Celestia said.

"Yes?"

"Watch over Rosemary and Zoey for me, please. Don't let them fall."

"Always."

She disappeared in a flash of blinding white Light, leaving Celestia to walk alone. Soon, the rain started up again, this time for real. It turned the mountainside into the wet dirt, but not enough to trigger a landslide.

So she walked in the rain, sword sheathed but mind sharp and at the ready.

Kiran and Zoey climbed side by side, Rosemary far ahead of them. She skipped on the nearly vertical parts of the climb, defying gravity at its finest. Now, she began to jump again.

"Some freak show going on up there," Zoey said. Kiran only grunted, grabbing onto a ledge and pulling himself up. The area was not particularly steep or that challenging of a climb, but the length was undoubtedly tricky. He glanced down for a split second, noticing both Ethan and Celestia had chosen to go around. There was nothing he could do about it, so he kept climbing.

Zoey followed Kiran's path pretty well, noticing he chose nearly all of the best routes.

"They teach this at the Academy?" she asked.

Kiran didn't respond, continuing to climb. He gritted his teeth, urging her to shut up with his mind. This was the first time since *then* that she had spoken to him directly. He could not see why.

"Yo!" she exclaimed, whacking Kiran's ankle to catch his attention. Kiran lost his footing and began to fall backward. He whirled his arms as he fell, praying for some balance miracle. For a moment, he thought that was it. It would be over, and he would fall to his death. Even so, he tried again to desperately hold on.

Nothing helped, and he detached entirely from the rock. The crushing force of gravity readied itself to flatten him on the ground, but just as he began to freefall from the mountainside, a rope tied itself around his leg. Zoey quickly commanded it to return back to her, pulling Kiran with. Slightly embarrassed, he grabbed back onto the place he had been before.

"I thought we took all of your stuff," he said, slashing the rope with his sword instantly. It fell from great height, plummeting to the ground as Zoey gave up on it as well. "And as far as I could tell, that bow was broken."

Zoey held up her black bow with both hands and immediately snapped it clean in half. She let go of it, and the pieces fell to where the rope had gone. *You're welcome,* she thought.

"The Brotherhood doesn't work like that, Kiran. You know that more than anyone."

Kiran turned away, climbing again. He did have a distinct idea of what Zoey was now referring to and feared there was no turning her away from the subject now.

"It's been a year or two, but oh, I remember," Zoey said, grinning. "You didn't catch me till the very end."

Kiran gritted his teeth, a bittersweet memory entering his mind. "Stop."

"What did you say again? 'She's a thief!' or some bullcrap? Jeez, and no one would believe you until now."

173

Kiran climbed faster. Zoey caught up quickly, her adrenaline pumping now.

"What did you tell them? 'Oh, the commander of the Bulls-Eye Brotherhood is a girl!' I bet they loved that one! You were just mad at the prank I pulled, right?"

"Ah, well," she continued. "You can't stay silent for much longer!"

Yeah, I freaking can, Kiran told himself and continued climbing.

22

"They're coming here *now*?" Frederick asked. He sat cross-legged on the cave floor, fire in his hand diminished significantly. Michael sat across from him in the same way.

Michael nodded. "All of them. Kiran and Ethan will be happy to see you."

Frederick glanced away. "I'm not sure I want to go back."

Michael raised an eyebrow, a little intrigued. "So, then, what *do* you want to do?"

Frederick fidgeted with his left hand, tapping his fingers in order as a pattern. "Ever since I left Topia, I've never thought about going back. This place, this mountain, is as peaceful as any place I could be. Nowhere else can give me this silence."

"But that's the not the full truth, is it?"

Frederick narrowed his eyes. "You're right, that isn't."

"There's someone you want to see."

"There is. But she's dead, and even resurrection isn't possible in this crazy world. I'm a Wizard, and that power is immense, but even so, I cannot bring life from those deceased. If I could...I wouldn't be hiding here at all."

Michael laughed. "You can't possibly believe either of those things, can you? Everyone in Topia thinks you're dead, including those walking here now. If you've survived-"

"But why hasn't she said anything? There's been no contact since we left. She could clear be on other sides of the city, for all I know. If she's alive. The chances are slim."

Michael stood, brushing the dirt off his orange shorts. "You see, there's a problem, Frederick."

Frederick stood as well, the fire growing. "What?" he asked, eyes narrowing again.

The blond haired boy looked to the ceiling, full of wonder. He turned back to Frederick, smiling.

"You don't have a choice."

And from above, the mountain shook violently.

Kiran cursed as he began to lose his footing again. A rumbling started in the mountain, rubble soon beginning to fall. The ledge he was holding onto broke off easily, but again, as he began to plummet downwards, a roped arrow caught his leg. This time, Zoey did not pull it back, so Kiran lay, dangling.

He tried not to look at the ground, a staggering drop away. It would surely kill him, no doubt at all.

Zoey struggled to hold onto her new bow, which she wrapped around her back. She climbed up further, but the mountain began to shake again. Ethan saying, "to hell with this!" flashed through her mind as the top of "outlying peak" started to crumble. She started to realize that maybe he had the right idea with going around, but it was too late now.

She jumped to the side, pulling Kiran with. His weight jerked her downwards, but she managed to keep a handle on the mountainside. Above, Rosemary continued to climb upwards, skipping over rough areas and falling rocks like a mountain goat.

Beneath, Celestia glanced upwards as soon as the first boulder broke off. It wasn't anywhere near the climbers, falling from the opposite side of the mountain. She stopped walking and drew her sword.

This isn't a natural avalanche or earthquake. Something is causing this for sure.

She watched the sky above the mountain closely, realizing all but the tip was below the clouds. She glanced toward Ethan quickly but paused when she realized he was now out of sight.

Probably took cover. Shows cowardice, but not a bad idea.

She readied herself, looking up to the top of the mountain. She swallowed nervously, already feeling a little nauseous from the height. She spun her sword once, then twice, then three times. Bending her knees, her eyes closed and her breathing slowed.

I can control my every movement, she told herself. Then, with one swift moment, she lifted off from the ground, bounding through the air and onto the side of the mountain. She swung her sword into the dirt, keeping hold. Her blade cut out chunks of soil and rock, and as it did, she clenched her jaw tightly.

Celestia made her way up the mountainside with giant leaps, digging her sword in when needed. A few rocks and even some small boulders came her way, but she easily knocked them down. A few times she stumbled to the side when the mountain shook, but always recovered within seconds.

Kiran and Zoey were passed quickly. Rosemary remained skipping upwards, and Celestia paid her no attention. She was locked in, all sights set on the peak.

At last, she came within range of the very top. The clouds began to part-

Oh, lord...

-and from them materialized a massive object in the sky. It was sleek, black, and hovering just above the mountaintop. Two huge engines sat on either side, red glowing balls of energy in the middle of them. Shaping almost like a disc, Celestia received a glimpse of her very first spaceship.

Her sword broke off from the rock, leaving her to plummet downward. Her grip grew weak, and her golden hair spread out in shimmering fashion.

How? How would the Anarchists be this close, and so soon? That's space technology as well. No way...

She free-fell for a few moments, glaring at the enormous machine high above. Her expression turned dark, and determination pulsed within her.

I'll destroy it all.

She flipped backward, the sunlight breaking through and glinting off her silver armor. Her grip tightened again, and she stabbed her sword deep into the mountainside. It left a large gash, moving down while opening the incision more. Celestia planted her feet firmly and looked back up to the great spaceship.

She glanced back to Zoey, who was now only a few feet away. She ignored Zoey's wide eyes.

"The first battle with the Anarchists," she said grimly. "Michael better get the heck out here soon."

23

"What did you do?" Frederick asked, eyeing the ceiling suspiciously. He could still feel rumbling, and the roof did shake. A few of the stalactites had fallen, but none were close to Frederick and Michael.

Michael looked to the ceiling as well. "I didn't do anything," he said. "The Anarchists are here."

Frederick's last bits of a grin faded and were replaced by a sour frown. He put his empty hand on his hip, still watching the ceiling with caution.

"Why would they come here, of all places?" he asked. The ceiling rumbled again, and a stalactite fell off in the corner of the room. It shattered into pieces of salt and moisture.

"You should know the answer to that," Michael responded. He stared at Frederick with curious eyes, arms crossed.

Frederick glanced at him bitterly. "You're the cryptic one to speak, eh? Look, I don't know how you convinced Kiran and Ethan to join with you, but you sure aren't clear about it. You speak in riddles, and it pisses me off." He placed a hand to his forehead, eyes glancing up. "If you want me to follow whatever plan you've got, tell it to me straight up."

"Telling apprentices the whole truth is the fault of a master."

Frederick laughed sarcastically. "You might be a master, but I'm no apprentice of yours. I follow the King, and you know that. He's the only person I would even consider my master."

Michael had no answer, so Frederick continued.

"If the Anarchists are causing that commotion up there, I'm a lot safer in this cave. It'll take them hours to even days if they want to find me, and even then I'll put up a fight.

"They won't find me here," he said assuringly and flopped back down. He sat cross-legged again, this time with his flame-hand resting nearly his center. It warmed him in the cold caves, which helped as it was eternally burning.

Michael shook his head. "You're right. They aren't looking for you. But they're looking for me. And that means they're coming here."

Frederick glanced at him, expressionless. "Then leave! Don't drag me into your messes."

"We need the Wizards to return to Topia, Frederick. I have placed great faith in choosing you, and I don't wish to regret it. The choice is ultimately yours, but I will warn you this: Stay here, and you will die with an unfinished life. Rachel is waiting for you, Leo is waiting for you, even the mystery of your parents is waiting for you. Do not let all of that go to waste."

Frederick stood, showing no reaction to Michael's words. He stretched his arms and twirled them a few times. The flame in his hand sparked strong. He walked past, brushing Michael's shoulder slightly. He did not glance back and began walking through the hallway ahead of him.

"Guess I better get away from you, then," he said, using the fire in his hand to light the way.

Michael did not follow or even look back at Frederick. "I wish you well, then, Frederick."

No response followed, and the firelight soon disappeared.

24

Celestia, Zoey, and Kiran watched as the Anarchist ship floated overhead, seemingly still. It loomed in massive size, a great machine waiting above.

Kiran frowned, already knowing the Anarchists had great technology. No one, however, expected something like this. At The Academy, there was no knowledge the Anarchists had aircraft, much less aircraft of this size. The Topian Government at the greatest had small fighter jets: transports with minimal firepower and speed, not to mention short-lasting. They costed more than they accomplished, and hadn't been used against the rebellion at all so far.

"This ship alone could be enough to destroy Lanon," Kiran muttered. "We have to get back to Topia immediately."

Celestia brushed off the dirt from her sword. "And what, get destroyed with it? We have to get rid of that thing now!" With that, she began sprinting up the mountainside once again, leaping when needed.

Kiran watched, his sword still sheathed. An ache started in his leg from the rope holding it. Zoey had pulled him back up as soon as the rumbling had ceased, letting him stand on the stone ledge she had chosen. Now they watched as Celestia made her way to the massive ship, sword in hand and hair flowing.

Zoey turned to Kiran and watched as he thought. She held out a hand.

Kiran looked at it and glared at her. She winked.

Kiran turned away, a bitter taste now in his mouth. He continued to half-watch Celestia, trying to make up his mind. Attacking now could possibly mean suicide, or it could mean an early victory. Going back to Topia would be the safer route, and there would be a chance at warning everyone before a potential attack came.

He started to turn away from the mountain, choosing that it might be better if Celestia stalled the Anarchists, while he-

A rope tied itself tightly around his wrist, restraining him back. He pulled violently against it, gritting his teeth. He then drew his sword, preparing to slice the thing to pieces, and perhaps take Zoey down with it.

But there was no time. Zoey jumped up to the next ledge, forcing Kiran to come with. Two black cords flung themselves from Zoey's wrist launchers, grappling hooks attached on the end of them. They dug into the mountain, and so began their ascent.

Kiran lowered his sword as Zoey dragged him up, instead using his feet to help speed up the climb. He hurried while doing it, shins scraping against the rock when he couldn't. Zoey flung herself upwards with her grappling hooks, launching herself and Kiran forward.

Kiran's side smashed into a jutting ledge, knocking the wind clear out of him. He wheezed, using his last bit of energy to slice the rope with his blade. Luckily, then, he caught his sword on the ledge he had hit, hooking onto one of the protruding rocks.

He hung there for a moment, breath returning. Zoey stopped, realizing that her extra weight was no longer on her. She turned, seeing Kiran pulling himself onto the ledge.

"Why did you make that idiotic move?!" she exclaimed, rushing down to him. She crouched on the area above, eyes wide. "I was helping!"

Kiran pulled himself entirely onto the ledge, still breathing heavily. He winced with a few of the movements, and fully collapsed on his back as soon as he could rest. After a few moments, he finally made eye contact with Zoey.

"I want nothing to do with that ship," he said.

"Really? Really?" Zoey looked at him curiously.

"Really."

"That's ridiculous! You're lying for some dumb reason, aren't you?"

"Yeah, I'm lying. But the reason isn't dumb."

"Oh?" She grinned.

Kiran glared. "The reason is that you're here, that's the freakin reason."

Zoey sighed, standing up. Her grin had faded. "Not surprising..." she muttered. "I can't believe you're still so bitter! Lighten up."

Kiran stood slowly, ignoring Zoey now. He winced again as a sharp pain hit his side. He stood there for a moment and started to turn away.

He found he could not, however. His entire body was immobile, all except for his head. He looked down, certain this was another rope Zoey had shot. He struggled against it but found no give in whatever was keeping him still.

It was not another trick of Zoey's, however. As he looked down curiously, he saw what was confining him. A dark aura surrounded his frozen being, all congealing near his shoulder and blasting outward in a straight beam. The beam shot toward the Anarchist ship, and that confirmed it to Kiran.

A force beam. I'll be in that ship in a matter of moments.

He looked at Zoey, and saw she was also trapped in one. Her eyes turned defeated, but Kiran did notice that her bow was inside the force beam, meaning it would travel to the ship with them. His sword was as well.

And so they began to dematerialize, appearing in an entirely foreign location.

Frederick stood outside the cave entrance, breathing outside air for the first time in what seemed like forever. He knew his days of bat meat and dripping stalactites were over, but he did not know how long these days would last. Deadly territory was ahead. The Anarchists were here, now, above him. Topia City could be in ruins within the week. Rachel could be dead or very much alive.

Rachel...Michael said he'd help me find her. If I do, and she's alive, then I will make sure Topia is saved. I can do it, too. But if she isn't, then I have nothing to truly live for. I won't have any reason to save the city she ran away and died from.

185

If then, Topia will surely be destroyed, and I'll be thankful for it. It'll place every lousy memory with no hope of redemption to rest, leaving it in dust and rubble.

No more would it haunt me.

He stared across the mountain valley, full of rolling hills as far as the eye could see. A great river lay in the distance, light forests running along either side. Great fields accompanied them, full of grazing, wild cattle. The creatures were beasts with horns, appearing cow-like, but not in the same way. Small birds fluttered around the area as well, observing.

The Anarchists sit on top of me, but I will not go. Michael knows it himself. I will not help-

"Until Rachel is found," he said out loud. He snapped his fingers, the fireball under them sparking to life. The ball glowed a deep orange, and then red.

Do I really need this? Do I really want their help? I...I do. Without them, I'll never stand alone. I need this flame to be put out. For now, it's necessary.

He raised his other hand to the sky, pointer and middle finger straightened. Between them sparkled electricity, and in his mind, he thought:

Let the electric fire dance through my breath, my body, but never my heart. Allow me to channel this raw, untouched source of energy, pouring it from my spirit outward. To which, I summon the King of Wizards...

The ball of fire in his hand sparked yellow, then blue. It morphed into a smooth ball, and inside a great storm of flame and lightning formed. The desert sands of it parted, and from within came a great yellow creature. It had scales of diamonds, eyes of galaxies, and teeth of shimmering golden light.

I call the King of Dragons.

A streaking pillar of yellow lighting struck the now orb of glowing fire in Frederick's hand, sending shockwaves through him. His hairs all stood on end, causing his ordinarily curly hair to strike upward in spikes. He gritted his teeth, fighting the urge to pass out.

Strength poured out from him, and at the last moment, he wanted to collapse. However, the electricity froze him in place, and he had no choice but to endure it.

Finally, it eased. His vision had turned pixelated and blurry, and now, it slowly started to regain focus.

Behind him bristled energy. The orb in his hand grew dark, then flared out in red once again. It returned to its fiery color, and Frederick found himself free of the last remnants of electricity. His heart began beating intensely. He turned and met face-to-face with exactly who he had planned to summon.

The leader of all Wizards, Master Timothy MacArthur.

The King stood appearing precisely as he royally should: Golden robed, a matching crown atop his head. Clear crystals, *All-Stone*, lay embedded in the five points of the crown. Dark brown hair fell from under the crown and behind him, but that was only a minor detail of the man they called Timothy MacArthur.

Frederick was more focused on the King's great eyes. They were equal to the orb Frederick had held moments ago, swirling spheres of lightning and flame. They flashed yellow and orange.

"You've made your decision?" the King asked, his voice booming. Even within it, Frederick could feel the electricity in the air, as if the King's words could cause lightning.

"Yes, my King," he said quietly. "I have."

"Explain to me your wish."

"I will recover Rachel Donovan, my dearest sister, and ensure that she is alive. If so, I will pledge myself to her protection. In return, I ask to have entire control over the flame burning in my hand."

"It will cease to eternally burn as long as you are fulfilling your requirement. Otherwise, it will come back with more force than you can imagine, and it will never leave you. Do you promise to find her and repair the Donovan name?"

"Yes, I promise." He closed his eyes, feeling the pact start to take place.

"And for your brother?"

"I.." he faltered. *Leo...*

He hadn't seen his brother in years, ever since he had left the city. Their relationship had never been as great as it could've, with Frederick and Rachel being the dreamers while Leo was the opposite. He never shared their wishes of becoming warriors. Business was a much better medium, and therefore they split.

"I pledge to include him in some way or form," he finished.

"Good enough," the King responded. "Then, I promise you this: As soon as you find Rachel Donovan, your mark will cease to exist. As well, your entrance to the Order of Merlin will be tested here. The Masters are watching you."

The King disappeared with another bolt of electricity, lighting up the area. Frederick nodded, clenching the fire in his fist. It burned now, white hot. He suspected the nerve endings in his hand would be beyond reasonable repair, a type three burn for sure. He squeezed the blaze once more, and then opened his hand. It stung.

He hardly acknowledged the king's comment about the Order of Merlin, not caring. The Wizards in that council were power-hungry, only caring for their own selves and their personal knowledge.

I'll be something even better than all of them.

He stood, looking out among the fields again.

It's time.

Ethan kept his head low while walking throughout The Unknown. It was a ship impressive for even his standards, but he had always known of it. In fact, Noah promised it would be his one day.

Masked Anarchists lined the halls, all armed and ready. When Ethan passed, they snapped to attention, waiting for his every command. He never said anything, though, as something else was on his mind. He now knew that this would be his first significant betrayal against his "friends."

It wouldn't be his final move, of course, and if all went as planned, his friends would never know. Not even Michael would be able to tell Ethan was the one orchestrating the entire event from the Shadows.

He passed quite a few rooms on his way to Noah's chamber, including a surveillance room, interrogation room, and Anarchist quarters. The Anarchists themselves were mainly odd, especially the ones on The Unknown. They didn't eat or rest often, but it was tough to tell. After all, every Anarchist was nearly the same aside from their weapons, and those repeated in similarity quickly.

They're so robotic. It's like being the only freaking human in the place.

He reached Noah's chamber, two tall, gray doors being the entrance. He grabbed the dark oak handles and pulled them open, entering the large room. Stone columns held up this area of the ship, swirls engraved in them. Ethan stepped through the first pair, walking along the path in the center of the room. The only windows were in this chamber, huge dark-stained windows on either side. They were one-way, impossible to see through from the outside.

Ethan walked up to the spotlight of the room: The Throne. It was pristine, jet black with shining speckles of gold. The bright sides curved in fancily, spiking up in the back. Two great wing-like masses shot out from the end, carved out by newly recruited Anarchists when the rebellion had sparked.

In the very center of the throne sat the Shadow Lord himself, Noah. He wore a dark, hooded cloak covering every square inch of his body. A shadow-like aura floated around him, an almost like an intense gravity.

Ethan walked forward, bowing slightly. Noah stood, the area around him rumbling as he did. At full height, he was only a foot taller than Ethan, but it seemed so much higher in reality. Noah waved his cloaked hand, a black glove showing from underneath. The black tile floor beneath Ethan began to change color, turning gray, then white, then clear.

Through it, Ethan could see his friends, each one contained in clear tubes. The room around them was dark, absent of any other people aside from two Anarchist guards. The guards stood silently by the two walls on either side of the tubes.

He could see Kiran, who kept attempting to force his blade through the tube, but it was no use. Nothing could penetrate this glass, as it had been instilled with every pain and death that had been experienced in the room. The tubes, were, in fact, torture chambers.

"You're going to torture them," Ethan said quietly.

Noah looked at him. "No...*you* are." He pointed a gloved finger at Ethan. He drew it back, closing into a loose fist. "But as you know...we do not use a standard method of uncivilized torture. You will give them every chance to survive."

Ethan turned to the hooded figure before him, chest pounding now. He smiled nervously, knowing this was it, a moment of decision and truth. A day where he would finally take what was rightfully his, and would get credit for his hard work. He would no longer be thrown to the side, an outcast. Kiran, Noah, everyone would be forced to see him.

"Don't fail," Noah said. The Shadow Lord smiled from beneath his hood, and whispered powerfully:

"Shadow Hand!"

A great, claw-like mass lunged from his cloaked arm, grabbing hold of Ethan and pulling him close. Ethan did not struggle, instead seeming oddly relaxed. The hand plunged him through the floor, letting go as he fell to the ground.

"Stay in the Shadows," he could almost hear Noah saying. *"They cannot see you there."*

He stood, masked entirely in the darkness. Looking to his friends, he first felt the pang of betrayal, but knew now was the worst time to feel empathy for them.

"Greetings, mortals," he growled.

25

Ethan scanned his "allies" in their respective chambers, noting that Celestia, Kiran, and Zoey were all glaring at him. He tried not to make eye contact, the daggers in the air nearly too much to handle. Instead, he looked to Rosemary, who lay sleeping peacefully in her chamber.

He paused, looking to the fifth chamber. It was empty, no sign of Michael, who should've been inside.

"Where is Michael Nebadon?!" he barked, doing his best impression of Noah. It strained his voice incredibly, but he had to do it. If Kiran were to recognize his voice, the whole cover would be blown.

No one answered, and to Ethan their acts were genuine. He had been with them when Michael had disappeared, and they hadn't seen him since. If their roles had been switched, Ethan in the chamber and one of them interrogating, he wouldn't have known either.

"No one?!" he bellowed, reminding himself to stay firm. He had to adopt a new personality, and it felt extremely odd. He knew with great fear that being his weak self would uncover nothing at all.

Again, no one answered. Kiran surveyed the room cautiously, his hands going from open to fist over and over again. His eyes scanned every inch of the ceiling and walls, as well as the guards on standby. Ethan could see a plan starting to form in Kiran's eyes.

I need to do something quick, he thought. *If I wait for him to come up with a strategy, he'll overthrow all of this.*

"Noah! What do I do?"

A significant presence formed itself in his mind, like a weight pressing onto his skull. He first resisted it, but then allowed himself to relax.

"Draw Michael out...," he could hear Noah whispering. *"Release the blonde girl...I'm interested to see what she can do..."*

"Really?!" Ethan thought. *"Celestia?"*

"Yes..."

Ethan glanced up to the Sisterhood Leader, who appeared more battle ready than ever. He face was twisted with anger, apparently itching for a fight. Letting her out would be giving her exactly what she wanted.

"You!" he shouted, pointing at Celestia with a cloaked hand. She looked at him, curious. He glanced back to the guards on either side, who snapped to attention. "Release her."

The guards nodded. They both turned, placing their palms on the walls next to them. Moments later, the transparent barrier around Celestia fell, sliding into the floor. She glanced around at it.

Celestia smiled, and leaped from the area she stood, no longer vulnerable to the chamber. She unsheathed her sword and twirled it. Turning to Ethan, she positioned herself threateningly.

"That was a mistake," she said confidently and took her stance. Her eyes glanced to the sides, watching the Anarchists guards. She thought it would be a custom of the Shadows to fight unfairly.

Kiran slammed his fist against the barrier holding him, and tried to shout out and catch Celestia's attention. He desperately yelled over and over, but it was no use.

Ethan flicked his wrist, and the walls on either side of the chambers opened smoothly. Ten more Anarchists rushed out from either side, armed with guns. Ethan had heard of the legendary bullet-deflecting blade Celestia held.

Let's see her prove it.

Celestia backed away, looking slowly to the Anarchists on either side of her. She waited, letting the soldiers prepare to fire.

Ethan snapped his fingers.

The first bullet rang out in an instant, Celestia crushing it with her sword with ease. Her sword had met it with unbelievable speed, a mere flash of silver in the air. The bullet sparked, flying off before crashing into the wall. Then a second came, and that one was launched away as well.

Celestia brought her sword back to her center, resuming her starting stance. She stared forward, eyes tilted up at Ethan. An arrogant grin crept onto her face.

Ethan exhaled angrily and snapped his fingers again. This time, every soldier fired twenty bullets in total. Celestia sliced her blade multiple times while moving in a blur. There were too many sparks for Ethan to count. After seeing that none hit, the Anarchists prepared to shoot again. Celestia was now growing in confidence.

Ethan snapped his fingers for a third time, now with extra force. The Anarchists moved to shoot, but before they even could, Celestia froze up. A weak gasp slipped from her lips, and she started to fall over.

Ethan's eyes widened as he saw the sword that now protruded from Celestia's stomach. It was a primary Anarchist blade, but now, it had an aura of Shadow energy floating around it. He didn't even have time to notice the sheer lack of blood on the blade's point.

Celestia herself glanced down to it in disbelief. Her eyes lost any remains of confidence, and instead, were replaced with shock.

Ethan grew a little faint, and his face paled. *"Noah...what did you do?"*

As Celestia fell to the ground, the figure behind was revealed. Ethan slowly recognized him, or her. Brown hair down behind her back, eyes that held an unknown gender within.

Zoey.

"I MADE HER AN OFFER," Noah announced, his voice booming around the room. The walls rattled.

"And I took it!" Zoey exclaimed, and Ethan could detect some human regret within. "Let us go!"

"KIRAN, CELESTIA, AND THE SMALL GIRL WILL BE LET GO," Noah announced. "YOU, HOWEVER, HAVE A BOUNTY ON YOUR HEAD, AND THEREFORE WILL NOT BE SET FREE SO EASILY."

Kiran, whose wide eyes were locked on dying Celestia, barely felt himself start to fall. The ground beneath him flapped open suddenly, causing Kiran to be thrown from the ship. The same thing happened with Celestia, and her body dropped from the sky.

Zoey glanced behind her, watching in horror as her allies disappeared. Her hands trembled. She looked frantically to the Anarchists on either side of her, who positioned their guns. She squeezed her shaking hands tightly into fists, knowing very well this could be her end.

"IF YOU CAN DEFEAT MY APPRENTICE, YOU WILL BE GIVEN FREEDOM," Noah boomed. Ethan's eyes widened again, and he shook his head in anger. *"Go to hell, Noah."*

"Kill her easily," Noah responded. Ethan nodded sadly.

He stepped from the darkness, a brand new sword in hand. He kept his eyes away from Zoey's, shameful. It was no use protecting his identity, as his red-hair wasn't very unique.

"You," Zoey said, voice starting to crack. Many years of keeping it low had finally started to get to her, now that she was speaking normally. She had masked it for so long, but it turned rough soon as her focus became absent.

Ethan nodded. He held up two fingers, looking toward the ceiling. Beside Zoey, two squares of black tile overturned. On top sat two silver katanas. Their hilts were wrapped in black leather, strange symbols engraved into them.

"Use them," Ethan said. "Use them, or I'll kill you with ease."

Zoey did not respond, gaze stuck to the floor. Ethan readied his own blade.

A moment later, he rushed at Zoey. She made no effort to pick up the blades, throwing Ethan off. He slowed in his charge, waiting for her to act sensibly. With his mind he desperately urged her to use the weapons, hoping she would somehow hear him. But yet, she did not move.

Then, an arrow stabbed into his shoulder, blinding pain for only a second. He felt his left arm now become practically useless, falling limp. As Ethan glared at her, Zoey prepared another arrow. Her bow looked good as new, even though it had been broken earlier. She notched the arrow and started her release.

A bullet shot into the upper limb of her bow, breaking it once again. The Anarchist who had shot it reloaded, his gun smoking. Zoey's hand stung, and she let her arrow drop.

"NO BOWS," Noah said. "THAT IS THE WEAPON OF A COWARD."

And in Ethan's mind, Noah said: *"End this quickly."*

"Use the swords!" Ethan assured. Zoey reluctantly bent down to pick up the blades. Her hands trembled as she held them, and as she pointed them forward, she could not push Celestia from her mind. She had stabbed someone so trusting to her, someone who was undoubtedly dead. Wanting to drop them, she held on.

The blasted Academy Warrior weapon...this is an evil way of killing. No one should die to this...But yet, I've already killed with them. And, for what? Will Kiran and Rosemary be safe now? They were dropped from such a height! That wasn't part of the deal.

Ethan walked steadily up to her this time, placing his sword in between hers. Some deep part of him was still holding on, telling him this was against the rules. It was blasphemy against Academy Warrior code and ideals. *To kill willingly, I now do.*

Zoey felt her confidence waning, feeling the threat of Ethan now pressing on her. She could sense the Anarchists aiming their guns readily, and knew that even if she were to defeat Ethan, they would shoot her down instantly. *They won't let me go no matter what.*

She looked to Ethan, eyes meeting as her swords dropped slightly. She could see the hurt in his eyes, sincere regret that she also felt.

Maybe there's time to save him. I can bring him away from the Anarchists.

She reaffirmed her grip. *Might as well go out making him think.*

197

Her swords clashed against Ethan's, prying it to the middle. She pulled, attempting an early disarm. It failed, but Ethan fell closer to her.

"You don't have to do this," she whispered, just loud enough for him to hear. He ignored it.

Ethan threw his force upward, turning to his left and sending both of Zoey's blades away. He shifted stance and stabbed with lighter force, hoping to draw Zoey in. She fell for it, letting her blades both strike down. Ethan's sword moved around, coming out of nowhere.

But just as it came inches from Zoey's face, he turned the sword to the flat side.

Zoey stumbled back, a ringing in her ears. She took a moment to regain her focus, a dizzying sensation still present. Her face grew bent with determination.

"They can't control you!" she shouted, walking forward again.

Ethan waited for her to approach.

"You could've ended it there," Noah told him.

"I know, I know," he responded.

Zoey sliced with both her blades, one toward his head and one toward his hip. Ethan blocked both, bending into a new stance with one leg bent and the other straight. It was what Gabriel had always taught for solid blocking.

It feels dirty, now, using it. Like I've contaminated it...I hate it. But even so, screw Gabriel. He didn't care for me anyway.

He smashed Zoey's upper blade out of the way, launching it high up. Zoey attacked with the other, but it was easily blocked. Ethan had the opening for a direct stab. He moved to strike-

I..can't...

-and kicked. Zoey fell onto her back, gasping for air. The wind had been knocked out of her when she hit the ground. Her grip weakened.

"A missed chance again," Noah told Ethan. *"Don't miss a third time."*

Ethan brought his sword high, preparing to strike down. He stopped, holding it still above him.

"No, no, no!" Noah yelled. *"Kill her now! Do not hesitate!"*

Ethan looked down to Zoey, and their eyes met for the last time. Zoey could see a great hurt in him, a blockage that was holding back a dam of Light. She took her last bit of strength to grab her swords.

Ethan struck. In what seemed like slow motion to her, she raised her swords to block. They formed an X above her chest, ready to catch the blade.

Ethan nearly smiled, seeing this wouldn't be over. His sword made its way down toward Zoey's block, and right as they started to clash...

Ethan's sword fell right through.

There was once a time in Zoey Mitchell's existence when she had loved space. Not just space itself, but the idea of space. A vast, expansive universe in which there were nearly no boundaries on exploration. Millions of worlds beyond her own, all with the possibility of being a new home.

One night, many years before she had assumed her role as a man and joined the Brotherhood, she took a minute to watch the stars. She had seen hundreds of midnights before, but this one was exceptional. She had leaned out her window on the third story of Hookhorse Residences, lacking her oddly cut hair now. That night it had been her most beautiful, flowing and reflecting the starlight above.

She had looked up to the sky in wonder, hoping to see her favorite stars. Diamond, always the brightest, sat in its usual place at the center of the sky. Altus, the one with a blue tint, glowed off to the side. She always swore that the star glowed with her heartbeat, pulsing at the exact same rhythm.

Then, in a moment of pure awe, Zoey witnessed something spectacular. A great golden light erupted in between the horizon and the sky, taking the form of some incredible star. She initially thought of a quasar, one of the brightest things in the universe, but shook her head at it.

It was something else entirely.

And as she now laid on the ground, consciousness fading and breaths slowly falling weak, she saw that same light. Even through the dark ceiling, she could see the night sky drawing close. That same quasar-like object shone above her, and it told her to close her eyes.

She did, and she was herself again.

Young and bright, a little star in an enormous night sky.

Zoey looked up, and white flooded her vision. Everything around her was void of color, from the floor to the sky above her. She could not tell if there were walls around her, as the white expanse seemingly went on forever. All was like a blank canvas. Nothing.

She turned around and yelped in surprise.

"I am sorry," Michael told her. He bowed his head low, blond hair sitting messily on his head. His blue eyes stung of a certain regret that was nearly inhuman, greater than Zoey had seen in...

What was his name...She asked herself. I...don't-

"Zoey," Michael said, bringing her attention. "Focus. You have a long journey ahead of you."

She frowned, eyes coming into realization. Her memories returned slightly, but she found certain aspects impossible. Every face in her mind was blurred, and even worse, no names could be matched to them.

But Michael...he's here, in front of me. That must be why I can remember him.

"What...what is this place?" she asked.

Michael sighed of relief slightly. "It's...well, a road." He turned, holding his hand out as if displaying the area. From where he stood began a stone brick path, moss creeping from beneath each crack. It curved like a snake far into the distance, and Zoey thought she saw a great lighthouse at the end of it.

Zoey smiled at it, and together they stood, looking down the road more and more. Then, Zoey's smile faltered.

"I'm dead, aren't I?" she asked defeatedly, a sudden tone of heaviness taking hold of her voice. Weirdly enough, saying the words didn't feel as real as they should've been. It was such a serious topic, yet now being here, it didn't feel that way to her.

Michael smirked. "That's a crude way of putting it. Think of it more as...embarking on a new journey."

He waved his hand again, and beside the road, which had sat empty against the white, there began rolling green grass. Fields upon fields of it went on and on, as far as the eye could see. Pink and purple plants popped up from the ground, sporting fruit unlike Zoey had ever seen. The sky turned a deep purple, and it became littered with glowing yellow stars.

It was beautiful, and it went on.

Michael helped Zoey take her first few steps as if teaching her to walk all over again. Once she could on her own, Michael let her go.

She walked along the path, starting this new journey.

The sword fell from Ethan's trembling hands, staying in Zoey. The area stuck into her chest was now bloodstained red, causing Ethan to back away. The silver katanas Zoey had wielded dissolved into black smoke.

"Noah!" Ethan exclaimed, voice hoarse. "Noah, what did you do?!" He bent over, clutching his trembling sword hand with his injured arm, but the physical pain was no more. He felt nothing in his body now, only coldness. He fought the urge to look at Zoey, knowing it would just scar him more.

"I've...I've killed her," he whispered. "I killed her with my own sword!"

"Retake it," Noah responded. *"Hold that blade again, I'm sure you'll find it interesting."*

Ethan shook his head, bending over further. He started to gag, feeling the dizziness begin to overtake him. A swift breeze would have pushed him over. He stumbled to the side, hands on his stomach. The Anarchists on either side steadily made their ways back into the wall, disappearing from view. The door guards, however, watched Ethan closely.

He fell over, using one arm to keep himself propped up. Flashes of Zoey zipped through his mind, and with each one he gagged again. His head began to throb, and it grew light. Just as he was about to pass out, something changed.

Strength flowed into him. It came like fire, burning in his chest and his lungs. He gasped, and the dizziness faded instantly. No more gagging, either. In fact, everything felt better than usual.

"What...is this?" he asked, bringing his no longer shaking hands up. He stood with fearful caution and had no problem doing so. His pale skin had become even paler than before, but aside from that, every aspect of his body was perfect. A weight had been added to him as well, vast energy storage at his disposal.

I could run across the city at full speed and still have energy left over for a riot. This is incredible!

His hand then shot up against his will, turning his wondrous grin into bent confusion. His legs commanded themselves to walk forward to Zoey, his hand grabbing hold of the blade embedded in her.

The sword erupted in black flame. Burning hot shadows surrounded every inch of the metal, turning it from material to plasma. It adjusted precisely to Ethan's wishes, and he nearly didn't care that his limbs could move against his will.

Noah's voice entered his mind forcefully: *"Be careful...it feels fantastic...but it's what I feel every day. Just wait until-"*

The Shadow Lord's voice cut off, and it completely disappeared. Ethan felt the weight inside his mind lift off and fade away. He laughed and hefted his new sword over his shoulder.

"No more voices in my head!" he announced.

Then the prickling started. Pins and needles crawled up every inch of his body, stabbing and scratching. No cuts appeared on his skin, but that was almost impossible for Ethan to believe. He dropped his new Shadow Sword, which dissolved instantly, and began losing his control again.

SOON YOU WILL UNDERSTAND THIS, a voice rattled in his brain. This one held ten times the gravity of Noah's.

Ethan fell backward, blacking out before he even touched the ground.

Noah fell to his hands and knees, eyes opening for the first time in many, many years. His vision blurred intensely, trying to hard to understand what was happening around him. He was slightly glad, however, because the view was pure. As he began to test his eyesight, he was somewhat fortunate. His chamber held almost no color unless he looked to the windows.

He vomited. It was only bile, clear from nothing being eaten in years. Noah felt the pains beginning to settle in almost instantly.

It's been forever...I can barely conceive...

He started to work his way to his feet but failed miserably. His arms were far too weak, not even capable of holding himself up. And never mind his legs...mere toothpicks. He glanced worriedly to them and winced. His calves were nearly nonexistent, skin and bone. He glanced at his arms and found them to be the same. Without the energy of the Shadows, he had no muscle.

He did manage to pull off his cloak, however, revealing black leather armor beneath. There he laid, splayed out on the cold, tile floor.

HE WILL OVERTAKE YOU SOON, a thundering voice inside his head said.

*He's too weak...*Noah countered. *I'm a much better host for you, father.*

LIES...YOUR LOYALTY IS WANING.

As long as I am the rightful holder of your power, my loyalty is eternal.

BE CAREFUL WITH WHO YOU TRUST.

Oh...I will be.

He closed his eyes, awaiting the spirit of the most powerful Shadow Being in existence to flow into him.

26

As Kiran fell from the great ship above him, The Unknown, a great force blasted into his side. Blinding light filled his eyes, so he shut them.

The force launched him off the mountain, but the fall slowed tremendously. As he reached the ground, there was no issue with the landing. He and his savior rested steadily to the solid ground, and Kiran relaxed a little. He wasn't sure if he was happy just yet, but he wasn't going to die from falling, and he supposed that was good.

"Can you stand?" a familiar voice asked. Kiran nodded slightly and felt the force leave him. He opened his eyes.

Michael Nebadon stood before him, nearly unchanged aside for the shine in his blue eyes. No longer was that twinkle of magic in them, the sparkling that made them unique. But even so, Kiran didn't care.

He threw a punch at the boy out of anger. "You left us!" Michael dodged, growing serious. Kiran threw another punch, but his aim was off even without Michael moving. These were attacks thrown by a chaotic mind.

"You-" punch. "Left-" punch. "Us!" punch. All three missed as Michael dodged them with ease. Kiran gritted his teeth, searching frantically for another weapon. Michael only watched concerningly.

Kiran found his sword still sheathed on his belt and quickly drew it. He swung wildly, forcing Michael to step back. Kiran aimed for the head, but his blade did not reach his target.

Michael threw up his arm in defense, tensing as the sword struck. It shattered on impact, pieces crumbling to the ground. Michael's arm appeared undamaged by some spectacular miracle. Kiran glumly dropped his broken hilt. For a moment, he couldn't speak, his words stuck in his throat. Finally, they poured out.

"What the hell even are you?!" he exclaimed, placing his hands to the sides of his head. "What kind of leader lets at least one, maybe two of his warriors die without even trying to protect them?!"

He bowed his head low, shaking it slowly. "Look, I don't know what your goal is right now, but it isn't on the line with what I expected."

Michael raised an eyebrow, lacing his fingers together. "What did you expect?"

Kiran looked up, grinning sarcastically. "I don't know! But I didn't expect to watch one of my new allies to get stabbed by another of my 'allies'!"

"Then you misunderstand the motive of the Anarchists," Michael said coldly. "They are a plague, corrupting others. It is the mere mission we are trying to stop. But, you also misunderstood Zoey in the final moments of her life."

Kiran sighed angrily. "So she's really dead, then? Is that what you're-yeah...that's what you're saying."

"Zoey did not betray Celestia for her own sake. She did it for yours."

Kiran laughed. "Yeah, okay. You're really pushing your 'wisdom,' you know that?"

"You and Zoey had history," Michael responded, ignoring Kiran's sarcasm. "We've got quite a ways to go before we reach Topia, mind sharing?"

Kiran hesitated, looking to the city. It stood proudly in the distance, and Kiran started to realize the sheer size of it. The Anarchists had a lot of power, but there was a lot of the city to take.

"Heck, why not," he said, and so he began.

"Remember Rachel Donovan?" Kiran asked as they walked, the city growing closer by minuscule amounts. He estimated they would reach their destination in about six hours, if they were lucky.

"Yes," Michael responded. He watched Kiran with curiosity.

"Well, in a weird way, she sparked this whole thing. If you remember correctly, Rachel left about two years ago. I was the last person to ever speak with her, and it was the night before she had left when I did. She lied to me about leaving, and then was gone."

Michael nodded along. "So, what happened after?"

"That's what I'm getting to," Kiran answered. "You see, her departure...it took a toll on me. I thought that I had something to do with it, that I hadn't been good enough to stop her. And, by association, to save her."

He paused, sighing.

"So anyway, after all of that, I faltered a little in my work. Made some minor mistakes, lost some respect. I couldn't focus."

"Seems reasonable."

"Yeah well, not to everyone. No one except for Gabriel knew about my final conversation with Rachel, so they couldn't understand my reaction."

"Why didn't you explain?"

"I didn't want to. That would be lighting the match for a completely new fire. I didn't want the media to talk to me at all."

Michael nodded in response.

"About a week after, I had a run-in with someone who finally took my mind off of Rachel."

"Zoey," Michael concluded.

"Yeah. She wasn't a part of the Brotherhood yet, but she had taken up the name of Z already. She had posed with her new 'identity' as well, one I couldn't see through. In fact, this whole mess was her initiation. She arrived at The Academy, asking if she could speak with me. I accepted, and we talked in private.

"She told me she admired my work as an Academy Warrior, and wanted to know if I'd help her with a mystery he was trying to solve."

He paused, sighing angrily again.

"It was completely bogus, but I didn't know at the time. She showed me pictures of the Bulls-Eye Brotherhood leader, someone named Captain Parker. He was on file, and she told me she was trying to find more information on him. She thought she had a lead.

"I let her check the files we had on Parker, showing her to the main database. I turned away for a few seconds to work on something else, and when I looked back, she was gone. I rushed to check the files she had been viewing, but they had been erased. In fact, everything concerning the Bulls-Eye Brotherhood was gone. I called in our tech experts to investigate, and nothing could be done about the missing information.

"She single-handedly pulled off the biggest information heist in Academy Warrior history. The hack chip she used, Brotherhood tech, took every backup and stored it on that hard drive."

"Were you punished?"

"No," Kiran answered, shaking his head. "Gabriel understood, and I was grateful for that. But...that wasn't the issue. That day, I slipped up. Let my guard down because I was hyper-focused on too many things.

"When I met Z...*Zoey* again, I couldn't believe it. I didn't want to. I hoped she would never bring it up since the attention was on her, but she did. Of course, it was when we were climbing the mountain...and then-

"MICHAEL!" He exclaimed, eyes widening. "Where are the others?!" He couldn't believe he had forgotten about all of them.

I've been distracted by this story! I-I need to find them.

"What do you mean?" Michael asked.

"Wha-What do I mean? Michael, the others! Ethan, Celestia, and Rosemary! Oh...Celestia's probably dead, isn't she..." A pang of remorse hit him hard, but he assured himself to stay hopeful. After all, he hadn't grown that attached to the Sisterhood leader. "Well, that still leaves two more!"

Michael smiled. "They will be waiting for us in the city, of that I am certain."

"How?! Can you read their minds or something?"

"Not at all. I just have faith."

"So...you're hoping they're waiting for us. That's all you have. Hope."

"It's all I need."

Kiran narrowed his eyes, but he found absolute truth in Michael's statement. "...right..."

He turned away, looking back to Topia, still a little uncertain. They walked on.

Rosemary opened her eyes, and her entire body felt sore. Her arms were heavier than usual, and her head felt like a bowling ball. She was on the side of the mountain, the great Anarchist ship gone. Dirt covered her hair, and her dress turned from green to muddy brown. As she looked to her hands, scrapes filled them. None were bleeding, thankfully.

She placed her forearms against the ground, trying to push herself up. Her arms screamed, and she was forced to fall back on her stomach.

I could do it...but I have to find Celestia soon. I have to do it now.

She rolled over onto her back, wincing. Bringing her hands to her chest, she knew that the pain would only exist for a little longer. She placed her palms together in a double prayer position, and said one word.

"Clarity."

She felt herself rise from the ground, utterly void of her injuries. As she looked around at her body, everything seemed in perfect condition. Her skin appeared glossier than usual, as if she was made of glass.

She walked forward and did not glance back. She knew what was behind her: A motionless, torn up version of herself, eyes closed and all. She would appear dead to anyone who found her this way. That body was only her life force, but her new one was her doppelganger. She could do almost anything in this form, but one scratch or injury, and it would pop like a balloon.

Time to find Celestia!

"My darling, you do not understand what you are," Elara said. She hovered above sleeping Celestia on the mountainside, eyes full of caring. She watched as Celestia's stab wound closed in on itself, blood never showing, as if she had none. It fused shut, but the area where her armor had been pierced remained.

"I hope you soon sprout your wings, as you should've long ago." She envisioned the council's decision to assign her here, to this odd recovery task, and wondered if they regretted it now. Would they even accept a reclaimed rebel?

"I so dearly wish you luck, Celestia."

And with a flash, she disappeared. Celestia launched upright at the exact moment, her breath heavy. She put her hands to her stomach instantly, feeling for the wound, but did not find it.

I'm...alive. Did I-no. It happened. It all happened. I was stabbed, betrayed. But...how?

She ran her fingers over the armor slit over and over, as if she expected it to disappear suddenly. Every time she went to

feel it, a sigh of relief came from her. She was still alive, but by what miracle?

She stood, pushing herself up with surprisingly minimal effort. She then panicked for a moment and glanced back to where she had been laying. Sure enough, her sword was still there. She picked it up quickly, never feeling so grateful to have her weapon. She nearly wished to hug it, but figured that wouldn't be the best idea.

It still had a few burn marks from deflecting bullets.

Ah, they'll disappear in a few hours. Always do.

Celestia took a moment to look around, realizing she was back down the mountainside, just near where the group had begun climbing. That had been only an hour or two ago, but it seemed like days. No one was over there now.

Let's see...If I was dropped from the ship, were the others as well? They must've thought I was dead...maybe that's why they disposed of me.

I need to find the others quick.

She set off, looking toward the city. Pretty soon, though, as she reached open land, she heard a voice.

"Celestia! Celestia!" a young voice called. Celestia whirled around, searching. Her face lit up as she saw Rosemary running toward her, but she didn't appear well. The girl seemed to be desperate, sprinting with urgency.

Rosemary hugged her instantly, burying her face in Celestia's side. Celestia laughed worriedly, needing to pry the young girl off her after a few moments.

"What's going on?" Celestia asked softly. Rosemary's eyes grew watery, but she kept back tears.

"This-this isn't actually me. I'm hurt..." the young girl said. "This way." She began leading Celestia back over to the mountainside. Celestia braced herself, knowing she didn't have any aid for health on her at the moment. If it was bad enough, they might need to head to the city.

When they reached Rosemary's physical body, Celestia winced. The girl was beaten up pretty severely, presumably from the fall down the mountain. Scrapes lined nearly every inch of her skin, and her dress was torn immensely. Celestia bent down and picked the young girl up.

Spirit Rosemary looked to Celestia cautiously. She knew that if her real self died, that was it. Her life would indeed be over. Her consciousness only really existed in that body.

Celestia grimaced and glanced up to the city.

She first shook her head, already having seen too much. based off the past few hours, she doubted the city would even be worth saving. If the citizens would join with the Anarchists and become mindless slaves, then what was the point of liberating them?

Unfortunately, as Celestia looked down to the dying Rosemary in her arms, she knew there was no choice. She could not heal these wounds herself, and the Sisterhood was too far; they'd never make it in time. The only option was the worst one.

"We're going to the city," she announced reluctantly. "For the very first time."

Rosemary smiled weakly. She looked to the silver mass in the distance. *Finally, I'll be back home.*

27

The sun was setting low over Topia, and the storm clouds were not pulling away. Still, only a light drizzle fell from the sky, nothing more. The loyal citizens stayed inside, however, as every day the Anarchists took over more and more of the city. Many speculated it would be only a day or two before the capital was attacked, and not many had faith the Anarchists would fail.

News reports said the Anarchists had conquered the entire lower half of the city, taking over all of Fiasco District and the lower half of Mysti District.

Upon hearing this news, Leo Donovan sighed. He clicked the TV off instantly, taking a moment to look around his living room. Living on the upper half of Mysti, the Anarchists were now nearly on the edge of his doorstep.

The doorbell rang. Leo glanced at it angrily. *Speak of the devil.*

He stomped over, looking through the peephole in the door. His eyes widened, but quickly narrowed after. For a moment, the peephole seemed to be a mirror of some sort, but Leo knew that wasn't the case.

That's not my hair. Jesus Christ, it looks terrible. All grown out like that, is it even a hairstyle?

He tore the door open, glaring. "What the hell do you want?"

Frederick grinned. "Great to see you too, brother."

"You come back after all this time!? You idiot of a Donovan..." He started to shut the door.

"Wait!" Frederick exclaimed, putting his hand out. "It's about Rachel."

Leo stared for a few seconds, searching for truth in Frederick's expression. He opened the door fully again.

"Come on inside. You're going to get killed standing on my doorstep at this point."

Frederick sighed of relief. He walked past Leo, glad to be out of the light rain. He stopped in the living room.

"You've been living well, I see," he noted.

Leo slammed the door shut, locking the deadbolt. "Since you and sis ditched me, I was the only one to take on dad's resources. Let's just say...he had a lot. Guess that's one thing I can thank you for."

He eyed Frederick suspiciously. "That's not what you're here for, is it? Money? I'll give it to Rachel if she needs, but it better not be for your gain."

"Relax," Frederick said, dismissing Leo's words. He sat down on Leo's couch, still glancing about the room. Leo remained standing, arms crossed as he watched Frederick pick at his fingernails.

"So then," Leo said. "What's the sitch? Make it quick, too."

Frederick looked to him. "I want to find her. Unfortunately, I have no idea about what to do or where to look," he said blankly.

Leo narrowed his eyes. "Why'd you come here, then? Did you think I'd be able to tell you where she is? I've got a lot else on my mind."

Frederick raised an eyebrow.

"The Anarchists have taken over every square inch of land south of here! They could be here, in this house, by tonight! Here you are, thinking about Rachel." He scoffed, looking away. "We can always look for her later on, but not now. If we were to focus on her, there'd be no city for her to come back to."

"It's that bad, eh?" Frederick asked.

"Just today the Anarchists took Fiasco and lower Mysti. Where have you been all this time?"

Frederick looked down, mind wandering a little. "Some cave...I don't really remember. I kept to-"

"And why now?" Leo asked. "Why, after nearly two years, come looking for us now?"

Frederick shook his head a little. "I need to do it now."

Leo sat down on the couch beside him. They sat in silence for a little while, both waiting for..something to happen.

"Well, are you expecting like a ghost's sign or something? Wait...did you even consider that she's *dead*?"

"Considered, didn't believe."

The doorbell rang again. Leo jumped up, leaving Frederick on the couch. He approached the door carefully.

"This time it might really be the Anarchists," Leo said.

"Why would the Anarchists ring your-"

"Shhh."

Leo looked through the peephole again, half expecting another version of himself to be standing there.

There were no blade twirling men in black, that was for sure. In fact, no one stood on Leo's doorstep. He opened the door slowly, peeking around it. He glanced down, eyes narrowing. A little slip of paper sat on his doormat, a white rectangle over the *I don't want any!* phrase that was embedded in cursive letters.

He glanced back to Frederick, who sat up. He jerked his head toward the open door, calling him over. Frederick hurried.

"What is it?" Frederick asked.

"Probably an ad, someone wanting to sell us something. I see they didn't notice the mat."

"Have you read it?"

Leo picked up the piece of paper and found it was folded. He quickly dismantled it, smoothing the creases out a little.

"It's a poem!" he exclaimed. "What kind of door-dasher leaves poems on people's doorsteps?"

Frederick shushed him and pointed to the words. "Read."

They read it in unison:

"For now the first time you have reunited,
"The identical twins of Donovan righted,
"I watch from above where the birds are quieted,
"And hope one day to be finally sighted."
        ~Rachel

Both Leo and Frederick's eyes widened, and they looked to one another.

"Holy crap she's alive," Leo whispered.

28

"And you say they'll be here soon?" President Leila Lanondek asked, watching the streets of Lanon from the window. They were nearly empty, with abandoned cars lining the sides of the roads.

Everyone hid inside out of fear from an Anarchist invasion, and they had the right to.

Leila herself was safe up here in Topia's Paradise, but even she would only be here for a short stay.

"Yes," Ethan responded, nodding. "Less than an hour, at most."

Leila sighed. "That's good. You see, I'm rather worried." She turned away from the window, icy blue eyes turning to Ethan. A great age showed in her expressions, decades of experience behind them.

"The Anarchists rule over half of the city now," she continued. "I'm not sure how much longer we can hold them off. They show no sign of stopping."

Ethan nodded solemnly. He had nothing to add.

"But," Leila continued. "If this boy, Michael, who saved my own life only a few days ago, returns...we may have a fighting chance." Graying hair fell to her shoulders, stripes of white within.

Ethan nodded again. He silently cursed, seeing Michael's return now. He would only have Kiran by his side, however. He's coming back with those he left with. That entire mission out there was futile...

Still, his mind kept flashing back to the moments in The Unknown. Kiran couldn't know about his allegiances, but he had to come up with an excuse soon. Both he and Michael would become suspicious quickly.

"President Leila, if you don't mind me asking, what force do we have against the Anarchists now?"

Leila looked thoughtfully around the room, eyes passing over the two bodyguards who stood at the door. Trying to remember the exact numbers her data collector had received, she said:

"Besides your near one hundred Academy Warriors, well...I'd say at least five thousand in the militant force. Those are MacArthur's soldiers."

Ethan nodded. *Not too many...there are about eight thousand Anarchists active.*

"There will be evacuations in Mysti District soon," she continued. "I'm just not sure where all the people will go. We don't exactly have extra space lying around.

"Oh, lord. This may truly be the end of an age. This planet is so old...so much history. I hope the Anarchists don't treat it too badly."

One of the guards stepped into the room, a thundering couple of footsteps. He stood six and a half feet tall, broad-shouldered and loaded with muscle.

"Michael Nebadon and Kiran Andon have been spotted just outside the city," he said in a low voice. "I suggest we invite them here."

Leila smiled. "Oh, that won't be necessary. We can meet in the capitol building."

"President, all due respect, but the capitol is not safe for you."

"Michael Nebadon is someone I trust," she said with slight irritation. "You and J.D. will stay close."

The guard nodded, returning back to his post. Leila looked to Ethan expectantly.

"You should come with. I bet you will be excited to see your old...*friends.*"

Ethan smiled nervously, wondering why she had said it like that. "Of course."

Kiran looked up to the massive building before him, a silver monstrosity. It started wide, curving in upwards to a point, where five spikes shot out in a pentagram. Great columns held up the overhang, which loomed above the front door. Five guards, dressed in tuxedos, stood at the ready. The largest one, nearly eight feet tall, stood guarding the golden door that led to the inside of the capitol.

Michael laughed, shaking his head. "Those men won't stop an army of Anarchists."

Kiran looked to him, glaring. "Maybe not, but they'll stop a few rowdy teenagers out of their minds. See the biggest one?" he pointed at the center man. "That's Cortex, considered the smartest and strongest man in all of Topia. Plus, no one knows what he looks like under that mask."

Michael peered at the man called Cortex, noting his over clothed appearance. No skin was showing on Cortex's body, his face covered in a type of gas mask. It stretched over his head like a helmet.

"A little like how the Anarchists dress," he noted.

"Don't go accusing!" Kiran hissed. "C'mon, let's go."

Kiran relayed the message Ethan had delivered twenty minutes ago in his mind, an urgent invitation to the capitol. This would be Kiran's first meeting in direct person with the President, but Michael eased his nerves a little. Kiran had been a guard assigned to her side many times, but now she would undoubtedly be focused on the blond boy.

They walked up the silver path, the guards watching closely. Cortex did not move a muscle until the boys were within a few feet of him. He stepped forward, towering over them.

"Name," Cortex asked. His voice did not match his appearance, being a little more high pitched.

"Academy Warrior Kiran Andon," Kiran stated, going to flash his badge. His hand caught open air, and as he glanced down at the right side of his chest, no badge was pinned to him. It must've fallen off sometime out of the city.

Kiran looked up uneasily to Cortex, putting his hand back down. Cortex only stared, expectant.

Then, oddly, the guard straightened. He stepped to his left, leaving the door unprotected. He swept his gaze away from the boys, resuming a blank stare forward.

Kiran raised an eyebrow. *He's just going to let us in anyway?* Michael shrugged and stepped forward. He opened the golden door, letting Kiran walk inside.

"Perhaps your name is that well known," Michael commented. Kiran shook his head.

"No. That was strange." He took a deep breath. "Doesn't matter, though. We're here for different reasons."

Michael nodded. "Indeed we are," he said blankly.

The inside of the capitol matched its outside well. Nearly everything was of silver makeup, from the tables to the lamps to even couches. Kiran almost slipped on the chromium floor as he walked in, Michael catching him.

"Careful," he warned.

The only objects that were not silver were the small plants off to the side. Even so, those were colored blue instead of green. A few were icy, nearly crystalline structures instead of plants. They were unlike anything both Michael nor Kiran had seen of any plant species.

"You've made it!" Ethan yelled from the center of the vast room. Kiran brought his attention over as he walked. Ethan sat on one of the silver couches, President Leila Lanondek nearby on one of the chairs.

Michael noticed President Leila's eyes following him closely. Those icy blue spheres, like his own but colder, tracking his every move. Of course, he had saved her life not too long ago, but he had done it to prove a point. He valued her life no higher than any citizen in the city, but others did.

They sat down on either side of Ethan. Kiran half expected the couch to be hard as silver would be, but it softened upon him sitting.

"Are you enjoying the feel of the capitol?" President Leila asked, her voice pleased.

"Quite...silvery," Kiran pointed out. "Are the walls and floor solid silver?"

"Oh, not at all," President Leila responded. "In fact, most of the silver is just a coating. A little finish on top."

"Must be-"

"That man outside," Michael interrupted. "Cortex. based off what I've deduced and what Kiran has told me, he's an intelligent individual, is he not?" He sputtered his words out, like a detective unraveling a mystery.

President Leila raised an eyebrow but nodded soon after. "He has a great aptitude for many things."

"Then why waste him on guarding your door? Why not put him as a general in your armies? One man outside will not protect you from an onslaught of Anarchists."

Ethan nudged Michael's arm. "Dude, that's a little frontal."

President Leila waved off Ethan. "It isn't imposing at all! A wise question, in fact. Why aren't you in my armies?"

Michael was not flattered. "Answer my question, if you will."

"Cortex does not want any part in my army, and that is the sole truth. If you aren't pleased with that, perhaps you should speak with him. He is a stubborn one, however."

Michael fell silent. He watched Leila Lanondek closely and began to narrow his eyes.

Kiran looked over to Ethan. Breaking the awkward silence, he addressed what had been on his mind for most of this evening.

"Where were you during that whole mess?" he asked, in reference to The Unknown. His words were tinged with a odd sense of tension.

"What...mess?" Ethan responded, leaning forward. President Leila watched with curious eyes, eyes that Michael in his own right watched.

"The Anarchist Ship," Kiran said. "The giant thing above the mountain? Nearly the length of twenty cars? Enormous thruster engines on the back?"

"Anarchist Ship!?" President Leila asked. "You mean, an aircraft?!"

"Yes. My friends and I were trapped on it. They let us go for some reason." Kiran looked over at Ethan, and then back to the President. "But he was busy with something else, apparently."

"I was walking away from the rest of you!" Ethan exclaimed. "You're the ones who decided to climb up the mountain like maniacs! I wouldn't have been surprised if we'd lost a member or two on that rock."

"The ship was huge. I'm talking bigger than the mountain peak. And...oh, jeez." *He doesn't know about Zoey...or Celestia and Rosemary, in fact.*

"What?" Ethan asked, noting Kiran's troubled expression.

"Zoey...she didn't make it out of the ship alive," he managed. His eyes strayed from making contact. "And, we're not sure about-"

"Rosemary and Celestia are right outside the city," Michael broke in. "If you will give me a moment..."

The area exploded with a flash of blinding light as Michael disappeared. President Leila yelped in surprise, shielding herself from the blast. Ethan did the same, but Kiran was used to it, and only turned his head.

"He can teleport?" President Leila asked. Realization crossed her face. "So that's how he reached the stage so quickly..."

Kiran and Ethan locked eyes, and they both grimaced.

Michael appeared just as Celestia crossed into Desertia District. Celestia stepped back, startled.

"Michael! Where is everyone? Rosemary..." She glanced at the sleeping girl in her arms, still scratched immensely. "She needs a healer."

Michael nodded. "We are all meeting at the Capitol. Let's move quickly."

They hurried through Desertia and into Lanon, Michael guiding Celestia through the streets. Only knowing the direction he was going in, the specifics weren't smoothed out. Michael was honked at by a few passing cars as he and Celestia sprinted across Ruby Street.

Celestia glanced down to Rosemary in her arms. The girl had collapsed part way through their journey back, her doppelganger form dissipating. She didn't seem fatally wounded, as no blood was showing on the outside, but the fact the girl was still unconscious...

Upon reaching the capital district, Celestia gained her first view of city security. Men of massive sizes guarded every building in Lanon, and she spotted what seemed to be The Academy. Through the glass doors, she saw tens of men and women wearing the exact same red uniform as Kiran had. *His counterparts,* she thought. Part of her wished to challenge them all, hoping one would prove a better match than Kiran, but she urged herself to stay focused.

Then, as they crossed onto the silver path leading to the capitol building, Celestia's eyes widened. Light reflected off every silver inch of the building, even though it was near sundown. It turned the building a beautiful orange, the skies above red and yellow.

Michael stopped at the golden door. Cortex had already stepped out of the way, allowing Michael complete access. Celestia stepped inside, but the blond boy did not follow.

"I'm going to be out for a little while," he explained, glancing to Cortex. "Go on in."

Celestia nodded and turned away.

Kiran jumped up from the couch. "He wasn't lying," he muttered. Celestia walked forward, and Kiran noticed the injured Rosemary in her arms. "You both lived." He looked to Celestia's stomach and noticed the slit in her armor.

And yet, she walked all the way here?

Celestia noticed Kiran staring at her stomach. "The blade went through, but yet..."

"We both survived," she finished, voice heavy. "I'm not entirely sure how, but we did."

The odd reality settled in for her: *I should be dead. Everyone thought I was, and I was left to die, but here I am now. I fell down a mountain as well! I shouldn't be here, but I must be grateful.*

She set the sleeping Rosemary on another chair nearby, moving the curly hair from the girl's face. She then turned to Kiran, who sat down next to...

Ethan.

"Ethan," Celestia said, tinged with confused anger. "Where were you during the Anarchist attack?"

Ethan raised his eyebrows in mock surprise. "I was walking around the mountain. I came back here once I realized everyone was gone. I'd figured you would be this way."

Celestia grunted. She glanced at the President, who sat quietly, observing. The woman watched Celestia with similar intrigue to Michael.

"Leila Lanondek," Celestia muttered.

"Here I am," Leila responded. "You must be Celestia. I've heard much about you from Kiran and Ethan. Leader of the...'Sisterhood,' you call it? Tell me, please, what do you do within that organization?"

Celestia did not respond immediately, sensing that her answer would be analyzed. She knew the Topia Government to be controlling and all-powerful, perhaps reasons for rebellion. The Anarchists nearly seemed right in this moment, breaking free of this dictator.

"The Sisterhood advocates for equality among gender. We stray from the city in order to keep peace within our ranks. Politics in Topia are rather...violent based off what I've seen."

President Leila smiled. "A legitimate cause. Now that that's settled, please, sit down with us."

"Actually, I have a more pressing concern. My...friend here, Rosemary, is in need of healing. She was dropped from the Anarchist ship, and suffered a large fall due to it."

"Of course," President Leila responded. "I can get you a healer." She closed her eyes momentarily and then reopened them. The front door opened immediately after, and two guards stepped in.

The guards approached Celestia. One reached for Rosemary, but Celestia stopped him.

"Actually, just bring me to the materials. I can heal her with the right ingredients." She was a little unsure, but she had seen loads of Sisters perform healing magic before. Even so, she didn't want any large men, with hardly any will or personality of their own, taking Rosemary from her. They would surely use her for some sort of experiment.

"Right this way," one of the guards said, a little surprised. Celestia scooped up Rosemary in her arms, and the guards led her from the room.

Kiran looked at President Leila, brow furrowed.

"Telepathy, of course," the president answered. "Don't tell me you've never met a person with it?"

Kiran paused. "Gabriel, but that was it. I thought it was unique to him. I had heard of a few of the Wizards being able to do it, but only will great energy. Gabriel, however, he could use it as easily as you."

"Well, who do you think taught me? I went through many years of mental training to possess the ability. Hours of strenuous concentration and focus, repeating phrases until they finally reached my target. Magic isn't an easy field, I'm sure you know. One thing has struck me odd, however, and that is my guard, Cortex, has it as well, but I'm not sure at all how he learned it!"

That explains a lot, Kiran realized. *If the Anarchists realize ways to communicate without speaking as well, their power will go unchecked. But based off what President Leila has said, it isn't easy to learn at all.*

They wouldn't be able to teach it to the masses.

"Do the Anarchists have strange abilities like telepathy? Magic we don't have?" he asked.

"I am never sure of everything they possess. I do know they have allies...some with rather, peculiar techniques. I've heard many rumors, none of which are true, of course, about Anarchists with glowing swords and cosmic abilities."

"What exactly do-"

"Ah! It's a little late for more questions, unfortunately. Tomorrow the entire military staff will be here for all your inquiries! It's growing late, anyway. You all can stay here tonight. There are nearly thirty bedrooms in this building, and only a few are currently occupied."

"Thank you, President," Ethan said. Leila Lanondek abruptly rose from her seat and began walking off with hurried strides. Kiran remained in mid-sentence, paused. He frowned, knowing he would have to wait until morning for an answer. It would be stuck in his head all night.

Cosmic Abilities...something along the lines of the Shadow Lord on that Anarchist Ship. The rest only had guns, lethal nonetheless, but no

magic. The Shadow Lord himself definitely had magical abilities. He
might even possess telepathy.

As night began to fall over the city, a few guards came inside to assist the three boys. They were led upstairs to separate bedrooms, where they settled. Kiran yearned a little for his apartment, even though this one bedroom was nearly more extensive than it. Everything here was foreign. The furniture and amenities seemed too luxurious, almost that they weren't meant to be used. It was like they belonged in a museum, far away from the touch of any human being.

Kiran glanced out the window next to the queen size bed, noticing he could see Desertia District from there. Streets lit up dimly, a few cars driving by late into the night. He watched for a long time, and from this perspective, the city seemed so peaceful.

But he knew...that beyond Desertia lay hordes of Anarchists and rioters. Burned buildings, defeated Academy Warriors and military. Money spread out in vast piles, some of it surely on fire, just in spite of the government. Broken car windshields, crowbars tossed aside.

And somewhere, deep in that whole mess, flew the great Anarchist Ship, and whatever Shadow Lord controlled it.

And, of course, unbeknownst to Kiran, the very apprentice of that Shadow Lord stood in the room next to him. He was blind, but Ethan could painfully see.

29

Frederick stared at the paper for a few minutes, reading the lines over and over again. Leo stood nearby, frowning and pacing. Every now and then he would light up with an idea, but quickly shoot it down in his own mind.

"Hmm. 'Above where the birds are quieted,'" Frederick quoted. "Seems to be referring to the sky?"

"Why would the birds be quieted though?" Leo countered.

"Birds live in the sky."

"Maybe she's really high up."

"She's probably on another freaking planet at this point. *Mars.* That's where she is. She's probably roaming around up there, waiting for us to fly up in a spaceship." He laughed slightly, thinking further about the ridiculous situation he had formulated.

Frederick didn't respond. He stayed silent for a few more minutes, scratching his head as his eyes started to glaze over a little.

"Whatever," Leo said. He stopped pacing. With exasperation, he realized it was nearly ten o'clock at night. "I'm going to bed. The guest room is down here too, if you're staying." He started to walk out of the room, but Frederick stopped him.

"Seriously?" Frederick asked, flicking the paper. "We need to find her soon, and that means spending some extra time."

Leo whirled around. "If she wanted us to find her easily, then why did she leave us a poem?" He stared blankly at Frederick for a moment, starting to let the exasperation take hold of him. "Plus, what's the rush?"

"What do you mean, 'what's the rush?' You said it yourself. The Anarchists could be storming in here any day now. Tonight, perhaps. I don't want Rachel to see the last bits of our home destroyed."

Leo sighed. "I'll sleep on it."

Frederick rubbed his eyes with exasperation, and in a tired voice, he called Leo back. "One more thing," he said. Leo paused but urged him to make it quick.

"Do you have coffee?"

Leo glanced back, eyes narrowing. After a moment, he realized Frederick was serious. "Yeah, I do. It's in the kitchen." After a moment, he asked: "Why?"

Frederick shrugged. "Always wanted to try it when we were younger. Never got the chance."

Leo shook his head sadly, and turned away. Frederick hurried over into the kitchen, where he sloppily figured out how to make coffee. Once he was finished, it tasted intensely bitter, but the caffeine startled him awake.

He looked back to the paper, putting his cup aside. He read the words over and over, still processing them. He focused on those last two lines in particular.

She has to be in the sky. I'll have to find a way...

Not the Anarchist ship. I'm not hijacking that thing.

He chewed at his lip, hesitating. His mind rushed back to Timothy MacArthur, but not the man he knew as King. Not the Grand Wizard, but the military general.

There's another way. But it involves fighting a war.

He folded the paper back up, placing it in his pocket securely. He paused again, making sure this was the right decision, and reassured himself it was the only way. Otherwise, Rachel would go undiscovered, and the Donovan name would be lost. He and Leo would surely be killed by an Anarchist Invasion, unless, of course, Frederick took advantage.

Stepping through the front door, a fire started in Frederick's right hand. This time, however, it was intentional.

Celestia watched Rosemary's chest rise and fall, the scratches over her face and arms slowly disappearing. It hadn't taken much to heal her, using a pinch of northern herbs and energy crystal to relieve the girl's pain, at least. Now, it was only a matter of waiting.

Celestia herself felt a little tired, but she didn't quite realize it. The day had been so chaotic and hectic that rest wasn't on her mind. Recurring images of Anarchists and the mountain flashed through her mind in a blur.

Her hand moved again to her gut, fingers feeling the torn bit of her armor. She wanted to press her fingertips to the matching spot on her skin, but she knew nothing would be there but a thin scar. Only a memory of the incident, somehow defying the time it takes to heal. Again, she thought about how she should be dead. There was no reason for her to be living, and of that she was sure.

She looked around the recovery room, a small and cold area mostly meant for dying patients. The hospital's materials had been vast, many substances Celestia had never seen before. The guards had left after a little while from her command, wishing to be alone with the young girl. They had agreed immediately, but Celestia knew they would keep a close eye on her.

After a few hours, her eyelids grew heavy. She drifted off and didn't awake until morning.

Kiran opened his eyes in the darkness, awakened abruptly due to some quiet noise. A slight murmur came from somewhere in the room, sounding almost like talking. Kiran grunted, hoping it would pass, but it did not. He struggled to his feet from his sleeping spot and came face to face with the window. He had fallen asleep while looking outside.

He turned, still hearing the slight murmur. Knowing Ethan was next door, Kiran knew that was always a possibility. The redheaded boy had a history of talking in his sleep, but it was never loud enough to cross rooms. And as soon as his eyes swept the room, he spotted the source.

Michael sat cross-legged on one of the silver chairs, clearly distressed. As Kiran drew slowly closer, he noticed Michael's darting eyes beneath his eyelids, as if he were dreaming. His forehead appeared creased with frustration, the corners of his eyes tight and clenched.

Every few seconds he would speak.

"-locked up, like that," he said in his normal voice. Then, Kiran hardly believing his ears, swore he spoke in Gabriel Lanondek's voice, saying:

"Of course. It's what you requested."

"It's hard to believe...will that really hold him?"

"It is impossible for him to break out alone, and those who will assist him are trapped elsewhere." Again, it was Gabriel's voice. It sounded as if Michael was having a conversation with the man.

"I'm not so sure..."

"Are you afraid he'll do it all over again?"

"Why wouldn't I be? He's still a raging demon, as they called him."

"You could cease his existence easily."

"What good would that do? Beneath everything that he stands for and lives for, there is always Light."

There was a long pause, and in his own voice, Michael said:

"I will come back for you, fallen system sovereign."

"Michael, Michael!" Kiran shook him awake, noticing the boy's face begin to distort extremely in discomfort. Sweat beads had even started to form.

Michael's eyes snapped open, and he fell back against the chair. His arms fell limp, noodles against the chair's armrest.

So...that's what you thought of me, he thought.

Kiran stared at him for a moment, hands on Michael's shoulders. Michael's eyes weakly fell on Kiran, and he became hunched over.

"Are you alright?" Kiran asked in a soft voice. "Who were you talking to?"

"I was only speaking with my past," Michael managed. Kiran could barely hear him, voice a murmur again. Deep breaths ensued, ones that sounded painful. "Do not worry."

Kiran took his hands off. Michael brought his head up, resting against the back of the chair.

Cortex was right. It's too much for me to handle, the blond boy thought.

236

"Michael," Kiran said, meeting the boy's feeble gaze. "I have a reason to fight in this rebellion. I don't want the Anarchists taking over my home and leaving it in ruins. Ethan has something to fight for here. So does Celestia, and even Rosemary...I think.

"...Zoey had a reason. We all knew what we were here for, but do you? Do you know why you are here?"

Michael merely stared at him, watching as the night sky shined through the room's windows.

"You showed up when the rebellion was already in full swing! Your first time to a city that is alone on this planet! Somehow, beyond whatever you will tell me, you've done the impossible!" Kiran exclaimed. For a moment he wanted to quiet himself for Ethan next door but decided against it. Quiet voices worked for quiet matters.

"I don't," Michael said defeatedly. He sounded distant, as if he was still talking to himself. "I don't know why I'm here."

Kiran frowned, and his enthusiasm faltered.

"But I do know something," Michael continued. "I do know that I am not here to fight this rebellion. When the time comes, I want you to know that I will not be on the battlefield. That will be your responsibility, Kiran. And whoever else will side with you.

"I...am not here to fight the rebellion," he repeated. "I am here to bring together those who will."

And, at that moment, he indeed did sound certain.

30

The night passed then on peacefully. Celestia remained with Rosemary, both dreaming without care. In Celestia's dreams, she could see Zoey always watching in the backgrounds, as if her ghost was passing through. Every time she went to interact with her, however, the spirit could never speak. It only smiled and waved.

Frederick arrived at the capitol building quickly, but he was not focused on the upper areas of it. Down under the ground, he knew, was a facility. One where Military General and *secretly Wizard King* Timothy MacArthur planned out his every move. Leo hadn't kept this a secret between his siblings a few years ago, and it had always stuck with Frederick. Frederick's training as a Wizard hardly ever included information about the military, and he assumed that it was the opposite on Leo's end.

He waited outside, keeping himself warm with the fire in his hand. He stayed by the trees and bushes out front, one eye always trained to the front door of the building. He decided to wait until morning to make a move, and after a little while, he grew tired.

He slept standing up, a skill he had taught himself after many years of cave living. Often, in the caves, there weren't places to sleep laying down, as stalactites above dripped water constantly nearly everywhere. Sometimes, a wall or a corner were the only options.

Meanwhile, inside the capitol, the night had quieted in Kiran's room.

Kiran could only sleep after a long time of staring outside again. Michael sat nearby, watching as well. The night passed slowly for the both of them.

Ethan had the most difficult time sleeping, as he lay alone on the queen-size bed. He did not use the blankets or sheets at all, merely laying flat on top. He moved from sleeping position to position, attempting to relax, but nothing worked. His mind remained active.

Moments in The Unknown flashed through his memory constantly, a movie he was forced to watch over and over. It always started with Celestia being stabbed, watching as the Sisterhood leader fell to the floor over and over. Each time Zoey revealed herself behind, Ethan didn't know if she would be herself, or Z. It never mattered though, because he would end up killing either one.

Every time he brought his sword down, and Zoey raised her block as an X, he hoped she would finally succeed. But every time, the swords dissolved as his blade passed through, and he cursed at Noah.

He relived it until his mind could no longer keep him awake, and the nightmares began.

Frederick awoke the moment the sun breached the horizon. No one had bothered him during the night, thankfully, and the fire on his hand had burned out. He suspected that most people who had passed by assumed him to be a homeless person, having nothing of value.

Sometimes, looking like a beggar is beneficial.

He glanced back at the capitol building and smiled. The two guards on either side of the door were sleeping, heads lolling to one side as they sat slumped. Frederick nearly wanted to make his move right there, running in full speed, but as soon as he took a closer look, his plan changed.

The eight-foot-tall guard still stood at the ready, still as a mountain. He stared forward blankly beneath his gas mask, arms crossed. Frederick ducked back behind his tree, shaking his head at that.

I'll need some sort of distraction, he realized. He looked to the street, watching as a few cars passed. The fire in his right hand sparked to life again. A big enough explosion would surely draw the attention of the guard, but that could wake up the other two guards as well.

I can handle the smaller ones, though. It's only the big guy I need to move out of the way.

He readied himself, knowing it was now or never. His movements acted themselves out in his head, from the moment he was throwing the flame to sliding into the bunker hatch.

Hatch lays underneath the doormat, Frederick recalled. *Leo said the code was...3-1-4-1-5...curses. The last digit...what was it? A 3? Another 5? The first five digits I'm sure of, but the sixth...*

I'll figure it out on the way. There are only ten possible combinations. Alright...let's go.

He took one final glance back at the door, making sure everything was in order. He turned to the street, spotting the parked car he planned to use. It was an older model, not finished with designs and metallic coating, but it would work.

He raised his hand and exhaled slowly. The flame grew larger and hotter, turning a deep red to hints of blue. He could feel the blaze now, but only of warmth.

He threw.

The blazing ball plunged into the car across the street, and after a few moments, hell broke loose within it. A tremendously bright explosion sent the machine rattling, fire bursting from the top. Parts detached quickly, sent skittering across the road.

Frederick shielded himself and looked to the front door of the capitol. The tall guard snapped from his focus and began running toward the car in a panic. One of the other guards followed, but the third stayed behind by the door.

Frederick sprinted faster than he had ever before. Faster than in Academy Warrior training, that was for sure.

He charged the guard at the door, throwing a scalding hot fist into the man before he could even react. The man let out a stinging gasp, a red mark across his face. He punched at Frederick in retaliation, but Frederick's bare arm blocked easily. As it did, Frederick flexed, sending furious flaming energy into the area. The guard pulled his hand away instantly, as if he had been burned by hot metal.

Frederick shoved the guard, sending him toppling backward. Before the guard could even get back up, he tore off the doormat.

His eyes widened as he realized Leo was correct about the trapdoor. It was a metal plate, a code dial in the very center, almost like a safe.

3...1...4...1...5.......frick! He fumbled to select the last digit, knowing the guard was surely right behind him. As he slid it between 1, to 2, to 3, and so on, his pulse quickened. He started with the following numbers and began to try each one. Every time, however, he had to enter in the entire code once again.

A cold hand grasped itself around Frederick's ankle and began dragging him backward. Frederick fought to break from its grip, kicking over and over. He just needed a little more time...

Finally, he entered the last possible code: *3...1...4...1...5...9!*

It clicked open, and the metal plates fell sideways. Frederick quickly, with one motion, tore his foot from the guard's grip. His momentum caused him to stumble forward, and he slipped into the trapdoor. He slammed against the side, his back meeting the sharp corner of the tunnel going downward. His hands grasped the walls for something to hold onto, and soon, his fingers began repeatedly banging against bars.

A ladder! He realized.

Only when he caught hold of what was seemingly the ladder did he remember to breathe.

He climbed down slowly, continuously glancing up at the open door. Any second he expected the guard to stare down at him, either ready to chase or let go.

Frederick reached the bottom before the guard entered the door. He spun around and was met with the worried gaze of a single man. It was the man he was looking for nonetheless, but other than that, he was alone.

Swords, shields, and even a few rifles lined the walls. Every now and then Frederick noticed a specialized weapon like a staff or nunchakus, but they were indeed rare.

And in the center, looking up from his notepad, was Timothy MacArthur himself. The King of Wizards was not wearing his royal outfit, but rather a suit and tie. A little golden badge sat pinned to his chest, a dragon breathing flame carved into it. Other than that, there was no way to tell if this man was a Wizard.

"Look," Frederick started, as Timothy slowly lowered his notepad. "I can explain."

"You know that wasn't necessary. I would've let you in," the king answered. He placed the notepad on the table in front of him and turned his full attention.

"I have a request."

"You could've summoned me using the call, but you didn't."

"A request I could only make in person. Right now, you have the funds to do practically anything. You are the leader, the gui-"

"Speak your request, but first-" Timothy, covering it with his other hand, flicked his right pointer finger. The littlest bit of friction traveled up his arm and into his body, where it expelled instantly. "The cameras are no longer watching or listening."

Frederick nodded. "Thank you. I believe I may know where my sister is."

"Have you talked with Leo as I demanded?"

"Yes. We both have the suspicion that she is...well, in the sky."

"How do you know this?"

"We received a letter from her, a poem." He pulled the little slip of paper from his pocket and handed it to MacArthur. The king frowned upon seeing it, and after reading, he sighed.

"You want a dragon," the king said solemnly. "Of course you do. Now, let me explain some history here:

"There have never been records of dragons on this planet. For a while, the natives believed, but later they were restricted to fantasy and myth. That is the truth here. There are no dragons within our reach."

Frederick shook his head. "Then where are they all?"

"Off-planet. There are many worlds beyond this one, as you know. Worlds much more impressive than here."

"You can't summon one?"

The king looked at him blankly. "A dragon cannot survive in space without a Wizard commanding them. Only that bond can keep them alive."

"So your other title of *Dragon* King means nothing in that sense? You-"

"It is a title, as you have said. I am granted no power beside my own skill from my crown. It is the way of every Wizard King. We do not have our powers because of luck, but because we show skill in the Wizard Arts. This crown holds no meaning beside the title it signals. I hope you can come to understand that."

Frederick glanced away bitterly. "If no material dragon can come to assist me, then I will call a cosmic one. You won't assist in the summoning of an off-world dragon? I'll bring one of the most powerful ones straight here."

Timothy laughed slightly out of absurdity. "The cosmic dragons do not respect the wishes of an apprentice Wizard such as yourself. Until you have proven yourself to them, they will ignore every call."

"Then why can't you call them?"

"I, as they, do not respect your wishes."

Frederick looked to him, disbelief on his face. He narrowed his eyes, fingers beginning to twitch.

"Don't be surprised," MacArthur continued. "Ever since you were inducted into the order, you have kept your powers hidden away. You make no effort to help-"

"Then I'll help!" Frederick interrupted, both hands growing hot. He flexed them, feeling the blaze ready to be set free. "I'll fight your stupid war, and prove whatever I need to prove! I'll kill as many wretched Anarchists as you need. Send me to the front line whenever you want."

The king smirked. "I can do better than that. In less than an hour, we will be having a war meeting. You are to observe and be ready for any and all orders. Wait patiently as for now, *soldier*."

Frederick swallowed visibly, and the fire in his hands snuffed itself.

He nodded.

31

When morning arrived, everyone was immediately invited down to the war facility by Timothy MacArthur. Notes had been left at everyone's doors, including the recovery room where Celestia and Rosemary were. The message was simple: *Be in the facility by nine o'clock AM.*

Guards created a path for everyone to follow, snaking down the staircase. Celestia reluctantly left Rosemary in the recovery room, knowing a meeting would only upset the young girl. She walked out from the medical rooms and into the center area, where they had spoken with the president the day before. She spotted the guards quickly and followed the path down the staircase.

Kiran and Michael followed, both hardly rested. Even so, Kiran still felt wide awake, and Michael assured himself that rest was unimportant. Still, a scarcely noticeable lethargicness hung in the air around him. He pushed it aside with every bit of strength.

Ethan was last, zombie-like in nature. Dark circles sat beneath his eyes, and his red hair shot out at awkward angles. A dark cloak covered his body, concealing almost the entirety of him. For a moment, he wanted to pull over his hood, but feared it would make him look a little too much like a Shadow Lord. His feet dragged against the ground and nearly tripped down the stairs.

Once inside the war facility, everyone gathered in a circle. General Timothy MacArthur stood in the center, scanning the room as it was filled. He gave each person a formal nod, thanking them all for being here.

"Now, especially for our guests," he said, gesturing to Michael and those around him. "There is breakfast available to all. Today we will be discussing a critical matter at hand: the Anarchist Rebellion. Therefore, all of you must be at your highest functioning levels."

"Is there coffee?" Ethan asked sleepily, yawning soon after. He leaned against the wall with his shoulder.

"Yes, there is coffee," the general answered. Ethan nodded gratefully, and his eyelids drooped further down. "Three minutes. Get what you need and return immediately."

Everyone rushed over, and only then did Kiran understand how hungry he was. The breakfast bar seemed incredibly more appealing now, and he rushed in. Soon after, he glanced at Michael, who wasn't eating.

"Bro you should eat somethin'," Kiran said in between bites. "It's been waaay too long."

Michael shook his head. "Later. I must focus, as of now."

Kiran shrugged, continuing to eat. He walked away from the bar and back to his spot in the circle.

After a few minutes, Timothy MacArthur clapped twice. "Now that that has been settled, I suggest we begin. First, I would like for our new recruits to introduce themselves."

Celestia grunted. "'Recruit' sounds like an insult. I have nearly enough experi-"

"Celestia," Michael cautioned. She backed off.

"I'm Academy Warrior Kiran Andon," said Kiran.

"Ethan," the redheaded boy muttered, sipping his black coffee. The other Academy Warriors had always judged him for it, with their cream and sugar-filled drinks. Only black coffee...nothing else for Ethan Catanzaro.

Timothy nodded to each one, the guards off to the side as well. "Pleasure to meet you all. I've heard great things about each and every one of you. I look forward to having some actual leaders on my side."

"The pleasure is ours, general," Michael responded. "Now, who are your representatives?"

Timothy turned, looking to the three guards on standby. "Introduce yourselves."

The taller two removed their glasses, revealing bright yellow irises. One had black hair, the other with white. Both had streaks of yellow, almost like lightning.

"Bolten," the one with black hair said.

"Blaze," the other said. They both nodded.

Michael smiled. "I welcome you. And the third?" He found himself asking only for his companions, as he already knew the identity. He prepared himself for it.

The third guard, shorter than the other two, removed his glasses.

He did not have piercing yellow eyes, but peaceful, blue ones. Kiran's and Ethan's faces slowly lit up with recognition.

"Frederick Donovan," the guard said. Timothy MacArthur nodded with him. Ethan nearly spit out his coffee, and Kiran started to step forward without thinking. Michael kept him back with his arm.

"Wait."

"Our plan," the general started. "Is to send all of you with respective teams of soldiers and Academy Warriors. We will take back our lower districts in one fell sweep. With all of your leadership, I expect this to be easy. Anything to add before I assign the teams?"

"What will we do about the Anarchist Ship?" Celestia asked. "It's technology I've never seen before."

"I'll knock it out of the sky," Frederick said, and everyone looked to him. "I'll blow it to pieces."

"There's your answer," the general said. Celestia didn't seem entirely convinced, but the look on Frederick's face was one of supreme confidence.

He better be careful, or pride is what'll knock HIM out of the sky.

"Anything else?" the general asked. Silence followed. Kiran and Frederick's eyes met, both serious. Kiran nodded, smiling within.

The first Donovan had returned.

Through the next two hours, General Timothy MacArthur laid the entire plan out. Ethan passed three cups of coffee, and Kiran nearly fell into a food coma once he had finally finished eating. The rest listened intently.

"The plan is simple enough," the general said, addressing all. "We will drive back the Anarchists forces first from Mysti, Fiasco, and Desertia. Kiran, you and the loyal Academy Warriors will handle Desertia. Frederick, Bolten, and Blaze, you will all be handling Mysti. Platoons of soldiers will support you. Ethan, you will have platoons to accompany you to Fiasco. All of you are to stay within your districts."

They all nodded.

"Top priority: evacuate. We do not need innocent civilians caught up in the cross-fire. Before any offensive moves are made, make sure all citizens are safe. No explanations for them are necessary. If they ask, tell them the rebellion is ending soon. If all goes well, they will be back in their homes by tomorrow or the day after.

"Then..." he met the eyes of each of them. "Take back our districts. Leave no trace of the Anarchist reign. Once the front districts are taken back, flood Hookhorse and Smith. That's where Celestia will bring her soldiers in to assist."

"I work better with women," the blonde leader said. "Personal reasons."

"Noted. Find the Anarchist operations base and eliminate it. We have reports that it is in Hookhorse district, but we are unsure. Search Hookhorse as best as you can, and search Smith with the same precision.

"There is, as well, a side goal. If any of you can capture an Anarchist, do so. As you all are aware, they have a knack for dissolving into ash after being defeated. If any Anarchist remains intact, even a dead one, bring them back to the capitol. If you yourself cannot do it, send the Anarchist back with a group of soldiers. Be steady and confident in your strides."

A silence of thought followed, everyone passing the orders through their heads. Michael stepped forward and broke the silence.

"I have one thing to add, if that's all right, general," the boy said. Timothy nodded immediately, stepping from his center position.

"Be wary of Shadow Lords," he began. Ethan glanced up, eyes widening. "If any of you are aware, the leaders of the Anarchist rebellion fit what I've learned to call 'Shadow Lords.' These supreme warriors hold blasphemous magic in their hands, being capable of fearsome tasks. They can cause pain to flare in a person's body with a flick of their wrists. They can control people in unnatural ways, voiding one of will. Their swords are fearsome to even look at, much less fight. Hold great caution.

"But do not fear them. They will only grow more powerful if you do."

A hushed silence followed, everyone nervously glancing to one another. Frederick glanced at Kiran, and the both of them watch unnervingly as Michael stepped from the center. Bolten and Blaze's faces grew severe.

"The Shadow Lords were a failed experiment of misguided individuals. They are the product of an evil reign in this world, so be very wary about their abilities. They will hold no mercy against you, and will feed off your life force long after you are defeated."

"How will we know when we see one?" Bolten asked.

"You will know," Michael responded quickly. "They will make it known."

"And how can we kill them?" asked Blaze. Ethan swallowed visibly.

"As you would kill a normal human. It will not be as easy as fighting an Anarchist, however. Shadow Lords focus on rage and weakness of others for power. Use that to your advantage."

Blaze nodded. "Very well."

Timothy MacArthur nodded. "Assemble at The Academy at two o'clock. Our attack will run through sundown and into the night. Our time frames will be laid out there. For now, do as you wish."

The room emptied soon after.

32

"It's been a while," Kiran said. Frederick nodded halfheartedly. "So-"

"Look, I'm sorry," Frederick broke in abruptly. "I didn't want to face the world of Topia anymore, that's all." He began walking off, hands in his pockets. Kiran followed.

"That's not all," Kiran said. "You owe me a major explanation, dude." They passed by Bolten and Blaze, who were whispering off to the side.

Entering the main room, Frederick began motioning for the door. He stopped as he started to open it.

"Fine. Just not here," he said, and they stepped outside. Cortex paid them no attention, and they walked down the front path.

"Good," Kiran responded, satisfied. "I have an errand to run anyway. C'mon, we can walk there."

Kiran took the lead, Frederick silently agreeing to follow. They walked without talking, both wishing to but never making an effort. A ton of questions circled Kiran's mind, sensible ones like, *how did you survive?*

But one giant question overshadowed them all, the question of Rachel Donovan.

Kiran knew now with near certainty that Rachel was most likely alive. If Frederick somehow managed to live beyond the city on his own for nearly two years, then the possibility was high. Rachel had always been the more resourceful of the two as well.

Frederick watched the bustling streets of Lanon, realizing he had never seen much of this area when he was younger. The Donovans had always lived in Mysti and never strayed far from it. Of course, when their parents had left, and the children were scooped up by Gabriel Lanondek, they had gone to live in Desertia. Only Leo ever saw the capitol.

Now it seemed almost humorous, seeing it for the first time and having the pressure to save it. He imagined hordes of black-clothed Anarchists sprinting through the streets. Like shadows engulfing an entire district with ease.

Must be what it's like for the lower districts.

They crossed a few streets before passing The Academy. Kiran paid no attention to the building, but Frederick found himself a little intrigued. Through the glass doors, he could see red clothed Academy Warriors nearly like Kiran. He looked back to the boy in front of him and frowned.

"Where's your sword?" he asked, noticing the empty sheath Kiran wore.

"Michael broke it," Kiran answered flatly. Frederick raised an eyebrow, but nothing followed.

They entered the northern part of Desertia, mostly housing. Kiran led Frederick through many winding streets, deep into the neighborhood. They stopped at one corner, Kiran staring across the street.

Frederick stopped next to him and followed his gaze. A two-story house sat across the street, identical in structure to those around it. However, lack of care for the place had put in worse shape, a few windows broken and a piece of the roof caving in.

Kiran crossed the street swiftly, still silent. Frederick followed, his focus on the house. As they neared closer, he could see spider webs stretching from the house's overhang and outward. Several of them were currently being knocked out of the way by a younger woman armed with a broom. Her dark complexion was bent in a grimace as she swept the porch clear of webs.

Kiran walked up the front sidewalk with cautious stride, observing the woman. She noticed him and Frederick approaching and ceased her activity.

Peering around at Frederick, she then looked to Kiran. "How can I help you?" she asked unenthusiastically. Her eyes flicked from the both of them, truly inconvenienced.

Kiran paused before answering. The formal way to greet an Academy Warrior was by "officer" or "loyal soldier." He let it slide this time.

"What's your name?" he asked flatly.

"Why would I tell you? Got somethin' against me? Someone's lookin' for me, ain't they...that's what I bet." Kiran knew from the accent she was from Fiasco district. Probably a refugee. Fiasco was

the third district to fall, and most of the area went up in flames. The
Anarchists truly decimated the remains of it.

"I am an Academy Warrior. I have the right to ask for your
name, and you must answer."

"Academy Warrior? Got no badge or sword, as far as I can tell.
That uniform doesn't do you any good farther than that. You're
lucky I haven't whacked you with this broom. Standing right here
you ain't any better than these cobwebs."

Kiran's hands began tightening into fists. Before he could make
any impulsive actions, however, Frederick tapped his shoulder.
Kiran glanced back, seeing the Wizard's eyebrows raised.

"Look, I'll make ya a deal," the woman said. "Tell me your name,
don't go on lying, and I'll tell ya mine. You first."

Kiran looked up at the house, recognizing the upper story
vividly. *I need to get inside, no matter the cost.*

"Kiran Andon."

The woman laughed for a moment, then stopped suddenly.
"Well, I'll be! How fascinating!"

"Follow through with the deal. This was my house once, after
all."

The woman leaned a little closer with one ear. "Was? Well, it
still is. Or your mother's, in fact. Name's Stacey Brown. I'm your
mother's caretaker."

Kiran's eyes widened, and Stacey laughed because of it.
"I thought my mother was in an institution. Why is she here, back at
this house?" He began speaking with his interrogative, demanding
edge, but Stacey only found it humorous.

"Oh my, you really haven't been keeping up with the old fam!
Quick, c'mon inside and see her again. She's only out of the

crackhouse because she ain't violent. Still a little tough to talk to, though!"

Kiran looked to the door, stepping onto the porch. It as the very same door as four years prior, broken oak, the corners termite-ridden. As it creaked open, Stacey apologized.

"Not much money to repair the place, I'm afraid. Gotta live with what'cha got."

Frederick followed behind as well. *What am I getting myself into?* he thought. *Some errand.*

Kiran stepped into the foyer, breathing in the old air. Satisfying, but also unsettling. As he looked around, almost nothing at all had changed since the day he left. For a moment, he wanted to run to the pantry and check for food, even though it was improbable.

It's probably stocked now... people are living here again.

In the living room, darkened from all except for a dirty window letting in fractured light. Kiran's eyes fell on the main table, chairs around as always. The house had never had a couch or resting area, that was all in the bedrooms upstairs. When in the living room, every action needed to be alive.

A woman with chocolate-brown skin sat at the table, eyes glossy. Her hair fell back messily and distraught, tangled in a number of ways. Her mouth moved a little as if she was whispering, but Kiran couldn't hear anything. He was glad, though, because whatever she would be saying would surely remind him of terrible things.

"Mae..." Stacey said, voice soft. "Remember Kiran? Your son?" She walked over by the frozen woman, placing her hands on her shoulders and massaging slightly.

Kiran stopped walking forward, looking expectantly to Mae Andon. Even now, pity was stale.

It's disturbing, yeah, but she never cared for me in the first place. I didn't feel for her then, and I don't now.

"Son..." Mae whispered. Hope sparked momentarily in Kiran, but it quickly died out. She was only repeating the word. Stacey looked up, not surprised.

"Sorry, but there ain't much I can do. It's tough for her to snap out of things, you know?"

Kiran nodded solemnly, still watching. His mother's hands were clasped together tightly on the table, trembling slightly. Her knuckles looked to be turning white.

Frederick stepped next to Kiran. "Hey, why did we come here again? You weren't expecting this...right?"

Kiran shook his head. He began to speak, but paused.
Mae Andon turned her head slowly as if it was on a swivel. Her eyes broke from their glossy nature, turning vivid. She stared, eyes incredibly wide. Kiran expected her to turn to him, but her sights were focused on Frederick.

"YOU," she boomed. He eyes widened, and her breaths grew heavy. Stacey watched in fear as Mae spoke again. "I SAW YOU."

Kiran turned to Frederick, motioning him to get behind. "Go upstairs. There's-"

"STACEY GET THIS BLOODY-"

"Get upstairs!"

Her voice was drowned out as Frederick sprinted up the staircase, heart pumping. Footsteps pounding against the carpeted steps, his mind scattered itself. Once he reached the top, he nearly dove for safety. He took a moment to rest against the wall, looking about the area he had entered. Breaths slowed as he brought his concentration elsewhere. A few rooms sat off to the side and forward. Within one he could see a bathroom.

Soon, Kiran began following up the staircase, keeping his eyes trained on his mother. As soon as she disappeared from view, he knelt. Pressing a few fingers to the bridge of his nose, he closed his eyes. His eyes grew watery from bitterness, and he fought back from them blossoming into tears. Frederick sat down nearby, slumped against the wall.

"Just be glad you still have one," he said. Kiran sniffed.

"One...what?"

"A mother. That's one of your answers, by the way. I left my home to remain with the only family I had left. And when both of my siblings started to distance themselves, that was it. I had had enough."

"But why not go after them...why not at least try?"

"Like you're trying with your psycho mom? I've talked to Leo since I got back, but he won't help me. Not in the way I think he should."

"Rachel."

"Exactly. I'm going to find her now. I think I have a pretty good idea of where she is. All I need is a ride."

"Good. Find her. I loved her the moment we talked that night, more than I've ever loved my mom."

Frederick laughed. "I don't even know if that's a good or a bad thing."

"Neither do I." He stood, Frederick copying soon after. They exchanged a slightly awkward glance. "Well, I better get what I came for."

"And what's that?"

"You'll see." He led Frederick into the room off to the right, what appeared to be a child's bedroom. A single twin bed sat off to the side, dust covering the entire comforter. A closed, mirrored, closet lined the far wall. Kiran walked straight to the desk, a wooden piece beginning to fall apart.

The single window in the room shed a little light on the polished oak desk, illuminating the tiny particles in the air.

Kiran grabbed the front of it and began prying up. Frederick grimaced as he tore the top off the desk, a splintering sound coming from the back of it. Kiran tossed the top off to the side, and reached for something.

He came back with a rope. It was sleek, black, and soon Frederick realized it was in fact, a whip. A silver handle coiled the cable around, a large button the side.

"A whip. Fascinating. You gonna fight the Anarchists with that?" he commented.

"Just watch."

He grabbed the handle, letting the whip unravel. He pressed the button, and it flared to life. A neon blue energy burst through it, electrifying. From it, Frederick could feel the charge in the air, a running power source. Kiran flicked his wrist, and the whip wrapped itself around one of the desk legs. It curled around the leg until taut, and Frederick saw the magic starting to work.

"It was my father's design. He had a prototype, of course, but this one is the real thing. I'm done with swords for now. I'll whip Topia into shape."

He tore the leg from the desk, sending splinters of wood nearby. The leg flew to him, and as he caught it with his open hand, he promptly turned the whip off. He dropped the leg to the floor, kicking it aside soon after. Then, with practiced skill, he wrapped the whip back up and slid his arm through it like a handbag.

"I'm ready."

33

NOAH looked dominantly over the city as if it was his child beginning to walk. A thin layer of dark smoke hung over the southern districts, shrouding them. He reached out, fingers just touching the glass wall of The Unknown, and smiled.

ATTACK THEM NOW, a voice boomed within him.

"Be patient, father. They will come to us," he responded simply.

DESTROY THEM AT THE HEART OF THE CAPITOL.

"A frontal assault? That would be a waste of our resources."

THEY ARE WEAK NO MATTER WHERE THEY ARE FOUGHT.

Noah frowned. "Why are you so determined to do this? Attacking the capitol now would leave everything else unprotected. We would need-"

EVERY ANARCHIST. OF COURSE. WHOEVER ATTACKS FIRST WILL SUCCEED. WAIT, AND THEY WILL BRING THE MOMENTUM TO YOU. BRING IT TO THEM INSTEAD.

Noah hesitated, unsure. Lives could be risked here, unnecessary ones. *Lanon is heavily populated.*

"We could lose many loyal Anarchists in an attack like this," he stated simply.

THEY VOLUNTEERED TO JOIN US.

"Over the threat of death."

MERE INCENTIVE.

"They want a new world! Not a wasteland!"

A WORLD WITHOUT GOVERNMENT IS NO WASTELAND.

"Then what is it, a paradise?"

INDEED. WITH MY AND MOSTLY YOUR GUIDANCE, TOPIA WILL BE REBORN. IT WILL BE A CITY WITHOUT BORDERS, PREJUDICE, AND LAW. IT WILL BE FREE FROM ANYONE'S CONTROL.

"Even ours?"

WE ARE NOT JUST ANYONE...WE ARE THE TRUTH.

Noah stared over the city, seeing many without them seeing him. The Unknown was invisible to all, a floating mass without color. It could not prevent a shadow, however, and that alone enveloped half of Hookhorse District.

He watched as the city-people moved throughout their daily lives, or so he wished. Deep down he knew that instead of going outside, people were shutting their curtains in fear. He knew that families were having dinner for possibly the last time, as their homes could soon be overtaken.

"We're destroying livelihoods," he muttered.

LIVELIHOODS THAT DO NOT MATTER. WE ARE RIDDING THE WORLD OF THE FLAWED WAYS OF LIFE, AND WELCOMING THE PERFECT.

"Who's to say we're the perfect ones?"

HAVE YOU THE AUDACITY TO SAY THAT STATEMENT? I AM THE HIGHEST PERFECTION, THE BRINGER OF ALL

RIGHTS, THE NEW PRINCE.

Noah shook his head a little, brow furrowing. "It's just...I don't want a part in this."

A pause followed, Noah staring beyond. In the slight reflection of the window, he saw himself, green eyes meeting themselves. They twinkled, and he knew what was coming. He relaxed, but cursed. He knew that there was no way to stop it.

THEN I WILL DO IT MYSELF.

"Celestia! Celestia!" Rosemary yelled, skipping through the main hall. Her shoes clicked against the silver tile floor, echoing off the walls. Her green dress was now gone, replaced by a plain white gown. She lunged at the Sisterhood leader, grabbing onto her waist.

Celestia jerked away for a moment, then relaxed. She patted the girl's head, smiling.

"You okay?"

"I think so!" she answered cheerfully. "What are you doing?"

Celestia looked to the staircase. "Was about to see if there are any extra weapons I need for the battle. Come with me. Maybe there's something that will interest you."

"Battle?"

"We're going to fight off the Anarchists, just like we promised. We'll take back the city, and form our dream. The Sisterhood dream. Even so, I'm going to need you to stay a little safer during this though, okay? We had a close call earlier."

"Okay! I'll try."

"Mhm." They followed the path down to the war facility same as earlier. This time, however, the room was nearly empty. Only Ethan stood in the corner, and Celestia paid him no attention.

Rosemary grinned to him, then looked to the wall of weapons with Celestia. The assortment was vast, guns and blades alike. Every gun shot only once before you needed to reload, none were automatic. That technology wasn't compact enough for personal carrying. The blades appeared to be steel but lacked the shine of Celestia's own. She hefted the Tritonyx, comparing it visually, and lowered it soon after.

She pulled one of the blades from the wall, and tossed it and the Tritonyx from hand to hand. The weight of the military blade was much lighter, but it seemed weaker as well. Celestia lightly banged the Tritonyx against it, producing a hollow sound.

"My sword is still far superior," she concluded sadly, placing the military blade back. "I'm done here. See anything you like?"

Rosemary put a finger to her chin thoughtfully. She scanned the isle of weapons, eyes lighting up as they crossed a dagger that hung from the wall.

"That one!" she exclaimed, pointing. Celestia grabbed it, a small silver dagger in a brown sheath. She handed it to Rosemary carefully, pulling it back at the last second.

"You will use it only to defend yourself, okay?"

Rosemary nodded. Celestia handed the dagger to her flat, resting on the palms of her hands. Her fingers closed over it. It wasn't the first time she had held a weapon, but it was definitely the first time she had one of her own.

Celestia noticed Ethan watching them, and raised an eyebrow. He sipped his coffee lazily, covering his eyes with the cup. As he began to finish it off, the entire facility trembled. The walls shook violently, metal crashing against itself.

The motion knocked Ethan forward, and he ended up spitting out the majority of the coffee he had drunk. The cup fell to the floor, and he reached out for a brace. He found the metal ladder rungs and clutched tight.

Celestia covered Rosemary with her entire body, getting low. She glanced around the swaying lights, waiting for another rumble. When none followed. She hurried to her feet.

"Let's go! Get upstairs," she ordered Rosemary and Ethan. They all thundered their way up the staircase and paused on the top step. Celestia watched as guards sprinted to the front door and outside, flooding the front lawn. Leila Lanondek stood in the center of the room, staring blankly. Cortex and another guard stood beside her at the ready.

Celestia walked to the front slowly and peered outside. She cursed silently and glanced back.

"Rosemary," she said. The girl looked to her, confused worry in her eyes.

"The little girl can stay with me, Celestia. She'll be safe," Leila Lanondek offered. Celestia glared at her, but then turned to Rosemary again.

"Rosemary! Get over here. Stay close."

She hurried over, torn dress brushing against the ground. Upon joining Celestia at the door, they both looked outside again.

A great black mass hovered above The Academy, what Celestia recognized immediately to be *The Unknown.*

34

"THIS IS IT, EVERYONE! TOP PRIORITY: EVACUATE
LANON, PROTECT THE CAPITOL!"

Timothy MacArthur lowered his megaphone, handing it off to
Blaze. Both Blaze and Bolten stood at the ready, awaiting orders.
They watched from the lawn of the capitol, keeping a close eye on
the Anarchist ship overhead. It loomed threateningly, but at the
moment, it hovered still.

When it had arrived out of thin air, shockwaves had blasted the
ground. Smaller buildings in Lanon had already collapsed from the
force, civilians trapped inside.

Kiran stood on the balcony of the capitol building, looking
through binoculars. He swept the city horizon many times, but
nothing was showing at first. Not long after the ship had appeared,
though, he noticed something dire.

A wall of pitch black, a mass of shadows, was steadily charging
toward the capital itself. Kiran's eyes widened, and he lowered the
binoculars immediately. Even now, with the naked eye, he could see
the wall.

"Timothy!" he shouted down below. The general looked up,
cupping a hand to his ear. "We've got Anarchists on their way here!"

The General grimaced. "Are you sure!?"

Kiran nodded vigorously.

Timothy sighed angrily and took the megaphone from Blaze.

"LOOKS LIKE WE'RE ON THE DEFENSE, EVERYONE!
ANARCHISTS ARE APPROACHING FROM THE SOUTH! STICK
TO YOUR STATIONS, AND PUSH ALL ENEMY FORCES BACK!

MOVE OUT!"

Kiran sprinted across the streets of Lanon, whip wrapped around his shoulder. Traffic had stopped on its own, no one daring to move at the sight of an oncoming invasion. Kiran passed many frightened eyes and minds. A small group of sensible people had fled from their vehicles, rushing for cover instantly. Mothers shielded their children on the way in as if expecting an air strike.

Kiran reached The Academy quickly, keeping an eye trained on the great Anarchist ship. It remained still, a looming beast in the sky, just breaking through the clouds. Crowds of people stood on the sidewalks, staring up at it as well. Kiran nearly had to force his way past people who were frozen from fear.

"GET INSIDE, EVERYONE!" he shouted at the top of his lungs, straining. Barely anyone truly heard him, and he had no choice but to keep running. He entered the Centre Lanon, where The Academy sat, mobbed.

He barrelled through the front crowds at the building, no time to apologize. He slammed against the front glass door, but it wouldn't open. Grabbing the handle and rattling, he hoped to catch some attention. There was movement inside, and Jeremy came running up.

Jeremy drew his sword but kept it low. He unlocked the door, and in a swift movement, allowed Kiran inside. A few of the mobsters tried to force their ways in, but Jeremy raised his blade in response. He locked the door again. The mobsters smushed themselves up against the glass, pounding to be let in.

Kiran suppressed any urge to let them in. The Academy would be no safer for citizens. It would be a prime target for the Anarchist forces, certainly.

He and Jeremy ran to the meeting hall. Once again, everyone stood inside.

"MacArthur has a very simple plan!" Kiran shouted once inside, catching everyone's attention. All eyes snapped to him, wary. "Our armies are focused on protecting the capitol! Commanders Frederick, Bolten, Blaze, and MacArthur will have the area fortified within the hour! We Academy Warriors will flank the Anarchists, and hopefully begin to surround their forces. We wait until they have struck first, and then we charge forth!"

"What if-" Walter began. The Warrior had a bandana wrapped tightly around his forehead, with a strange symbol marked on the center.

"-No what ifs! We have a full-scale invasion at our fingertips, and there's no time to waste!" He pointed toward the ceiling. "That thing hovering above us right now, it's powerful. I don't know what it can do exactly, but my guess is that it could take this place down in a matter of seconds. However, we need eyes on it at all times! Do not forget about the threat it poses. However, we need to be out of here immediately!"

He waited for a few nods, and continued:

"Walter and Dynai! You two stay here and guard HQ." Dyni nodded swiftly, but Walter did not.

"Kiran!" Ethan yelled. "Can I guard with them?" He worried his attempt would not work, but it would make everything easier if Kiran just said yes.

"Ethan, we need you on the battlefield!"

266

"I need to stay here." He cursed, knowing that Kiran wouldn't believe him until a well-fabricated lie was created.

So as Kiran watched him worriedly, staring him down, Ethan offered:

"I just want to be here for the very end, I guess," he lied. "It's been my home for a long time, and I figured I'd spend the most important part of my career guarding it." It hurt a little to say that, considering much of it was true.

Kiran gravely nodded. Ethan readied his brand-new sword. "I'm counting on you to lead this, Ethan," Kiran added. Walter started to protest but was cut off once again.

"REST OF YOU, WITH ME!"

He backed out of the room quickly, Jeremy already at his heels. He unraveled his whip, spinning it slowly at his side as he ran. Slinging it over his shoulder, he charged outside.

Eighty Academy Warriors followed.

35

Frederick took a quick glance to Bolten, who stood 100 yards away. They locked eyes and nodded. Bolten's gaze was torn with grim intent, as if he was already envisioning the destruction to come. Frederick held the same mindset, and unfortunately, could very vividly see what was to come. It made sense for the both of them, as the Academy Wizards had always held an air of foresight.

Frederick turned back to the soldiers gathered around him, a mass of nearly one hundred under his command. Being the least experienced, he had the smallest group, but it was more than enough.

"Captains," he said, addressing the five men before him. "I only ask of your best work. We're fighting for a city today, perhaps the last in the world. And for some of us...we're fighting for much more than that. Family." He was unsatisfied with the short speech, but time was of the essence.

The captains nodded. The center one looked to the four to his sides, jerked his head in their directions. The others split, gathering the soldiers around them. Most were dressed in red and silver, weapons hung at their sides. Only the captains held guns.

The center captain looked back to Frederick. "Do you have confidence we'll win, sir?"

Frederick sighed. "They outnumber us, but we have the skill. That's all I think."

The captain nodded and turned away to join his platoon. The five platoons spread themselves in a thick wall in front of Frederick. He stood behind them, but knew that would not be for long. They were gathered in the wide open square of Lanon, not the Centre but near. Diamond Street ran down the center of the square, going south. The dark wave of Anarchists approached from it, still at least five minutes away.

Timothy MacArthur had split Frederick, Bolten, and Blaze into the three sections of the square. Frederick took the right, Bolten the left, Blaze the center. MacArthur himself hung back near the capital, in case anyone broke through.

A few minutes passed, and as the Anarchist armies grew closer, and the Topian soldiers stood waiting, clouds began to gather overhead. The sun poked itself through in a few places, scattered light throughout the city, but it would soon grow weak.

Just as the sky turned dark, the first Anarchist and Topian clashed blades.

Celestia threw herself into the battle, faithful in the fact that Rosemary would not follow. She had ordered the young girl to hide in one of the nearby buildings of Upper Mysti, guarded by two soldiers of her choice. So now, Celestia could fight without worry.

With even the first Anarchist she faced, a smile crossed her. She defeated him in an instant, the first casualty of the battle. More Anarchists rushed her, and quickly did they fall as well. The ease of combat kept her light and aware, as if she was still getting warmed up. Her blade smashed down any Anarchist's with impressive strength, dealing wounding blows in the blink of an eye as well.

The entire district had been evacuated, but to Celestia, it seemed anciently desolate. Plenty of Anarchists had already smashed open car and apartment windows, looting whatever was inside. She advanced forward to meet them as they stuffed their pockets.

As she parried one blow and struck down the twentieth Anarchists, prepared for the next attack. An unnatural pause followed, and as she glanced around, no more Anarchists had begun to approach her.

Her eyes narrowed as she saw where they were funneling. A huge crowd of black-clothed warriors crowded one of the medical buildings, and were smashing down the front door.

Rosemary.

Do they know she's in there? Is this on purpose?

She hurried over and began her work.

The Anarchists whirled around, and one caught Celestia off guard. She blocked his attack just barely and sliced clear across his chest. She deflected two more Anarchist blows as a few more moved from the building. Two quick slashes sent the attackers down. As more crowded around her, more fell. Her heart rate increased, and her stances deepened. As each Anarchist swung to strike, they were faced by two of Celestia's own.

The next few Anarchists approached slowly and readied themselves to attack. After a brief stalemate of no movement, the Anarchists started to take action.

Celestia glanced over to the front of the building, taking advantage of the last few Anarchists' hesitancy. The door to the building shattered in a rain of glass and the breakers jumped through. Celestia darted at the Anarchist to her right. They exchanged two strikes, with Celestia overpowering on the second. The Anarchist stumbled back into his comrades, and Celestia took the opening.

She sprinted to the building, diving through the shattered door. A shard sliced part of her shoulder, but she could barely feel it. The Anarchists were steadily making their way through the main hallway. The building was some sort of medical center, offices on all sides and a second floor for other operations. Luckily, the Anarchists were going in the wrong direction of Rosemary.

Celestia rushed up the stairs as quietly as possible, glancing back continuously. She knew the attackers outside would be following soon, but she needed to find Rosemary ASAP.

She turned the corner to the left wing, and upon entering the room, her eyes widened.

"Rosemary!" she yelled, turning away from the empty room. The soldiers who had been guarding her lay unconscious on the floor, their blades taken. The table in the room had a streak of red across it, and a few of the chairs had been knocked over.

There was no response.

"Kiran shouldn't have put me with this job! He hardly has any power over any of us!" Walter exclaimed. He slammed a fist against the wall, the front door glass shaking slightly. The crowds outside had dissipated, even though the immediate threat was away from Centre Lanon. In fact, the Anarchists almost held a wide berth around the area.

Of course, Ethan, who sat silently a couple feet away, knew exactly why. If the plan were to work, there would need to be no one at all around The Academy, aside for those he could destroy easily. He eyed Walter and Dynai carefully.

"Cut your freaking whining," Dynai remarked. "You're nearly a grown man." She wasn't of age herself, being the same as Ethan and Kiran. Walter, however, had just turned seventeen.

"He shouldn't have put you on this job either! This is rookie work."

Dynai hefted her sword. "It's easy, and that's the point. We get to sit back and watch the fire."

Walter frowned, beginning to pace in circles. Ethan bounced his leg against his chair, glancing around the room and outside non-stop. The time that Noah had mentioned was drawing nearer. The moment the signal came, he would have to spring into action.

As Walter and Dynai's bickering started to fade into the background, Ethan began running over the scenario in his head.

I-I'm going to stand up, and slaughter the both of them, right here. It will be easy, swift. I w-won't hesitate, I'll follow through. If they resist, I will overpower them. If I cannot outduel them, I will kill them will the power of the Shadows. There will be no escape. I will regain my energy...and...hunt down the rest of my...friends...

Kiran...Celestia...Rosemary...even Frederick. Then...once they're...g-gone, I will hunt down Michael. Noah will be proud. I will be proud. The city will be mine...and...h-his. We will rule as master and apprentice, and everyone will bow b-beneath us.

Everything is right...but why does it feel so wrong? It's almost...too easy...

He glanced up to the bickering Walter and Dynai, arms crossing steadily. Behind them, in the distance, raged a battle seemingly so disconnected at the moment, but yet closer than ever. In the distance, smoke had already begun to rise. It was only a matter of time.

The night was consuming Topia, and the time would soon come. As Ethan waited, his adrenaline began pumping as his heartbeat grew faster and faster. His leg bounced continuously, a nervous action.

Out of the corner of his eye, he saw someone step into the back of the room. He stopped for a moment, fearing it was Noah, but it was not. In fact, it was the opposite.

Michael Nebadon walked swiftly into the room, stepping from

the winding staircase. Ethan stood immediately, Walter and Dynai noticing and turning as well.

"You," Walter growled, beginning to approach the blond boy. "What do you want?" He drew his sword.

Ethan hurried to block Walter with his arm. "Let me talk to him." Walter glared at him for a moment, silent, and then backed off. He sheathed his sword slowly. Ethan sighed of relief and looked to Michael expectantly.

Michael stared for a few seconds, a great thought in his eyes. He appeared to be sizing up Ethan again, as he did the first time they had met.

"I've had someone betray me before," the boy said flatly. Ethan's eyes widened a little, and he affirmed his sword grip. "I knew it was to happen, as I do now. That time, I allowed it. And it resulted in my death.

"Of course, I was destined to perish anyway. The betrayal was not necessary, and yet it happened." He frowned, glancing off to the side. As he looked back to Ethan, his blue eyes seemed nearly fake.

"Now, Ethan, it is necessary. But not for me, for you. I will not stop you from doing anything that is in your best interest. If you want power, dominance over others, and the strength of a thousand men, you are choosing the proper path.

"If you truly believe doing this will solve the great problem within you, I support it. If you believe that this will redeem yourself of a tragic past, go ahead. I will not stop you from seeing your own Light. Do it for your sake, not mine."

Ethan frowned, eyes wandering. "I-I don't understand. You are asking me...to defy your own wishes?"

"Do not do it for me, do it for you."

Michael then turned, beginning to walk away. Walter motioned to follow, but Dynai assured him not to.

Ethan looked down, mind torn.

Do not do it for me, do it for you. For your sake, not mine. It's another one of his blasted riddles. What the hell is that even supposed to mean?!

Then, a horn sounded.

NOW NOW NOW! DO IT! IT IS TIME! Noah commanded. Ethan tried to resist, clenching his fists tight and shutting his eyes, but it was no use. An overwhelming control flowed over him, a cold ocean wave of darkness. His eyes flared a bright green.

Walter narrowed his eyes a little, watching Ethan struggle against himself. He prodded the redheaded boy slightly with his sword expectantly as he watched. Dynai had her back turned to the situation, and was watching outside. She had a slight suspicion that the horn signaled something for the Anarchists, and that they might be on their way here.

Walter poked Ethan in the side, and that set off Ethan's internal alarm. His eyes turned deep neon green, and the rest of his skin stung with shadows. A thin outline around him turned smoky, and a force seeped into his mind.

Ethan snapped, and within a moment, Walter's sword was flying across the room. Dynai whipped around just as Ethan raised his sword to Walter threateningly. She did nothing as Ethan slashed at Walter's chest. Walter stumbled back, gasping, a tear through the front of his shirt.

"What the...Dynai, help!" Walter cried out as Ethan swung again, this time over Walter's head. Ethan glanced at Dynai sideways, expecting her to attack him next.

Dynai only smiled, nearly impressed. Walter coughed.

"Don't tell me..." Walter's eyes widened, and he backed away. "What is this mutiny?!" As Dynai smiled further, and Ethan watched her suspiciously, he turned and ran.

Ethan launched his free hand forward, and a burst of Shadow power launched from it.

"Shadow Hand," he said. The energy stretched out into a great hand, void of light, which wrapped itself around Walter. He held him tightly, keeping a focus on Dynai.

"Why have you been smiling?" Ethan asked, feeling nothing as Walter struggled against the shadow hand. "Your friend is in great danger."

Dynai remained smiling, eyes sparkling maliciously.

"I could kill him in an instant!" Ethan threatened, beginning to crush Walter slowly. Walter yelled out, squirming even more. Dynai did not move, nor cease grinning. "Why aren't you doing anything?!"

"I don't care," Dynai stated. "Kill him, and leave it be." She lost her smile.

Ethan gawked at her, then glared. He snatched his hand back, and as Walter rocketed toward him with the shadow hand leading, stabbed his sword forward. It pierced Walter immediately. Ethan turned to it and focused all strength on his blade.

"Summonus, summonus, blasphemous, blasphemous...," he whispered. He repeated it thrice.

His sword exploded in black flame again, this time consuming the dying Walter. The Academy Warrior turned to ash, funneling into Ethan sword as if it was a vacuum. An essence draining power.

Dynai snickered. "So you're the Shadow Lord. Gee, Michael really was right. Is that why he showed up?" Then, in a more serious tone, she asked: "Does he know?"

Ethan turned toward her, not answering. He glared again, bringing his sword into striking position. Dynai raised an eyebrow, her own blade still sheathed.

"Easy there, bud," Dynai said. "Don't go on attacking me, too."

"Give me one reason I shouldn't," Ethan growled.

"For one," she said, counting off her fingers. "We have a common interest."

Ethan watched her expectantly.

"You see, I need to kill Timothy MacArthur. Special reasons."

Ethan raised an eyebrow. "You do? The man you are fighting for?"

"Well, every Wizard in the world knows killing the Dragon King makes you the Dragon King. Or Queen, in my case."

Ethan could not find himself too surprised, but that itself was information he wasn't aware of. "You're an undercover Wizard."

"Of course. The Wizard class is by far the most powerful. Ever since the rift, however, I figured I'd study the Warriors as well. Plus, the Wizards haven't been well respected lately, have they?"

"Then why do it now?"

"A new age is beginning, Ethan. No matter which side prevails today, the end result will be a new Topia. It'll be one where the classes may start fresh. If so, I will begin this age by taking the throne!"

"MacArthur's protected by hundreds of soldiers."

"Child's play."

"You are calling this war child's play?"

"I have no goals in this war. Like I said, either side would result in my benefit. MacArthur is my only enemy. And anyone who tries to keep him from me."

Ethan chewed his lip, debating on striking the girl down right here. He knew it could be easy, but the way she spoke seemed oddly sincere. It was if this one girl would face the currently most bright man in the city alone.

"Then we have a deal?" Dynai asked. "We help each other?"

"We will remove his armies. You will remove him," Ethan settled. "It will be excellent to have the new Dragon Queen on our side."

She smirked, amused by the flattery. "Yes, it will."

36

The Anarchists began gaining momentum as the sun fell toward the horizon. It shone over the Sisterhood, blazing light through the great forests. Then, as its light spread along the lines of Topia City, the Battle of Lanon raged on.

Kiran forced himself to finally back off, latching onto and disarming one last Anarchist. He threw the blade clattering to the side, and quickly snapped his whip against the man's chest, sending him to the floor. Nearly two hundred of the soldiers dressed in black pressed forward toward the capitol, all of the Topians retreating as far as they could. MacArthur shouted orders on his megaphone, but most of the direction was left to the commanding officers.

The Academy Warrior numbers were kept high enough, only two of the eighty fallen so far. Of course, many had been badly wounded, but the casualties were slim. Kiran estimated nearly fifty were set to continue on. Some had run off to assist Frederick, who struggled to push the Anarchists away from Diamond Street. Bolten and Blaze's armies were nowhere in sight, probably off assisting Celestia.

Kiran ducked behind a corner as the battle fought on, Jeremy crouching nearby. They looked to one another, nodding.

"Any new plans?" Jeremy asked. His silver sword was stained with black ash, the signature dying mark of the Anarchists. Whenever one of their soldiers was "killed," they dissolved before anyone could stop them. Only their weapons did not disappear.

Kiran shook his head. "Nothing. At some point, we'll resort to a new strategy, but not yet. We still have some ground to give up. They're losing more soldiers than we are, but their numbers are still much higher."

Jeremy glanced at his blade. "You think these guys are actually dying for real?"

"What do you mean?"

"They crumble like burnt logs. How do we even know we're reducing their numbers?"

Kiran frowned, not truly knowing the answer. He thought a little, saying: "I suppose it's the only option we have. They seem to care about surviving, or else they'd just pile themselves on top of us.

"And even if they were somehow coming back over and over, we'd still be doing the exact same thing."

Jeremy looked away. "Would we? I don't know if I'd fight an enemy that couldn't die."

"I would," Kiran responded, seemingly more of talking to himself. "I'd keep going even at that point. Not much else to lose once you've gone that low."

"I suppose."

Kiran stared at the ground for a little bit, listening to the clashing nearby. Academy Warriors, Sergio at their helm, fought against hordes and hordes. Outnumbered nearly four-to-one, the odds of victory were slim. Even so, as Kiran had said, there was nothing else to lose. This was the final stand.

"C'mon," he said, standing. He jerked his head in the direction of the battle. "Let's go!" He bounded off, Jeremy following after some hesitation.

Kiran jumped behind the third line of Academy Warriors.

Slinging his whip over his neck for stability, he cupped his hands around his mouth. "Draw back! Move to Emerald!"

The Academy Warriors all backed up swiftly, falling into retreat formation. Sergio and a few others occupied the Anarchists at the front, while everyone else hurried for cover. They all turned a corner, the same one Kiran and Jeremy had been moments ago. Warriors in red flooded the street.

Kiran cursed as the Anarchists picked up speed, starting to surround Sergio and his partners.

"Sergio! Get back!" He rushed into the middle to help, launching out his whip as he slid beside the other Academy Warriors. They watched in curiosity as Kiran snatched and slashed with his contraption, pulling Anarchists' swords from their hands and even throwing them at others. The seven of them fought in unison, but the soldiers in black kept coming.

Kiran began to tire, his arms aching. Even adrenaline couldn't keep his fatigue from settling in, and his technique grew sloppy. He missed one attacking Anarchist outright, and the man took advantage. Only when Sergio intervened was the threat diminished.

The group defended on, the other Academy Warriors outside the mob attempting to break through. It was no use, however, and they were no more than a nuisance to these ravaging mobsters.

Then, the first arrow was fired. It sliced straight through the head of an Anarchist, leaving a puff of black smoke in its wake. From there, the arrow fell to the ground, golden fletchings on a golden shaft.

Another followed. Another puff of smoke filled the air. Then, yet another arrow struck down an Anarchist. These arrows, however, were black and blue colored.

They rained upon the great scene, striking down Anarchists left and right. They were thin needles in the air, the light of sundown glinting off their metals. It was a shower that turned the warriors to dust, and none could resist. The arrows intentionally strayed from Kiran and his allies, which confirmed Kiran's suspicions.

He glanced up to one of the buildings and wasn't sure if he wanted to smile. A slender teenage boy stood on the edge of the tallest building, nearly ten stories, a dark blue cloak rippling in the wind. Dark brown hair flowed as the wind did, eyes shining as an orange glow. A purple bow pointed down at the crowd was in his left hand, right hand hovering by a quiver of thin gold arrows.

The black and blue ones aren't his... there must be more archers, but how many?

As Kiran glanced around to more of the buildings, he counted six more archers positioned. Each held a fearsome gaze upon them, confident but not proud in their work. They stood still in the wake of their destruction, like rulers upon their empires.

Every last Anarchist on Emerald Street was defeated in a matter of seconds.

"Well I'll be," Sergio remarked. "It's Captain Parker and his Bulls-Eye Brotherhood."

Captain Parker wasted no time on top of the building. He signaled to his men, calling them forth, and slung his bow over his back. Then, he swiftly bounded from the rooftop.

Kiran watched in wonder as the Brotherhood leader shot two curling ropes from his wrists, small metal clasps on the ends of them. They smashed through two windows on the closest buildings, slowing Parker's fall. Descending smoothly, he landed just outside of the Academy Warrior circle.

As Kiran called everyone forth to meet, Parker came alone. Instead, the Captain had his Brothers keep guard on the buildings surveying Emerald Street. Jeremy silently admired this tactic.

Kiran, Jeremy, and Sergio met with Parker in the center of the now Anarchist free land. Sadly enough, it had been revealed that not every Academy Warrior had been saved by the Brotherhood, two younger warriors being defeated on the outside of the mob. Their friends held a quick ceremony in honor.

Kiran nodded to Parker. "First off, thanks-"

Parker reached into the side of his cloak, waving Kiran off. He produced a square shaped object, what appeared to be a wooden picture frame. He held it out to Kiran, waiting for a reaction.

"Michael gave this to us late last night. He told us what happened with...*her*, and...I'm dropping anything that was against him-*her*," he said.

Kiran felt a slight rush of shock run through him as he looked upon the painting, many questions flooding his mind. He examined the incredible quality, as if it was a real picture.

There's no way. This would've had to be taken in the afterlife. He can't...do that can he?

"Yeah, it's impressive," Parker continued. "Not sure how he got it, and I didn't have the time to ask. It's yours, now."

Kiran glanced up, brow furrowed. "You're sure? Michael gave it to you for a reason, I bet."

Parker shrugged. "I'm returning it. Not to him, but to you. based off what I've heard, she died for your sake. Plus, if she'd come back, or gotten captured, I would've had no choice but to get rid of her anyway. There's plenty of pressure around here. Many eyes watching my choices, many people wishing to see me fail."

Kiran hesitated, but took the painting from Parker's hands. He looked at it for a short time, still taking it in. For once, Zoey looked peaceful, finally free of whatever chains she had been bound to. Kiran knew it would serve nicely in The Academy's main hall, accompanying the other masters. Of course, that would mean the great Warrior HQ needed to be still standing at the end.

He glanced up, thanking Parker again. The Captain nodded. Kiran handed the painting to Jeremy.

"Keep it safe," he said. Turning to Parker, he seemed a little relieved to have it out of his hands. Another bit of pressure taken from him. He addressed Parker blatantly. "So, will you help us further? There's a struggle on Diamond that we need assistance with."

Parker grinned. "I'll see what my brothers and I can do."

Kiran turned back to Jeremy and Sergio. "Rally everyone. Tell Frederick we're on the way."

As dusk began approaching, and the air grew cold, the battle continued. Celestia still chased after Rosemary in upper Mysti, where the Anarchists swarmed without contest. The battle on Diamond worked as a standoff, neither side taking hold of the area. Wave after wave of Anarchists fell, but their numbers were still considerably higher than the Topians. And with each oncoming battle with the next group of Anarchists, more Topians were killed.

Suddenly, as the moon soon became the only light, a new one soon sparked. It was not Michael's, as Kiran hoped when he saw it in the sky. Instead, the light was lightning, a thundering bolt streaking through the air. It rattled the ground and the buildings, every soldier and Brotherhood archer feeling it beneath their feet. The bolt zipped to a skyscraper in Centre Lanon, visible to all on Diamond.

Then, it *jumped*. It bounced from rooftop to rooftop, an electric burst at every bounce. As Frederick began to watch it closer, noticing the irregularity of it, his eyes widened. There was something, organic about the bolt's movements, as if every bounce was a choice. As it drew closer north, to where he and his men were situated, another odd thing showed.

The bolt's on fire, Frederick realized. He instantly brought his wrist up, tapping on his wrist communicator.

"Bolten!" he shouted. "Blaze!"

"Yes?" Blaze responded in a gruff voice.

"Are you seeing this?"

A silence followed, suspenseful as Frederick wondered if Blaze shared the same views as him. If he was to be-

"A Wizard," Blaze concluded. Frederick agreed gravely.

"And he's heading straight for MacArthur."

"Will we need to help?"

"No! You stay, I'll go. At least someone has to." Frederick leaned over to Kiran, who was barking orders across the front lines. "You can handle this on your own, right?" he asked the Academy Warrior.

"Of course. Do what you need to do," Kiran responded.

Frederick stood, ending the call with Blaze. He turned from the battle and began sprinting toward the capitol. The bolt moved at nearly twice his speed, but it was still in the distance. Hopefully, he would be able to reach MacArthur before it did.

His mind ran to every possibility, but none stood out to him. Unless the Shadow Lords had a Wizard under the wraps for quite some time, as the lightning technique being used was powerful, no one came to mind. Bolten, Blaze, MacArthur, and Frederick himself were the only four. That was how had it worked for years, just the four of them training in secret.

Apparently, until now.

He arrived shortly, hands already growing warm. The great reserved legion of the Topians flooded the Capitol Streets. He maneuvered through them, occasionally yelling out that MacArthur was in danger. Not many of the soldiers took him quite seriously, as many of the captains ordered their troops to stay put.

MacArthur stood at the steps of the capitol, hands behind his back in a professional standpoint. Cortex, as planned, was downstairs, guarding the President. The other two guards were still with MacArthur, also as planned.

Frederick hurried to them, disregarding any shouts from the men who did not recognize him. MacArthur held back the guards as Frederick approached, noticing the lightning at the same time.

As Frederick was within reach of the front doors, the lightning struck. It exploded in a great shockwave, knocking everyone to the floor in a mile radius. Platoon after platoon fell to their knees, and Frederick was even thrown on his back. An instinctive brace scraped up his arm, but there was no time to acknowledge it.

MacArthur was the only one not to fall. His guards had been thrown sideways and were not making an attempt at getting back up. He looked down upon them disappointingly and frowned.

Frederick watched as the bolt turned human, solidifying into someone he hadn't seen for years. An old classmate: *Dynai Riddenwood.*

The coconut-brown skinned girl, now bristling with electric energy, glanced back at Frederick. She glared, irises a beautiful yellow, and turned back to MacArthur. Her hand shot out, pointing.

"MACARTHUR!" she bellowed. "YOUR CROWN IS MINE!"

Timothy MacArthur threw off his facade, needing it no more. He stepped forward, elongated strides of an experienced fighter. His blond hair turned electric gold, his great crown forming atop. His suit burned away, a red cape billowing behind him and silver armor running underneath.

Dynai yelled out in a burst of rage, her hands positioning themselves. She raised her back arm, ran it just below her chest, and shot it forward. Her back leg came up until she was horizontal.

Electric Fire, Frederick recognized. A great burst of flame, accompanied by flashes of lightning, blasted from Dynai's hand. MacArthur put his own hands out, fingers extended, and allowed the electric fire to flow into him. Static electricity rippled up his arms. Bringing them over his head, he redirected it back at Dynai.

Frederick struggled to his feet as the bolts crashed just behind Dynai, who had scurried out of the way. He backed off as Dynai sprinted to MacArthur's left, bounding into the air. Her entire body bristled with electricity as she let down a hailstorm of flame. MacArthur waved away the blaze with a simple hand and returned a bolt of his own.

Meanwhile, as they raged back and forth, the Topians had begun to rise to their feet again. None had seemed to be actually injured, only stunned by the blast. As their captains regained control, the back line made an agreement. The captains yelled out in command, and the back line charged Dynai.

The first attackers were quickly decimated. MacArthur shot three great bolts of flame at Dynai, but to his dismay and utter shock, she deflected them into the oncoming soldiers. All were knocked down swiftly.

With each great strike, they dealt back and forth to one another, red and yellow lit up the night, and in the distance, everyone could see it.

Frederick ducked away, watching as Dynai easily handled herself against MacArthur and the soldiers. She alternated strikes, never letting the soldiers come within range of attack. If they ever began crowding, she dropped and swept the area around her with one leg, creating an uproar of flame from the ground.

But as she did, she never appeared to begin tiring. More and more soldiers fell back, but she did not yield. Even so, MacArthur stayed on his feet, a distracted Dynai never catching him off guard. Here, she was occupied, but it still wasn't enough.

Frederick glanced down at his own hands, still glowing bright red. He closed his eyes and snapped his right-hand fingers. A spark lit in his palm, blossoming into a small blaze rather quickly. He held up his other hand and concentrated. He imagined the flame leaping from one hand to the other, and as his eyes opened slowly, that became a reality.

Dynai can't handle too many distractions. I have to do this before the soldiers fall.

288

He stepped from his covering place, hands burning. A little bit of his mind yelled for him to go back, to not get himself involved in this. But deep down, he knew, that once Dynai was done with MacArthur, he would be next. Then Bolten, Blaze, and anyone else who stood in her way.

He ran forward and released four consecutive strings of fire. With each blast, he snapped his leg upward, colliding it with his corresponding palm.

"Flame Burst!"

The strings all rushed toward Dynai, little zips slightly slower than the electric fire. She blocked three simultaneously, an unconscious move, believing it to come from MacArthur. However, she turned her back as the fourth trailed, moving to strike a group of soldiers close by. The flame drove itself into her back, a scalding burst of energy. For a moment, her body tensed up, and she collapsed to the floor, wincing.

Frederick sprinted forth, the soldiers surprised, but elated.

"Don't just stand there!" he exclaimed. "Arrest her!"

A few soldiers hesitantly ran to the fallen Dynai, who was still struggling to get up. The soldiers forcefully bounded her with rope, minimal restraint, but seemingly enough. Even so, MacArthur ordered the soldiers to leave her on the ground. They did, and both he and Frederick approached.

Frederick got there first. "You traitorous Academy Warrior! All this time, you've been plotting to take the crown? How'd you even know about the Wizards?! We've been in hiding for nearly a decade!" He lit with rage, hands heating up as well as his face. Dynai did not smile, nor laugh. She appeared to be no madwoman, but sensible in a different way. A deep recognition showed on her face as she watched Frederick.

Then Frederick remembered: Dynai and Rachel had been best friends during academy days. Of course, Frederick had known the traitor as well, but not nearly to the extent of his sister. Now, as they looked so similar, it was obvious Dynai was thinking of Rachel Donovan.

"Don't insult me, *Donovan*," she spat, words venomous. "You're less worthy of the crown than I am."

Frederick gritted his teeth, glaring. "That crown is MacArthur's! Not yours, not mine. It belongs to him, to him-" he paused, seeing the King himself shaking his head slowly. "What?"

"Any challenge must be accepted. If it is not, surrender is the only other option."

Frederick glanced at the floor, overthinking it. MacArthur now seemed antagonistic as much as Dynai, as if this was supposed to happen, fate as it was. Still, his confidence in the King was no less than before, and he was still certain that victory was inevitable.

"Stay out of this," Dynai said, but it could've been a sly taunt with the way she spoke. MacArthur nodded again, which Frederick took as a slight betrayal. He turned away, beginning to storm off, when a flurry occurred behind him.

Dynai slipped through her ropes with the aid of a small dagger that had been hidden up her sleeve. As they unraveled around her, the dagger released from her hand. It spun at Frederick's back, but it did not hit him.

For when Frederick turned, he gasped. His eyes widened as he rushed to catch the falling MacArthur before him, the dagger stuck in the King's chest. Frederick tried to call out for help with the soldiers, but it was too late.

Instead, he watched helplessly as the crown atop MacArthur's head slowly dissolved, gold fading into the air. Dynai stood, triumphant. She laughed greatly, and slowly rose her hands to the sides of her head.

Frederick wanted so desperately to kill her now. He brought his hands up from MacArthur's dying body and felt the flame arise within.

His palm bristled with energy, but as he reached out to attack, nothing happened. Weakness and bitter defeat clouded his concentration, and his hope faded. He could only watch.

The crown, gold particles glimmering through the air, congregated above Dynai's dark hair. Between her rising hands and topping her grand smile, the particles solidified. The great crown formed, jewels and all.

"I...," she said, fascinated with this feeling. "Am the Queen."

37

Ethan appeared in a black flash, nearly invisible to the night. He strode across the street, carelessly looking forward. The buildings on either side of him held desolate auras, some abandoned, some as hideouts. Anarchists had overrun every square inch of Upper Mysti, leaving no survivors in their wake. Even those who were running for their lives had been struck down, all by Noah's orders.

Ethan reached the makeshift Anarchist base, a few overturned cars blocking the roads to form a circle. In the middle there sparked a fire out of a trash can, leaving the smell of burning rubbish. No one cared, however, as every Anarchist had his or her nose covered. About twenty of them crowded the base.

The young Shadow Lord entered through the side, the Anarchists beside him nodding. He walked up to the fire and called for attention.

"Grinks!" he yelled, a fat man turning around, startled. The rotund general was one of the only without a mask, but the smell didn't seem to bother him. In fact, he was most certainly drunk, and began to saunter his way over to Ethan.

"Hey there, junior," Grinks said, taking a swig of the bottle in his left hand. He adjusted the general's cap atop his head and looked to Ethan.

Ethan sighed, debating on correcting the man, but knew it would be pointless. At this stage, almost nothing he could say would impact him. It would go in one ear, and out the other.

"How do we plan on capturing the Sisterhood leader?" he demanded, hoping this question would make it through Grinks's muffled head. The question did appear to stump him at first, but then he snapped to life.

"Ay, right, right," the general muttered. He stumbled his way over to one of the overturned cars and gestured to a small figure. Ethan followed him, curious, and upon seeing who the figure was, he knew the plan would be foolproof.

Rosemary sat, bound to the point where she could not move, tape over her mouth as well. Her eyes were not blindfolded, so they glanced around worriedly. Upon seeing Ethan, they froze with fear.

292

"Well done," Ethan said, almost having a tough time believing it. "She has a dirty trick of being in more places at once. Did you check for that?"

Grinks paused, puzzled again. A slight delay previewed his answer, but he nodded positively. "Yeah, I believe so. A-actually, A'im nearly certain." He looked at Rosemary for a bit longer, then placed a grubby hand on her head. "Yep, that's her alright."

"The leader is on her way here?" Ethan asked. "She knows where the girl is?"

Grinks nodded. "Yep."

"And we have men stationed every which way?"

"Sounds 'bout right."

"And...one more thing," Ethan said, a little quieter. He whispered something quick into Grinks's ear, Rosemary unable to hear it at all. Grinks smiled widely, tossing up his drink after hearing it.

"Brilliant! Jonah chose right!" He bellowed with laughter, polishing off whatever was in his bottle. Ethan could not resist at least a smirk, half because of Grinks calling Noah, *Jonah*. This brought a little lightheartedness to Ethan's mind, allowing him to relax a little as if this was all a joke.

Grinks waddled off, saying he was going to rally everyone up. He grabbed another drink on the way, nearly dropping it as he did. Ethan, meanwhile, turned back to Rosemary.

They met eyes, and while Rosemary's were only filled with fear, Ethan's were filled with long-lasting guilt. A new question posed him, one that he had been pushing back for the longest time. He knew, that now was the time for it all to end, for the mission, Michael, even Kiran to end. Only he would remain, and for now, would that question remain as well.

Can I do this?

In Upper Mysti, Anarchists lined the rooftops. They crowded building floors, huddled behind doorways, and crouched in alleys. Their weapons were out, glistening silver in the night. Predators, awaiting one single prey.

And so Ethan waited, pacing back and forth in front of Rosemary, pulling up every memory on Celestia. Her fighting techniques, her stature, her every way of thinking. He tried to nearly become her for a moment, something that Noah had taught him to do years ago. To understand your enemy would be to defeat them.

Of course, he hadn't been there to meet Celestia originally. Kiran would be the one holding that knowledge, but there was no time now. At first, she had seemed brooding and distant, and she still seemed to be. After a while, however, Ethan had noticed Celestia's open attachments to Rosemary and then Zoey. A caring that she did not initially portray, something new to her cold disposition.

There was that moment on The Unknown, where Celestia was brutally betrayed by Zoey. Celestia had somehow survived, and Ethan could not explain it. Some magic seemed to be at play, for she could not have lived through the injury any other way. It was if the injury had merely never happened.

His mind turned to the more recent news. Celestia had shown no weakness so far against any Anarchist soldier, cutting down all in her path. She was a bull on a rampage throughout Upper Mysti, and a trap might be the only way of stopping her at all.

Then, there was her sword. The Tritonyx, the bullet deflector, now the Anarchist destroyer. The great blade that could not be outmatched by any Anarchists'.

But mine...even with her skill, I can defeat her in a duel. The power of the Shadow Sword is still unknown to her, and it will be her doom.

Lightning lit up the sky nearby, but Ethan paid it no attention. He knew it was only Dynai, on her way to destroy Timothy MacArthur. If she proved successful, the battle would soon be over.

In the corner of his eye, Ethan then caught the flash of light. It was surely not the lightning, too blinding to be so. This light was pure white, devoid of any colors. It was the light of Celestia, certainly.

He paused, waiting for it again. Where it had been, only the rooftops served as a clue. Anarchists were already stationed up there and would handle the threat at a moment's notice.

Ethan fully turned to watch, and his suspicions were confirmed. Celestia Triton's great blonde hair shone brilliantly even in the dark of night, her mind set on rescuing Rosemary, and that only.

Ethan smiled nervously.

She's close. So, so, close. If I can just get to her soon enough, everything will be okay.

Celestia interrupted her constant thoughts to knock an Anarchist sideways with her blade. She continued to sprint forth on the dark rooftops but allowed herself to light the way. A thin bubble of glowing energy surrounded her, but it had no purpose other than for visibility. However, if an Anarchist caught her off guard, she could harden it and deflect the blow.

She cut down Anarchist after Anarchist that jumped at her from hidden points, never stopping. Hardly did any of them pose a threat to her own life, but all did to Rosemary. Celestia knew that the young girl could be slowly dying at this moment. Wherever she was, it wasn't good.

Finally, a fire started to come in view. It smelled now of burning rubber, and Celestia had the urge to clutch her stomach. She nearly fell off the side of one of the buildings, and moved to pinch her nose instead. Fighting one-handed would be a challenge, but it was the lesser evil.

As her blade clashed with more Anarchist weapons, she kept a slight focus on the fire. Around it lay overturned cars and rubble from buildings, serving as a sort of shield. After one more Anarchist was launched off, Celestia herself leaped.

The building was only two story, so she landed smoothly. She rolled out of the action and quickly started to make her way to the burning circle. Jumping up onto one of the cars, she knew Rosemary had to be close by.

To her relief, the young girl sat directly below her, still bound. She moved to jump down, but paused. There were still Anarchists about.

A figure walked into the circle, darkness following them. The fire cast an undertone on the red hair of Ethan Catanzaro, and his murderous eyes.

"Ethan!" Celestia exclaimed. "Quick! Help guard me while I free Rosemary!" She looked at him expectantly, a little unsettled by his watchful gaze.

"That...is something I cannot do," he responded, words icy. With each word he hurt inside, watching as Celestia came to a realization. He drew his sword slowly, but this time, it lit with black fire. Dark, burning intentions on the blade, prepared to strike down any light.

"A Shadow Sword..." Celestia muttered. "How long?" she demanded. "How long have you been with them?" Her eyes turned dark. "*How long?!*"

"Always," Ethan said, breathing heavily. "From the very start."

He did not await Celestia's reaction. "*PAIN!*" he yelled, hand outstretched. Celestia was blasted from the top of the car and tumbled down the street. Her sword flew out, stabbing itself into a lamppost not too far away.

Rosemary screamed beneath the tape as Ethan turned to her. She struggled against the bonds, but they were too tight for any greater movement. He hefted his blade and began to pray.

Summonus, summonus, blasphemous, blasphemous.

Then, with one simple strike, he drove the blade into Rosemary's chest. They both yelled out in pain, Ethan from an influx greater than he could understand, Rosemary from a loss of power. The Shadow Sword exploded, darkness flooding everything in the area around them. Sound turned to muffled noise, the light dimmed until it was hardly there. Everything was covered, still as night.

Tears poured from Rosemary's eyes, and soon they fell from Ethan's. The redheaded boy gripped the blade until his knuckles turned white, and he clenched his jaw tighter than ever. His eyelids fell heavy, and he soon could not keep them open. Gravity pressed down from every angle onto him, forcing him to kneel.

He bowed low, both hands gripping his blade for support. He trembled, feeling a cold, dark impulse start to rush through.

And the weight of the world fell onto him.

38

The trashcan fire exploded, a pillar erupting into the air. It reached high into the sky, a terrifying sight to all. A yellow glow enveloped the city.

Kiran looked up to it with worry, the unnatural essence of it a concerning sight. He, Jeremy, and Sergio had taken advantage of a short pause in the battle, as the Anarchists finally began to draw back. Their numbers were dwindling, fleeing as the Bulls-Eye Brotherhood littered the battlefield with arrows from the rooftops. With every archer, there was a stationed Academy Warrior, aside from Captain Parker himself.

"I'll be fine," he had insisted.

Kiran now watched as the blaze in the sky died off, but smoke still drifted through the night. It had come from over in Upper Mysti, where Celestia was stationed. For a moment, he made the connection she could be responsible but dismissed it as intentional.

He turned to Jeremy. "Any reports from MacArthur?"

The Academy Warrior glanced at his wrist and was only granted a black screen. A puzzled look crossed his face. "Nothing," he said, and tapped the screen twice. It remained black. "Wait a minute..."

He glanced toward Sergio, who was giving orders to a few rookies. "Serge! Check your communications!"

Sergio looked back, pausing for one final order. The rookies turned and hustled off to their posts. He looked to his wrist, and narrowed his eyes when his watch did not light up. There was no response at all, not even a low battery sign. He shook it violently and cursed when nothing happened at all.

He shook his head to Jeremy. Jeremy looked to the ground, contemplating. He glanced at Kiran sideways, and they met eyes solemnly.

"All communications are down," they aid in unison. Kiran turned instantly, looking to one of the buildings close by. He cupped his hands around his mouth and began to yell.

"PARKER!" he exclaimed. The Brotherhood leader heard him, but only due to archer's instinct. He looked down, and seeing Kiran wave him over, leaped from the rooftop. He gracefully shot more ropes from his wrists, and swung right next to the Academy Warriors. His purple bow was nowhere in sight, but like the rest of the brothers, could be conjured in an instant.

"What's the issue?" he asked. "Do we need to press further?"

"Not yet. Have your men keep watch over the city, but there's a more pressing matter."

Parker raised an eyebrow expectantly.

"All of our communication lines are down," Kiran said. "No contact with MacArthur, and no news across from Mysti district."

"I can check out the deal with MacArthur. Is Mysti in need of attention?"

"That's for you to investigate."

"Alright then. I'll give the order."

He turned and quickly launched a grappling hook into the building beside him. He zipped up to the roof and signaled to the brother a few rooftops down from him. He then bounded off toward the capital, a messenger in the night.

Celestia crawled her way forward, fingers clutching to every groove she could find in the broken street. A layer of soot marked the side of her face, scrapes surrounding it. Her blonde hair did not shine as it had before, darkened by not only dirt, but pain. A dark cloud surrounded her, unlike anything she had ever felt.

Whatever Ethan had hit her with, it was energy-draining. Her muscles had collapsed with agony, frozen and only so much as spastic. Just some last remaining spark of willpower forced her along.

She listened to the chaos around her, some bitter monster Ethan had created. Spite reigned within her toward the boy, but in pure honesty, she was not surprised. If Michael had not seen it himself, Celestia would be shocked purely at that. Now, as she held it in her mind, she wondered how she had not seen it sooner. Every word the young boy had said was filled with regret and hurt, qualities only the Shadows would exploit.

Oh, if Elara could see this now.

And if the pure thought inspired her, she threw a final hand out for her blade, and sighed of relief when she felt the soft grip. A comfort rushed through her as she brought The Tritonyx close.

"Get up, Celestia," a voice ordered. Celestia didn't have to look to know it was Ethan's. She slowly pushed herself up, a newfound strength with the magic of The Tritonyx flowing through her. She rose to full height, but her energy was not completely replenished.

She thrust the Tritonyx out with one hand, pointing it directly at

Ethan's face. "Betrayer, I will destroy you." Her voice was low.

Ethan looked to his Shadow Sword fatefully and affirmed his grip. "You know you can't. You've seen what I can do."

Celestia smiled nervously. "Maybe, but I don't care." Her eyes flared, and she ran to attack.

Ethan darted forward, his blade striking up in an instant. Celestia smacked it down, but immediately felt a vibration run through her. Her heart skipped a beat, and everything trembled. Soon, it went away, only just in time for the next strike.

Ethan threw his hilt into the side of Celestia's head, sending her staggering sideways. It hurt him just as much, but he did not show it. Celestia's vision blacked out for a split second and returned with stars.

Their blades then clashed, interlocking. Celestia's raw strength would've won any other day, but Ethan had the upper hand. His reborn sword, the shadows licking out like tentacles, began to consume The Tritonyx. It wrapped itself around, the two blades becoming one.

Celestia grunted and kicked with all her force. Ethan was thrown off, the blades tearing apart. Celestia charged forward, aiming for Ethan's sword hand, but he evaded just in time. They parried back and forth a few more times, before Ethan gained an opening again. He threw his hand forward, sword by to protect.

"*Shadow Hand!*" he exclaimed. A dark, glowing set of claws lunged out from his palm, grasping onto Celestia's right leg. She made an attempt to sever it, but Ethan pulled violently. Celestia was slammed to the ground, the wind leaving her immediately. A pathetic gasp escaped her, and before she knew it, Ethan was standing before her.

"R-rosemary..." Celestia managed. "W-what did you do to her?" Her voice was weaker than a whisper, hardly intelligible. Ethan knew what she was asking, anyhow.

"I'm sorry," he responded, and it was genuine. Killing one of his companions hadn't been fun, more or less easy. And now, he soon would be forced to do it again.

Celestia exploded with rage and used more of her energy reserve to roll backward. She sprung up from the ground and raised her sword high.

"I'm going to cut you down, you bloody murderer!" she exclaimed. She charged forward, determined. "I'm going to slice clean through that grin of yours, I'll-"

Her last breath escaped her, and she found talking no more among her abilities. Every aspect of her grew weak, and her eyes steadily trailed down. As she saw the darkened Ethan, his head low, she felt the urge to attack again.

But she could not move.

Her hands fell limp, arms becoming mere noodles attached to her body. The Tritonyx clanged to the floor, sparks flying just from its contact.

Celestia fell to her knees, and as her hazel eyes came down to her chest, she already knew what would await them.

Ethan's blade, deeply embedded within, was taking her very life force. There was nothing she could do, absolutely nothing. Hope, it was gone. Promise, broken. Will, long lost. Nothing...nothing left at all.

And slowly, she evaporated into black dust as Rosemary had, ashes in the air. They soon fused back together, but now attached to Ethan's Shadow Sword. The redheaded boy smiled weakly, knowing the battle was won here. The war was not, of course, but this very battle, with possibly the most threatening member of Michael's party, was won.

TAKE THE SWORD, a voice beckoned. IT IS A TROPHY.

Ethan walked over to the excellent blade and picked it up swiftly. He held it in his left hand, Shadow Sword in the right, and raised them both.

Three down, one to go.

"Kiran..." he muttered. A slight laugh escaped him, followed by another. And another, and another, and another.
Soon, he could not stop, and his insane laughter echoed into the night.

39

Frederick's lack of energy merely lasted for a few seconds longer.

"YOU MURDEROUS REBEL!" he screamed, sending wave after wave of fire toward the smiling Dynai Riddenwood.

The Queen now hovered just over the ground, her golden crown bristling with electricity. Beneath her feet roared white-hot flames, as if she was a rocket lifting off. Her eyes had turned electron-yellow as MacArthur's used to be, a single black lightning bolt running through the center.

She dismissed Fredrick's every attack easily, a single wave dispersing the blazes. He palm seemed immune to any heat that touched it. But even so, Frederick pressed on. With each attack he grunted, throwing pure force each time. His flames grew sloppy, but every time he ceased to attack, MacArthur flashed through his mind.

The Topian Soldiers kept their distance, seeing this was no longer their fight. A few had come to take the general away, even though he was beyond saving. None now chanced the possibility of Dynai turning on them. The Anarchists were enough.

Dynai's smiled wavered as Frederick continued to press on. "You are no more than a pest, Donovan! Mere sparks you throw at me! Your king is dead, I am now your ruler! I hold the crown over all Wizards! MacArthur has passed his rule to me!"

Frederick's nostrils flared as a dragon's would. He stepped back with one leg, never ceasing to glare at Dynai, and brought his arms up to the side. Slowly, as Dynai began to process what he was performing, it was too late.

Frederick drew his right arm across his stomach in an instant, swinging up his back leg and shooting himself onto his other. Fire built up and rocketed out of him with enormous force, taking his energy and turning it into electricity.

"*ELECTRIC FIRE!*" he screamed, and the great blaze released within him. It barreled into Dynai with force, but it dissipated as quickly as it had been sent. She brushed the remaining bits of static electricity from her clothes and narrowed her eyes. Frederick held back, eyes widened in shock.

It did nothing at all? That was my full force, there's nothing left in me. He even went to doubt the possibility of him performing electric fire again. He felt drained, void of more energy inside him.

"You foolish Wizard. You're a disgrace to your kind, and to all your kind in the universe. I am the supreme, the QUEEN! Even

304

though our numbers are low in this world, you are alone in your efforts. Even Bolten and Blaze will bow down-"

"We will not!" Bolten announced, stepping from the crowd of Topians. They backed away from him, forming a circle. His fingers bristled, and he prepared to strike. Even before he could, however, Blaze threw himself forward.

He charged through the crowd and threw his arms forward in rapid succession. Five bolts of lightning zipped through the air, all catching Dynai off guard. Several burn marks seared her new golden cape, but she retaliated nonetheless. Roaring electric fire smoked the ground beside Blaze, who had already evaded.

Bolten turned to attack from behind, sending two swift bolts into Dynai's side. She was stunned, a simple zap, but it left time open for Blaze to strike.

He ran up from behind, reared his fist back, and punched. As he did, his fist engulfed with flame, a red-hot brick smashing into Dynai's back. She yelled out and fell to her hands and knees. As she scrambled forward, Bolten and Blaze slowly began to surround her.

Bolten glanced over to Frederick, who stood, stunned. "Frederick! Help us out! This was the fight you started!" He kept his hands raised in a defensive posture, despite Dynai's apparent weakness.

Frederick snapped into focus and ran up beside Blaze. Blaze motioned to strike again, but this time, Frederick held him back.

"No," he said, looking to Dynai. She watched as the hurt in his eyes took form, and smiled oddly. His eyes turned dark and grim. "Let's make her suffer."

Dynai's smile turned weak, and she turned away to escape. The three Wizards slowly made their way to encircle her, almost reaching the Capitol's front steps.

"I would warn against that," Bolten cautioned. "The longer we wait, the more time she has to think."

Blaze growled. "He's right, Frederick. We should kill her now."

It felt a little odd to Frederick, as they seemed to refer to him as a superior, despite disagreeing. He thought it to make sense after a moment, however. This was his fight. MacArthur had died to protect him. It was only right that he take the mantle.

"No," he said gravely. "We burn her to death."

Bolten and Blaze both objected simultaneously, but Blaze backed off to let Bolten speak. The Wizard approached cautiously, holding a hand out.

"Frederick, we need to get rid of her as soon as possible," he spoke like a trainer calming an animal on the verge of rabidness. Blaze, meanwhile, kept his sights on Dynai, who now awaited them, seemingly too weak to even crawl. She remained smiling, however, watching Frederick and Bolten go back and forth on what to do.

"Guys," Blaze said. There was no response, so he yelled louder. "Guys!" Bolten and Frederick snapped to attention, and both raised their hands in fighting position. Dynai had started laughing, and it soon turned into a cackle.

"What are you doing?" Frederick demanded. Bolten urged him to make a decision, but he was ignored.

The smell of smoke slowly drifted into the air, much stronger than it was usually. Frederick's flames almost always left behind residue, but never to this extent. Now, it started to take form, a fog looming all around them.

"She's bristling!" Bolten yelled, his hands igniting. As he announced it, the sparks around Dynai grew stronger, becoming little embers of flame. Some shone blue, others an electric yellow.

Frederick's eyes narrowed as two embers flashed purple. He realized that she was building up energy for something great...and if they waited much longer, there would be no option. He was convinced.

"Okay, we go with your plan!" he yielded. Bolten glanced back and nodded. "On three!"

"Fools!" Dynai yelled, voice hoarse. "The three of you killing me-"

"One!"

"-at the same time-"

"Two!"

"-will send the crown to DRACO!"

Frederick lost his flow. The electric fire that was building up, his energy for the executing blow, failed. "STOP!" he yelled, but it was too late. Bolten and Blaze released their combined electric fires.

Red flame mixed with yellow electricity, engulfing Dynai. She seized up, but only in dramatic fashion. The fire left burns scattered across her body. She twitched as searing as searing flame drove into her, turning her dark flesh red. The fire finally dispersed, and Frederick watched, hopeful.

She was, unfortunately, very much alive. Without Fredrick's assistance, the killing blow was no more than a harming one. Dynai's worn face managed an eerie smile, and she spoke two words:

"Too late."

Then, from the sky, there swooped a beast of enormous size. Every Topian soldier cowered at the sight of it, but the three Wizards stood their ground. Frederick watched in amazement as the beast, a red, glowing string at first, descended upon them. It solidified, and darted to the weakened Dynai.

The beast curled around her several times, its long, snake-like body scaly and shining red. It's enormous head loomed high, disapproving eyes looking down upon Frederick, Bolten, and Blaze. It had glowing blue irises the size of dinner plates, smoothly shifting from the three Wizards until finally settling on Frederick in the center.

Long, white whiskers rippled in the wind from the beast's face, little albino noodles about. Frederick realized they were actually more like stingers, that of a jellyfish. Capable of paralyzing in an instant.

"The Cosmic Dragon," he muttered, staring up.

"*A* Cosmic Dragon," Bolten corrected. "There's three. This one before us is the red one, *Aka*. Lord...I'd never think to see it in person! It's only a part of a trinity, however. The others must be even more astonishing!"

Even so, to Frederick, this one seemed impressive enough. Dynai disappeared within its grasp, and it threatened to take off. Frederick motioned to stop it but knew he would stand no chance at all. Attacking a dragon of that power would be suicidal, so he let it be. They would be forced to take the crown another time.

The dragon, Aka, lifted off, red wings flapping powerfully. Wind smashed the ground, and no one dared to step beneath. With a wingspan of nearly 50 feet, the beast spiraled into the air, disappearing with a flash.

Frederick glanced at the burned-out hole in the ground, where Dynai had been, and frowned. Not much left to do. He turned to Bolten, still processing what had happened, and sighed angrily.

"I have to get to Kiran. We need the appropriate chain of

command to activate. The general is dead, so a commander must rise in the ranks. And if that may be me, I will assume MacArthur's position."

"Frederick is on his way here," Parker said, calling back his ropes. They snapped at his wrists, but he showed no reaction to it. Worry had already taken hold of his expression, and his mind was completely full.

"We'll be ready for him," Kiran responded, nodding. "It looks like the Anarchists are starting to fall back. Those rebels have lost too many. Our numbers are decreasing as well, but we'll make do. We've done our part."

Parker glanced at the floor, some struggle apparent on him. Kiran noticed this and questioned it.

"You alright? We'll need support when we push the Anarchists back to Hookhorse and Mysti."

"My brothers and I are leaving."

Kiran met his gaze and frowned. "What?"

"When we agreed to fight with you, we didn't expect dragons."

Kiran raised an eyebrow. *Was that what the lightning was?*

"And, we did not expect Wizards," Parker continued. "This fight is beyond what we stand for. We have done what we can against the Anarchists, but I will not die to a Wizard.

"If I were you, I'd pick my allies to be those who I actually know. Based off what I've seen, you don't even know who Frederick Donovan actually is. And, you didn't know who MacArthur was, either."

"I don't understand, Parker."

"Ask Frederick. I'm leaving."

Before Kiran could respond, Parker sent his grappling hooks into two nearby buildings. He swung away, into the cold morning, and disappeared shortly after. The rest of the archers soon vanished as well.

Kiran glanced worriedly to the other Academy Warriors, who all stood to block Diamond Street. The Anarchists had drawn back quite a while ago, but since Jeremy and Sergio had taken control of Bolten and Blaze's forces, the cloaked rebels still pressed elsewhere. The communications were still down across Topia, so he hadn't heard from Ethan or Celestia. He assured himself all was well.

As he awaited Frederick's arrival, he watched the Academy Warriors tend to one another. While most guarded, the injured and a few others were set aside. They helped heal wounds, inspire one another, and care. It was beautiful, seeing the Academy generations mix, members of his class and others being partners out on the battlefield. Each and every Academy Warrior was still just a human, and that was an advantage. The Anarchists were alien, inhuman and robotic.

But, even so, Kiran saw hurt in many of the young Warriors' eyes. Some of their friends had died on this day, and there was no time for proper burials. Later, when there was time, perhaps they would. Some, though, would never be found.

None will, if we don't succeed.

A few minutes passed before Frederick arrived. The Donovan Twin hurried up, breaths short and fast. His green shirt was riddled with burn holes, and an undying ember was dwindling in the brown curls of his hair.

310

"MacArthur's dead," he said bluntly. "Someone else needs to take command."

Kiran paused before answering, still processing the first two words. It was almost if he didn't hear Frederick clearly, as the idea seemed so unreal. And the way Frederick said it so lightly, it was almost if he didn't care.

"How?" Kiran asked, voice low.

Frederick glanced away. "I can't really explain." He assumed a sarcastic smile.

Kiran leaned in close, holding Frederick's gaze. "The general's dead, so you say. I need to know how." What Parker had said kept replaying in his mind, and now he knew Frederick was lying to him. *MacArthur wasn't who you thought he was.*

Frederick hesitated, but seeing there was no one else close enough to hear, he went ahead.

"Back during the Academy days, you remember when Leo was recruited by MacArthur?

"Yeah."

"So was I. While Leo, however, was recruited for business and perhaps a spot in the army, I was not." He paused, taking a deep breath. *Half the Topian Army already knows. What's one more person?*

"Timothy revealed himself to be the legendary Wizard King, the one we were taught about scarcely. It was honestly a little anticlimactic, seeing as the King was shown to be nearly a god. It was said he had power like no other, but even today I learned that wasn't true. He took me on as an apprentice and trained me in the ways of the Wizards. He told me, that if the crown were ever in danger, I would help him protect it."

"And did you?"

"One of our own, Dynai Riddenwood, revealed herself to be a challenger for the throne. I ran back to help, and just as we were arriving-"

"We?"

"Bolten and Blaze are Wizards as well. They've always been, long before I. Posed as soldiers in the army. We ran to protect MacArthur, but I was far ahead of them. MacArthur and I defeated Dynai, but..."

He envisioned the scene in his head for a brutal moment, but pushed it away. "She went for me with a dagger, and MacArthur jumped in the way. Just a trick, playing on his emotions."

"He sacrificed himself for you."

Frederick nodded silently and brushed a little bit of ash from his forehead. The black dust smeared into his hair, a streak of black in brown.

"It better be worth it," Kiran muttered, looking out toward the lined Academy Warriors. He turned back to Frederick, and with finality, he said: "Tell Bolten and Blaze to push forward. I'm in charge now, and we're taking hold of the lower districts. Bring Sergio and Jeremy back here. They're taking care of the Academy Students."

"What about you?"

Kiran looked up to the dawning sky, warm light beginning to rise. The Unknown still loomed above The Academy, threateningly poised for attack. Even so, it had been lying dormant for the entire battle, with no sign of any activity within. Kiran knew, however, that the Anarchist leaders would be inside.

"I'm going to the source," he said. "We've lost too much. It's time for this all to be put to rest, for it to end. I will fight my hardest in there, and bring down the Shadow Lord who has disguised himself so far." *And I'll avenge Zoey, I guess,* he added in his mind. *Least I can do.*

Frederick paused before nodding solemnly, and started to turn away. Kiran stopped him.

"One more thing," the Academy Warrior said. "Where is Dynai now?"

"Dynai was rescued by the Cosmic Dragon...Aka, I believe it was. We didn't get the chance to finish her off." In his own, he knew that was a lie, but couldn't face it now. He would need a little more time to mourn first.

"Hm."

Frederick walked off, hoping to catch Bolten and Blaze on their ways to the warfront. Kiran kept his gaze on The Unknown, and prepared himself. He knew that only he could afford to enter the great ship, but it would be a test like no other. Inside were beings he hadn't even met, but he knew Michael would be with him.

Some tiny bit of him just knew. It knew that no matter the task Kiran faced in the darkness, Michael would help him shine the light.

As for Celestia, Rosemary, and Ethan, Kiran hoped they would join him. He had no time to find any of them and notify each one of them, however. The only thing he could wish for would be that they notice The Unknown lowering its hatch.

They'll welcome me with open arms, he thought. *It's a risk, but I'll offer myself up on a silver platter, and they'll be forced to take me in. The only problem is getting to the leader. The one who killed Zoey is in there.*

I'll find him.

40

Ethan's eyes widened as he saw the view below him. The Academy stood tall, but The Unknown was very high up. The dark floors of the main hall had rippled apart, to reveal the city underneath. Down south he could see Desertia, which was one of the only districts mostly intact. There had only been slight opposition to the Anarchist takeover there, and while pillaging and looting were necessary, no combat was.

The Academy sat right on the border of Desertia and Lanon, but it blended in with the former. Ethan had sent Anarchists to occupy it, but the Topian armies were beginning to approach. All seemed to be now heading in favor of Topia. Even despite the fall of MacArthur, the Academy Warriors remained strong.

Then why the hell is Kiran doing that?!

Kiran stood on top of The Academy, waving his arms. He looked like he was preparing The Unknown for landing.

"HOW CONVENIENT," a voice boomed, deep from the halls. "YOU SHOULD BE GLAD, ETHAN."

"I should be," he agreed, still watching as Kiran waved his arms. "I should be."

"YOU CAN END IT HERE."

Ethan smiled weakly. He unsheathed his sword and looked unnervingly at the blade. His old one shattering flashed through his mind and knew Kiran could easily outduel him. *He has a strange new weapon as well, so I hear.*

"He's stronger than the others," he said.

"BUT HE'S FIGHTING IN *OUR* SHIP NOW. YOU CAN USE THE PHYSICAL DISTORTION ANOMALY. IT IS LEVEL NINE, BUT IT WILL DRAIN YOUR POWER, HOWEVER."

"Will I survive?"

"USE THE SACRIFICES YOU HAVE PREPARED IN YOUR SHADOW SWORD. BOTH SHOULD BE SUFFICIENT IN ENERGY."

Ethan glanced at his sword again and imagined the two souls within, swirling. Celestia and Rosemary. Both were sources of immense power, but he could not bring himself to use them lightly. A part of him was still attached to them, merely out of pity now. He had killed them, and they would not go to waste.

That's the best I'll do for them.

He turned and commanded a few of the Anarchists on standby. They rushed to the walls, and two on either side placed their hands firmly against the dark marble. A third motioned to activate the containment field, but Ethan interrupted.

"No," he said. "Beam him up as he is."

The Anarchists hesitated, unsure.

"And once you've started the sequence, leave this room! Do not reenter!"

He watched as the ship rumbled slightly, and Kiran began to portal up. The Anarchists rushed out hastily as Ethan had commanded them to, shutting the large oak doors behind them. Twenty seconds later, Kiran appeared out of nowhere.

He stumbled forward and snapped into fighting position. He detached his whip from his belt and threw it open. He pointed a stiff, gloved finger at Ethan, and nodded.

"Let's go, Shadow Lord."

Ethan kept his face low, hood still covering most of his features. The Shadows cloaked him elsewhere, and he sheathed his sword. Hoping Kiran would not recognize him by stance, he took a new one. One he called, *betrayer faces the betrayed.*

"How 'bout taking off that hood before we get started? I'd like to know who I'm fighting."

There it is, the overconfident side. It's my advantage, now. In training, it was something I couldn't exploit. Whenever we sparred, I had to let him beat down on me with the blasted attitude. Now, no holding back. I can do whatever I want.

He outstretched a dark hand and prepared to mutter what "Noah" had told him. The words hesitated on his lips, ready.

Kiran narrowed his eyes. "Guess I'm going to have to tear it off."

I can't let that happen, Ethan thought. *He can't ever know.*

"*LEVEL NINE ANOMALY!*" he yelled, voice intentionally low. "*PHYSICAL DISTORTION!*"

For a moment, nothing happened. Ethan's body sapped of energy, and he nearly fell to the floor. He fought hard not to have to use his reserves, and was successful.

Then, the room around them lost all color. The walls shifted and wobbled, disorienting both Kiran and Ethan. Ethan's mind rushed to a desert, and that's what soon came into view. Above, a dark blue night sky expanded across, seemingly as real as the sky outside. Stars dotted it like tiny spots, gleaming white. The desert around them turned rust-red.

Kiran regained himself and looked around. "It's like Mars..." For a moment, he worried that he could not breathe, but found that was not the case. A cold breeze washed over him, and he readied his

316

whip again.

"Nice trick," he told Ethan. "But it won't do anything."

Ethan raised his hand again, but before he could command the environment, Kiran lunged forward. As he did, his whip trailed close behind. It flared to life, electric blue. He snapped it forth, forcing Ethan to dive out of the way.

Ethan took control of the sands and swirled his wrists toward the ground. The red dirt opened beneath Kiran's feet, and he fell through. Nearby, the sands collapsed again, and Kiran was launched through the air.

He landed on his side, but quickly got back up. "Illusion tricks! You're just a Wizard!"

Ethan opened the ground again, but this time, Kiran was too quick. He dashed forward, dodging two more of the opening holes, and attacked with his whip. He aimed for the front hand, and it wrapped around successfully.

Kiran smiled. The whip pulsed, and Ethan yelled out in pain. The part around his wrist singed his skin, leaving stinging burn marks. He lost all control for the sands and lost most feeling in his hand.

Ethan backed off, but Kiran didn't let him rest. He pulled Ethan toward him, before finally releasing. The Shadow Lord skidded to a halt and stomped one foot. The sands erupted again, this time in a wave. Kiran was thrown backward, slamming onto his back. The wind was knocked from his lungs, but he soon returned to his feet.

Ethan let his hand fall limp, and hesitated to draw his blade. The power of the illusion was beginning to fade away, as he could not keep supporting it. The shadow sword beckoned to him and forced Celestia and Rosemary into his mind. Their energy, their life force, it could all be used.

Kiran's whip caught Ethan off-guard and wrapped itself around Ethan's hood. He pulled it tight, and it pulsed. Ethan clutched at it, trying to pull it off, but was only burned. Finally, it ate away at his hood, consuming it until it eventually fell off.

He stood, face exposed. He knew there was no use covering it anymore, and awaited Kiran's reaction.

The Academy Warrior was initially elated when the hood fell, but as he recognized the face beneath, happiness dissolving. It was replaced by a not anger, nor frustration, but minor disappointment.

He laughed slightly. "Can't say I'm surprised." But even so, it was a lie. He had hoped against it, but now, here it was, before him. A wretched reality that proved to be the truth. A ton of questions swirled in his mind, but he suppressed all.

Ethan frowned, glaring. "That's it?!! That's all you have to say?! You're...not even surprised?!"

"Doesn't' matter, right?" Kiran asked rhetorically. He wanted to explode with rage, but what he wanted even more was to show Ethan no satisfaction. He would beat him at his own game. "I'm not here to fight against somebody, I'm here to fight for somebody. You've fallen into their game, the game we've been playing for weeks."

"That's all this is to you? A hellish *game*?"

Kiran's lighthearted act faded away. He glared at the traitor before him and sighed angrily. Ethan was sincere, and he decided he better be as well.

"You're a pawn," he said. Still, he did not want to give Ethan the satisfaction.

"No," Ethan muttered. "I am a king in this...*game*, so you call it."

"Just as weak, different title. We've trained so well for this, Ethan! Over four years the both of us trained to fight against the shadows!" Now, he no longer could spare Ethan his disappointment. "We have been shown a myriad of ways to resist them, but that's done nothing to you?" He frowned. "I'm almost, confused."

"You never paid attention to me," he growled. "I worked just as hard as you did, but received none of Gabriel's praise. I'm glad he's gone. The moment he left was the moment I broke free."

"Free from what?! Some jail cell you built around yourself?!"

The area around them changed from the desert; the reddish sands melted away. The sky turned from purple back to the black ceiling, and the floors matched it. They were back in The Unknown.

Seeing the inside of the room again, Kiran finally recognized it. "This is the same room..." He glanced up to Ethan and frowned. "So that's why you weren't beamed up with us! You were already here, plotting all of our deaths. Standing right where you are now." He swallowed his own bitter words and even seemed disgusted.

He looked at the center of the room, and a vivid memory crossed him. *Zoey...*

"You did worse than that," he continued. "This means...that it was you who killed her." He stared at the spot for a long time, as if he could see Zoey's corpse still there. The greatness Michael and even Parker had shown of her was disgraced, mutilated. Her once shining star overshadowed by Ethan.

"Celestia?" Kiran asked. Ethan didn't respond, but the Academy Warrior could tell. He was the first Ethan had met so he would be the last to die. "Rosemary too. You killed both of them."

But not Frederick, he thought. *I bet he didn't even try. Coward.*

"So what's next? After you kill me, what'll you do next? Go after

Michael, I bet."

Ethan sighed angrily, starting to grow tired of this. Each word Kiran said was another shot at his decisions, without Kiran even wondering if he had regrets for them.

"Well, Michael's going to be glad. I'll stop you before you even get near him, of course, but let's pretend you win. What will you even say to him? It was us, us he started with. He chose us to begin a new age, and apparently, he only chose one of us right."

Ethan could feel his Shadow Sword beginning to form in his hand. Kiran's last comment had sparked something new.

"Heck, what would he even say? How disappointed he'll be. He chose you, Ethan. You say you've done this because you didn't get recognition? Michael picked you out of nearly tens of thousands of people in this city! That isn't enough?"

Kiran stared at the boy blankly. "That isn't enough?! To be hand selected from the faceless city around us? There are individuals everywhere that could've easily joined my side at this, but Michael chose you!"

Ethan's Shadow Sword erupted from his injured hand, the pain no more. It shimmered in its usual black flame, but now, two tiny dots of light flickered within.

"He knows!" Ethan barked. Kiran readied his whip, eyes glancing from the boy to his blade. "Michael knows!

"In fact, he's probably watching us right now. Watching as his two apprentices fight on opposing sides. When I told him, he wasn't mad. In fact, he gave me permission."

"He would never!"

"He did. No objections. He let me go ahead and-"

"He let you go ahead and destroy yourself. He let you become a monster on your own terms. Who else have you killed?"

"Walter. But you're glad-"

"I'm not glad about another Academy Warrior's death, damnit! You think, that just because I disagree with someone, I'd kill them?

"Well, actually, I think you do! That's the sad reality you're living in! It's precisely what you've been doing all along. Killing anyone in your path. For hours on end now, I've been leading Academy Warriors to their deaths, all at the hands of you. Each Topian that dies out there is on your name.

"Listen, Ethan. I'm offering you this one chance to surrender. Tell the Anarchists to back off, and that'll be the end of it. You can leave in your special ship, and go elsewhere."

Ethan didn't respond. He only raised his Shadow Sword.

"If that's the route you're going to take, fine," Kiran said. *This time, the goal is absolute victory.*

And so they clashed.

Krian snapped his whip forward, but Ethan easily knocked it out of the way. He leaped over the next swipe and chased ahead. He pursued Kiran for a short time, blocking strike after strike. They danced a little, but finally, Ethan caught an opening.

Kiran's whip snapped the air just above his head, but instead of ducking and letting it go by, he sliced for it.

A third of the whip lost its glow and fell to the floor.

Kiran's eyes widened, and he quickly forced himself to recover. He sent three more slashes at Ethan, but the last one was a mistake.

The young Shadow Lord was ready, and he quickly cut another section of the whip off. He dashed forward, closing Kiran's distance, and struck a devastating blow. Kiran stared solemnly at the now sparking whip hilt he held in his hand, the rest of the whip wholly severed. Ethan swung for Kiran's head, but the Academy Warrior ducked just in time.

He rolled backward, feeling the air of the Shadow Sword cut the area above him. He flung himself sideways as the blade dug itself into the dark floor. He stood, and immediately felt Ethan press forward. Ethan sliced back and forth, each dodge more energy-draining than the last for Kiran.

Finally, Kiran felt the coldness of a wall hit his back. He seized up, and dove to the side, letting Ethan leave a deep incision in the dark marble wall. Ethan brought up his other hand, and yelled:

"*PAIN!*"

Kiran dropped to the ground as tens of blades were seemingly driven into his body. Every angle of him screamed in agony, as the sharp points pierced further and further down. As he struggled to glance about his actual body, he saw no knives of swords at all. Even so, he still felt it with insane realism.

Ethan rose above him, blade at the ready. Kiran started to finally relax, the effects already wearing off. Relief washed over him, and the sight of Ethan preparing to strike him down was almost ironic bliss. If Ethan just killed him now, he would never need to feel that pain ever again.

And so Ethan raised his sword high above his head and prepared to swing downward. Kiran closed his eyes and welcomed it.

And so it came.

41

"Kiran," a voice said. It was soft, like the voice of a swift breeze. And true to that, it came quickly, lingered, and drifted off. In the air, it danced for a little while, the syllables a simple rhythm.

"Gabriel?" the young Kiran asked, thinking he recognized the voice. He stepped forward in the field of grass around him, keeping his eyes on the man far in front of him. It was a shorter figure, with darker hair and bland clothes, much as the Academy Master had worn. But while Gabriel was a little rounder, this figure was skinny.

Kiran ran to the figure faster, seeing as he did not answer. Kiran was confident that the man was the one who had said his name, even from afar. It made sense, and there was no one else around. In fact, only these rolling green hills could be seen in the distance.

Kiran reached the figure quickly. "Gabri-"

The figure turned unnaturally, spinning without moving his feet. It was not Gabriel, but someone Kiran had never seen before. Then, the figure's features started to change.

Black hair turned blond, and hazel eyes turned blue. His body morphed multiple times before finally deciding on a form, and stuck with it.

Michael Nebadon stood before Kiran, similar to how he had near their first meeting. He raised his right arm, and placed it in the shape of an L. "Attack," he said.

"What do you..." Kiran trailed off as his old sword materialized into his hands. He raised it against his will, as if he was merely a puppet on a string. Like a replay, the sword raised up, and just like it had days before, smashed itself into Michael's arm. The pieces fell

Casey Hartley   Salvington's Soldiers

as sadly as they had previously. Kiran glanced down at them, little shards of metal on the grass.

"Don't focus on those," Michael said. "Focus on my arm. Can you copy it?"

Kiran nodded and raised his arm to match. Michael waited for a few moments, then came over to inspect. He adjusted Kiran's arm a few times, and let him consciously hold it there.

"Good," he said. "Now, just hold still as you do it. It's important to practice."

Kiran nodded and focused hard on it. He concentrated for what seemed like days, before finally, the world around him changed.

His eyes snapped open just as Ethan began to swing downward. He raised his arm to block, precisely as Michael had shown, and he felt something crack.

For a sickening moment, he was sure his arm had been cut in half, but no pain followed it. Instead, the crack was from the sword itself. Ethan looked feebly at it, seeing the jagged white fission within it. It opened wider, and then, in a flash, the sword disappeared.

Ethan felt every last reserve of energy pour from him outward, and without even enough to stand, he dropped to his knees.

As he did, Kiran struggled to his feet. He reached out to prop himself up with his right arm, but the moment he put weight on it, pain rushed through his body. He collapsed on his side, feeling as his arm began to throb constantly. It was broken, for sure.

He waited for the pain to die down a little. It did, but he was forced to use his left arm for support. Careful not to fall over, he took a final glance at Ethan.

"I'm sorry," he said and walked off.

Kiran motioned for the oak hall doors, but as he gripped the cold, metal handle, a pulsation of light came behind him. He whipped around, fearing it was Ethan back for more. It was not.

From the shattered Shadow Sword there came two tiny spheres of golden light. They swirled in the air for a few moments, like little stars in the sky. An invisible wind pushed them over to Kiran, where they planted firmly in his uninjured palm. Deep inside each one, he could see a figure, one of an armored woman, and the other of a young girl.

He closed his fingers over them, keeping hem hidden. They felt like marbles now, but not as cold.

"I'll get the two of you out of there," Kiran promised. He turned back to the door and pulled it open. For a moment, he considered just beaming himself down, but he knew that would not be enough. He needed to bring the ship down for good.

He hurried through the halls, knowing there were more Anarchists about. He ducked from view, keeping close to the walls. Peering around one of the dark corners, he quickly jumped back. It was just reflex, however, for the Anarchist in the hallway was not on his feet.

Kiran hurried over to him, and his eyes narrowed. The Anarchists only seemed to be stunned, not dead.

Someone else is here.

This placed an extra aura of caution around him, but he continued on. He kept his steps quiet against the tile and heard no footsteps of others nearby. In fact, most of the ship was eerily silent, only a slight whirring sound of the engine. It was in the distance, and Kiran had a little trouble tracking it, but found he was soon going in the right direction.

It grew louder, going from a whir to hum, and then to a growl. After passing a few more unconscious Anarchists, he found the engine room. Inside was a great silver machine, rumbling with every moment. He walked up to it and froze.

A pair of green eyes met his from the far side of the room. Kiran cursed. The man was an Anarchist. Even so, he did not wear a complete mask over his face. All but his eyes and hair were covered, dark black streaks of the man's hair falling over his forehead.

The man raised a gloved finger to his lips. That's when Kiran realized the man held a dark blade and was holding it close to the engine.

"He'll hear us," the man said quietly. "When he does, we will die."

Kiran could barely hear what the man was saying over the engine's rumbling, but he understood.

He clenched the glowing marbles in his hand tighter, clutching for their warmth. The man began to scan the walls carefully, so Kiran figured he'd do the same. Unsure of what he was looking for, the search was nearly useless, but it gave him some distraction. His arm still throbbed, but it was very distant.

The man looked back to him, eyes wide. "He's latching onto someone else..." He was speaking more to himself than to Kiran, but he continued. "I believe I am free." He smiled oddly, as if he didn't understand his own words.

"Free from who?" Kiran asked, noticing the man had lost his

cautious stature. "Are we still being listened for?"

"No," the man said. He sighed of relief and resumed back to his work. He flipped up a latch and stabbed his sword through it quickly. An unsatisfied sound came from his lips, and he drew his sword back.

Kiran, now feeling out of place, took a step forward. The man immediately turned his sword to him.

"Do you need help?" he asked.

The man glanced from the latch to Kiran, deciding. "Yes, actually." He seemed a little ashamed to admit it.

Kiran raised his uninjured arm in the air, as to show he was peaceful. The man narrowed his eyes.

"Why are you doing that?" he asked, holding his sword readily.

"You're not afraid I'm going to attack you?"

The man shook his head. "You are injured, as by your arm. I can sense anyone's pain, and where it is in their body. Yours is nearly everywhere, in fact. No man in that much pain will put himself through more conflict unless he is indeed insane."

Kiran had never heard of magic like that, not even the Wizards having it. *Must be the tricks of a healer.* He lowered his arm and walked over to the far side of the engine. The man showed him a series of slits and tubes that extended from it.

"I will ask you this, though," the man added. "Why would you want this ship to crash?"

Kiran raised an eyebrow. "I am an Academy Warrior. I am against any Anarchist creation."

"But it will plummet right on top of your headquarters if it does fall. You are fine with that?"

"It is my building to sacrifice." In his head, he added: *Michael*

329

wants a new age, so when it comes, even the Academy must start fresh.

The man nodded and put his hand over a small latch. He slid it down to reveal a circuit board, exposed completely. "This is a failsafe," he said. "This ship will go down the moment this thing is broken."

"Why is it so easy to access?" Kiran asked.

The man looked back to the doorway, where one of the Anarchist guards lay unconscious. "There are guards everywhere. It was not easy."

"None of them will betray and bring the ship down?"

"They are all controlled. They are hypocrites."

The man released the latch, and it slid back upwards in an instant. "That's the issue here," he said. "This is designed for two people to destroy. This is where you come in."

"What do I need to do?"

"Hold down the latch while I stab through it."

Kiran frowned. "Why couldn't you just rip the thing out?"

"It has an anomalous barrier around it. If you were to try, he would find and kill you immediately. You would not be able to defend, no matter what your skill. There is, however, another way. I take it you're familiar with the Academy Sword techniques?"

Kiran nodded, realizing what was needed. "Of course. I've been trained in the first five."

"Academy four is needed to pierce this barrier. Hold it still."

Kiran slid down the latch with two of his fingers, gripping the warm marbles tight with the others. He exposed the circuit board, and the man readied his blade. He twirled it twice before beginning the form.

"How do you know so much about this ship?" Kiran asked.

"Because," the man answered. "Up until thirty minutes ago, I was the one in control over it."

He stabbed, and the circuit board split in half.

The engine ceased to rumble.

42

Just as Kiran turned from the hallway leading to the hangar room, Michael sprinted through. He glanced back hurriedly, as if expecting something to rush from behind. His blond hair fell messily from distress, but his blue eyes remained in hardened focus. Footsteps pounded through the rooms, and a few unconscious Anarchists lay beside the walls.

Michael skidded to a halt as he saw the hangar bay entrance open. He made the decision quickly, the sights inside catching his eye. A dark streak of blood was smeared against the silver handle, so Michael slipped through.

His eyes widened as a figure lay gasping for air, crawling steadily toward him. The hangar doors themselves were discreetly closed, blending in purely with the ground. The only sign of the room's purpose was the two buttons on either side of the room.

Michael inhaled sharply as the injured figure met his eyes. *Ethan.*

"Curse you...Michael," Ethan growled, voice torn and deep. His eyes flared a malicious green, and his face was slowly distorting with ark static.

I'm too late for him, Michael realized. *He's already being controlled.*

"Michael…" Ethan said, beginning to claw his way over. "I am going to tear every last Academy Warrior apart!" His red hair started to grow black streaks, an essence of shadows misting around them.

"I," he continued. "Will destroy every last Wizard and Archer as well!" His hands started to morph, fingernails turning to claws. His hands themselves swelled to a huge size, becoming monstrosities. Michael wondered if Ethan would even notice, but the Shadow Lord was too focused on rage.

"Once I kill Kiran, I'm coming for you! I'll destroy all of Topia, all that you've fixed! Everything you've fought hard for, I'll break it down! You are a false prophet and a traitor! I'll end your reign!" He lunged forward, but before he could even get within ten yards of Michael, the blond boy quickly shut the door and disappeared from view.

Michael pressed up against the door, keeping it shut. He closed his eyes, and a few teardrops began to form in the corners of them. He willed himself to pull them back in, but his thoughts grew louder.

I should've stopped Ethan when I had the chance, or at least stopped Kiran from fighting him. It's a curse, isn't it…I bring chaos and death wherever I go.

I will break the curse.

Ethan, I will come back for you.

He whipped around, and from his hands launched two ropes of blinding light. He wrapped them tightly around the silver handles and tensed when the doors rattled. From inside, he could hear Ethan struggling for consistent breath, slamming his body against the door over and over.

"Be patient, friend," Michael said and turned.

Now...for the final apprentice to be found.

Her brown curls fell like rings, but sometimes, they fell like waves.

"No, no," the girl said, her voice exasperated. "That's lame." She twisted the knobs on her guitar, tuning the pitch until as perfect as could be. The notes rang out in symphony even though she didn't command them to. It was just her curse to bear. "It's poem-ish, not song worthy."

She looked at the empty theatre seats in front of her stage and sighed. Her guitar fell limp in her hands, and she placed it off to the side. Setting it gingerly on the hardwood stage, she leaned back. She rested her head against the wood, arms interlocked behind. Her eyes closed, and she let her mind wander.

I really wish they would give me an audience, she thought. *Even just a few Anarchists would be nice. Even if they hated my music, there would be someone else here with me.*

She stared up at the stage ceiling, a silver series of bars holding up bright lights. Cords rushed down from every angle, all to their respective amps and speakers. Even though they were readily available, she never played electric. Always acoustic.

It's been...I don't even know how many days. So much time has passed outside of here, I wish I could just look out the window and see something other than what's inside. But...the walls are still barren.

She glanced to either side of her, seeing the tiny closets that were the stage exits. One of them was just a bathroom, but the other was where she kept her other stringed instruments. An ukulele sat in there, accompanied by many others, including a mandolin and a harp. She seldom played them, as her guitar always her favorite and on stage.

She thought about going to sleep, a common thought she had. It solved the monotony of boredom, and dreams were always exciting. Full of wonder at night, he brain was, but not in the day. Even though she almost saw nothing new in her life now, the past filled her every sleeping moment. Stories of her twin brothers, her time at the Academy, even her dismal parents.

Her stomach began to growl, which was odd.

I haven't eaten breakfast yet? It seems a little late now.

She sat up, looking to the door on the far end of the theatre. There was a box embedded into the door, which her captors would often place her meals into. She had never seen them aside from when she was first imprisoned, but they managed to keep her from starving.

She thought about it for a moment, and even without the aid of a clock, she was sure it was past the usual time for breakfast. Meals were the only way she could keep track of vague time, and it was still a challenge. But, however, it was definitely past time.

I wonder if-

BOOM. The entire room rattled, and the lights above her head swayed. Everything around her flickered into static for a moment. She waited...careful.

BOOM. One of the lights above her broke off and crashed a few feet away. She gripped her guitar tightly, hoping to use it for defense. A quick thought gave her the urge to run for the theatre seats and away from the stage, so she made a break for it.

BOOM. The quake knocked her from her feet, letting her fall back onto the wooden stage. She rolled to the side as one of the light holders broke off from the ceiling, smashing into the scene. Each light shattered, and a few even broke from it and crashed through the stage itself. A speaker cord ripped off, now a live wire dancing in the air.

Finally, the chaos began to slow down. She sat up, still holding her guitar. Her jeans now had two huge holes at the knees, and the stage backboard had a massive tear in it. Her yellow symbol, two R's with their flat sides touching, had been defaced. The stage was utterly ruined.

She sat still, wondering if yet another quake would rock the room. Even her electric guitar with the master volume turned to max couldn't shake the place quite like that, and she had tried. Of course, she had been nearly deafened by the sound, but it had been a worthy shot.

The door started glowing. In the cracks of it, the outline against the black walls, there shone a brilliant light. She stood with wonder, and soon the door fell down gracefully.

A golden, warm light filled the entire theatre and stage. A shorter figure stepped from the light and smiled.

The figure was a boy probably a year younger than her, with golden blond hair and shimmering blue eyes. His mere gaze was enough to entrance, as if he was going to lead you straight into the promised land of God.

"Rachel Donovan," the boy said. "It's time you are set free."

Michael led a very confused Rachel out of the burning Unknown, straight into the heart of The Academy where it had crashed. A massive opening had been torn in the hull of the ship, which they soon walked out of. The great ship shone brilliantly in the rising daylight, and it was already so lifeless in nature.

Rachel's entire body felt weakened now, as her hunger grew.
Even so, during the past year, she hadn't made very many efforts to

exercise.

The light of day nearly burned her upon impact. Her pale skin hadn't felt such light in the longest time, and she was shocked at how warm it was. She began to feel weak, and despite being taller than Michael, held onto him for a little support. At first, she had been hesitant to trust this mysterious boy, but her fatigue quickly took over. Michael steadily guided her over to the main lobby.

Academy Warriors rushed about, mostly standing in awe of the great ship. Much of the building had been destroyed, the southern half a pile of rubble. For now, the rest seemed stable, but once the ship would be removed from the area, it would undoubtedly topple.

Michael started to bring Rachel over to one of the benches by the front desk, but she refused.

"Outside," she said. "I don't want to be in here."

Michael nodded, and they walked out through the front doors instead. They were a sight to see, with many of the Academy Warriors and Topian Army soldiers staring oddly. A few might have thought they recognized Rachel, but none went out of their way to say hello. They were all too focused on the crash.

Kiran was at the lead, and he had already sent soldiers and Academy Warriors to inspect every bit of the ship inside. Apparently, as soon as the machine had crashed, all of the Anarchists inside had disintegrated. Ethan was gone as well.

This made Kiran certain the redheaded traitor was still alive, and capable of movement. If he had found some way to escape the ship before it had crashed, then he could still be in the city somewhere.

Kiran himself had escaped through a back entrance, with the mysterious ninja-like man.

Once they had landed atop one of the buildings neighboring The

Academy, they had immediately rushed downstairs to gather the armies. The man had excused himself for some "time" and promised he would return later.

"Holy crap, Kiran," a voice behind him said. The Academy Warrior whirled around to see Jeremy and Sergio jogging toward him, expressions shocked. They stopped just behind him.

"Hey guys," Kiran said, turning around.

Jeremy looked to him worriedly. "We're taking charge of this, okay?"

Kiran laughed. "Guys, I've got this!" He started to turn back.

"Your arm is broken. You look like you've been hit by a bus!"

Sergio nodded in agreement. "Get some rest."

Kiran sighed and glanced at his arm. It had started to swell almost immediately, and now it looked sickening. It was no longer his arm, but a purple and red thing attached to his body. He winced just looking at it.

"Alright," he conceded. "Maybe I do need some help."

"There are a few ambulances over there," Jeremy said, pointing around the building. "They'll help you out."

Kiran thanked them both and began to walk off. Sure enough, white ambulances were huddled around the front of the building, attendees helping anyone nearby. A few soldiers in the area had been hit by debris, but other than that, the space had been mainly unoccupied before the crash.

He forgot all about his arm once he saw the scene in front. Near one of the benches stood Michael Nebadon and Frederick Donovan, talking to a girl sitting on the bench. She was huddled in a dark blanket, brown wave-curls running along her head. She looked terribly different than the years before, but she was unmistakable to

Kiran himself.

Rachel Donovan.

He sprinted forth, arm yelling out, but he pressed the pain away. Michael saw him first, then Rachel.

 Frederick did not look to him. Frederick's mind was deep in thought about what his dearest sister, someone he hadn't seen in years, presumed dead, had just told him.

"I'm so happy to see you," he had said. *"Leo and I got your letter a couple days ago."*

She had looked so confused, as if he had spoken in a foreign tongue. *"I don't understand. What letter?"*

Frederick had fished the piece of paper from his pocket, determined to show proof. He showed it eagerly but was greeted with a similar response. Rachel read the letter multiple times but shook her head.

"I didn't write that."

Frederick turned the paper so he could read it, and it was the exact one that had appeared on Leo's doorstep. The words were all there. Her name was still at the bottom.

"But...then...who did?"

43

YOU DARE TO STAND BEFORE ME? The voice boomed. The figure rose from his throne, a slender being nearly ten feet tall. He radiated a force of gravity to his mere form, as if the room was bending toward him. Jagged green eyes pierced forward, and long green claws complimented them.

Noah stared at the throne blankly. "You no longer have any power over me. I do not fear you."

The figure's eyes glared, peering down at him as if he was a pesky insect.

MICHAEL MAY BE PROTECTING YOU FOR NOW, BUT EVEN HE IS WEAK.

"He has me on his side now. Countless Light Beings will stand up to your plans."

YOU USE THAT CURSED TERM IN FRONT OF ME? I SHOULD SMITE YOU THIS INSTANT.

"You are no god, father. You are making the same mistake your predecessor did."

FOR EVERY BEING THAT IS LIGHT, THERE ARE TEN WITHIN THE SHADOWS. THEY ARE LURKING AROUND EVERY LAST CORNER, AND WILL HUNT THAT BOY DOWN.

"I will not let them."

THEN THEY WILL HUNT YOU DOWN AS WELL. AND ONCE THEY HAVE, IT WILL NOT BE LONG BEFORE THE OLD PRINCE WILL BE REBORN, AND THE SOVEREIGNS WILL RETURN. THIS TIME, EARTH WILL FALL UNDER

OUR CONTROL PERMANENTLY, AND WE WILL
DOMINATE EVERY CORNER OF NEBADON ITSELF.

"You have high expectations."

THEY ARE FEASIBLE TO MY EXPANSIVE MIND, BUT NOT
TO YOURS. THE SHADOWS WILL SPREAD AMONG EVERY
REGION OF SPACE, AND THE NEW ORDER WILL BE
CREATED. ONCE WE HAVE DONE THAT, WE WILL
CONQUER SALVINGTON ITSELF.

"I hope I am there to see you fail."

YOU WILL BE THERE, TO WATCH EVERY BIT OF WHAT
YOU SEE AS "LIGHT" BE DECIMATED IN ONE SWIFT BLOW.

TAKE THIS INTO ACCOUNT, NOAH: HOW WILL YOU
EVER STAND UP TO A BEING LIKE ME? MUCH LESS FOUR
OTHERS. WE WILL BE THE PENTAGON OF THE NEW ORDER,
AND WE WILL LEAVE NOTHING FOR YOU-

Noah's eyes snapped open, and a splitting headache rammed
him instantly. He calmed himself down, pressing fingers to his
temples. He massaged them for a little while, circular motions
consistent. It eased the pain after a little while, and he sat up.

The corner of the room was empty, and looking around it, Noah
realized it must've been some sort of meeting hall. A large stage sat
off to the far side. A few microphones had fallen down in their
stands, now laying feebly on their sides.

He stood, and exited the room swiftly.

No one paid him attention, and it was not on the soldiers and
Academy Warriors' own will. Noah's cloak held a dark aura around
himself that clouded the mind of anyone who spared a glance at him.
Otherwise, he knew the questions and perhaps violence might
overwhelm him.

Kiran greeted him (on Noah's own accord) as soon as he stepped outside. He hated the sun, but bore it now, as a slight thanks.

Kiran shook his hand, saying:

"I don't think I ever caught your name."

Noah nodded. "I am Noah...son of...Val."

Kiran laughed. "Nice to meet you, Noah, son of Val. I'm Kiran." He now had a strong cast wrapped around his arm, a sling holding it upright. With his free hand, he gestured to a bench nearby, where Rachel and Frederick sat, talking.

Michael hovered nearby, a caring in his eyes as he watched. Noah relaxed a little upon seeing Rachel and nodded to himself. He caught Michael's gaze for a long time, and they both smiled internally. Michael winked, so Noah turned back to Kiran.

"It's been a long day."

EPILOGUE

Nearly a week had passed before Kiran realized the glowing marbles were still with him. After some time he had stored them in his pocket, needing his free hand for almost everything. He tried to give them to Michael, but the boy refused.

"They are your friends. Take care of them as you would yourself."

Kiran didn't entirely trust himself to, but he had no other choice. Frederick didn't want them, and he was busy with Rachel and Leo nearly every day. Jeremy and Sergio were occupied, still commanding the deconstruction of The Academy. The Unknown had been removed after a few days, and sure enough, the building had crumbled soon after. Now, it was a matter of clearing the debris. As well, they were responsible for taking back the southern districts, but weirdly enough, that wasn't much of a contest.

Without The Unknown, the remnants of Anarchist society had crumbled almost instantaneously.

So Kiran placed the marbles on the dresser by his bed, and wished them goodnight every time he closed his eyes to rest. They never responded, of course, but he liked to pretend they could hear him. He wanted desperately to free the both of them, but it was an anomaly neither he nor Michael could undo. In fact, Michael seemed reluctant to even mess with it.

As he looked inside the one containing a tiny version of Celestia, he thought back, for the first time, about what she had told him at Outlying Peak. Her past was still a confuddled mess, and Kiran did wish she would one day explain. But then again, she did say she would die.

Elara finally appeared in Kiran's apartment a few days later. She informed him that this stage was all a part of their "rebirth." She told him it was like death for them, but since they cannot die, it was only a temporary state.

When Kiran asked how that was even possible, Elara had not answered. She merely bid him farewell and disappeared in a shimmering flash.

She cannot die? Does she even know that? Or, has everything about death from her only been lies?

So, as a result, he was still left in the darkness there.

But every day, Michael showed him some new aspect of the Light. They began to spend a lot of time learning and studying together, as a master and his student. It still felt odd for Kiran, being taught by someone his own age, but he ignored the feeling. Michael held the same thousands of years of wisdom that Gabriel once had, and Kiran suspected there was even more.

So it was not surprising when Michael announced that a brand-new Academy would be opening, a place for training the new age masters. He sanctioned it to be built away from the city, in the mountain ranges where The Unknown had been first spotted.

Kiran asked about the Sisterhood forest and Crescent Island, but Michael deemed those exclusive to Siona's Sisterhood. They were empty at the moment, but Michael seemed confident in their safety.

Three weeks after, Michael, Kiran, and Noah had departed for the mountain ranges with twenty Academy Warriors. Frederick offered himself to stay in the city, taking the position Timothy MacArthur once held. Bolten and Blaze returned to be his two high generals. Jeremy and Sergio had taken the rest of the Academy Warriors to begin the new police of the city, what they referred to as The Topian Guard.

The new Topian Guard building would be replacing The Academy's ruins. It would be three stories, unlike The Academy's seven, and would operate much differently. Smaller offices would be opened in every district, but those had been put on hold for now. Michael had made a final request of Frederick to abolish the old district lines, and instead separate the city into three new districts.

Lanon would expand to cover not just the capital, but the old Desertia and Smith Districts as well. New Desertia would be where Mysti was, fusing with Chuckle District as well. Finally, Insension District would fuse Hookhorse and Fiasco Districts. Each district was set to elect a new leader. Governors, they would be called.

Frederick wanted to run, but he could not be the militant leader and one of the Governors simultaneously, so he backed down. Insension elected an old man by the name of Mal, a ginger fellow with the tendency to rant for long periods of time. Desertia elected Jeremy Gonzalez, even despite the Academy Warrior's hesitancy to run. Jeremy reluctantly then yielded all of his power as a policeman to Sergio, placing him in charge of keeping the city safe. Police Chief Sergio, he would be called.

Lanon had the most difficult time deciding.

But then, Leila Lanondek returned. She had been found unconscious in the capital some days after the last battle and had been kept in the hospital for nearly two weeks. Two hours after the election announced for Lanon had been released, Leila woke up.

She was elected Governor of Lanon two days later. There was no contest. Even despite her failure at stopping the Anarchist Rebellion, she was deemed fit to lead.

A month passed, and the Academy was constructed outside of Topia. It was a series of temples and dojos attached to the side of the mountains, with platforms and staircases being carved out. Michael had started class a day later, but much to Kiran's surprise, handed the torch of teaching to him.

"I barely know anything!" Kiran exclaimed.

"You know more than they do," Michael said and walked off. So Kiran taught, and having no idea what to do, taught what he had learned on his very first day: what it means to be an Academy Warrior.

Of course, the Academy Warriors before him had already undergone most of these beginner lessons, but no one objected. They followed along to his standards, and soon enough, training had gone well under way. Soon enough, Kiran wished to open the Academy up to all three classes, welcoming the Wizards and Archers. He contacted Frederick and Parker, who both responded with cryptic answers. Even so, Kiran remained hopeful that they would one day rejoin the Academy.

Michael, however, had not just given Kiran the permission to teach for apparent reasons. He needed a little time to himself.

His last moments with Ethan rushed through his mind over and over. The words pounded within him, and he fought hard to not be affected by them. Even so, he found remnants of truth within them.

I couldn't save him. I chose him and Kiran to be at my side, but now only Kiran was saved. I could've tried harder, been more direct with my words. Maybe that would've stopped him from betrayal.

What am I thinking?! That's precisely what the rebels believe in. The Shadow Lords treat indirect learning as weakness. It is their enemy and the Light's specialty.

348

It is the truth of learning, and I must continue to spread it to those who still care.

A few nights later, Michael and Kiran met outside the main dojo. They stood on the wooden deck that sat suspended over the mountainside, and from there Kiran could see where he had fallen off multiple times. He looked up and saw the vast expanse of stars above.

"Do you want to explore the stars, Kiran?" Michael asked, staring up with great longing. His golden blond hair was in an upward swoop, streaks of shining light shooting upward. Kiran could almost imagine Michael's hair being its own star in the sky. It would glimmer bright enough.

"Sure do," the Academy Warrior responded. "But they're so far away."

"Once Topia develops spaceships, exploration will be easy for all. I've witnessed it happen many times. It may take ten years, a hundred years, or even a thousand. Every example is one I've seen."

Kiran looked to him, surprised. "So you've met aliens?! And they have space technology?"

"Of course," Michael answered, still looking up. "I've met nice ones, violent ones, smart ones, nearly every adjective fits a species I've met. Some are even still colorful."

"So...you're saying there's thousands of inhabited planets out there?! With species of humans well beyond our own?!'

"Oh, more than that." He looked to Kiran. "And you know what?"

"What?"

Michael spread his grin wide, teeth shiny. His blue eyes sparkled even in the night, orbs of wonder and discovery. Kiran nearly swore he could see space in the boy's irises that night, even though it was probably just a reflection.

"We're going to spread the Light to every single one of them."

<u>ACKNOWLEDGEMENTS</u>

Now, I know I thanked everyone who helped on this project toward the beginning, but that was brief.

This beyond two-year project began with a few short stories I wrote for school, nothing more. If not for the praise that my teacher, Kojo, had given those stories, this book may not have been written.

Actually, let me back up even farther. In sixth grade, I *hated* writing. Absolutely *despised* it. But, when my mother forced me to take a creative writing class led by Miss Erin, my imagination sparked to life. Without that class, this book may not have been written.

Justin took that class with me. When I talked about my ideas with him (honestly I can't remember his responses), those ideas became realistic. Without him being there to talk to, this book may not have been written.

Justin led to Hanna, who created this book's beautiful cover and the glorious illustrations within. Without those illustrations to push me forward and live up to what they depicted, this book may not have been written.

To family members, to friends, to classmates, to teachers, so many people made this book happen. Without the never ending questions, support, and feedback, none of this may have happened.

Thank you, really. Thank you to everyone.

I have one final group to thank.

This book was heavily inspired by what is called *The Urantia Book*, published by The Urantia Foundation. The world depicted in that book was one that interested me beyond anything ever before. Despite them not knowing about this and perhaps never being able to see it, I thank them.

From Michael to Gabriel to Seraphim to Salvington, *The Urantia Book* showed me a world that was truly astonishing. It offered a brand new perspective to the universe that I had never envisioned prior.

I apologize for any inaccuracies that may have showed during this book. My intention was not to follow *The Urantia Book* exactly. I merely drew inspiration from it.

To the Urantia Foundation, if you ever read this, I hope that this book has met any of your standards. I enjoy all the work that you've done and in no way wish to undermine it.

Note: Again, in no way at all do I wish to detract from or demean *The Urantia Book*. To any reader, I would recommend at least researching Urantian Philosophy. It's worth it.

54774935R00212

Made in the USA
Columbia, SC
04 April 2019